Finding Faithful

Finding Faithful

A Christian Romance

Vicie Annette Allison

Trilogy Christian Publishers

A Wholly Owned Subsidiary of Trinity Broadcasting Network

2442 Michelle Drive

Tustin, CA 92780

For information, address Trilogy Christian Publishing

Rights Department, 2442 Michelle Drive, Tustin, Ca 92780.

Trilogy Christian Publishing/ TBN and colophon are trademarks of Trinity Broadcasting Network.

For information about special discounts for bulk purchases, please contact Trilogy Christian Publishing.

10 9 8 7 6 5 4 3 2 1

Library of Congress Cataloging-in-Publication Data is available.

ISBN 979-8-89333-505-7

ISBN 979-8-89333-506-4 (ebook)

DEDICATION

This book is dedicated to my parents, who were
protective and supportive, and to the girls
who have lived life with faith.

TABLE OF CONTENTS

PROLOGUE:
THE 1918 FAITHFUL LADIES BOOK CIRCLE

The fire crackled wisely as the ladies swept in, armed with their finger sandwiches, lemon squares, and delicious cocoa bars. Tea was ready, and the table set. On a rainy, cold fall day, everyone was glad to be inside and cozy.

The home had been a rather small log cabin, but gradually, my uncle had enlarged it and added an upper level. Now, it was considered one of the nicer homes on the ridge. I just loved it for the memories that it contained.

It was a monthly book circle meeting, like most that were held in Faithful, Oregon. The usual ladies were present, including Lydia McVale, my mother; my aunt Maddie; Beatrice, the infamous town busybody; Mary Alice Thomas, a beloved and graceful lady; my cousins, Mary and Penny; Mrs. Margaret Ruth, my upper school teacher, and, of course, the lady who would always be "My Miss O'Brien."

On this particular Saturday afternoon, we had taken on Oliver Twist with all of his forlorn miseries and travails. Mr. Dickens' masterpiece was our most ambitious discussion to that date, but Miss O'Brien, considered our circle leader, was unusually quiet.

My mother, in her true "mothering" and curious nature, commented on how brutal the life of an orphan could be and that the "Poor House" and orphanage system of England was not so different from many of the situations that young girls had found themselves living out in America.

Aunt Maddie found Nancy's relationship with Bill, a tale not too dramatically different from the *Ladies of the Evening* in towns, mining camps, and saloons throughout the western coastline.

Mrs. Beatrice rolled her eyes at both ladies before interjecting her usual overbearing but sometimes astute opinion. "For heaven's sake, you two," she began. "Why not just stay with the story?"

Oliver is a mistreated orphan. Fagan is a thief who preys on children, and Nancy is little more than a tramp. As in actual life, no one really cares about any of them until Oliver is lucky enough to meet Mr. Brownlow.

"Ladies, not everything has to apply to life today. Although," she said with a sly smile, "there have been several people in this town who could be compared to Oliver, himself, as well as Nancy (and with that, I could have sworn she cast a sidelong look at Aunt Maddie)."

"In fact," she continued, "I believe I grew up with an 'Artful Dodger,'" she said, as she gave a slight look at Miss O'Brien. This, I took to mean my uncle, who had at one time possessed the reputation of being a bit of a con man.

Seeing that both my mother and aunt Maddie were beginning to heat up with silent resentments and knowing that I was thinking of my Ned and what he had endured in his early years, I hoped that someone else would jump into the discussion. Stabs of remembrance and resentment seemed to be coming out.

In fact, Aunt Maddie was at the point of explosion when Miss Mary Alice intervened. "Beatrice, every town, village, large city, and community does indeed have these same social indignities and atrocities somewhere in their past or present. I don't think that anyone was necessarily trying to draw a parallel between the story and our town, although they are there to be seen if one searches their heart. I, personally, however, as you first pointed out, would prefer to dwell on the story and the fact that it has helped to bring about social change."

Our Mrs. Margaret Ruth sat with her usual "knowing smile" and waited her turn before speaking. "I think that Bill Sikes should be examined," she said, almost casually, before really making her theme known.

"It occurs to me," she continued, "that his demeanor and behavior were not a great deal different from that of a master with a slave. Although he must have had some degree of love for Nancy, he basically simply uses her. Then, he brutally beats her to death, and, of course, all of this is based on a cruel lie carried by none other than Fagan. We mustn't forget Mr. Bumble either," she added. "I find him to be a typical town character, lapping up any bit of power that he can find. I'm sure he didn't care where the orphans wound up or why any more than the others. Well, just offering some 'food for thought,' ladies," she smiled and finished.

Still, my Miss O'Brien remained quiet.

My cousins, Mary and Penny, exchanged sisterly glances. As different as they were, they shared the bond of silent communication.

Mary, always serenely beautiful, remarked on the unique and beautiful use of language and style that Mr. Dickens used in his writing before continuing.

She looked thoughtful for a moment and added, "Also, let's not forget the characters that seem to represent absolute good and kindness, such as Rose, Oliver's aunt, and Mr. Brownlow. Indeed, it is almost biblical how Oliver Twist takes in the absolute good and bad of life. If my children, God forbid, were in these circumstances, I would hope that they would be helped by the kindness of others. I really think that most of the characters held on to their own kind of faith." (I always admired and longed for the quiet and peaceful self-confidence that Mary seemed to have.)

Penny, however, stated that while reading the book, she wanted to meet the "Artful Dodger" and have an adventure or two with him. Somehow, I believed that Penny could have set Fagan straight.

It was my turn, of course, as I was quite often still overlooked until the end of a discussion. I wasn't quite sure what I could add. I was thrown by the fact that Miss O'Brien still had not responded.

"Well," I began, "in many ways, this is just the tale of a young orphan boy in the 1800s in England, but I also think it portrays the different roles that people play in life. Some are hurt through no fault of their own, but they overcome. Some use other people through farce and manipulation. Others are a bit on the shady side in order to survive (but their hearts are good), and others get to be the hero.

"And," I hesitated, a little unsure of how to proceed, "maybe some people get to be all of the parts at one time or another," I finished and looked down at the table, a bit afraid of the reactions of the rest of the group.

Miss O'Brien smiled and broke the all too daunting silence, "How insightful. That was a marvelous observation."

I dared to look up and met with several approving nods and smiles.

"What a good summary!" Mrs. Margaret Ruth said.

"You know," Mrs. Beatrice whispered far too loudly to Mrs. Margaret Ruth, "no one thought she'd ever be able to learn."

My mother looked at her, opened her mouth to speak, but then looked as though she was unable, and I declare that my aunt Maddie looked at the fireplace poker as though she would soon wield it on Beatrice's head. Then, my Miss O'Brien spoke again.

"Well, after that well-spoken philosophical comment on this month's literary choice, I think we should allow her," she said, standing and motioning to me, "to choose our next book."

Thankfully, I did have a choice in mind. "I've always wanted to hear opinions on Jane Eyre," I said.

"Oh, I'd love to read that book!" Mrs. Mary Alice smiled and said as others agreed. "And please come to my house this time," she added.

"School teachers and intellectuals!" Miss Beatrice said and rolled her eyes yet again, looking as though she might spit in disgust.

I then decided to stay and help Miss O'Brien rearrange the chairs and clean up a bit, although she had denied help from everyone else. I, of course, had the ulterior motive of simply wanting to visit with her before I went by my mother's house to see about her.

As she filed by, Aunt Maddie whispered to me, "We're going to tell Beatrice that the next meeting had to be moved to your house, but secretly tell everyone else that they should show up at Mary Alice's as planned." She then grinned in her trademark mischievous way.

The ladies then followed Maddie out the door, thanking "Kayleigh" for the lovely time. She smiled and nodded.

I touched my Miss O'Brien on the sleeve when the others had left and asked her why she had been so quiet.

She motioned to the two chairs in front of the fireplace, and we sat down side by side. She shook her head briefly and then began what would be a painful tale. We sipped tea, and I listened and watched as she stopped and started a story that could have rivaled poor Olivier's, or perhaps surpassed him. It is a tale of finding the faithful in this life.

PART I: KAYLEIGH'S JOURNEY

CHAPTER 1: 1873—LEAVING IRELAND

"Woman overboard!" a deckhand shouted out. Kayleigh and her mama knew that it was young Miss Crowley. Constantly belittled by her father, frustrated by the conditions on the boat, and taken with a bad cough, it was not a complete surprise that she took her life, but the resolute sadness and hopelessness of it hit Kayleigh hard. She kept remembering her father's words from a year ago, "Look for the brightness and the humor in life. It's always there if you but look for it."

It was hard, though, to live that message when those around you were so negative. Remarks such as, "Well, she's gone now. If she doesn't drown right off, the sharks will have a go at her." Somehow, it seemed a strange foreboding to Kayleigh, like jumping from one difficult life to another.

However, the spirits of most of those on board were not yet overcome. Couples still embraced while children played on the crowded deck. Often, a man dressed in a thread bare jacket and worn brown trousers played the flute in cheerful tunes.

It was an arduous passage, at best, from Ireland to New York, as the cold Atlantic lapped the sides of the large carrier ship. Cargo ships passed in the light of day, rusted and worn but plowing along like grumpy old men.

Sometimes at night, beautiful, sleek ships went sailing by like what Kayleigh imagined to be swans, carrying a cargo of the wealthy and what Mama called the "well to do."

Kayleigh was usually dressed in a green woolen overblouse and a heavy blue woolen skirt. Her stockings were worn but concealed, and her shoes were heavy brogans, so often worn by the little girls of Ireland.

At almost nine years of age, Kayleigh was a pretty, petite strawberry blonde. Her eyes were a bluish-green, which often drew more attention for her than she wanted. With her small, freckled, upturned nose and bright, cupid bow smile, people sometimes thought of her as a little girlish and naive, but once they came to know her, they also recognized her as a very smart and capable girl.

Her mother, Kathleen, was a beautiful woman. She was aware of it but did not flaunt it or attempt to live off of it. Like Kayleigh, she had strawberry blonde hair and startling blue-green eyes. Her features, however, were a bit more chiseled, with high cheekbones and a heart-shaped jawline that could tilt in a very alluring way. However, an intelligence about character and men was not her strongest asset.

Kayleigh had already taken notice that Kathleen was weak where men were concerned. She tended to allow them to take complete charge with no attempt at having her own way. As Kayleigh's grandmother had warned her, "I know that you are very young, but try to steer your mama in the right direction. She has little sense about the wiles of men."

Kayleigh thought that her mother was still in love with her father and always would be, but he had given way to his own weaknesses. Namely, he liked "the drink," and he liked to talk politics, and the two would come together in the wrong place and at the wrong time quite often.

Finally, one day, after being missing for two nights, Kathleen and her mother found him hanged in the town square on a bright fall morning. His beautiful, strong, slender frame twisted with the wind. His curling brown hair blew about with the breeze, and his crystal blue eyes remained closed.

Kayleigh had loved her daddy, although, even at nine years of age, she knew he was not to be counted upon, and she lived in fear that death would overtake him; but, oh, when he was at his best, his Irish stories and songs could charm even the hardest heart! How she missed him and her grandmother.

Kayleigh's grandmother was a tiny thing of barely five feet, whereas Kathleen was slender and five full inches taller than her mother. Kayleigh would one day be somewhere in between the two women, measuring five foot two inches in height.

All three, though, had the reddish blonde hair, high cheekbones, and emerald, greenish eyes of many Irish women. Kayleigh's "gifts" from her father included a smattering of freckles across her nose and what her grandmother called her father's "speculative grin."

"The boy always looked as though he was figuring the answer to a problem or how to work a deal," her grandmother had once reflected, "but it was lovely, though, when the boy smiled."

Kayleigh's grandmother, Kate, had been her rock of stability. She had run a little china and clock shop for quite a time, and Kathleen and Kayleigh both begged for her to close it and come with them to America. She declined, though, saying, "I'm too old now. I will close the shop soon, but I must find a good buyer, which in today's market will not be easy." She, then, uneasily gave Kathleen her inheritance from her father, the same man that Kate continued to light candles for and whose portraiture she kissed each night.

She talked sternly to Kathleen about how a large part of the money needed to be set aside for the passage to America and the rest for her and Kayleigh to find a place to settle. Next, she sewed a small pouch with a strap for Kathleen to wear under her skirts and shift.

After she had finished her handiwork with the pouch, she gently pulled Kayleigh aside and told her, "Kayleigh, I love you more than anyone or anything. It is breaking my heart to part with you.

"You're an old, wise soul placed in the body of a child. Your mother is not good with men or money, but she is a good soul. Watch her and try to steer her from harm and parting with the money. Just do your best. She can also be stubborn when it comes to making her choice.

"We're all teetering on the edge of poverty, my love. I've left myself just enough money to live out my days on what was our farm, and, hopefully, I'll sell the shop.

"If I sell it, my love, I'll be arranging for the money to go to you, but don't repeat that.

"In fact, if there's any way, I'll find a way to make more money."

She held her finger to the side of her nose. "Remember, it's our secret. I'll get a letter to you, and it will be like a riddle so that you'll know where the money has been placed, but no one else can. Your mother never cared enough to learn her native tongue, so I'll use the Irish so that you'll decipher the terms. If you're made to read the letter aloud, do not read it truthfully. I'm giving you full permission to read it like a simple letter of love.

"However, you won't come into the money until you're twenty-five. By then, God willing, you should have found a home and a trustworthy man." She drew Kayleigh close and kissed her. "Oh, how I love you. Stay away from 'the drink' and be a good and hard-working lass."

Kayleigh understood their situation as well as she could. Mainly, she knew that she and her mother were on a big, crowded, and smelly boat and that she missed her grandmother desperately. She was a keen observer of life, though, and a good judge of character.

The families, children, single men and women, and crew members passed by, walked to and fro, and sometimes made an impression. One family, in particular, seemed to always be headed in her and Kathleen's direction.

The "widowed father" and three boys continually seemed to be coming up to them, with the father chatting with and charming Kathleen.

He was an evil one, though, that Nolan O'Connor, and so were two of his boys, Matthew and Marcus. All three had that cruel, twisted line of a mouth. Their dark, straight black hair hung in bowl cuts, and their brown eyes were continually drawn into cruel squints.

Their father, Nolan, however, did have a good build, lean and strong, whereas his two older boys were stocky, bordering on fat, with barrel chests and large bowed legs. The youngest son, though, Luke, was handsome, with light brown hair, high cheekbones, and green eyes.

He was fifteen, but he seemed so much younger. In fact, Kayleigh was the one who did much of the talking and directed him on how to interact with others. She felt so safe with him. He was kind-hearted and seemed amused with everything she did. He was truly the big brother that she had never had.

She hated how Nolan O'Connor looked at both Kathleen and herself. There was a sly cruelty there that gave her a chill, and he was never very clear on how his first wife had died.

"Mama, that is not a good man," Kayleigh told her mother.

"You leave grown-up things to the grown-ups, Kayleigh," she would admonish quietly but sternly.

"I would," Kayleigh thought bitterly, "but you're not a very grown-up person."

If she had known the meaning of the word "leer" at that point, she would have pointed out to her mama that both Nolan and Matthew were leering at her, but she had no words for it, and it was doubtful that her mama would have believed her.

Kathleen was so enthralled with Nolan and his promises about New York that she was completely blinded to who he was. However, he revealed his true self more than once in conversation while on the boat, but Kathleen seemed to completely disregard it. Once, she commented that it was "touching" that

Nolan's boys had biblical names.

Nolan rolled his eyes and answered, "Their mother was constantly praying, reading the Bible, and on her beads when the pitiful creature wasn't coughing up blood. I think Matthew was some sort of tax collector or such," he continued, "and Mark was one of the followers, but Luke was a doctor." At this final comment, he laughed and pointed at his youngest son.

"Can you imagine that one practicing medicine?" He slapped his knee and laughed almost hysterically as the two older boys followed suit, mimicking and laughing at the expense of poor Luke.

Luke hung his head, and Kayleigh patted his shoulder. This scene would play out again and again for the two.

Kathleen and Nolan were married on the boat, and everyone seemed to think that it was perfect. In their view, a young widower had found a young widow, but Kayleigh knew that trouble was coming down the road. Her young heart and head had become worried as never before.

Luke pulled her aside one day and whispered to her, "You just stay close to me, 'Little Bit,' and I'll look out for you. My brothers ain't never up to no good, and Pa ain't no better, but I'll protect you as best I can."

"Get over here, idiot!" Nolan called out to Luke. Kayleigh noticed more and more just how cruel his father and brothers were to him.

Kayleigh had a little book of the ABCs, verses, and poetry that her grandmother had packed for her. In truth, she could read anything that she put her hands and eyes to, but these were the only books that she had.

So, often, she would sit with Luke and teach him to read. He was her one true friend, and it pained her to know that he had never been to school or learned to read.

"Now ain't this somethin'?" he would grin and say. "Here I am, fourteen years old, and you, only nine, but you're teachin' me to read." Her sweet, gentle Luke would be imprinted in her soul forever.

They were all coming closer to New York, and most on the boat ran over to the rails to watch in wonderment as the Statue of Liberty came into sight. Kayleigh wondered and hoped in her young heart that this new country and city would be what she and Mama needed.

Not long before they all disembarked for Ellis Island, she pulled her mother aside and asked her about the money. "Oh, Nolan will take care of that," she said cheerily. "You're not to worry. He wears the money pouch now, and he'll take care of us," she finished with a child-like, trusting smile.

"Oh, Mama!" Kayleigh cried. "You shouldn't have done that."

"Well, now, how was I to keep it from him?" she questioned. Then, seeing that Kayleigh did not understand, she said more gently, "It's all for the best."

When Kayleigh and her new "family" were released from Ellis Island, she had hoped and dreamt that they could find a home that would be large enough for her to have her own room, but she soon found out how foolish that was.

Nolan had flashed money about like the arrogant and complete fool that he was. He was going to "make his 'big deal' here in New York." Instead, he was snookered at every turn and responsible for the situation that the family found themselves in.

The tenement that they rented had three rooms. Two were small bedrooms, and the other was a small kitchen. The landlady, a very thin, wrinkled, and bitter woman, told them roughly that it was "better than what most in Brooklyn have."

Kathleen and Nolan were in one room, and the boys were in the other, barely larger than a good-sized closet. Kayleigh had a palette in the kitchen, and, at night, she would talk to her mama while she put a blanket over a rope hanging from the window to the front door. In this way, she had some privacy, but not a lot.

At night, she would lay awake and write stories in her head and view the stars that shone through the sliver of window still uncovered. She wondered what it would be like to live somewhere with green grass and mountains in the distance rather than to be enclosed by noisy streets and bickering family and neighbors.

One day, Nolan announced that they would all get jobs. "Matthew and Marcus will come with me, and we'll find factory jobs. Luke, go to restaurants. Go around the back and ask if there's work for taking out trash and bussing tables. Save some of the food for us and try not to look like such a sniveling simpleton.

"Kathleen," he continued, "take your little spoiled burden and look for cleaning work," he ordered, "and I want a proper meal on this table when I get back.

"As for you," he said pointing his dirty index finger in Kayleigh's face, "you'll call me Pa and do as you're told. Don't think for a minute that you're prancing off to some school because you're not, and back talk me once, girl, and you'll wish you never had."

CHAPTER 2: 1876—LEAVING BROOKLYN

Kayleigh, Kathleen, and Luke made the most of their situations. The three of them had a silent agreement to make the most positive experience possible out of what had been dealt to them.

Kayleigh and Kathleen began to clean apartments and a few very tiny homes. Sometimes Kayleigh would linger a bit as they walked, with longing gazes at the schools from which well-turned-out little girls emerged and polished little boys walked with pride and the knowledge of their breeding.

The two of them made a game out of cleaning by seeing who could clean a complete room most quickly and efficiently and by making up stories about the apartments and homes where they worked. Then, amid the work of cleaning and dusting, they would give each other knowing looks about their stories and the people who resided there.

Later, taking the trolley home, conversations ensued, such as, "Mr. O'Shane's cat sounded as though he was throwing up a mouse," or "Mrs. Rhineheart probably never allows anyone to even sit in those expensive chairs."

Once home, the money earned for the day was turned over to Nolan, who held out his hand like a guard taking a prisoner's belongings; however, his wages, along with those of Matthew and Marcus, could be spent in any way they chose, such as alcohol, gambling, or "playing a con." Kathleen managed to put just a few pennies away each week in a pocket she sewed into Kayleigh's petticoat that was stored in her little trunk. This gave Kayleigh hope. Perhaps one day, just she and Mama and Luke could leave.

Luke's job turned out to be an adventure for Kayleigh, although probably more of a humiliating experience for poor Luke.

Being Luke, though, he made the best of the job. He endured the admonishments of Mr. Gambino when he yelled, "Hurry up in clearing that table, slow boy, or I'll sack you and hold your wages," along with the sneers and arrogant looks of those who saw him as less than a man.

Actually, Kayleigh had helped him get the job. They had tried several restaurants, going around to the back while poor Luke struggled to explain that he was looking for work. Kayleigh tried coaching him but eventually just took over. At Mario's, she gave her most angelic smile and asked if any work was available for a strong young man willing to clear tables, take out trash, or do any other needed chores.

Mario, himself, smiled and, charmed by the "little Irish girl," agreed to start Luke the next day. "Mr. Gambino will tell you what to do," he said in an amused tone. "Oh, your wages will be at the end of the week, and you and the little girl may have a free dessert every Wednesday."

Mr. Gambino appeared at the door. In contrast to Mario, a round, jovial dark Italian, Gambino was tall, thin, and had a pinched, disgusted look about his face. "You'll be here at 8:00 in the morning, and you'll do anything you're asked, from bringing in food from the market to clearing tables, carrying trays, and taking out all of the trash. You understand?"

"Yes, sir," Luke answered timidly.

Kayleigh met Luke at the back door every Wednesday after that, and they enjoyed tiramisu or cheesecake or cannolis before walking home. Fortunately, the restaurant was close to their building, and they shared talks about their days and their hopes for better lives.

Sometimes it was just too much. It was the continual press of people, too close, too hungry, too angry or repressed, just too much of every human condition. So they also made a game of things to escape the smells and life of the streets, with bodies packed too closely together and the smells of food, tenements, and factories.

Luke knew that Kayleigh wanted to go to school more than anything, and Kayleigh knew that Luke wanted a farm out west and a good wife. She understood how lost he felt in the city and how cramped and overshadowed he felt while with his brothers.

As small as their goals would seem to others, to them, they were unreachable dreams. The iron hand of Nolan O'Connor overshadowed everything, and they both knew it.

Kayleigh would not be a little girl for much longer. At eleven years, she was already beginning to understand how the world worked and how men often thought of women. She already saw her mother beginning to lose hope. Kayleigh knew that her mother had stopped her secret, thinking about how to leave Nolan.

It was a hot, sticky August night, and Kayleigh had lain on her pallet for what seemed to be a long time. There was a slight separation between the dirty kitchen curtains and the blanket hung around Kayleigh. She could see the stars again, and so she counted the ones that were visible until she fell asleep.

She awoke to a feeling of choking and suffocation. A large, dirty hand was over her mouth, and Matthew was pressing down toward her, holding a knife, while Marcus watched with a sneer. Instinctively, she bit the hand and screamed as loudly as she could before she was struck full in the face by Nolan and cut at the base of her neck by the knife.

Then, there was Luke, rushing into the kitchen, followed by Kathleen. He was shouting and pushing and hitting at Matthew. Kathleen was gripping the table, her long hair braided, falling across her thread-bare gown. She had her hand to her mouth, unable to even scream.

There were complaints among the neighbors, and nine months later, after Kayleigh had delivered a baby, Nolan announced that they were leaving New York because he had a "lead" on work in Canada, as well as Minnesota.

He purchased a rickety wagon and a wheezing horse to pull them out of New York and toward the Canadian border. They traveled for what seemed an eternity.

They had all been together that day. Kathleen, Nolan, and the baby rode up front, with Nolan driving the horse. Matthew, Marcus, Luke, and Kayleigh rode in the back of the wagon. They came to Toronto after five days. Kathleen held the baby, and Kayleigh tried to keep from throwing up in the back of the wagon.

As they pulled in and stopped at a Catholic nunnery in Toronto, Marcus looked back at his step-sister, Kayleigh, and sneered as he said, "This ought to teach you to quit being a bad girl."

"Mama, what's he talking about?" she cried to Kathleen. "What is this place? I haven't done anything." She was beginning to get hysterical.

"Get out!" her stepfather, Nolan, screamed. "Marcus, get her out!"

Kayleigh was trying to sit up and move when Marcus came around to the side of the wagon and kicked her in the back into the road. "Get out, girl!" he screamed. As she was pushing herself up to her knees, Luke hopped off the wagon to help her up.

"Get out of the way, stupid," Matthew jumped out of the wagon and yelled.

"You shouldn't be treatin' her that way!" Luke cried. "She ain't never done nothin' bad. You all treat her awful!" Kathleen had begun to cry softly.

"And you, Mama," he said, pointing at Kathleen. "She's your daughter, and you don't do nothin' to help her!" It was beginning to rain, and Luke, the one step-brother that she trusted, had his arm around Kayleigh, walking her toward the sanctuary within the cathedral.

"Mama, help me!" Kayleigh begged.

With downcast eyes, she managed to say, "Kayleigh, it's for the best. You'll be safe," before Nolan backhanded her in the face, and the baby cried softly.

"Come on, Little Bit," Luke said softly, and he walked her toward the convent. "I'll come back for you as soon as I can, but right now, I'll get you settled."

The two nuns who met them were opposites in every way. The older of the pair was smiling, and her gentle, round face was friendly. She was short and a bit stout but walked at a fast clip. Her sweet voice was a mix of French and Irish accents.

"Well, who would this be?" Sister Immaculata, the older and the plumper of the two, asked gently.

"This is my sister, Kayleigh," Luke answered. "Our Pa and Mama are outside in the wagon."

"Well, what a good brother you are to bring her in," the Sister commented quietly with a smile while gently taking Kayleigh's hand.

"Where is the baby?" the younger woman, Sister Evangelina, asked abruptly.

"Sister, please," Immaculata whispered.

"Well, we might as well be out in the open about it," Evangelina insisted. "We all know what these girls have done. We know what they're like," she said with a knowing sneer directed toward Kayleigh.

"I'm not a bad girl," Kayleigh pleaded. "I could stay with Mama."

"She's not bad," Luke said loudly. "Something bad happened to her. She don't need to be here for long. I can come back and get her."

"We'll be the judges of that," Evangelina said in a precise message of authority.

"Please, Luke," Kayleigh begged, clinging to him. "Please take me out of here. Don't leave me!"

Luke knelt down next to Kayleigh, his tall, lean frame next to her tiny, vulnerable body. He whispered into her ear, "I can't take you right now, but I'll be back for you. I swear it. I got to get away from them first, myself."

"Don't let them hurt the baby," she whispered while tears of resignation streaked her face.

"They won't hurt that baby. I promise," Luke hugged her with tears in his eyes. "I'm sorry I couldn't do no better by you, Little Bit." He took her face in his hands and whispered, "Don't lose your faith. I love you."

Evangelina pulled the two apart. "Let's go now, no more of this," she said.

"Evagelina, I'll take her to the room with the other girls," Sister Immaculata said as she again took Kayleigh's hand and smiled sweetly at Luke.

"Come along, *ma chère*," she said quietly, "let's get you settled. Do you have any other clothes?" she asked.

"I have nothing," Kayleigh said quietly.

The weeks dragged onward, bleak and dark as the winter skies above the cathedral now used as a mission and hostel for "wayward" girls. Kayleigh kept herself to herself, not trusting the girls that she shared a dormitory with, or the sisters, except possibly Sister Immaculata. She wanted to trust her. She wanted to trust someone, but experience had taught her differently. So, she prayed every night for two things: for Luke to come back for her and for Cassidy, "Cassie," the name that Kathleen had chosen for the baby, to be safe.

Some of the girls stayed only long enough to deliver their babies and move on, with or without the child. Others stayed as Kayleigh did because there was nowhere else for them to go.

The two years that Kayleigh spent there were not totally wasted or spent in pain. She learned rudimentary French, household skills, such as cooking, basic mathematics, and a good deal about the Bible.

Her nun-like uniform was practical, but it did not hide the fact that she was becoming a beautiful young woman, and the plain head kerchief did not hide her curling strawberry-blonde hair.

Sister Immaculata was protective of her and occasionally requested her to help in the nursery with the newborn babies or the toddlers. The good Sister knew that Kayleigh might one day have her own child, and this training would help her.

Father Simeon and Sister Evangelina, however, had a special, more sinister arrangement. She would bring him the prettier girls who had caught his eye, and he would help promote her gradually to Mother Superior.

When she came for Kayleigh, she explained that it was time for her to make a private confession to Father Simeon. She further informed Kayleigh that she should follow all of his instructions completely.

Kayleigh followed obediently, hoping that she might ask him about the possibility of finding her stepbrother, Luke, but she soon learned the real intent of this private audience. Although Father Simeon looked like a sweet, plump French Papa, he was anything but that idyllic character.

"That will be all," he said rather abruptly to Sister Evangelina before he turned to Kayleigh.

"So, petite fille," he began, "do you like your stay here so far?"

"It's fine, sir," Kayleigh said quietly.

"Just fine?" he asked with a series of "tsk, tsk, tsk" following. "Well, surely we can make it better than that, ma chère. For young women who are obedient to me, I can see that many privileges are given. Do you like sweets and pretty frocks or visiting the theater?" he asked in a manner that made Kayleigh shiver.

"I have no need of anything, Father," she replied.

"Well, let's not be so hasty," Father Simeon countered. "You may have need of something you never even imagined," he grinned maliciously, revealing two prominent yellow front teeth.

On the other side of the cathedral, Sister Immaculata had begun to look for her little charge so that they could make their regular rounds with the infants and toddlers.

As she passed the corridor connecting the girls' dormitory to the chapel, there was a tall young man quietly making his way in the same direction.

"You are not allowed here, young sir," she started to say when he stopped and held up his hands to show her that he had no weapon.

"Sister, please help," he appealed to her. "I'm Kayleigh's step-brother, Luke, and I just want to make sure that she's alright. Will you help me?"

Suddenly, the remembrance of him, the day that he brought Kayleigh, flooded back to her. He had seemed so gentle and truly concerned for Kayleigh.

"Well, young man," she said quietly, "as a matter of fact, I can't find her right now, and I'm beginning to be concerned. I shouldn't allow it, but since you're here, you can help me look for her."

"Yes, ma'am," he nodded and fell in step with her.

Since the sister had already searched the chapel and dormitory, as well as the nurseries, they headed to the opposite side of the cathedral to search the church itself when they heard a scream.

"Leave me alone!" Kayleigh screamed as Father Simeon ran one hand up her skirt and began to place the other hand over her left breast.

As she began screaming, Father Simeon placed one hand over her mouth, pinching her lips together so that she could not bite him.

Hearing the piercing scream, Luke and Sister Immaculata both began running toward the Father's study behind the main sanctuary.

"Let go of my sister," Luke screamed as he burst through the door while Sister Immaculata stood frozen in shock.

"She went wild while I was trying to take her confession," Father Simeon explained, "and I was just trying to restrain her."

"Get away from her!" Luke screamed as he began to slam the priest down and punch his face.

The Father's face was beginning to resemble raw meat when Kayleigh placed her hand on Luke's shoulder. "Please, Luke, let's just go. Please just get me out of here," she pleaded.

He turned to Sister Immaculata, "Is this how you run a sanctuary? These girls have been through enough. Don't you care?"

"I didn't know," the small Sister said, crying. "It will never happen again," she said angrily, looking at the priest. "I'm reporting this to the diocese."

"You ain't no man of God!" Luke hissed at the priest.

Luke took Kayleigh by the shoulders and began walking her away. He had a horse and a small wagon tethered in the back of the cathedral next to a small alley.

"Is there anything that you need to collect?" Luke asked her.

"No, Luke," she answered and hugged him tightly.

"There now, Little Bit," he said soothingly. "I told you I'd be back for you."

CHAPTER 3: 1878—LONGING FOR FAITHFUL

"This will be a long trip," Luke advised Kayleigh as they rode along in the wagon, "but I've saved some money for it, and I know how to get back to Pa and Mama. You don't have to worry no more."

"I never worry when I'm with you, Luke," she said, "but I don't want to be around Pa."

"I know, and I understand, but I'll be there. He ain't so quick to take off on me anymore," he said with a newfound look of determination.

"Did you and Pa fight?" she asked.

"No," Luke answered, "but he knew I was about to, and I wouldn't back down. He ain't calling me stupid no more."

"Do you think I'm stupid?" he asked Kayleigh in a low, soft voice.

"No, Luke," Kayleigh sighed, "we've been over this. You just have to take a little more time with your reading and writing."

"Did the priest hurt you, Kayleigh?" Luke asked, completely changing his thoughts and conversation as he frequently did.

"No, but he would have," she answered. "Thank you, Luke."

"Of course, Little Bit," he said with a sideways smile at her. "You're my little sister. I'll always look out for you."

"Don't make me be around Pa or the boys, Luke. I mean it," Kayleigh said, trying not to cry.

"I won't," Luke assured her, but Pa's finally on to something that will make him and us money. He's playing cons similar to what he played in New York. Only he's playing them with a traveling carnival. Or, as some are putting it, he's a 'top con.'

"I don't get involved with that part of it. I work for the carnival, but it's mainly by helping to set up when we get to a new town and by fighting in the ring with anyone who wants a try. I've got a friend now, Joey O'Dell. We put the tents up and take them down. He helps me some with setting up the boxing ring, and sometimes he boxes himself.

"See, I'm a fighter, a boxer now. I take on smart-mouthed Johnnies that'll pay a nickel to go one round with me in the ring. Now, they ought to know better than to take on a New York ruffian. Don't you think, Little Bit?" He laughed and looked at Kayleigh.

"Isn't that dangerous, Luke?" Kayleigh asked.

"I haven't been beat yet," Luke grinned. "Look, Kayleigh," he said, noticing the worried look on her face, "I'm just gonna' be around Pa and my brothers long enough to make my own stake. Then, you and I will leave with Mama and Cassie," he spoke soothingly and confidently to Kayleigh.

"Is Cassie alright?" Kayleigh asked. Her voice again was shaky, and she again was at the point of crying.

"She's growing, and she's so sweet," Luke said with a faraway look in his eyes. "She has a little problem, though," he said carefully. "She has little tremors and spells where she just stretches out and shakes."

"Does it hurt her?" Kayleigh grabbed his arm, her eyes turned to him in desperation.

"No, Little Bit. I don't think so, but I wanted you to know so that you could help her."

They rode on, sometimes in complete silence, and Luke longed for how Kayleigh had been back in New York when they rode the street cars and ran the streets of Brooklyn. She was a chatty magpie of a little girl with him, and he loved it. Now, though, she was withdrawn, morose, and nervous.

He stopped the wagon just as they entered Ontario. While leaving the wagon at a livery stable, he made inquiries about finding an affordable hotel or inn. The innkeeper gave Luke a speculative look, which was not lost on either of them, but neither Luke nor Kayleigh cared at that point. They were brother and sister, and they were both just bone tired.

Once they were settled, he gave Kayleigh one of his shirts to use as a nightgown. She went behind a little dressing screen in the room and changed while Luke spread out a quilt on the floor. Kayleigh also handed him a pillow and spare coverlet from the bed.

She stretched out in the bed and went to sleep more quickly than she had in two years. She was with Luke, and she felt perfectly safe.

The next day, they ate in the hotel. Both of them were half-starved, and Luke managed to get a smile and laugh out of Kayleigh when he declared an eating contest. Luke won, but not by much. He put away four more pancakes and one more egg than Kayleigh did. Even the cook and hostess were entertained and impressed.

Luke paid for the meal and the room, and they began walking toward the stable. "Kayleigh," he ventured, "we need to buy some things for you. You need another outfit to wear and a nightgown, and…I don't really know," he said, blushing. "I mean…I just think that uh…you're going to need some girl things. So, my thought was to get you to a dress shop and get one of them shop ladies to help you. I can't afford much, but probably enough to get you started."

Kayleigh smiled at him and squeezed his arm. "Thank you for everything, Luke."

The shop that they decided on turned out to be a blessing. The Irish lady in charge took an interest in Kayleigh and Luke, their Irish accents, and their situation. She outfitted Kayleigh with a skirt, a blouse, a nightgown, underclothes, stockings, shoes, and a woolen cape. (Luke had explained that they were headed to Minnesota and other states that would have cold winters.)

On their way again, Kayleigh asked Luke just what Pa had begun to do that was bringing in money.

"Well, now keep an open mind and ear," he said. "Pa is working with a carnival, the Dream Town Carnival, that goes from town to town. It's owned by an old man named Abraham Randolph, just Mr. Abe for short. He's pretty fair, but he walks about barking orders like Pa when he's full of himself.

"Anyway, we're making good money setting up the carnival, and we've got our own wagons to live in. This way, Mama can keep Cassie in the daytime, and Matthew, Marcus, and I can make a living.

"Mama helps out the seamstress lady some. That fetches a little money. You'd like the main seamstress for the carnival. Her name is Fancy, and she's a real nice lady.

"Pa's got a sideline, of course. He runs two games. One is a ring toss for prizes, and one is the cup game, or shell game. The carnival gets a cut, but he gets his part, too."

"What will I do, Luke?" she asked, wondering if she would be put to work and if she could ever go to school again.

"Well, I suppose just help Mama," he said, looking puzzled. The truth was that he had not reasoned this part out.

They were quiet for a while as they approached the American border. After a time, though, Luke asked Kayleigh a question.

"Kayleigh, I've been wondering. Well…that is. One of the ladies who is working with the carnival seems interested in me. She's a little older than me by about four years. Do you think a woman could ever want me, to marry?"

"Oh, Luke," Kayleigh said earnestly. "Don't you know who you are and what you have to offer? You're handsome, strong, hard-working, willing to help a woman, and you're a really good man. What more is there for most women? You have it all."

He blushed and said quietly, "Kayleigh, you always was a smart one, and even though I'm twenty years old, I swear it's like you're older and wiser than me. Thank you for what you just said."

"It's just the truth of it all," Kayleigh offered. "Any woman will be lucky to have you."

They made a few more stops along the way before pulling into Minnesota and making their way toward the young city of Minneapolis and the Dream Town Carnival. Carnivals had not yet swept the country, but they were beginning to find their way westward and to the south, as was everything else.

Once they had stopped, Luke pointed out the wagon where her mother and Cassie were, and she jumped down and ran as fast as she could.

"Kayleigh!" Kathleen said, shocked, "My colleen, I thought to never see you again!" She reached to pull Kayleigh in for a hug, but Kayleigh pulled back and reached for Cassie.

"I'm going to hold her," she told her mother in a challenging way. "I want to hold her."

"Of course," her mother agreed, "she needs to take to you. Right now, she'll only go to Luke or me."

She scooped up the small child, noticing how tiny and frail she was. Usually, Cassie wailed if anyone other than Kathleen was holding her, but instead, with Kayleigh, she studied this new young woman tentatively. Then, a wide grin began to light her face and her blue eyes. She nuzzled her head into Kayleigh's shoulder.

"Oh, she knows you, lass," Kathleen said barely louder than a whisper. "I thought perhaps she might call you 'Sissy.' Don't you even have a hug for your own mama, Kayleigh?" Kathleen pleaded with her eyes.

"You didn't stand up for me or protect me, Mama," she answered. "That's what a mother does," Kayleigh said, close to tears, as she put Cassie back on her pallet.

"I swear I'll do better by you, Kayleigh," Kathleen begged. "I didn't know he would sink so low. When he started up through Canada, he told me that he was looking for work. I didn't know about the church and the mission."

Kayleigh looked at her mother with a fresh pair of eyes, those of a maturing young woman. She and Kathleen looked a great deal alike. Their hair, eyes, and stature were similar, but Kathleen's eyes did not seem to have quite the spark of curiosity about life that Kayleigh's did.

"You're weak, Mama," Kayleigh said bluntly, "and I will not live in the same wagon with him, but I do plan on being around Cassie and protecting her. If he or Matthew and Marcus ever try to harm me or her, I'll find a way to kill him," she warned.

"Why have you even stayed with him?" Kayleigh asked.

"Well, now, what do you think I was going to do?" Kathleen asked with a trace of bitterness. "I was, and I am, a woman with no money and no family," Kathleen replied. "Luke has been the closest thing to a son to me. With his quiet, shy ways, it just took him longer to find his voice. He stands up right well now to Pa and Matthew and Marcus. Pa and I don't even sleep in the same wagon. He bunks in with Marcus. Matthew sleeps in one of the tents, as does Luke," she explained.

"Did he know that Luke was going to fetch me?" Kayleigh asked with her eyes full of questioning fear.

"He does now," Kathleen answered. "Just try to stay clear of him. Most days, he's busy with the carnival business, but sometimes, he does stomp about, reminding us that he's in charge."

True hatred burned within Kayleigh with each quick breath that she took. She was changing. She would never be a child again, not that she ever had much time to be one, but anything trusting in her seemed to be leaving. She would live her life for Cassie and herself, and whatever little acts and tricks she had to use as a cover, so be it.

After a time, Kayleigh began to find her way about the carnival. It reminded her of life. It could be shiny, exciting, exotic, even beautiful on the outside, but on the inside, it was full of sad tasks, illness, tricks, and poverty. This came along with an unbalanced dependence on others to keep the secrets of the different identities that people had taken on to stave off the reality of who they were.

She picked up odd jobs, or in ticket sales, and sometimes as "Mr. Leonardo's" sketch assistant.

Because she was well-liked, things went pretty well until Luke decided to leave and search out a farm or a homestead for himself and his soon-to-be bride, Gloria. When they left Minnesota, they would go to South Dakota, where land was available.

Gloria played the part of an opera singer from the "northern provinces" of France. Her tight red dance actually brought more young men to her exhibit than her actual singing. Professor Gallant, the "barker" for the attraction, billed her as the "Angel of the Opera."

In truth, Gloria was from the Bronx, and Professor Gallant was a former school teacher from Chicago whose students had beaten him up before he was fired. They were an odd business pair, but Kayleigh liked them both and was glad that Luke had found love in Gloria.

With Luke gone, Nolan began to come around Kathleen and Cassie more often. This meant that he was beginning to be around Kayleigh also and that Matthew and Marcus began to show their cruel faces more often also. The two would look at Kayleigh lewdly and make suggestive or downright ugly remarks to her.

She was beginning to rely more and more on Peaches and Pop, who ran the singing group and the band musicians. They were a good, honest couple without any children, and they cared about Kayleigh. They offered her shelter, music, and love, but they could not completely protect her from her stepfather and brothers.

It was at this point that she was coerced into pick-pocketing. The three men threatened to take Cassie to an orphanage if Kayleigh did not comply. She finally, in fear, tried her hand at this questionable "trade" one Saturday night and actually did well, targeting older, more well-to-do customers.

However, when she refused to do this a second time, they shut her into a trunk until she agreed to continue again. The next time, though, they found her in jail. When Peaches and Pop found out about her situation and understood what she was being forced to do, they confronted Nolan.

The couple then came to her rescue and bailed her out, telling her to come and stay with them on the far side of the carnival, away from the games and attractions. This way, she would be away from her stepfather but could go to see about Cassie.

At night, when the carnival had closed down and the stars dotted a clear sky, she might sleep in the wagon with her mother and little sister or stay in the wagon with Peaches and Pop. In either setting, she would peer at the stars, imagining beautiful mountains that seemed to call to her

Again, she dared to think that life was beginning to be a more stable proposition, and she breathed a sigh of relief when Luke returned just before they moved on.

Winter had set in when they reached Wisconsin. Kayleigh thought that she had known winters in Brooklyn and Canada, but this was a different combination of snow and cold. It was, however, a great comfort to be in rented rooms for a time. She, Cassie, and Kathleen had a room together, but she knew exactly where Peaches and Pop were, should she need them.

Nolan, Matthew, and Marcus sneered at her when she crossed their paths, but they knew when they were outnumbered by those who cared about Kayleigh, Kathleen, and Cassie. Kayleigh came to rely more and more on Luke, Gloria, and Peaches and Pop.

Pop had taught her to play the fiddle and piano that last spring in Minnesota, and to his delight, she was a natural. She began to perform in their shows, and they also discovered that she could sing. They were, therefore, the main money makers for the Dream Town Carnival during winters.

They usually performed in taverns or in churches if they did their hymnal selections. The carnival took their cut, which bothered Pop to no end, but all of the musicians and singers were paid.

Kayleigh had little money of her own, but she did keep a little secret box. It was sewn into the lining of her small trunk, and her mother had given her the small bit of money that she had hidden in Kayleigh's petticoat while they were in New York. It also contained her earnings and a few little poems and songs that she had tried to pen.

It was at this time that Kayleigh came to understand that Pop was going blind. She became his eyes, fetching his fiddle or guitar, leading him to his place on stage, or making sure that he turned in all of the money earned to Peaches.

As the carnival resumed, Kayleigh turned fourteen, and there were things that were becoming firm in her mind. She wanted a profession, and she wanted to be respectable; and, more than anything, she wanted to go back to school. She knew that she had a good mind, and she knew that she would make a good teacher.

Professor Gallant had talked to her about getting into a teacher college in South Dakota and offered to help her prepare for the training and exams that followed. He offered her books and all of his knowledge, which was a good bit. It was a true tragedy that he felt driven out of his chosen profession.

Kayleigh was elated and had a plan. Since Luke and Gloria were going to homestead in South Dakota and had offered to let her, her mother, and Cassie live with them, she could be with Cassie and go to school, but, as with most things in Kayleigh's life, another episode was about to unfold.

It was the last night of the carnival in Wisconsin. She would miss Peaches and Pop and some of the other carnies like Professor Gallant, but mainly, she just wanted to start school.

Luke had told her that he would help get the packing started after his last fight. Kayleigh asked him not to fight again, but he insisted that they needed the money.

She made her way to the boxing ring to see his last round. According to the crowd, he had already knocked out three men in a row and caused one to just walk away after the second round. He felt his worth and raised his gloves when Kayleigh walked up.

Then, a man approached the ring that Kayleigh could only silently describe as a giant. She glanced across the crowd to see Gloria's wide-eyed look of fear. This could not be a fair fight.

Luke sized up the man and made an immediate decision to take a fall in the second round if he couldn't last the giant out. It sickened him that he would be losing the nickel that the man would pay, plus another that he would be paid for winning, but he also knew that he had little chance with this man.

Luke was wiry and fast, so he managed to dodge and weave away from the giant for the first round. He was mentally planning his strategy for the second when the giant sucker-punched him in the jaw. He started down, and the giant kicked Luke's legs out from under him and then kicked and stomped his ribs.

"No!" Kayleigh screamed. "No! Let him alone."

Part of the crowd was staring at her while the rest was mesmerized by the fight. Suddenly, Nolan flew through the crowd along with Matthew and Marcus in tow. They shoved and pushed people out of the way indiscriminately. Kayleigh and Gloria both ran to the ring from opposite sides.

Kayleigh was tiny but fast, and she reached her stepbrother first. With her eyes ablaze, she dared the giant to come any closer. She knelt down beside Luke.

"Little Bit, is that you?" he asked. "I can't see so good," he spoke barely above a whisper.

"It's me, Luke," she answered as tears streamed down her face, "and Gloria is here."

Gloria took his hand, trying to keep her voice steady and calm. "It's me, love," she said softly. "Lie still and think of all our wonderful plans."

Three men from the crowd had pushed the giant back, and he stood with them at the opposite corner of the ring. Nolan and the brothers, for once, stood silently behind Kayleigh.

"We need a doctor!" Kayleigh screamed.

A man emerged who had been a medic in the Civil War. He knelt next to Luke and took the pulse at the base of his neck. Kayleigh could see from the look on his face that things were not good.

"He has internal injuries," he said to Kayleigh and Gloria. "He's probably bleeding internally, and it would not be good to move him."

"Pa," Luke said so softly.

"What, son?" Nolan asked, and for once, the man seemed to have some genuine emotion.

"Don't you or Matthew and Marcus ever try to hurt Kayleigh again."

He turned then to Gloria. "I love you, darling, with all my heart. You find a good man and a good life for yourself." Gloria bent her head and sobbed.

"Little Bit," he said, "take care of Mama and Cassie and you," and with that, he let go of life.

They buried him in Wisconsin. Pop and Peaches helped pay for the burial and advised her to stay close to them as the carnival continued through Wisconsin. Kayleigh knew that she had no choice but to move with the carnival, but she yearned for an education more than anything. At night, she often curled up at the foot of Peaches and Pop's bed. She often dreamed of a place surrounded by mountains. "Where was this place?" she wondered again and again.

She would awaken and pray. She had never completely abandoned speaking to God, and the prayer was usually the same, "Dear Lord, lead me somewhere…somewhere where people are gentle and accepting of each other, understanding of differences (not perfect, but oh so close). Please, show me this place and my purpose, and please, for once, let me feel safe. Please lead me to the faithful people of this life."

CHAPTER 4: 1880—ALONG THE WAY

Wisconsin was a blur of activity as spring set in. The carnival was up and at its best. Later, Kayleigh would barely remember that time. Her longing for Luke was so strong that it overshadowed much of her life. Many people missed him, but especially she, Gloria, and Joey O'Dell.

Joey had black curling hair, and the rumor was that he was part Cherokee. His large dark brown eyes were heavily framed with dark lashes, and his eyebrows were jet black and expressive. He wore a dark mustache, which set off his high cheekbones, and his body, at six foot three, was lean and muscular. "Madam Daring," the fearless dancing horses ring leader who often rode standing on bareback horses, once said, "he makes a young woman think of things she's never had, and an older woman think of things forgotten or gone."

Joey had thought of Luke like a brother. He admired the goodness in him and the perseverance in his work. Together, they had torn down and put up the carnival over fifty times. They would talk as they worked, and he knew, as well as anyone, of Luke's hopes with Gloria and his concerns for Kayleigh and Cassie. They laughed a lot, and he missed him more than he would ever let on.

Women approached him like shells washed up on a shore, and he usually seemed rather uninterested, but he did wonder about Kayleigh. So, sometimes, he stole glances in her direction, wondering if she was as sad as she sometimes looked.

Kayleigh would later vaguely remember going into Madison for a day or two. The weather was pleasantly cool, and the carnival took in more money than it ever had. She saved as much of the money as she could, but her thoughts were occupied with other things, such as her lessons with Professor Gallant and her concerns over Cassie. (She had not yet really taken notice of Joey O'Dell.)

At almost four years of age, Cassie did not seem to be developing normally. She was still so frail and small, and the doctor in Madison called her shaking difficulty "epilepsy."

He cautioned that it would remain a problem for most of her life, if not all. He showed Kathleen and Kayleigh certain techniques to use with her and recommended a special medication to help with it. However, he made it clear that there were no easy answers.

There was still little known about how to help patients with this disability. He also pointed out that although many people with this affliction were highly intelligent, some were damaged from birth or from seizures and were always childish. Kayleigh and her mother looked at one another in a mixture of sadness and confusion. What would they do?

Kayleigh had turned fifteen, and one day, she was helping "Madam Daring" with her ledger and balancing the tickets with "the take," or the sales. Her act was one of the most popular, and she was a good friend to have. She possessed both people skills and business sense, in addition to her horseback skills.

Suddenly, Joey O'Dell appeared at the tent. His plaid flannel shirt and dungarees somehow seemed to fit him better than they did most men. His black eyes sparkled, and his voice was charming. "How are sales?" he smiled and asked casually.

It seemed to Kayleigh that he was as tall as the tent and that his presence dominated everything. She took in the look of him, the slow smile, and even his scent. He smelled like a hard-working male, yet he also smelled a bit like the bay rum that some men used after shaving. She blushed suddenly and looked away, realizing that she was beginning to stare.

"Not bad," Madam Daring replied. "The sales in Madison really helped. By the way, do you know where we're headed next?"

"Yes, Mr. Abe Randolph wants to continue south, so I guess we'll be going by way of Indiana next. Apparently, he wants to wind up all the way down in Florida," he explained. "His son, Ike, however, has plans of going west. Word is, they may split the carnival between the two of them.

"Personally, I'll be glad to get to Tennessee. That's where my people are, and I haven't seen my mama in some time," he smiled and looked at Kayleigh.

That's why he always seemed to have the hint of a southern accent, Kayleigh thought. *He must have grown up there.*

"How about you, Little Bit?" he turned and smiled at Kayleigh. "What do you think about moving south?"

In truth, she had not thought about where they were going. She just went, and now, somehow, she felt tongue-tied, as though anything that she said would be wrong. However, it did not escape her that he had used Luke's pet name for her. She finally mustered up the courage to reply, "I think that will be fine. Maybe I can go back to school at some point."

"That means a lot to you, doesn't it, Kayleigh?" he asked.

"Yes," she managed to reply.

"Well, you know what else might mean a lot to you?" he smiled as he delivered the question.

"No, what?" she asked, mesmerized by his voice and tone.

"Just having some fun," he replied. "Here we are in the middle of a carnival, and I bet you've never just walked through it on a busy night and enjoyed it," he said, still smiling at her.

"Um, I need to deliver these sales to Mr. Randolph's office," Madam Daring said, giving Kayleigh a rather approving look. "I'll be back in a half hour."

Kayleigh could feel herself blushing. What should she say?

"I tell you what, Little Bit," Joey gave her another very direct look, as though sizing up her maturity, "meet me right here at the entrance to the Fortune Tellers tent tonight, about 7:00. Instead of working tonight, I'll walk you around the attractions. We'll talk and just have a good time."

"But I really need to make money for my mama and sister," Kayleigh could hear the desperation in her own voice.

"Are you singing tonight with Peaches and Pop?" he asked.

"No, not tonight," she answered, "but I was going to help at the gate."

"Well, how about this," he proposed, "we'll work the gate together for an hour, and then we'll walk about. What about that?" he asked.

"Alright," she agreed. "That sounds…fine."

He stooped as he went through the tent flap and turned, "Tonight, at the gate, then," and he was gone.

Kayleigh was surprised that he even showed up at the gate, but he did, handsome as ever. Kayleigh had tried to "dress up" a bit, as best she could. She wore her best blue skirt and a white silk blouse that Peaches insisted on loaning her once she had "gotten wind" of the plan from Madam Daring.

Her mother insisted on putting her hair up for her. "Now look at the young woman you are in the mirror," Kathleen instructed as she smiled, and all of the more mature ladies of the carnival seemed to have a stake in this encounter.

Of course, they couldn't talk a lot while minding the entrance to the carnival and selling tickets, but she and Joey exchanged looks and smiles and a few comments as those attending strolled in. After two hours, Mr. Randolph and his wife took over.

Marcus and Matthew took their turns next. They were both their usual snarling selves, perhaps even more so. "Keeping the gate" had not been part of their evening plans, but this was what Joey had worked out with Mr. Randolph. (Kayleigh was grateful that she would not have to see either one of them.)

It was a beautiful clear night, and the slivered moon was beginning to shyly reveal itself. As they walked along the midway, Joey commented on how pretty Kayleigh looked. After a while, he began to hold her hand.

"You should get out and about more often, Kayleigh," he said and smiled. "You're allowed to have a little fun, you know."

They took in the sounds, sights, and smells of the crowded little carnival. Mingled among the attractions were booths with fruit pies and meat pies, and "Dr. Healthful," actually, Herman Jones, a short middle-aged mustached barker who stood in heeled boots on a small platform, called out to all who would listen to how the wonders of his back pain elixir stopped the pain. (Kayleigh thought it best to keep it to herself that she actually drank some of this from time to time for her own back pain, which had persisted since her step-brother had kicked her in Canada. Little did she know that it simply consisted of water, sugar, strong tea, and molasses.)

The press of the crowd thinned at some points and grew at others. As they approached the left side of the carnival grounds, many were being drawn to "Samson the Strong Man" or "Zelda the Bearded Lady" and her sister with huge feet. "Gwendolyn the Sword Swallower" was also popular, as were the

"Little People" dressed as clowns.

Children were most often drawn to the "Great Performing Elephants," just as older patrons were drawn to "Pop and Peaches' Gospel Review." All ages, however, found the acrobats fascinating with their flips, tumbling, and mid-air jumps.

Young men stood in a long line to get into "Professor Gallant's Angel of the Opera Show," with speculative remarks about just how tight the opera singer's dress might be. In truth, Gloria was still so saddened that she now merely wore a simple black dress. Still, the "Strong Man," who had adopted the biblical name, Samson, was called upon at times to free her from the advances of one or more of the young men.

Samson was blind in one eye and completely deaf. Onlookers just assumed that he was aloof, but the carnival people knew the truth and the pain of his loneliness. He had taught Kayleigh to use sign language, and she had tried to encourage him to go back to school, but he seemed set on his path with the carnival.

As Joey and Kayleigh began to walk toward the right, they grew closer to the "Game of Chance," which Nolan ran. Kayleigh watched on in dread at her stepfather as he barked out, "Come on! Come all! Take a chance and win a prize!"

People gradually made their way either to Matthew's ring toss or the shell game that Marcus ran. "Either way," Kayleigh thought, "it's all a con."

Seeing Kayleigh with Joey, Nolan stopped and sneered. "What is this, O'Dell, your yearly pity night of walking around a homely girl?"

"I'm not pitying anyone," Joey said, giving Nolan O'Connor look for look.

"Well, you couldn't possibly want her. She's a cold old maid in the making. Don't you know that?" he asked with a nasty laugh which set his lip in a curling leer.

"Look, old man," Joey said, standing barely an inch away from Nolan's face. "If I ever hear you talk that way again, I'll beat your face in, and I'll enjoy doing it."

Kayleigh took his arm, and they continued walking. The night sky had turned a velvety black, alight with thousands of stars. Cigar smoke wafted in the breeze. They were approaching the boxing ring when Kayleigh stopped and froze in place. Suddenly, everything was too much. The sights and sounds, her stepfather's comments, and the place where her brother had died were all crowding around her.

"I know you really loved him, Kayleigh," Joey said softly, "and he really loved you. It's alright to grieve, but it's also alright to move on. And don't ever let anyone tell you that you're not a pretty, smart, sweet girl 'cause you are. Your stepfather is a cruel idiot, and he's helped ruin Matthew and Marcus. They're just as mean as he is.

"The truth is that he's jealous of you, and he wants you, and so do your step-brothers. They're all three twisted." His face changed, darkened somehow as he continued, "You're doing right to stay away from them. I know what it's like to have hateful brothers," he said bitterly.

Kayleigh had tears in her eyes. Someone finally understood and cared. She could stay with this man forever and finally be safe and happy.

They continued walking, and after a time, they wound up at the "Quick Sketch" show. Mr. Leonardo sketched whatever a patron was willing to pay for a ticket and see come to life from his deft and talented hands. She doubted that his last name was really Leonardo, but she liked his choice.

Joey paid for a ticket, and Mr. Leonardo beamed as he said, "Oh, and what do you want to see, sweet Kayleigh? What can I sketch for you?"

"Could you draw beautiful mountains with stars above them?" she asked.

"Yes, I think I could manage that," he smiled.

She watched as he sketched, and a scene grew simply from what she had described. She was amazed that he had captured her dream in almost every detail. Then, as he was finishing, he took the sketch from the easel and turned it from her sight as if he had a secret that he was not quite ready to share.

He slowly turned it around, and there, at the foot of the mountains, was a bit of a ledge with sun streaming through pine trees. A couple walked hand in hand. There was not enough detail to distinguish their features, but to Kayleigh, it was her and Joey.

They thanked Mr. Leonardo and commented on how talented he was. He looked very directly at Kayleigh and commented, "I've seen some of your drawings too. You are quite good and should work at your gift," he advised.

She blushed and said, "Thank you," as she and Joey walked on. By now, they were back at the wagons and small tents, away from the actual carnival. It was time to say good night, and Kayleigh found herself feeling very nervous.

Joey took her very suddenly in his arms. His face gently scratched her face as he kissed her cheek. Releasing her, he said, "Don't ever think that no man would want you. You have a beautiful soul and a sweet prettiness."

I will love you forever, she thought silently, and she expected nothing in return.

When Kayleigh looked back in later years at her time spent in the carnival before it split in two, she would remember Joey O'Dell the best. His smile, his eyes, his voice, his tall, lean frame would all come back to her. She had loved him that much. It would leave her, though, always questioning whether she was seeing love or simple concern in a man's eyes.

CHAPTER 5: LEAVING WISCONSIN

The carnival found its way through the smaller towns of Wisconsin that spring and summer. Sometimes, it moved slowly like a snake winding through the grasses, but sometimes, it picked up a bit of speed and, from a distance, looked like a wagon train of pioneers. Of course, these pioneers were anything but your typical bonneted mamas and farmer-type men.

Kayleigh continued to help take care of Cassie. The little girl had not had a seizure in over six months, which gave both Kathleen and Kayleigh great hope. The child had also gained some weight, and her color was better.

In fact, Kayleigh and Cassie looked a good deal alike. Both had greenish blue eyes, cupid-bow lips, and a pixie-like, upturned nose. Cassie, however, had dark brown hair, and there was a lively, attentive quality absent from her eyes. She charmed many, though, simply with her sweetness and concern for others.

Kayleigh was wearing a plain white shirt, a straw hat, and a simple light blue skirt. Kathleen had put the hat on her at the last minute, and, for the first time in a long time, they had shared a tender moment. It reminded her of the boat from Ireland when her mother would place a bonnet on her head and say, "Put this bonnet on to keep those freckles from getting any more ideas about settling on your face."

She had the reins and was driving the horses as Cassie leaned against her. "I love you better than anyone, ever, Sissy!" she beamed up into Kayleigh's eyes as she spoke in her childish cadence.

"I love you, Blossom," Kayleigh said gently, using her pet name for the child. "You stay with Mama and me always, so you'll be safe. Now, take your thumb out of your mouth," she said softly. "You're almost four now, a big girl."

Cassie obeyed and pointed excitedly. "Look, Sissy, it's Fancy! Can Fancy ride with us? I like it when she and Mama sew together."

"Well, we'll slow down and ask," Kayleigh answered, but Fancy was already beginning to ask.

"Hey, can a girl get a ride to the next city?" she asked and grinned while shading her eyes with her hand and peering out of her bonnet. "I can spell you on the reins, too," she said and flashed her smile again.

"Well, climb on up and keep us company for a time, and then we'll see," Kayleigh smiled in return.

"The three rode along chatting. Fancy was always dressed impeccably in the style of the day, with a pretty flowing skirt and colorful blouse or a dress taken in beautifully at the waist with a silken bodice. Her dark hair was usually braided into a coil at the nape of her neck, and she seemed to never miss a detail of life or the stitch of her needle as she made and mended the carnival costumes.

Fancy looked at Cassie and smiled warmly. "How's my Cassie today?"

"Good," Cassie beamed as she removed her thumb from her mouth again. "You have very pretty brown skin," she said.

"Cassie!" Kayleigh admonished.

"It's all right, Kayleigh," Fancy soothed. "I know that I have brown skin," she looked directly and kindly at Cassie, "and I'm alright with it. In fact, it's just fine. It's a part of who I am."

They all three smiled at that, and Kayleigh reflected on how fine and pretty Fancy's features were. From her high cheekbones to her full lips, she was a beauty with a figure that matched.

They chatted away the hours and took turns at the reins. This gave Kayleigh time to check on Kathleen, who was in the back of the wagon. Kathleen sometimes looked ashen and defeated again, which worried Kayleigh greatly.

In the evenings, though, if they had not reached a city yet or weren't opening the carnival that night, various campfires would be made, and groups would gather around. Kayleigh looked forward to this all day, sitting next to Joey, holding his hand, and talking about their days of traveling or what she and Professor Gallant had shared in the readings with him.

One evening, they were parked in a green plain, beautiful to the eye. The cold was leaving Wisconsin in favor of a full spring. Farms dotted the neighboring countryside. An occasional cowbell could be heard. Peaches and Pop sang gospel songs softly while the banks of the fire crackled and popped.

The clear night sky revealed millions of stars like a proud mother gently pulling the bed covers back to show a friend her beautiful children. Kayleigh looked at Joey as though he was her very life, and it did not go unnoticed by others.

Fancy slipped up to the group so softly that there was a surprise in seeing her expressed good-naturedly by the group. Samson, Peaches, Pop, Gloria, Madame See-All, Kayleigh, and Joey looked up and smiled.

"Might I join?" she asked tentatively.

Everyone in the group murmured welcomes as she sat down between Joey and Pop. "It's good to have some time before the business of tomorrow," she commented.

"That it is," Joey agreed eagerly, and there was something about how he looked at Fancy that was not lost on Kayleigh.

"I've always wondered, Joey, just how you came to be with this traveling enterprise?" Fancy smiled.

"Well, that is a story," Joey said with a hint of bitterness. "My brothers and I went down to the docks in Memphis to unload a shipment for our Pa. My brothers got to talkin' with Mr. Randolph, who had come in on a steamship to do some barking for his carnival and to see about buying supplies.

"My baby brother, Ben, was with me, but then I didn't see him. I turned around and saw that he had gotten ahead of me. I started to call out to him when I felt a blow to my head. The next thing I knew,

I was waking up on that steamboat in Minnesota. When I finally came to myself and realized where I was, Mr. Randolph showed me a contract that my brothers had signed. If I did not serve seven years with the carnival, my father and mother's house would be foreclosed on. The mortgage had been signed over to Mr. Randolph by my oldest brother.

"Pa and Mother were holding on by a thread as it was. The crops had not been good. That contract is almost up. I've made this same carnival circuit seven times. When we leave here, I'll be heading to Tennessee. I have some things to attend to there."

The group fell silent in shock, "Well, that does it for me," Pop said, breaking the silence. "I'm throwing in with young Mr. Randolph, the son. The west sounds good to me."

Samson, lip-reading the conversation, nodded.

Kayleigh studied Joey's face by the firelight. *I'll go with Joey*, she thought. *Mama and Cassie can come too.*

"What about you, Fancy?" Joey asked, leaning toward her and smiling. "How did you wind up in this traveling world of characters?"

"Well, in a way, my story is similar to yours," she said quietly, "except that I was running and looking for protection. I heard that the carnival needed a seamstress, so while the carnival was in town, I gathered up my courage, went up to Mrs. Randolph, and showed her some of my handiwork. In that way, I showed what I could do and secured my position."

"And what town did you leave from Fancy?" Peaches asked in her high-pitched mountain accent.

"Nashville," Fancy replied. "I taught in a school for black children and also did seamstress work for white people. I was making a good living but also being continually harassed by a young white man who wanted me for his mistress. After a time, it just became more than I could bear," she finished with tears glistening at the corners of her eyes.

For a time, they all shared about how they had come into the carnival. Kayleigh noticed that Joey had not taken his eyes off of Fancy since she had spoken, and she stole furtive glances at him. That night, Peaches told Pop, "Joey and Fancy will not be with the carnival much longer. They'll find a way to be together. It's sad that Kayleigh never saw that he was only offering her friendship."

Pop stopped in his tracks before beginning to undress for bed. Having not seen the signs, as others around the campfire had, he was taken aback. "Lord be with little Kayleigh," he said, and Peaches nodded.

The next week, most were not surprised when Joey and Fancy announced that they would break away from the carnival and go their own way through Iowa and Missouri into Tennessee. Even Kayleigh knew from seeing them together and not having Joey to walk with anymore that the two were together.

It was early one morning, and Kayleigh was beginning to practice her fiddle with Pop and Peaches for the evening show. Fancy walked quietly up to her and asked her to talk. "We can talk here," Kayleigh replied.

"No, please, Kayleigh," Fancy answered. "Let's step down from the stage."

Once they were out of hearing distance, Fancy took Kayleigh's hands in hers and said, "I'm sorry about all of this. It just happened, I guess. You are one of the best friends I've ever had, and the last thing I wanted was to hurt you. Can you forgive me?"

"What's to forgive?" Kayleigh answered carefully and tightly. "He loves you, not me. It happens."

"That's not completely true," Fancy said, looking very directly into Kayleigh's green eyes. "I think he loved you very much, just differently. I also think you did him a world of good."

"Well, that's fine," Kayleigh forced a smile. "I hope that you are both very happy. He'd be a fool not to love you and leave with you."

With that, Kayleigh turned to go.

"Wait, Kayleigh, can Joey come and talk to you?"

"If he wants," she turned her head back and answered. "He's never needed to ask permission."

"All right, I'll tell him," Fancy said sadly. "Can we both hug goodbye?"

"I'm already on my way to practice," Kayleigh said matter-of-factly. "As I said, I wish you the best." She would regret not hugging Fancy much later.

Fancy turned in a resigned way. Joey attended Peaches and Pop's "Mountain Gospel Show" that night and waited for Kayleigh to come off stage. She had been careful not to catch his eye in the audience and was making her way off stage when he caught up to her.

"I need to talk to you, Little Bit," he said from behind her.

"Please don't call me that," she said. "That was between Luke and myself. I'm happy for you and Fancy, and I give you my best wishes. Now, if you'll excuse me, I need to get back to Cassie."

He touched her arm gently and turned her to face him. "Please forgive me and know that I love you. I probably always will, but there's a likeness between Fancy and me, and I know that she's lived through enough to help me go back and face what I need to face in Tennessee. We're not going to have an easy time of it, but I've never gone the easy way. Please forgive me."

"There is nothing to forgive," Kayleigh said, looking deeply into his dark eyes, eyes sometimes hard to read. "We didn't have much more than a friendship, and, by the way, let me assure you that I've already lived through more than enough and will continue to. I hope you'll be happy," and she managed to keep the tears in.

He stopped, kissed her on the cheek, and left.

Throughout the days that followed, Matthew and Marcus began to taunt Kayleigh again. "You shoulda' known no man would stay with you," Matthew jeered, but Kayleigh was beginning to stand up for herself and discovered that she had quite the tongue when she wanted.

"Well, I know women can't stay away from short, fat men with hick bowl haircuts and sneers for faces, but somehow they've managed with you and Marcus."

They looked at her in shock as she walked back to her wagon. If they wanted a fight, she would give them one. Pop had already loaned her a gun.

The following week, the Randolphs made an announcement about their separate plans. Mr. Abe Randolph would go on toward Tennessee by Illinois and Kentucky. His plan was to take the carnival all the way to Florida and possibly stay there for quite a while.

The younger, Mr. Ike Randolph, had westward dreams and would be taking the carnival members who wanted to come along back through Minnesota onward to South Dakota, Wyoming, and Idaho.

"Mama," Kayleigh instructed as she picked up Cassie, "please help me pack and tend to the horses. We're going west."

"Yay!" Cassie shouted and clapped her hands.

"Well, I hope so," Kayleigh said. "I hope so."

CHAPTER 6: 1881—TURNING POINTS

The plan was to backtrack through Minnesota before heading to South Dakota. To Kayleigh's disappointment, Nolan, Matthew, and Marcus also decided to go westward. However, the three had never been a part of any real friendships or gatherings within the carnival, so her contact with them was limited, and she now felt that she could protect herself or turn to friends for help.

So, she, Kathleen, and Cassie bonded with those who had cast their lots with Ike. That included Kayleigh, Peaches, and Pop, along with Samson, Madam Daring, Professor Gallant, and Gloria. In this way, Ike actually had the main players for his carnival. He would have what he needed for his enterprise. However, his father would need to rehire and build his crew again.

Ike reminded Kayleigh of General Custer, at least the sketches she had seen of him or the stories she had heard of him. He had the flowing blonde locks, the piercing eyes and angular features, and the perfectly groomed facial hair. He was slim but, at five foot seven inches, not a big man. Much like his father, though, he could command a crowd and lead with know-how.

No one really questioned his knowledge, since he had grown up in the carnival, or his confidence, except Kayleigh, and this was only within her own mind. She sensed his insecurities. He was a good man and not really a show-off or brash person, but he could paint a picture with words and make promises that would be hard to fulfill. As the more experienced "Carnies" would say, "He knew how to play the game."

They did a few somewhat prosperous shows in Sioux Falls and Rapid City, but the state of South Dakota seemed more sparsely populated to her than others, more open with expansive prairies. Then, suddenly, they became stranded near Springfield.

Snow flew in slanted arrows, dissipating and freezing on the ground, then tufting and piling into inch upon inch. To his credit, Ike led them to a boarding house that he had already staked out. The owner, part Sioux, was a thin, petite woman with graying coal-black hair, and she agreed to rent out her entire upper-floor rooms. Since she wasn't doing a booming business anyway, she had to fake a business-like demeanor while inwardly celebrating.

For Kayleigh, Kathleen, and Cassie, most days were filled with the chores of everyday life, maintaining themselves and helping with the carnival wagons and livestock. Even little Cassie helped with small chores and, of course, continued to be her sister's shadow.

Blessedly, the three O'Connor men were in the downstairs rooms and could be avoided in the daytime. They often did the heavier chores before finding and patronizing the local tavern, often even in blinding snow.

One morning, when the snow had finally stopped, Professor Gallant pulled Kayleigh aside and told her of the Southern State Normal School in South Dakota. Every night, they studied, and he tutored her in math, English, and geography as he prepared her for the entrance exams.

Sometimes, in the afternoons, she would drink tea and talk with Ike while he downed coffee in the small dining room of the boarding house. She learned that Ike had been married and had a son, but his wife decided that the carnival life was not for her, or the boy, and returned to her mother in Indiana. He hoped to get back to her one day.

Kayleigh told him of her ambitions, and she was flattered that he honestly listened and gave his opinion. One evening, he advised her, "Kayleigh, don't settle for a man that 'might be good enough.' You deserve better. Even if you don't ever find him, it's better to be on your own with a few loved ones about you than miserable with a mean-spirited man."

"Yes, Ike. Believe me, I know," Kayleigh responded. "Just look at my mother."

As the cold snow and ice bent to the will of spring, the carnival people began to unthaw themselves and reveal their plans made during the harshness of winter.

Gloria had found a suitor, a boarder who had always reminded Kayleigh of Luke with his shy, quiet ways. They had decided to marry and find land for a farm.

Kayleigh was accepted at the South Dakota Southern State Normal School, and with the monetary help of Peaches and Pop, she would begin school for teacher training. (She promised them continuously that she would pay them back, and they said that they would write when they were settled so that she would know where to send the money. However, they made it clear that there was no real need or hurry. They just wanted her to fulfill her ambition.)

Securing a post as an English teacher, Professor Gallant would teach in the same school. He had his degree and all of his credentials approved, and no one bothered to contact Chicago.

"What will you do without Professor Gallant and Gloria?" Kayleigh questioned Ike with a tinge of worry in her voice.

Ike and Kayleigh were both sitting together on the boarding house porch. Ike had just announced his plans to press on, and most knew that Kayleigh would be staying in South Dakota, which would put an end to a short-lived rumor that the two were becoming romantically involved.

He smiled at Kayleigh and answered calmly, touched by her concern. "I'll just find another fast-talking man down on his luck and a pretty girl desperate to get away from something or someone.

"You, though," and he pointed at her and smiled, "had better become a teacher!"

Kayleigh smiled and watched as the carnival reassembled and moved onward. It reminded her of a story that she had once read about a waking giant, finally ready to begin life again.

Samson and Madam Daring, along with Nolan, Matthew and Marcus, would go onward with Ike, along with Peaches and Pop, the cook, and a new seamstress they had picked up along the way.

Kathleen and Nolan came to an unspoken agreement that she would stay wherever Kayleigh was, and he was pushing on to Idaho with the carnival. Whether he would continue with the carnival from there was uncertain.

Saying goodbye to Peaches and Pop was very difficult. They were the parents, or grandparents, that she had never had, but Kayleigh was beginning another chapter and secretly keeping her desire to find the faithful people in life.

CHAPTER 7: MITCH AND ZACH

Kayleigh was, as usual, pushing ahead as fast as her mind and body would allow. She needed work, so she began working as a waitress in an inn. During her second week, weary of pinches, grabs, and other unwanted attention, she noticed two young men from her classes at the Normal School.

Mitch Herd sat amiably at the piano, his tall, lanky frame always accentuated by the length of his long legs. The cane that he usually walked with was propped against the piano, and he wore his usual dark suit, but, with the enhancement of a colorful bow tie, somehow, Mitch was never somber in his appearance. He also had dark hair and dark brown eyes, but, oh, what a huge, engaging smile. So, just as some were ready to compare him to "Ichabod Crane," the smile took that imagery away.

Even with his angular features and large nose, there was something still handsome and charming about him. He was also self-effacing and humorous, so never usually seen as a threat unless dealing with a renegade male.

His friend, Zach Asher, gave his trademark lopsided grin as he stood. He was not exactly plump, but somewhat close. His build was short and stocky, and his face was that of a bad little boy with a rounded Irish chin and mischievous blue eyes.

The two had a comedy and singing act, which was, for the most part, failing. When they passed the hat, it usually came back empty.

As she swiftly thought about approaching the two, she scanned the inn, which was always crowded with lonely farmers. Kayleigh had just pulled a man's arm from around her waist and reminded him that she couldn't fetch food and be held back by him.

 She was working up the courage to approach the two men and ask about the possibility of becoming a part of their "act." She knew that with a woman's voice and presence, their routine really might take off.

The "gentleman" holding Kayleigh, however, had other ideas and was gradually moving his hand upward from her waist. While Kayleigh wrestled with him, yelling for "Big Rosco," who took care of the farmer patrons who were becoming progressively physical, and telling him continuously to "Stop!" the owner came out to investigate.

Mitch had already begun to take action, though, as he came off the piano bench, leaving his cane behind. He headed toward the farmer while Zach ran behind him as fast as his stubby legs would allow.

Amid the chaotic scene, patrons were yelling for either the farmer or Mitch, similar to witnessing a good prize fight. Most had thought Mitch would not have a chance, but it soon became apparent that he had toughness beyond his handicap.

Finally, as Mitch and the farmer were getting ready to throw punches at one another, Rosco emerged from the back room and quickly stepped between them, his broad chest separating the two.

Now, the owner, a tall blonde Swede named Gustav, snapped to life and began barking orders. "You," he said, pointing to the farmer, "get out, and don't come back!" "You," he pointed again, this time at Mitch, "go back to piano playing! And you," he pointed at Kayleigh, "are fired."

Before Kayleigh could defend herself, Mitch interjected, "Now just a minute, Mr. Gustav, Kayleigh was trying to get away from that man pawing her. She didn't cause any of this," he said.

"You know what," Gustav said, becoming red in the face, "all three of you are fired. So take your little short friend and your girlfriend and get out!"

Thinking it best not to explain at this point that Kayleigh was not his girlfriend, Mitch motioned to Zach and Kayleigh, and they quietly left the establishment.

"Now what?" Kayleigh caught herself saying aloud. "I'm out of a job, and I didn't get a chance to even ask you about…"

To her surprise, Mitch and Zach were both grinning. The whole scene seemed to have had no real effect on them or their emotions. "Are you always this happy?" Kayleigh asked.

"Oh, you mean that hubbub back there?" Zach asked. "That's nothing. We'll find something else. Besides, we got to meet you. We've had a bet going for two weeks on who would be the first to talk to you. We have most of the same classes with you at school."

"Yes, I recognized you while you were playing and singing at the tavern," Kayleigh said suspiciously, "but why would you want to talk to me?"

"Are you kidding," Zach grinned.

"Zach!" Mitch said and pressed his fingers to his lips, indicating that Zach should stop talking. He cleared his throat and said, "We merely thought that it would be the polite thing to do to make proper introductions with everyone."

"Yeah, right," Zach blushed and laughed. "We do that with both the beautiful girls and the bookish men. It's all the same."

Kayleigh smiled and began before Mitch could do any more backtracking, "Well, I wanted to ask you if you'd consider me in your act. You see, I have some experience with entertaining, and I play the fiddle, sing, and also play the piano—a little. Also, I could help you write some of your jokes and maybe be a part of them. What do you think? Your act might really take off with a lady as a part of it, and, selfishly, I wouldn't have to wait tables anymore."

Mitch cleared his throat again, but this time more humorously. He held out his hand as if it contained a printed contract, "Madam, if you would but sign on the dotted line, I'm sure an agreement could be reached. In other words, let's go try our hands at the other inn and boarding establishments."

"One other thing," Kayleigh said, holding up her hand. "How do the school administrators feel about you and Zach doing this act?"

"Well, we don't actually use our real names when we do the act. We go under the pseudonyms of Professor Iknowmore and his assistant, Imalittledaft, and if anyone should come in from school, we quietly tell them that we won't tell if they don't. After all, they're not really supposed to be in an inn un-supervised either," Mitch reminded her.

"And that's worked for you?" Kayleigh questioned.

"So far, so good," Zach said. "But, if you want, Mitch and I can wear beards, and we could find a dark wig for you," he grinned yet again.

"Actually, that's not a bad idea," Kayleigh said. "But, first, let's go see if we can get hired some-where."

In the end, Gustav's sister, who owned the nearby boarding house, hired them after they gave her a little impromptu performance. Her conditions were: "You'll not be drinking or eating my food. You strictly get the money you get from passing the hat, and if you don't bring more customers in, you're gone. I'm hoping you do, though, because then I could really rub my idiot brother's nose in it."

CHAPTER 8: GETTING EVERYONE MARRIED EXCEPT HERSELF

For once, things seemed to be going so well for Kayleigh, her mother, and Cassie. Kayleigh, Mitch, and Zach were finishing school and began to practice teaching at the nearby elementary and upper schools. They also earned a bit of pocket money while performing in the other inns and boarding establishments.

Kathleen made money doing seamstress work and became sought after for the dresses that she could make from a simple sketch or catalog picture. In this way, she could keep Cassie with her and work.

All was well until Kayleigh began to realize that Mitch was falling in love with her. For quite a while, she did not even admit it to herself, and then the little indications of infatuation began to tell on him. He would linger a bit long after they had finished a show, or he would stand a little too close to her when there was no reason for it.

Although Mitch was charming, sweet, and handsome (in an unconventional way), she knew that she could not return his feelings, although she often wished that she could. As for Zach, he looked on somewhat intrigued, sometimes with his trademark grin, but never commenting on the situation to Kayleigh.

Then, she hit upon a plan. On Tuesday and Thursday nights, she taught sign language at the small school for the deaf that had been independently formed at a church. She earned a wage with this instruction, and she had met a few young women who would be eligible for Mitch and Zach.

She began to tell Mitch about this very beautiful young woman whom she taught to sign. At first, he seemed uninterested or always had "a previous engagement," but one week, they went with Kayleigh to her class. The beautiful young woman was Rosemary, and Kayleigh was right about the match. Mitch was smitten almost immediately.

Rosemary was born beautiful, Rosemary Cantrell, perfect, and privileged. For the first year of her life, her parents showed her off in her pram as they walked about the streets of Idaho Falls, proud of her and their situation in life. Then tragedy came when she was stricken with a fever that robbed her of her hearing.

The young couple made the rounds of doctors, trying desperately to find some way to restore her, but it was a permanent loss that needed training and adjustments. The two had trouble accepting this diagnosis.

Still a beautiful child who grew into a beautiful young woman, she had dark eyes, much like velvet. They were intelligent and knowing eyes but also thoughtful and sensitive, and she longed for education. Indeed, she had taught herself to read with the help of a kind older woman who drew pictures for words and patiently showed them to Rosemary.

Her brunette hair curled perfectly about her face, and her smile was infectious. With all of the difficulties that life was presenting, she never lost that smile. It was a strong means of communication, especially when she went to South Dakota.

Slim and lithe, more than one young man had been interested in her until they found out that she could not hear and did not speak. Then, sadly, among several of the more unscrupulous young men, other thoughts set in about her, and it was because of this that her parents sought a protected situation for her. However, if the truth be told, they were both tired and disappointed at the prospect of continuing to raise her and care for her.

So they found a boarding situation for her in South Dakota and a small school for the deaf. Heartbroken at how her parents were dismissing her, she bravely went to her classes and tried to learn how to sign, but it was not until a bright little strawberry blond teacher arrived that she was actually determined to learn this language. In her heart, she was not sure what she loved the most, learning this new communication or this spunky new friend, Kayleigh.

More students began to assemble, both hearing and non-hearing, and the sessions became a bit of a social gathering as well. Kayleigh was an engaging teacher, and Rosemary, a talented baker, usually brought something sweet for afterward.

The romance blossomed gradually. Rosemary was falling in love with the young, tall teacher, but she was also canny enough to know that he was somewhat in love with Kayleigh. For this reason, she was cautious, but his continual attempts to talk to her through sign language won out until, one day, he signed the words "I love you" to her.

Now, Caroline O'Hara, whom Kayleigh had chosen for Zach, was a different matter. She could have slipped entirely out of anyone's notice, except as the plump little charwoman who cleaned the church where the sign language lessons were conducted, but Kayleigh noticed her.

Caroline could have had a chip on her shoulder or an attitude of indifference, but she smiled and waved at those who entered the church, and she had a comical side. She sometimes did a little pirouette with her mop to the entertainment of some of the students. It concerned Kayleigh, though, that Caroline did not attend classes sometimes. Then, one day, Rosemary explained that Caroline had to make sure every nook and cranny of the church was clean before she could go to class, and, with so many coming and going with muddy shoes, it was not always possible.

Then, on one night of her little pirouette routine, it hit Kayleigh like a runaway carriage that this was the girl for Zach. So, she and Mitch hit upon a plan to get Zach to join in on lessons. They also decided to pitch in on cleaning the church after lessons were finished.

Zach and Caroline were so drawn to each other that others in class looked on with joy and gladness for the two. They also sometimes laughed. This was a bit of a comedy pair, if ever there was one. They drew from one another.

The matches were made, and a bond was formed between all five. The couples were happy and dedicated to one another, but they were also forged into an unspoken agreement that Kayleigh was always to be protected.

Kayleigh was a good matchmaker. She just didn't use that ability for herself.

Now, the real test came. The three teachers needed jobs, and Wyoming seemed to be a wide-open adventure.

CHAPTER 9: 1884—THE SECOND TEACHING POST

Kayleigh was nineteen years old in 1884. Wyoming had a reputation for giving equal rights to women, including the right to vote. Of course, no one really explained to Kayleigh that this was passed mainly to attract women to the area and make the ladies of various brothels happy. It wouldn't have mattered, though. She was ready for a change and thought that this would be good for Kathleen and Cassie.

Headed for Rock Springs, with the old carnival wagon and some questionable horses that the three teachers had pooled their resources to buy, Kayleigh took in the cottonwood trees, the Indian Paintbrush flowers, and the scattered cattle ranches that they passed. She was in awe of the landscape and curious about the people who abided in these open spaces.

Their assignments in Rock Springs sounded promising. The town was in the county seat of Sweetwater. Sweetwater was known as the leader in coal mining, the Pony Express mail system, and the railroad industry. However, again, what no one had bothered to tell the three, Rock Springs was also known for outlaws and sometimes violent disagreements among the miners.

It took a while, but Kayleigh settled herself and her mother and little sister in the house next to the elementary school. Mitch and Zach were assigned to two small shanties nearby, not far from the upper-level school. None of these residences were particularly well built or attended to, but the three made homes of them.

Sometimes, in the evenings, she would take a chair and sit outside admiring the stars and praying again to find faithful, kind people. She leaned back and wrapped an old blanket about her.

The night was lit with moonlight as she prayed: "God, are men ever faithful to women? Are friends, who start as friends, ever faithful to one another, and do you really care about what people have done to us, the injustice, the humiliation, and the long-lasting consequences?"

The sky began to rain like a woman shedding silent tears, and she was reminded of one of the verses that she had learned in the convent:

"Be still, and know that I am God: I will be exalted among the heathen. I will be exalted in the earth" (Psalm 46:10, KJV).

She gazed up at the rocks that appeared carved against a smoky dark sky and at the steep mountains that framed the countryside. There she spied him, a young Sioux Brave, stopped silently on horseback and seemingly doing the same thing that she was.

Bare-chested but clothed in buckskin, his glance met hers briefly before he returned to studying the sky and taking in the night air as she had done. He then rode away as quietly as he had come.

Kayleigh had heard that his tribe was very faithful and loyal to one another, and she wondered why white people so often found this impossible.

School began well, and Kayleigh was fascinated by the children. In many ways, it was a typical school, with its neat rows of desks with their ink wells, the potbelly stove near the front, and the teacher's desk a bit elevated in front of the blackboard.

But, the mixture of children was what intrigued Kayleigh. Here before her were Chinese children, White children, and children of Indian Territory heritage. Most were well-behaved. They knew the regular school rules, and usually, there were not too many corrections that needed to be made.

It did concern her that some of her older boys, the nine and ten-year-olds, played outlaws and "The Wild Bunch." This usually involved hiding behind rocks and the outbuildings and jumping out at each other with sticks used like guns. She had to admit it made recess interesting but a bit distressing.

During her second year in Wyoming, the tales of shoot-outs and violence became more talked about, both among the young and old. In fact, as Kathleen reflected, there was a wild tone that prevailed in the entire town, and Kayleigh was beginning to have more and more trouble with her older boys as she tried to reign them in from fighting in the schoolyard and disrespectful remarks.

One afternoon, the children had left, and Kayleigh was finishing her grading while sitting at her desk. Two of her students had "clapped" the erasers, and another had swept and helped clear the ashes in the stove. Everything was in good order.

Suddenly, she could hear gunfire in the distance. Instantly, a window shattered. Kayleigh ducked down below the desk.

Across the main street, Mitch and Zach, who dismissed their students an hour later than the elementary school, told all the children to "Get down!" while they, too, ducked near the desk.

Kayleigh was shaking so hard that it was hard for her to collect her thoughts, and she did not initially notice that the bullet had grazed her leg. As her head cleared a bit, she wondered where the blood was coming from. Then she realized it was her own leg, which had soaked the right hem of her skirt with a deep red. *Oh, my poor mama and Cassie*, she thought as she became increasingly more dizzy.

She barely had time to take that in, though, before the door swung wide open, and a man in a cowboy hat jumped in and landed near Kayleigh. His face had a dark beard. He was tall and lanky in a black shirt and pants. A dirty white vest encased his chest, and the spurs of his boots were dangerously near Kayleigh's waist.

He grinned, revealing tobacco-stained teeth, tipped his hat, and said, "How are you, mam? I believe I've seen you about town. You and me are gonna flop here awhile until this commotion stops. You understand?"

Kayleigh tried to nod, somehow noticing that her hair had come completely down and her blouse was ripped. This had not gone unnoticed by the outlaw, who grinned appreciatively but did not linger with his gaze or comment on her appearance. "Well now, what's going on with your leg?" he motioned with one hand toward the blood stain while removing his gun from its holster.

"I believe I was hit by a bullet," Kayleigh managed to say, although her breath was coming in gasps.

"Well, let's take a look and see," he said while already lifting her skirt.

"Please, I can take care of it later!" she said.

"Not unless you fancy bleeding out, honey," the man continued, grinning. "I'm just gonna tear off part of your petticoat and tie it off. In truth, it don't look that bad, but it does need to be stopped."

He proceeded to do exactly what he had described while Kayleigh looked on helplessly. "My name is Jeremiah, by the way," he said, and he looked expectantly at Kayleigh.

"Oh, well, my name is Kayleigh O'Brien," she managed to remember and repeat.

"Oh, you got Irish in you then. Well, my mama was what they call Black Irish. That's where I got my dark hair and eyes." He tied off the bandage he had made rather expertly and looked at her as though studying her.

The barrage of bullets began again, and they peppered the front of the school while others came through the windows and the wall boards themselves.

"You'll have a hard but interesting life," he said as though he were almost in a trance. He was still leaning over her as he continued, "You will find your faithful man, honey. Pay attention to that man you meet at the well. Is Kayleigh your only given name?" he asked.

"My middle names are Naomi-Rebecca," she told him, the confusion clearly showing on his face. "The Irish sometimes give multiple names," she said, unsure of how much to tell him.

His grin grew wider. "Of course they do," he said softly. "Well, I'm considered a bit of a seer, but now it's time for me to keep fighting this old crazy war for turf and territory."

He crawled on his belly to the first side window and shot until his gun needed to be reloaded. "I'm going out your back door, darling. Say a little prayer that I make it."

"You'll get killed!" Kayleigh screamed.

He looked back briefly, "Probably, honey, but that's just the price. Not everybody wants to hear the good news, but may the Lord bless thee."

She could hear the bullets ripping into Jeremiah before she passed out.

CHAPTER 10: LET'S TRY IDAHO

Mitch and Zach, visibly shaken themselves, helped Kayleigh "come to" and got her up. "Let's get you to the doctor," Mitch said.

"No," Kayleigh said, stubbornly refusing. "Mama is very good at treating wounds and stitching. I can't afford a doctor. I'll be fine."

"As you want, Kayleigh, let's just all get home and check on our families," Mitch said.

Kayleigh hobbled toward the house in between Mitch and Zach. The street looked beaten and battered, with buildings scarred by bullets. The sheriff and mayor were out directing men to remove bodies and clean up.

The three made their way up to the door of the small house. "We're going to check on Rosemary and…" Mitch began when they saw Cassie on the floor in the middle of a seizure and Kathleen kneeling over her, trying to steady her. "Oh no," Zach said with genuine worry.

"Just go on home, both of you," Kayleigh said. "Mama and I will settle her. Thank you for helping me."

Kathleen looked up into Kayleigh's eyes. "We can't stay here, Kayleigh. It's not good for any of us."

Cassie was beginning to settle and whimper when Kathleen caught sight of Kayleigh's wound. "Och!" she cried, "Both of my daughters hurt in one day! What has happened, Colleen?"

"I was grazed by a bullet, and a man named Jeremiah helped me. It's stopped bleeding, but it needs to be cleansed and stitched," she explained.

"Let me see it," her mother ordered. "Oh, Kayleigh, this is more than a mere graze. This came right at the big vein in your leg. You are blessed to be alive. This Jeremiah fellow saved your life. Let me get Cassie to bed with her medicine, and then I'll attend to your leg. In truth, though, you should be going to a doctor."

"We can't afford that, Mama, and you know it. I'll be fine," Kayleigh met her mother's frightened look with her own assured one. "Now, let's get about attending to Cassie."

The three teachers made it through the rest of the school year, although jittery and subconsciously waiting for the next onslaught of violence. Even though both the mayor and sheriff had assured that things were under control, and Mitch and Zach were grateful that both they and their spouses were well and untouched, the damage was done.

As Kathleen described it, Cassie had gone into hysterics, followed by a seizure, and Kayleigh's leg would be scarred and a bit weakened. "She is blessed that an infection did not set in," she repeated to anyone in town who cared to hear.

After a meeting with the mayor, who tried to assure them that it was unlikely that the violence would occur again and highlighted that they were in the center of a thriving coal and railway economy, the three remained unconvinced.

During the last month of school, Kathleen made a generous fried chicken dinner for Mitch and Rosemary, Zach and Caroline, as well as, of course, Kayleigh and Cassie. They enjoyed each other's company while the unanswered question hung in the air: "Where would they go?"

Suddenly, Mitch slapped his hands together and said, "Let's try Idaho!"

"Do you mean it, Mitch?" Kayleigh looked both hopeful and doubtful at the same time. Zach, however, was grinning like the Cheshire Cat.

Rosemary turned to Mitch, smiling and waiting, "I've already made inquiries to Idaho Falls, and it seems that they are in need of an elementary teacher as well as two upper school teachers. Zach and I won't be in the same school, mind you, but maybe that's for the best," he said and winked. "We tend to get into a bit of mischief, but there are three positions open. I received the letter today via Pony Express," he assured. "Now, what should I reply?" he asked, looking speculatively at Kayleigh.

"Mama?" Kayleigh turned to her mother.

"Yes!" Kathleen exclaimed and clapped her hands. "Don't you know by now that I'm with you five always?"

Caroline giggled and clapped her hands like a schoolgirl, and then Cassie asked, with fear in her quiet little voice, "Am I coming too? I've tried to be good."

Kayleigh gathered the little six-year-old to her and answered quietly, "Of course, my love. You go where we go."

That night, she saw him again, the Sioux Brave who liked the evening as much as she did. They looked at each other again, and she thought she detected the slightest smile as she waved goodbye. It was as though he knew where she was destined to go, and, for some reason, Jeremiah came to her mind. When the bodies were cleared away from the gunfight, his was never found.

CHAPTER 11: 1886—IDAHO FALLS

Kayleigh was twenty-one when she began her teaching experience at Idaho Falls. It was a predominately Mormon town with schools run predominately by the Mormons. This was fine with Kayleigh, although she was not a Mormon, and neither were Mitch or Zach.

She was relieved that Nolan and her step-brothers were nowhere to be seen. Although the reports were that they traveled through Idaho Falls with the carnival, they did not seem to have put down roots in this land.

The beauty of the town's landscape was unquestionable, and the Mormon temple was impressive. There was something, though, that silently bothered Kayleigh. Most of the town's people were so welcoming, but a few of the women were very standoffish, as if they viewed her as some type of threat.

This seemed to filter into a few of the girls and boys, mainly the upper elementary school nine and ten-year-olds. There was a palpable attitude that she was not to be taken seriously or that she was someone who might cause a problem.

Mitch and Zach were aware of it, too, because the same attitudes seemed to be applied to them from Zach's group of eleven through fourteen-year-olds and Dave's fifteen through eighteen-year-olds. It was not just irritating and demeaning. It was sad. All three teachers were trying to put forth a more modern and needed curriculum, and Mitch was basically creating a Normal School for the local young people who desired higher education.

Rosemary, however, reconnected with her parents and helped care for both of them. She seemed happy, yet grappling with the situation, when Kayleigh signed with her.

In Kayleigh's case, she had the distinct feeling that rumors were being spread that she was after a man, anybody's man, or husband. More than once, she caught the girls whispering and caught a few phrases like, "Just came here to get a man or become someone's second wife," or "Who does she think she is? I'm not doing anything she says. Did you hear her accent? She's got some kind of scar on her neck, too."

The younger students were usually not so difficult, but these "little snits," Kayleigh's private name for them, were poisoning the class. Had it not been for the fact that Kathleen and Cassie were happy, she would have gone ahead and applied for another position for the following year. As it was, she was hopeful that "the tide would turn" and things would settle out.

One Mormon couple was especially kind and helpful to her and Kathleen and Cassie. The Langley couple rented them the small house that they lived in and did all that they could to help the three of them. They were one of the few Mormon couples who ventured outside of the community and were friendly with non-Mormons.

Of course, Kayleigh did not know at that time the difficult scene that had just unfolded for the Langleys. Although others in the community knew of the fall that Josiah and Mavis had taken in the eyes of the church, she and other newcomers had no knowledge of or reason to wonder.

It had begun with an elder's meeting. Josiah, who had fought many a battle for the Mormon faith, this time was fighting within his faith. When he stood in front of the temple elders to address the duties of the Mormon Church and its place in the community, he knew that he might well lose his standing. On this day, he had taken on a topic of great dissension, namely, the practice of polygamy.

"My brothers," he began, "I know I approach a difficult issue, but I feel that I can keep silent no longer. This should not continue. This practice of taking more than one wife demeans the first wife and often involves taking little more than a child bride. I, of course, think that our faith should be continued and spread, but I do not accept this particular tenet. If the members in Utah want to continue this, let them, but let us take a stand here in Idaho.

"I would also address our conduct with newcomers and those not in the faith. I would remind all that they are also God's children. It grieves me to witness, even the very young girls shunning or making hostile remarks about those who have just joined the town or those who have been here but do not share our faith."

His wife, Mavis, sat in a pew in the sanctuary, hearing a few bits and pieces from behind the closed door of the meeting room. She grasped her hands together even tighter, fearing that her Josiah may have taken on too big of a battle this time. In fact, when he emerged with the news that he was no longer an elder, she was not surprised.

So, it was that the Langleys began to help Kayleigh, Kathleen, and Cassie. Having no children of their own, they were both drawn to Kayleigh's goodness and determination and to Cassie's forever child-like goodness.

Mr. Langley reminded Kayleigh of drawings that she had seen of Abraham Lincoln. With his long legs and arms and his rather homely but wise facial features, he could have been 'Ol Abe's brother. There was a warm charm to him, though, also reminiscent of Mr. Lincoln.

Mavis was a rather tall woman with plain features. Many mistook her as cold when they first encountered her, but she was a true soul who cared for others and warmed to them as she came to know them and help them.

Mrs. Langley helped Kathleen find clients (mainly non-Mormons) for her seamstress skills and often helped her in minding Cassie. Mr. Langley offered advice about the upkeep of the small house and often simply came and did repairs.

They were also helpful in identifying which people in the community would be supportive and kind and which would be more difficult to deal with fairly. Although this was of help in a monetary way, it did not help with classroom matters.

The children who "had it in" for Kayleigh still did. Even though she had pulled some of them aside and carefully talked with them one-on-one, they persisted. Then, things seemed to change for the better. Mitch and Zach invited her to attend the local Presbyterian Church with them and their wives.

Kathleen had already found a Catholic church, which she took Cassie to, but Kayleigh had concerns from the past about attending there.

The little Presbyterian Church, however, was actually a welcoming experience. In fact, where one young man was concerned, it was more than welcoming. It was an immediate attraction to Kayleigh. Although she did not seem to notice it, Rosemary and Caroline did and began to immediately hatch a plan to get Kayleigh and this young man together—and quickly.

Adam Babulus was a newcomer to Idaho Falls. Of Italian descent, he was the very definition of tall, dark, and handsome. Like Kayleigh, he had decided to try a religion other than Catholicism.

He was now grateful that he had since he was experiencing an immediate draw to Kayleigh: her blondish red hair, her complexion, and, of course, her body. He was glad that his father, Santino, had all but given him the boot out of the vineyard he was trying to establish in California if there was any chance for him with Kayleigh.

It was decided rather quickly between the women as they signed and smiled that a dinner at one of their small homes with Kayleigh and Adam might do the trick, and it was a good dinner. Kayleigh was surprised at how interested Adam was in her, and Adam used all of his charms to capture her attention. In fact, after his thanks were expressed for the dinner, he suggested that he walk Kayleigh home. The two women were delighted. Mitch and Zach were both amused by their wives' plotting and hopeful for Kayleigh.

It was a beautiful night, and he explained the simple term "Bella Notte" as he slowly walked Kayleigh home. He carefully revealed that his mother was part Irish, and he had always loved her reddish hair. He then told Kayleigh that he wound up in Idaho because he had a friend who thought that he could find work on the railroad. Adam proved himself good at repairing the rails and so always managed to find work.

Kayleigh found herself telling him about her days with the carnival (leaving out the sad or negative details), her time at the South Dakota Normal School, and her mother and little sister. It was wonderful to finally have someone to talk to and share with.

It was also wonderful when the children, who had been bothering Kayleigh and misbehaving, began to "straighten up," realizing that she neither wanted nor needed a Mormon man. In typical fashion, when their parents stopped speculation, so did they.

They had the beginnings of a romance, with short kisses on the cheek, long walks and dinners, and church times together. This went on over the course of two months. Several things bothered Kayleigh, though. Adam seemed to have a roving eye and not a good deal of tolerance for differences.

The one time that Kayleigh had introduced him to Cassie, he seemed uncomfortable and nervous. He also noticed Kayleigh's scar one evening when she wore an open-collared shirt. He seemed to have a slight cringe at that small imperfection.

Then, one Sunday, as they left church, it became overwhelmingly obvious that a woman, new in town, was looking at Adam and watching Kayleigh as they walked back home. Although the two did not speak, Kayleigh knew that they had history together. Later, when she asked about the woman, he said, "Do not worry so much, little one. I cannot help it if the women look."

That Saturday, when they were set to attend a dance, Adam did not come. Kathleen continued to fuss over the dress that she had made for Kayleigh, and Cassie was fascinated with the preparations until it became clear that he would not be coming.

When he did not call for her on Sunday morning, Kayleigh became concerned that he had been hurt or sick, but then the reason became crushingly clear. Adam was walking with the woman she had seen, but not to church. They were looking passionately into each others' eyes and clearly headed for the hotel.

Kayleigh then understood the absolute insensitive cruelty of some men. She had known the pains of interpreting a friendship as something more, the brute abuse of brutish men, but this was something different. This was rejection simply because someone more desirable came along. *I'm done*, she thought. *This is enough.*

She walked back toward the little house, stopping at a favorite tree. She sobbed there as she had not since she was a little girl, wiped her face, and headed home.

Later, Adam would try to lamely explain to Kayleigh that he would always care for her, but this was a more mature woman, ready for "the physical love."

I could have been, Kayleigh thought. *I wanted to be, but then I would have felt even worse when he left me for another woman.*

CHAPTER 12: 1888—LEAVING IDAHO FALLS

Although Kayleigh would have loved to leave Idaho Falls after that experience, she reasoned that women were treated far worse, far more often, and that she desperately needed a job. So, in the end, after much thought and daydreaming of yet another place, she stayed into the second year.

Then, one morning, before Kayleigh made her way to school, Kathleen stopped her, still in her gown. "Could you take Cassie with you for a day or so, love? Mama's lumbago is flaring up something awful. She's already dressed," she added as she motioned to Cassie.

"Please, Sissy! Please!" she pleaded. "I want to go to school so bad. I'll be so good!" She grabbed onto Kayleigh for dear life, pressing her little freckled face and upturned nose into Kayleigh's middle.

"Well, I can hardly say no, can I?" Kayleigh asked, and she picked up her books and lunch, took Cassie's hand, and left.

It broke Kayleigh's heart once more to see how anxious Cassie was to see other children. However, before they actually entered the school, Kayleigh pulled her aside and spoke very gently to her.

"Cassie, these little girls and boys don't know you yet. You'll need to sit close to Sissy at first and remember that you are a big eight-year-old girl now. Do you understand, Blossom?" she asked.

"Yes, Sissy," Cassie said solemnly.

She entered the school room, seated Cassie near her desk, and greeted the class, explaining that her sister would be attending school with her for a few days, and she hoped that everyone would make her welcome.

Cassie gave a huge smile to all, which, sadly, did not help. The older girls and boys were already whispering and sneering in the back of the room. However, several of the six-year-olds smiled back and gave her shy little waves.

The day continued, and Kayleigh shared her lunch with Cassie and allowed her to play with the younger children. As far as her little sister was concerned, it was a good day, but Kayleigh worried about the next day.

She tried to explain the situation to her mother, but Kathleen, fatigued and still in pain, waved it off, saying, "You know how children are. Things will be better tomorrow," and, actually, things were a bit better the next day until lunch and recess.

"Teacher!" one of her first graders cried. "Abigail fell and hurt her arm!"

"Cassie, stay here," she turned quickly to her sister before going to attend to the child.

After inspecting Abigail's arm and cleaning it, she discovered that it was barely a scratch. Then she heard Cassie's wailing and saw her sitting with her hands over her ears as the older children circled around her, pointing their fingers and yelling, "Dummy, dummy!"

Kayleigh ran over to the circle of children, "All of you go home!" she yelled. "Every one of you go home now!"

They stopped and stared at her. Finally, one of them broke the silence, a boy who looked as though he'd parted his teeth in the middle along with his stringy black hair.

"My mama aint' gonna like it one bit if I get sent home," he sneered as the gap in his front teeth looked even wider.

"Davis, tell your mother I'll be glad to talk to her any time, but you're not going to torture other children. Now leave!" she screamed. "All of you!"

As they filed quietly away, Kayleigh helped Cassie up and ushered her and the younger children back into the schoolroom.

That afternoon, Kayleigh released the younger children and came out into the yard holding Cassie's hand while the wounded little girl turned her face into Kayleigh's waist and sucked her thumb.

"Mama," one of her second graders yelled as her mother approached to walk her home, "Brother, and a lot of boys and girls, pointed at Cassie and made fun of her. Then she had a shaking spell in the schoolroom."

Mothers who had just worn angry, ugly sneers on their faces changed rather suddenly. Some, without saying a word, simply took their young children and left quietly. Others turned around and left. A few inched their way forward, mouthing comments like, "Teachers shouldn't bring children with problems," or "Teachers shouldn't just send children home," before taking their own younger children.

Then, Davis's mother came forward, her front teeth and flat parted hair matching his. "Don't never yell at my Davis again," she hissed.

"Don't ever send him back," Kayleigh returned.

"I'll be sending my husband by," she said before turning away.

"I'll be bringing my gun around," Kayleigh replied.

A look of pure shock came over the other woman's face as she stomped away.

That evening, after Cassie was settled, Kayleigh told her mother that she was "done with the town."

"I'll finish out the last two weeks of the school year," she said, "but then, I'll be finding something else. You and Cassie are welcome to come, but I know that you really like the town." Kathleen looked sad but resigned.

The next afternoon, there was quite a commotion on the path leading from the school to the town. Kayleigh left the schoolroom to see what the shrieking was about. There, the entire group of students who had berated Cassie was being hit with eggs, seemingly from the tree above.

As they screamed and ran away, Kayleigh came up closer and started laughing softly. Looking up, she yelled, now that the children were completely out of sight, "Zach, come out of the tree."

He sheepishly climbed down, and as he did, Mitch came ambling up. He leaned over toward Kayleigh, his lean frame hunched a bit, as he lowered his voice, "I didn't come up with the idea or tell Zach to do it, but I did buy the eggs."

At that, the three laughed. Kayleigh laughed the hardiest, partly because of the situation and partly because of the two men standing side by side, the tall, seemingly dignified dark-haired man with the cane and the short, roundish man. Mainly, though, she simply found it very funny and justified.

"No one hurts our Blossom," Zach said with his lopsided grin. The three went their separate ways, still laughing.

There are times in life, however, when a break must be made from those that you have depended on. For Kayleigh, this was that time.

She made quick inquiries to Boise and soon had a reply. She advertised as a "Circuit Teacher" because, after all, that was what she had become, someone who had only stayed in one position for a year or maybe more.

So it was that Kayleigh would begin in an elementary school there in the fall. In the meantime, she tutored students who wished to pursue Normal School, and she helped in the General Store.

This brought in a little money, but she promised her mother that she would send a large portion of her check to her and Cassie each month when she was settled in Boise.

She was neither excited nor nervous about the new position. Her emotions were drifting like smoke, slowly and aimlessly, neither happy nor sad. The only thing that piqued her interest was the possibility of riding the train into Boise. That reminded her of her grandmother's expression, "a spot of fun."

Cassie cried hysterically the day that Kayleigh left with her one valise and a few books that she had kept. She had already sent her trunk ahead to the station. It was heartbreaking when the little girl clung to her older sister as though her very life was leaving.

"I love you, and I will be back," Kayleigh promised. She turned away quickly, unable to look at her "little sister's" tears a moment longer.

To her surprise, both Mitch and Zach were at the station to see her off.

"Write and tell us what you think of Boise, Kayleigh," Mitch said, trying to sound casual. She knew that he was finding it difficult, as was Zach. This was the first time that they had not accepted teaching positions together.

"Hey, Kayleigh," Zach grinned. "Let's get together and do the act again sometime." He tucked his head so that Kayleigh could not see the waiver in his smile.

"Of course," Kayleigh tried to smile, holding back tears. She hugged them quickly. "Try to stay out of trouble, you two," she said and quickly got on the train.

In a way, the train reminded her of the carnival wagons grouped together and sliding through the prairie grass, but it was a bit too modern for that comparison. It was a dark machine of precision, an unleashed animal that had waited for its meal of coal and its mission orders to forge ahead.

She took out the letters that she had saved in her drawstring purse and began to read them again. Some were beginning to be battered and a bit tattered, while others were still in good condition. (In fact, she sometimes feared that someone else had handled them.) However, it often calmed her to read over them again.

Kayleigh's letters from those that she had held dear were few and far between. Between her moving and the possibility of those that she hoped to hear from moving, she often wrote a letter that received no response or received one letter, then never again.

However, through all of her different posts, she always heard from Peaches and Pop, her grandmother, and, oddly enough, Mr. Leonardo and Dr. Healthful.

She heard from Peaches and Pop because they had given her a forwarding address in Colorado. She had heard from her grandmother because her post address in Ireland never changed, and her grandmother would write to whatever return address Kayleigh sent her. Next, she sometimes heard from Dr. Healthful because he had franchised his product, Dr. Healthful's Back Elixir, and she was a regular customer. (This was a secret that she kept carefully and always managed to have forwarded.)

Mr. Leonardo, however, was a complete surprise. Apparently, according to his letter, he was preparing to become a part of an "Artists' Colony" in Canada and wanted to know if she was interested. Of course, as he explained it, each artist would have to "put up a little cash," but he assured that there would be a school and that there would be more opportunities to show and sell their paintings.

In truth, Kayleigh was intrigued and decided to stay in communication with Mr. Leonardo. Who knew? At some point, it might be the best living situation for the three of them. Plus, it gave her hope, "an ace in the hole," something to dream about.

Her latest letter from her grandmother, however, had concerned her:

My dearest Kayleigh,

I was glad that you moved from Wyoming to Idaho.

Although Wyoming sounds most adventurous, it also sounds rather dangerous for two women and a child. Of course, I'm also quite glad that O'Connor and his sons are gone.

How is your health and Cassie's? I worry so over both of you and, of course, Kathleen. It also grieves me to think that I will never meet little Cassie.

Sadly, I have not been well, my love, so write to me soon, in hopes that I will read your precious letter of family news.

Have you found anyone yet? I know that it's not absolutely necessary to be married, but a partner can help to make life easier (if it's the right one).

I have recently sold the farm and the house, and I went to live with my bossy cousin. It is actually not so bad. It's just not home. Of course, I will be eternally grateful to the British lady who bought the china shop and for the money that your grandfather was able to leave me.

I was able to save and invest the money, and I'm quite pleased with the results. I tried to tell your grandfather that I was actually quite good with money, but his male pride kept me from ever participating in money affairs.

You will hear from me in due time concerning the value of your inheritance unless the Brits find a way to cheat me, which I don't think that they'll be able to do. Mainly, though, I hope that you will be settled and safe. Keep your faith and stay away from the drink.

Love always,

Grandmother

She would receive a letter from her grandmother again, but it would not be for some time, and it would not be in reply to a letter that Kayleigh sent to her in Ireland. The obvious conclusion broke her heart, and Kathleen, in typical fashion, refused to even talk about it.

Later, Mitch and Zach would reflect that it was good that Kayleigh left when she did. She did not have to witness the next return of Nolan O'Connor and the two soulless men that he had produced or the way that they began to terrorize Kathleen and Cassie yet again.

CHAPTER 13: 1888—BOISE, JUST ANOTHER TOWN?

Kayleigh was twenty-three when she checked into the hotel in Boise and began getting settled. The front desk clerk and the staff were nice, and because she was the local teacher, part of her room rent was paid along with her meals. This was the arrangement that had been made and kept for years.

Boise also seemed to be a bit more progressive than some of the other cities she had taught in. The school supplies for the children were better stocked, and she didn't have to dip into her own pocket quite as much. In addition to the supplies, the books and curriculum were well established and current, but the best part of Boise, which would live on with Kayleigh, was Margaret Ruth.

Petite, with raven dark hair that contained a hint of red and dark blue eyes, Margaret Ruth had a fiery delivery to her lessons and an intense knowledge of subject matter and strategies. The best part, however, was how ready she was to share with Kayleigh and help her get settled. Together, they were forging a partnership in both work and fun as Margaret Ruth handled the fifth to eight-level students, and Kayleigh, once again, had the five-year-olds to ten-year-olds.

It was fun to have someone to exchange ideas with, and since Margaret Ruth had taught elementary students before, Kayleigh looked forward to her guidance in everything from teaching the ABCs to geography lessons. It was a relief to know that she had the right ideas but simply had never had many of the needed supplies until now.

School was not the only fun that the two had, though. Margaret Ruth knew where the best "party" spots were around Boise. True, it was no San Francisco, but you could have a good, clean game of cards at someone's house, and you could attend a sponsored dance or a good church dinner.

"Don't you worry that someone might see you at a few of these 'parties'?" Kayleigh asked Margaret Ruth one day.

"Well, as I informed one gentleman who was curious about the same topic as we played cards, 'I won't tell that I saw an elder in the church if you don't tell that you saw the little school teacher.' That seemed to be enough. Besides," she said, raising her arms in a shrug, "I don't smoke, speak lewdly, or gamble," she concluded.

(Kayleigh laughed. So far, she hadn't seen or heard anything that compared to the Dream Town Carnival.)

It was then that Kayleigh happened on another idea: Margaret Ruth would be great in a comedy act. She had a good singing voice and a sharp wit, and she was not shy. Well…it was an idea. Kayleigh would keep it in the back of her mind for later. Everything was going well until two things became more demanding: Reverend Perkins and the Board of Education.

Reverend Perkins preached at the largest Baptist Church in town. He was a handsome, blonde-haired, blue-eyed single man of Swedish descent, often pursued by the local young women.

However, he was secretly quite shy of women. So, while his sermons were well written and his delivery usually fascinating, his love life was lackluster due to his general inability to talk with women or follow up on an obvious overture. Several women who were originally brimming with entrapment plans and follow-up marriages gave up on the Good Reverend. Rumors were, sadly, beginning to circulate.

Then, the Good Reverend Pharis Perkins spoke with Kayleigh after one particularly strong sermon about the value of honesty and welcomed her to the church. His lingering looks were obvious to Margaret Ruth, but Kayleigh simply thought he was being nice. When he mentioned that they would have dinner on the grounds after the next Sunday's sermon, Kayleigh nodded and said that she hoped it would be enjoyable.

Walking back to the hotel, Margaret Ruth suddenly turned to Kayleigh and said, "Catch a clue, kiddo. Reverend Perkins has eyes for you. Believe me, many have tried, and none have succeeded, but you've got the inside track."

"Why?" Kayleigh asked. "I didn't do anything to attract him."

"Well, that's even better," Margaret Ruth said knowingly. "You didn't have to work for him. He's just offering himself willingly.

"You've got to go to the church dinner on the grounds next Sunday and just see what happens. It could change your life."

The next Sunday was a beautiful day, with plenty of sunshine and hungry men, energetic and running children, and hurried women trying to keep up with both the food and children. It was also the end of the school year, and Kayleigh and Margaret Ruth greeted students and parents.

Margaret Ruth spread a blanket out for herself and Kayleigh after delivering the bread that they had baked to the main table. They bowed their heads as Reverend Perkins led a beautiful, if somewhat long, prayer before walking about and greeting others.

One of the elders' wives brought him a plate of food with a glass of lemonade, and he gradually made his way over to Margaret Ruth and Kayleigh. "May I join you ladies?" he asked politely. Kayleigh had to admit to herself that the Reverend was a good-looking man, and it was charming how he quietly approached them.

They all chatted for a while, although Margaret Ruth did most of the talking. Then, after a few minutes, Margaret Ruth wiped her hands on her napkin and said that she had seen someone that she wanted to talk with. She excused herself sweetly and left the two on their own.

"Well," Kayleigh started, "I don't believe I even know half of these people. I forget sometimes how big and bustling Boise is and how large a congregation you have."

"I guess 'growing' might be the word for both the town and the church," the Reverend replied and returned the smile.

"Well, that's always a good sign," Kayleigh agreed, trying to keep the conversation going. "By the way, what is your first name? I'm afraid that I haven't heard it used a great deal."

He smiled and took a sip of his lemonade. "It's Pharis, with a Ph."

Kayleigh raised an eyebrow and looked a bit perplexed. "Could I ask about your name? What I mean to say," she stumbled a bit, "is, well, I met a Ferris in Minnesota, but his name was spelled with the typical 'Fer.' I don't think I've ever seen it with the 'Ph.'"

Reverend Perkins gave a brief laugh and said, "Well, my mother thought it would be more biblical with the 'Ph.'"

"Oh, okay," Kayleigh replied, but her thought was, *Isn't "Ph" the beginning of 'Philistines,' 'Pharaoh,' and 'Pharisee'?*

A horseshoe game began, and Reverend Perkins was called upon to participate. "Come on, Pharis," one of the deacons called out. "Let's get a game going."

"Yeah, Reverend, come on," a young boy called out.

He looked at Kayleigh in a questioning way, to which she smiled and answered, "Go ahead, Pharis. I think the crowd will revolt if you don't."

He gave her a genuine and engaging grin, which she had never seen on him before, like a young boy glad to be allowed to go out and play. Reaching over, he gave her hand a brief squeeze before sauntering over to the game.

Perhaps there was more to the good Reverend than she had thought. She would have to give this another turn about in her mind.

That summer was filled with letters from her mother and Mitch and the attentions of Pharis Perkins. He was attentive and sweet-natured and seemed proud to have her on his arm, especially at church. Margaret Ruth smiled inwardly, thinking that she had brought the two together, but she also longed for someone of her own.

Kathleen's letters reported that she and Cassie were fine. Cassie had not had another episode, and between the money that Kayleigh sent her and the seamstress work that she brought in, life was going well.

The Langleys helped her with Cassie and often shared their meals with the two of them. They tried to interest Kathleen in the Mormon faith, but as Kathleen wrote in her letters, "I'm afraid that Catholicism is just ingrained in my Irish soul."

As for Mitch, he regaled her with tales of Zach's antics and their students from the upper school. Kayleigh sensed an undertone, though. Mitch seemed to be increasingly more dissatisfied. There was an unspoken desire to move on, a restlessness that was not being appeased in Idaho Falls. Then, he struck a hard blow for Kayleigh in his third letter that summer.

Nolan O'Connor and Matthew and Marcus were settling there, and he was afraid that they were threatening Kathleen. Kayleigh wrote in return that she would be coming back to see about Kathleen and Cassie as soon as she arranged her train fare back to Idaho Falls.

She had opened a small account in the local Boise bank, and she withdrew enough for the train fare and for her mother and Cassie's monthly rent and food allowance. This was almost all of her funds from her last paycheck. She clutched her small drawstring purse in her gloved hands and watched the scenery move past as the whistle blew. What was she going back to now? Once again, nothing was clear.

Arriving at the depot, she both hoped that someone would meet her and hoped that no one would. Which would be better? What if she walked right into her stepfather and step-brothers as she walked to her mother's tiny, rented cottage?

She had to admit, though, that her heart was lightened when Mitch and Rosemary met her. Rosemary embraced her so closely that neither could breathe for a few seconds. Mitch gave her a brief sideways hug and grinned.

"Girl, I'm glad to see you," he said and smiled, but not his characteristic huge grin. Then, he took her valise and put his other arm around Rosemary while she took Kayleigh's hand. Together, they walked toward Kathleen's home.

"Oh, my Colleen!" Kathleen cried as she opened the door. "How I've missed you!" she said, beginning to cry as she embraced her daughter.

"Me too, Sissy!" Cassie yelled while she jumped up and down, "Me too!"

The little girl had grown a bit, and, at ten years of age, she was pretty with her long brown hair and huge bluish-green eyes but very frail. Kayleigh grabbed her and held her close. "I've missed you so much, Blossom," she said. "You are my sweet flower."

Mitch and Rosemary smiled on the scene, and Mitch made polite remarks about needing to buy supplies in town as they eased out the door. Kayleigh could have sworn, though, that he subtly nodded toward Kathleen before leaving. Then she understood. As her mother raised her gaze to Kayleigh's own questioning look, she could see the bluish and purplish bruise still rising around Kathleen's right eye.

"How did this happen, Mama?" Kayleigh demanded. "And don't tell me that you had a slight 'accident,'" Kayleigh warned.

"Why are you beginning to yell, Sissy? Please don't be mad at us," Cassie begged.

"I'm not mad at you, sweetheart," Kayleigh soothed her. "I'm mad at the person who did this."

"Oh, well, that was the bad man, Daddy," Cassie said.

"Shh…Cassie," Kathleen warned.

"Well, he is," Cassie countered. "Daddy is a mean man, and he took our money after he hit Mama. It was the money you sent us."

"Cassie, please!" Kathleen begged.

"We didn't have nothin' to eat for a while. Mrs. Langley gave us food," she said with tears in her eyes.

Kayleigh could feel her face reddening (the sometimes curse of a redhead), and she wanted to see Nolan O'Connor dead. She wanted to be free of him once and for all.

The night was moving in, and Kathleen, wordlessly, was beginning a small dinner for the three while she hummed an old Irish tune. She turned after a time and smiled. "Oh, Kayleigh, things will be well after a time. You'll see. The Lord will take care of us."

Kayleigh was not sure whether to pity her mother or further resent her for the choices she had made in her life. Either way, it was always evident that her mother did not live in reality. She never really had, but it was far worse now.

After dinner, Kayleigh bolted the door. "Mama, tomorrow morning we're going to the bank and open an account, in my name, with permission for you to make withdraws from it. You'll need to get Mitch or Zach and Mr. Langley to go with you when you make withdraws. They'll, at least, offer some protection. Then, we'll go to the sheriff and explain to him how Pa has brutalized you."

Kathleen sighed. "You can try, love, but Nolan has charmed the sheriff into thinkin' that I'm weak in the head and left him so that I could be with other men. I doubt that he will even listen."

Kayleigh's mouth hung a bit open for a while. "Why did you not write me of any of this?" she questioned with desperation in her voice.

"You were settled for once and had a young man," Kathleen answered, "a preacher, no less. I wanted you to have that without worries."

"I will always be concerned about you and Cassie, Mama," she said, trying to keep her voice in control. "We'll also go see the Langleys tomorrow."

Kayleigh hid her purse under the mattress of the bed that the three of them shared that night. Her plan was to start to the bank the next day as soon as she and Kathleen had a bit of coffee and all three of them were dressed. They could eat after the banking, but, as most plans went where the three of them were concerned, these would be no different, ruined before they started.

They awoke the next morning to a hard banging at the door, followed by the unmistakable yelling of Matthew and Marcus, "We know you're in there, Kayleigh. Either let us in, or we'll break out a window."

"Oh no!" Cassie began to cry and shrank under the bed. "The mean brothers are back." Under normal circumstances, Kayleigh might have laughed, but the child was right, and where they were, the father was not far behind.

"What do you want?" Kayleigh yelled while wrapping her thin robe around her.

"We know you've got money, Kayleigh, and it should be part ours."

"What are you talking about? I don't have any money," she lied, "and if I did, it would be my hard-earned teaching money."

"We know the old lady in Ireland is sending you money. That's Kathleen's ma, and Kathleen's married to our pa, so by rights, it's ours," Marcus snarled.

Kayleigh's mind went back quickly to that last day in Ireland, standing in her grandmother's kitchen and the letters that they had written through the years. "When you are twenty-five…" echoed in her memory, but with her grandmother's death, she had ceased to even consider an inheritance, not that she had ever thought much about it.

"Kayleigh, don't argue back and forth with them," Kathleen had whispered and half hissed. "They're goading you on."

No sooner had the hushed words escaped Kathleen's mouth than the sound of a rock hurling through the large front window made its way to the two women's ears, crashing through glass and landing just short of their feet, while Cassie whimpered and shook under the bed.

Then, suddenly, he was there, just as fierce and cruel as always, while he kicked out the window with his boot. Nolan O'Connor made his way through and entered the room.

"Well, now, if it ain't 'Little Miss I'm Too Good for the Rest of You.' Where is it, Kayleigh? Where's my wife's money?"

"You're terrifying the child!" Kathleen pleaded while Nolan advanced to Kayleigh.

"I don't know what you're talking about," Kayleigh managed to say. By this time, Matthew and Marcus had entered. Both leered at Kayleigh's nightgown and robe. "You been entertaining?" Matthew asked with a laugh and a sneer as Marcus joined.

"Cut that foolin' about!" Nolan warned. "Now don't keep me waitin'. Where is it, Colleen?" Nolan demanded. "And, you," he pointed at Kathleen, "keep your mouth shut!"

"Again, I don't know what you're talking about," Kayleigh said, standing her ground. (But she wondered if they had somehow read her letters or contacted someone in Ireland.)

"Let's have a look about the bed," Matthew said. "Women always keep things about the bed."

"Just leave," Kayleigh warned, "before Mama starts screaming, and I call out to the neighbors."

With that, Matthew quickly pulled the terrified Cassie out from under the bed and held a knife to her neck. "Does this bring back memories, Colleen?" he sneered.

Cassie screamed hysterically as Kayleigh lunged for him, and he pulled the little girl to the floor.

"Shut up, you little misfit," he yelled at Cassie.

Then, turning, he shouted at Kayleigh, "Did you learn nothing from the last time that we cut you? This time, it will be your face." Kayleigh pulled her purse out from under the mattress and flung it at him.

"Take it and leave!" she screamed, her voice becoming more shrill, more out of control.

"Not just yet," Nolan said, his voice a low, ugly note. "Count it, Matthew." Marcus laughed as Matthew counted each bill and coin.

"That ain't no fortune!" Marcus barked. "That's what she makes tending children and putting on airs."

"Take it," Nolan snarled. "It'll have to do till she gets what the old lady has left," he said more calmly. "We'll be leaving now, ladies, but I'll be back in a month. Have the money then, Colleen, or I'll let Matthew make good on his promise of cuttin' you."

When they were gone, Kayleigh took Cassie in her arms, sat in the old creaky rocker that the previous tenants had left, and rocked her gently in front of the fireplace. Mercifully, the child had not had a seizure. "It will be all right," she promised her.

Kathleen sat with her head in her hands, gently crying, "how are we going to make it?' she asked Kayleigh. "We needed that money for food and rent."

"I don't know, Mama, but I'll think of something," she said wearily, fighting back tears. "Right now, I don't even have money to get back to Boise."

However, Kayleigh being Kayleigh, she had a plan already forming.

CHAPTER 14: GETTING BACK TO BOISE

After they were dressed, with a bit of coffee for fortification, Kayleigh took the three one-dollar bills that she had hidden in her shoe, transferred them to her purse, and ushered Kathleen and Cassie to the Bank of Idaho Falls. Once there, she asked one of the tellers, in a tone barely above a whisper, what the minimum amount of cash was required to open an account. She then requested to see the manager.

The teller was a thin middle-aged man dressed in a standard black suit, with reading glasses perched halfway down his nose, traditional of the day, but there was a small smile almost viewable on his thin lips. It was kind and reminiscent of his childhood when his older sister took charge of the family's modest finances. He turned to the area in back of his teller cage and gave a slight head bob to the man studying ledgers.

The large man adjusted his cravat and waistcoat and came forward. With his thick hair parted in the middle and his full-mustached face, he looked a bit like a villain that Kayleigh had once seen in a book that Margaret Ruth had lent to her. His smile was kind, though, and Kayleigh appreciated that.

"Let's just step over here to my desk," he motioned, "and tell your mother and little sister…" he questioned, with one eyebrow raised, "to join us also."

"My name is John Thurman (J.T.) Grainer," he said and offered his hand.

"I am Kayleigh O'Brien, and this is my mother, Kathleen O'Connor, and my little sister, Cassie O'Connor," Kayleigh managed the required introductions.

He motioned them to chairs, and when they were seated, he settled his large, rather bulky frame into the rolling chair behind his desk.

"I'm sorry to be in such a hurry," Kayleigh said hurriedly. "I'm just very concentrated on trying to open an account." Mr. Grainer smiled, and she noticed that he had warm, intelligent brown eyes. She also noticed that he was subtly eyeing Kathleen. In truth, he simply wondered about the situation.

He had some knowledge of Nolan O'Connor and thought it was a shame that such a cruel man was probably intimidating all three. He also took notice of the bruising under Kathleen's eye.

Kayleigh was not sure what to make of his reaction, but she forged on. "You see, I cannot open the account with much, only a dollar, but if your bank allows wire deposits, I can gradually build the account up when I go back to my teaching position in Boise."

"So, a teacher, eh," Mr. Grainer smiled. "Well, I think that could be arranged, and I can see there's more by the look in your eye."

"I don't want my stepfather, Mr. Nolan O'Connor, to have any access to the account, but I would like Mr. Josiah Langley to have full access to it at my direction," she stopped and held her breath.

"Well, I think, knowing both Mr. O'Conner (at this, Mr. Grainer's lips pursed into a somewhat disgusted expression) and Mr. Langley," (his expression returned to its pleasant demeanor), "that can be arranged, but I will need Mr. Langley to come in and co-sign at his convenience."

Kathleen eyed Kayleigh with a somewhat sad and disappointed expression, but Kayleigh refused to meet her gaze. "That will be fine, Mr. Grainer. I'll have him come in as soon as possible."

"Alright then," the large man smiled, "let's begin the paperwork and put your dollar to good use.

From the bank, the three walked to the bakery, where the smell of freshly baked rolls and other breads overwhelmed their senses and those of many others in town.

"Sissy, I'm so hungry," Cassie said softly.

"I know, Blossom," she answered. "Let's go get three rolls." At this suggestion, Kathleen was almost as joyous as Cassie.

They devoured the rolls, and Kayleigh pocketed the rest of the money next to the remaining one dollar that she had, knowing that they would need dry goods and enough food to make it for a while. "Mama," she said, turning to Kathleen and keeping Cassie behind her, "we need to see the Langleys now."

"That's a long walk, Colleen," Kathleen remarked. I'm beginning to worry about Cassie. I don't have much of her calming medicine left."

"Well, let's go first to see Mitch and Rosemary, Mama," Kayleigh pointed up the street toward their home. We'll be close to the Sheriff's Office after that.

"Well, they're a sweet couple and all, but why?" Kathleen looked perplexed.

"Cassie can sit down for a while, and I can ask Mitch a question," Kayleigh explained.

"Oh," Kathleen replied suspiciously. "And by the way, I'm still not happy about my own name not being on the bank account."

"It's for the best, Mama," Kayleigh reassured, "and by now, you should know it," she said, giving Kathleen a very direct look.

Kayleigh knocked on Mitch's door only once before Rosemary came bounding to open it. She signed excitedly that she was so glad to see Kayleigh and embraced her. She then signed for Kathleen and Cassie to come in and brought out a cherry pie. Cassie's eyes grew as big as saucers.

Hearing the chatter and gleeful sounds of Cassie beginning to eat her slice of pie, Mitch came into the room. The small front room was cheery, with a red checkered tablecloth on the kitchen table and a small fire snapping in the fireplace. Light shifted in through the small, curtained window of the front door.

"Well, if it isn't two of the most lovely ladies in Idaho Falls and a 'Boise Beauty,'" Mitch said, flashing his big trademark smile.

Cassie grinned in between bites, and Kathleen blushed. Kayleigh, though, gave her customary reply to Mitch, "You're full of the blarney and then some."

He and Rosemary laughed. "Well then, to what do I owe the honor?"

"I'm in some financial trouble, Mitch," Kayleigh began.

"Oh, Kayleigh, no!" Kathleen cautioned. "We didn't come to ask for money."

"I did," Kayleigh answered. "Mitch, Nolan robbed me last night and threatened us. I need a loan, a loan, mind you, of the fare back to Boise."

"Kayleigh, of course, Rosemary and I will do anything that we can for you, but we can't give you much. We just don't have much. However, I'm thinking if Zach pitches in a bit, together we could get the fare for you." At this, Rosemary shook her head in agreement.

"Oh, thank you, Mitch." Kayleigh sighed in relief and then beamed. "That's a load off, good friend."

"Come back by or, better yet, let me know when your train is set to leave, and we'll meet you with the money at the depot. That might be a bit safer," Mitch concluded.

"Yes, Mitch. I agree," Kayleigh answered. "Now, I hate to ask a favor and leave, but we have a few more things to settle up."

"That's fine," Mitch flashed his smile again, and Rosemary signed, "Take care, my sister."

"I will, dearest," Kayleigh signed back, and with that, they trekked toward the Sheriff's office.

Sheriff Blocker had an arrogant stance, face, build, demeanor, and voice. He was the type of man who bullied other men and thought that women instantly fell in love with him. In the meantime, he viewed women as inferior servants. Children were even less. He had abandoned four already in his limited life.

Cassie cowered behind Kayleigh, knowing instinctively that this was not a good man. Kathleen looked at Kayleigh and rolled her eyes as if to say, "I tried to tell you."

"Can I help you, ladies?" he sneered as his deputy snickered.

Physically, the two were a complete juxtaposition. The sheriff was tall with dark hair and eyes and a perfectly groomed pencil-thin mustache. The deputy was short, heavy set with an overflowing belly and a balding head, which he tried to cover up with about ten strands of hair.

"Perhaps," Kayleigh said, trying to look taller than her five foot two inches. "My mother and I were robbed last night, and my little sister was threatened at knifepoint."

"By who?" Blocker asked in a scoffing tone.

"By my stepfather and step-brothers," Kayleigh said.

"Are you sure they weren't just teasing a bit with you? And, from what I hear, you owe them a good bit of money," Blocker sneered.

Kayleigh could feel her face heating up with anger. "Holding a knife to a little girl's neck is not teasing," she said with her voice rising, "and I assure you I owe them nothing. That's an outright lie."

"The way he told us," the deputy knowingly interjected, "you was always in trouble with one man or another, and he and his boys was always having to bring you back."

"That's a lie!" Kathleen screamed. "My daughter has never been that way. She is the only thing that has stood between Cassie and I starving or never having a roof over our heads! Don't ever say that about my daughter again, you useless man. Men like the two of you shouldn't be in the law. The law should be after you!

"My husband is a thief, a liar, and a wife and child beater, and, if you won't listen to me, maybe you will to a few good armed men that I can summon for help.

"Let's go, Kayleigh. Cassie, come here to Mama," Kathleen finished and turned on her heel.

Kayleigh followed her mother dumbfounded. Never had her mother defended her as she had just done. Perhaps her mother did have more of a backbone than she usually displayed.

"I'm so tired," Cassie cried, "and I don't want to be around the bad men anymore."

"We've got to get her home, Kayleigh, before she has an episode," Kathleen looked tired and worn herself.

"Yes, Mama, you're right," Kayleigh said wearily. "I just need to make one more visit to make sure you'll both be taken care of."

"You're not thinking of going to the Langleys, are you?" Kathleen questioned.

"Yes, Mama, we've got to have help, and they can provide us with a loan—and perhaps more," she added quietly.

"Perhaps more of what?" Kathleen demanded as they walked toward the small house that Kathleen had tried to make a home.

"I'll discuss that when Mr. Langley can talk to the three of us," Kayleigh cautioned.

The two women swept up the remainder of the broken glass and nailed an old board over the ruined window. They settled Cassie then and put her to bed.

After a time, Kathleen went into the small bedroom and curled up next to the child, and Kayleigh fell asleep in front of the fire, determined to wake up early enough to walk to the Langleys. Her plan was in mind.

When Kathleen awakened, she found the coffee brewed and a note from Kayleigh telling her mother that she was going to speak with Mr. and Mrs. Langley and then to the depot to find out when the next train to Boise could be expected.

With the change that she had left, she would buy a few more rolls to take to Kathleen and Cassie for their mid-morning meal, and, hopefully, she would have something else in her possession.

Much of her plan went well. She had made the long walk to the Langley farm, an idyllic setting of open grass and pasture with mountains in the background. After talking with the couple, she completed her other tasks and had her small breakfast with Kathleen and Cassie, but when the Langleys pulled up to the small house in their horse and buggy, she could see Cassie brighten as Kathleen seemed to fold into herself.

Kayleigh pulled up chairs near the fireplace for the Langleys, and Kathleen stopped herself from offering them coffee, remembering that they did not "indulge." Cassie then hugged the couple and sat between them. Mr. Langley cleared his throat and began.

"Kathleen, Mavis, and I have great affection for you, Kayleigh, and little Cassie. You are not safe, though, since your husband has decided to settle in Idaho Falls." (Otherwise, he's often seen just wandering about and up to meanness.)

"Word is that his boys have a farm at the edge of town. Sometimes, he stays with them, and sometimes he, or all three, go into Oregon and work off the coast with the big fishing boats.

"Either way, he can't hold on to money, so he'll be back for yours. I don't know a lot about your finances, mind, but I suppose you're living off of what Kayleigh sends you and your seamstress wages, so he's robbing both of you and endangering all of your lives.

"Mavis and I would be glad to take you and Cassie in." He quickly continued on before Kathleen, her mouth ajar, could interject.

"We have the room and provisions, and we could see to it that the child had more medical care. Kayleigh has made a promise to pay for the room and board, plus she will send extra for clothing when she can. I've co-signed the bank account, so I would have access to these funds when needed," he finished.

Kathleen said but one word, quietly but firmly, "No."

"So you would endanger your own child?" Langley asked in a somewhat loud voice, uncharacteristic of him.

She collected herself and said quietly to Kayleigh, "I will allow Cassie to stay with the Langleys if I can come to see her every week, but I will not leave. I finally have a home to call my own. Although I know that I don't fully pay for it, it makes me feel better. Besides, I can almost pay the rent with my seamstress wages, and from what I heard in town, he's taken off again."

"Am I not stayin' with you anymore, Mama?" Cassie's eyes were filling with tears, and her voice and her mouth trembled.

"It's for the best, my love," Kathleen said as Cassie ran over to her and she took her in her lap.

"The bad men will come back, but this way, Mama will take care of them so that they don't hurt you," Kathleen smiled and kissed Cassie.

Mavis, silent until this point, nodded her head. "Mama will still be your mama, Cassie, but this way, Josiah and I can keep you safe."

Kayleigh looked at Mr. Langley, and He remembered the other part of the agreement.

"Mavis, take the child outside for a time," he leaned over and spoke very quietly.

When the two had left, Mr. Langley lowered his voice again and spoke. "Kathleen, I thought that this might be the case, so I've brought something." With a small gesture toward his coat, he withdrew a small derringer pistol from his inside pocket.

"Do you know how to shoot, Kathleen?" he asked.

"I do," she answered, almost scoffing. "I've known since I was a girl, although I prefer a rifle myself," she said knowingly. "You can blow a head clear off with that, you can."

Kayleigh and Josiah looked on in shock as Kathleen gave a slight smile. I actually have a shotgun dismantled under the bed. It was his, and I took it when we left South Dakota. I've kept it broken down for Cassie's sake, but perhaps it is time to reassemble it. A Winchester is said to be a good rifle."

"Well, we'll take the derringer and talk this over, Mr. Langley," Kayleigh said with more assurance than she felt. "If you and Mrs. Langley could return in the morning, we'll have Cassie ready," she said, choking back tears.

"Alright then," Langley agreed. "Let me call Mavis back in, and we'll sort things out."

Cassie was subdued but accepting when she returned to the small house. She hugged the Langleys bye and agreed that she would "see them in the morning."

The three readied for bed and held Cassie tightly between them…They were at the side of the bed, ready for prayers, when they heard the makeshift boarded window being pushed and beaten in, accompanied by the drunken and slurred language of Nolan O'Connor.

"Get in here with my money," he screamed.

Kayleigh quickly picked up the small derringer, pushing Cassie behind her and in front of Kathleen. Then, making her way into the small front room, the gun raised, she screamed, "Get out or I'll shoot you!"

O'Connor's laugh was a loud, vicious, hateful, and mocking sound. Cassie covered her ears while Katherine held her tightly. "You don't have the gumption or the sense. All three of us—Matthew, Marcus, and me—could have had you years ago if it hadn't been for Luke. Tell me, what do men think of the scar running down your neck? Do they like that?"

Kayleigh was barely aware of the gun going off until she saw, through a smoky haze, the shattered mess it had made of Nolan's shoulder. Blood had exploded out of his arm and covered the wall behind.

"Stay in the bedroom, Cassie," Kathleen whispered to Cassie as the child climbed into bed and pulled the covers over her head.

Grabbing at his shoulder and doubled over in pain, Nolan looked at Kayleigh with pure shock as Kathleen entered the room.

"Get out," she said clearly and flatly. No emotion was present.

"Where am I supposed to go like this, you old mule?" he sputtered.

"I don't know, and I don't care," Kathleen hissed. "Go out in the street and die for all I care. Get out before I shoot you myself!"

He staggered to the door. "You'll both regret this," he screamed.

Kayleigh and Kathleen watched as he ran back toward the road to his sons' farm, and that was the last Kayleigh or Cassie would ever see of him.

There was little sleep to be had for the three of them, but they sat together in front of the fire and dozed and talked.

Kayleigh gently reminded Cassie that she would be leaving the next day for Boise and that Cassie would be going to the Langleys. Both women assured Cassie that Kayleigh would be back and that Kathleen would come to see her each week.

When the child had drifted off to sleep in Kayleigh's arms, Kathleen assured her, in low tones, that she didn't think Nolan O'Connor would be a problem again, whether he was dead or alive. Kayleigh had her doubts and kept the derringer at her mother's urgings. Kathleen still planned to reassemble the shotgun.

Kayleigh and Cassie hugged and kissed Kathleen goodbye before leaving in the buggy. Their first stop was the depot, where Mitch and Rosemary were waiting for Kayleigh.

Kayleigh shook Mr. Langley's hand and gave a quick hug to Mavis (Mavis was not the hugging type, and Kayleigh knew it).

"Keep that derringer with you, Kayleigh," Langley admonished. "You never know what dangers might befall."

Then she lifted Cassie from the buggy and embraced her tightly.

"I will be back soon, Blossom," she assured Cassie. "Be a good girl and obey the Langleys. I love you."

Cassie was resigned to the situation this time, and that hurt Kayleigh more than anything. "Okay, Kayleigh. I'll be good," she promised. She kissed her older sister and got back into the buggy.

Kayleigh waved as the buggy left before turning to Mitch and Rosemary. Mitch smiled, as did Rosemary, both trying to be as pleasant as possible under the circumstances.

"Zach couldn't come, Kayleigh. Caroline is a bit sick, but they both send their love. Between the two of us, we have your fare," he grinned. "We all just hate to see you go again," he said, and Rosemary nodded, signing her love for Kayleigh.

"I love all of you," she said, hugging the two and dabbing at her eyes. "It's just for the best," she said, thinking to herself, *now more than ever.*

CHAPTER 15: BACK IN BOISE

Again, Kayleigh watched Idaho Falls slide away with the mountains standing stalwart in the background. The stretches of tall green grass seemed to be waving their own goodbye. She knew that she would be back around Christmas, but it didn't console her pain. How quickly things could change, and often did. Kathleen and Cassie were now separated.

She allowed herself just enough time to contemplate these things before making her plans for her return to Boise. School would be starting in a few short days. Perhaps she could work in the General Store for a short time, in addition to the school.

She owed the Langleys, Mitch, and Zach, and, of course, she had to support her mother. Then, there was her own board and food. She was in debt, and things would be tight.

"Fool!" she cursed herself. "Why had she taken most of her wages with her? And what was Nolan talking about concerning an inheritance?" Had her grandmother really known what she was saying and offering? It was all so long ago. She had always assumed that there was no money.

As Boise came into sight, she was thrilled to see Margaret Ruth standing on the platform and a bit shocked to see the Reverend standing with her. She had wired ahead to Margaret Ruth of her arrival and had hoped that she would meet her, but Reverend Perkins, she hadn't expected.

He withdrew his black, rounded hat, approached the train as passengers departed, and offered Kayleigh his arm as she emerged. "We have all missed you, dear," he said in a somber tone.

Kayleigh stole a look at Margaret Ruth, who rolled her eyes and crossed them. It took everything Kayleigh had not to laugh.

"Well, it's good to be back," Kayleigh said and sincerely meant it.

The three made their way to the hotel, chatting about recent town events when a short, rather swarthy man began to approach.

"Reverend, could I speak to you?" he inquired.

"My young lady has just returned, sir," Perkins said rather abruptly. "You'll need to approach me tomorrow."

"Pharis," Kayleigh began, "if you need to speak with this man…"

"Nonsense, dear," he replied. "It's just some general business, and it can wait."

"Well, alright," she agreed, but Margaret Ruth wore a very skeptical look. Something was up, but she wasn't quite sure what.

Margaret Ruth turned to Kayleigh and Pharis when they reached the hotel. "Well, I'll just check in with Mr. Oslo at the front desk. Good night, you two."

"Pharis leaned in for a brief kiss with Kayleigh at the door to the hotel. He looked about furtively before his lips barely grazed her cheek. "I know you're tired after your journey, dear. We'll talk again tomorrow. Let's say around 10:00 a.m."

Kayleigh smiled and thought again of the relief of a warm bed and a fresh nightgown. She wished him a good night and went in and spoke with Mr. Oslo so that she could check back into her room.

Mr. Oslo eyed her a bit differently, his pinched face twitching with the desire to tell her something.

"How was your trip, Miss O'Brien?" he inquired.

"Fine, a bit busy, but fine," Kayleigh answered.

"I see," Mr. Oslo said cautiously.

"You know, I just think the world of you, Miss O'Brien," Mr. Oslo started, leaning a bit over the desk. "That's why I think you ought to know. There's a man who's been asking after you in town, snooping about, you might even say."

Kayleigh hesitated before answering, "Well, thank you for letting me know, Mr.Oslo. If you'll excuse me, I'm anxious to get settled and get rested."

"Oh, of course, my dear, of course," he nodded. "Shall I get the porter to carry your bags?"

"No, I'm fine," she said as she quickly made her way up the stairs.

After she placed her valises in her room, she went softly down the carpeted hall to Margaret Ruth's room.

"What took you so long, kiddo?" Margaret Ruth asked. "I really need to talk to you."

"I could tell you had something to say," Kayleigh replied as she sat in the petite Victorian chair opposite of Margaret Ruth's matching chair. The small fireplace had a cheery fire. Not every room had a fireplace, but Mr. Oslo always made sure that the teachers who roomed there had one.

"Well, it's about that little bearded man who's been wandering about town, snooping into corners of your life. However, speaking of snoops, I'm sure our Mr. Oslo has already made mention of him," she concluded.

"Yes, but I don't know what this man thinks that he knows or why he is doing this. Is he a detective? Did someone hire him?" Kayleigh asked in confusion.

"Indeed, someone did hire him," Margaret Ruth said, leaning forward and looking very directly into Kayleigh's eyes. "Reverend Perkins hired him."

What?" Kayleigh said, her mouth slightly ajar and her fingertips digging into the arms of the chair.

"I overheard Perkins talking to him in the lobby one morning. He made it clear that he wanted to know not just your 'history' in Idaho Falls but also as much as he could find previous to that. His name is Caleb, something or other, by the way." Margaret Ruth paused and looked quizzically at Kayleigh, waiting for her reply. "What will you do?'

Kayleigh suddenly looked exhausted and overwhelmed. To be truthful, she had barely even thought about Pharis during her time in Idaho Falls, and now her thoughts of him were anything but kind. Why would he do this? If she had just had more time and trust in him, she would have told him anything.

"I'm going to bed, and tomorrow I'll be talking to Mr. Perkins. The next day, I'll go to church, although it may not be the 'Good Reverend's' church, and the day after, I'll return to school and teach my students."

Margaret Ruth smiled and said, "Good for you, Kayleigh."

The next day was a sunny and cold Saturday. Reverend Perkins arrived at 10:00 a.m., exactly, to see Kayleigh. She noticed that his handsome appearance was overshadowed by a look of sadness and disappointment, and somehow, smugness and a touch of evil were present, too.

"Let's walk for a while," he suggested.

She nodded, and they headed toward the outskirts of town, a lovely place where they had walked before, with a good view of the mountains in the background. She dared to think that this might be the mountains of her dreams, but then again, why was he checking up on her?

"Kayleigh," he began, "you are lovely and dear, but, as I'm sure you know, the wife of a reverend must be above reproach. You, my sweet girl, have a rather colorful past, complete with a carnival life and questionable parentage."

At this point, Kayleigh began to speak, but Pharis put his hand up and continued. "I might be able to overlook that part of your history, but your 'little sister' would be problematic. She is not right and prone to speak out in embarrassing ways. Also, some in your past have come to wonder if she is indeed just your 'little sister.'"

Kayleigh looked at him in shocked disbelief, as if he had struck her. Indeed, his words were hurting more than the blows her stepbrothers had sometimes inflicted on her.

"Then, there is the matter of your stepfather being shot," he continued. "Speculation is that this was your doing, in a temper fit of rage. Although I would keep many of these secrets, I'm afraid that sooner or later, the truth would come out. However, I do have a proposition. Even reverends have their needs, and until I find a wife, or even afterward, you could be my mistress, or, shall we say, 'second wife.' No one would have to know. I have an aunt who has gone senile. You could watch over her in Twin Falls, and I could 'visit' you quite often. Of course, I would provide for both of you, and she has an estate of her own. What are your thoughts?"

Suddenly, every negative thought that Kayleigh had experienced over the "Good Reverend" began to emerge. "I think you're a smug, arrogant, hypocritical idiot," she shouted. "I'd rather die than be involved with you. Frankly, you bore me, and I hate it when you call me 'dear.'"

He stared at her in disbelief and said, "Such language, Kayleigh. Do you not know that our Father is listening?" he said, gesturing to the sky.

"Do you not know that He just heard you ask me to be a mistress?" she countered.

"You could lose your school position over this!" he was shouting now.

"And you could lose your church over what you just said to me," she said in a low voice of rage. A look then came over his face as though he had not considered this.

"And by the way," she said with a voice shaking with hatred, "you might want to actually try going up to women and talking to them instead of looking at them at a distance and expecting them to come to you. It won't work forever. Your pretty looks will begin to age, and more and more ladies may begin to wonder if you actually desire a woman." Dumbstruck, Perkins stared as though in a trance as she continued. "Say one word about me, and I'll let the whole town know what you offered," she added as she began to walk away. "Come after me now," she spun back around and looked at him, "and I'll scream bloody murder. Stay away from me, you conceited Bible Thumper."

With those words, she turned and ran. As she approached the edge of town, she realized that she had to calm herself in order to stave off any rumors about her state of mind and emotions. Other rumors would be coming soon enough.

I'm done with men, she thought.

CHAPTER 16: I'VE HEARD OF FAITHFUL

Kaleigh was in danger of falling into an even deeper depression than she had experienced in the convent. This was compounded by a strange feeling of foreboding of the unknown, brought on by the short, swarthy man she had first seen when she returned.

He stopped her one day on his way out of town, introduced himself as Caleb Spivy, and asked if he could speak to her. He then detailed how he had been hired by Perkins as a detective to find out what he could about Kayleigh's background.

"I didn't like doing it, ma'am," he confessed, "but money is money. Anyways, I think you should know that I uncovered somethin' that you should be aware of. There's some kind of money matter to be settled. It's being settled by some law firms out of London and Boston. You don't need to look into it. They'll find you. That's all I can say, ma'am!"

In the meantime, all she knew to do was to work in the school each day, surrounded by the joy, the hurts, the frustrations, and the secrets of schoolchildren. This kept her busy until the evening when she and Margaret Ruth would share a meal in the hotel dining room and then talk for a time before returning to their mutual rooms, dreams, and sadness.

Margaret Ruth, who was usually very optimistic and naturally joyful, had confessed to Kayleigh that she sometimes felt that her life lacked the love that she had thought would have arrived by now. She knew that, at thirty, her chances were slim.

Kayleigh, for her part, had adopted a new mantra, "Keep to yourself and keep going," but often, she wondered what the point of keeping on was. Then, she would remember Cassie and her mission was clear again.

"It's like my daddy used to say, Kayleigh," Margaret Ruth said one night. "I'm free, healthy, well-fed, employed, and housed. What do I have to complain about?"

"Yes," Kayleigh agreed, "but I'd like it better if I weren't in debt and in the same town with a 'respected' man who propositioned me."

"Forget him," Margaret Ruth said, rolling her eyes. "He'll get his one day, and you won't be in debt forever." She paused then and quietly asked Kayleigh, "Have you known all along that I'm mixed race?"

"What difference does it make, Margaret Ruth?" Kayleigh queried. "You're a good, beautiful person."

"My father was a big German man who loved talking, laughing, and life. My mother was what they called a 'quadroon' from New Orleans. We moved a lot. After they both died and I came to Idaho, speculation stopped, for the most part, but I have to confess, I feel as if I'm always looking over my shoulder, waiting for someone to point out the truth.

"I tell you, though, I'd gladly go back to the remarks and whispers just to have my parents back. I loved them that much," Margaret Ruth paused then, close to tears.

Kayleigh took her hand. "Dear friend, it shouldn't matter to anyone, and no one has to know, but if it does become known, it provides a clear view of who is worth your friendship and who is not. I shall miss our friendship greatly."

The next morning, a letter and a wire came in the same day, parallel and non-intersecting, as Professor Gallant had once described a geometric figure to her. The letter was from Mitch. He had decided (which meant that Zach had also decided) to leave Idaho Falls.

Apparently, his lack of devotion to the Mormon faith, or any faith for that matter, had "come home to roost" and filtered down to the biting remarks of students and parents. He had also, as he put it, "dared to discipline" the sheriff's son, who was now ostracized in town and continually disrespected in the classroom.

"So I heard of this place called Faithful," he wrote. This actually meant that he had seen an advertisement in the newspaper for three school teachers in a town called Faithful, somewhere in Oregon. They had a need for one lower school teacher and two upper school teachers.

"Would you be interested, Kayleigh?" he asked, and she could sense his desperation between the lines.

She replied, "Yes, Mitch. I would. This situation has become 'awkward,' and a new post would be yet another start. Tell me where to send my references, and I will." (She did not try to explain her amazement that the town was actually called "Faithful.")

So, the flight to Faithful began. That night, after composing her letter and listing her references, Kayleigh dreamed again of beautiful stars and grand mountains, along with gentle people who were helpful to one another. When she awoke, she thought, *The dream and the place never go together, girl, you know that.*

Still, there was always hope. The hope of a good, faithful man was now gone in her mind, but the hope of one town that could be a good home still held true, and if this town did not prove to be the one, she had her "hold out" of the artist colony in Canada.

The next day was the last day of school before spring planting and summer work, which would take the children away until the beginning of fall. Kayleigh had gathered her books and contemplated the contents and heftiness of her school trunk when she entered the hotel, and Mr. Oslo called out to her from behind the registration desk.

"Miss O'Brien! Miss O'Brien, please stop."

"What is it, Mr. Oslo?" Kayleigh asked with genuine concern. She was anxious that nothing had happened to Margaret Ruth or that there were no unwanted messages from the Reverend, who had already sent a few, offering his apologies.

"It's a telegram, ma'am," Mr. Oslo said with his beady blue eyes gleaming and longing to hear the contents of the message. He slung back the hinged reservation table and stepped out as though he had the most crucial of news.

"It really came yesterday, but you didn't go by the office, and they've lost their regular boy who delivers them. So, it was just delivered a few minutes ago."

"Oh," she managed. "Well, thank you. I'll take it upstairs. The disappointment was evident in Mr. Oslo's face, but whatever the contents, Kayleigh did not want the whole town privy to her business. It was bad enough that the telegraph office knew the circumstances of her mother and sister.

She took off her hat once she reached her room and began opening the telegram. She edged closer to the chair and sat down quickly as she read the contents:

Please return to Idaho Falls as soon as possible.

You have an inheritance issue that must be settled for your and your mother's safety. Come straight to the bank.

J.T. Grainer

Scenarios of danger ran through her unbridled mind for a flash of seconds. Calm thinking then prevailed, and she dared to think that perhaps her grandmother had spoken in facts. There was an inheritance. She needed to leave, and more quickly than she had already planned, back to Idaho Falls, then forward to Faithful.

CHAPTER 17: 1890—RUNNING AGAIN

This time, the clacking of the rails seemed to match the beat of Kayleigh's heart and the momentum of her anxiety. She was only eight when her grandmother told her that she would have an inheritance, but the few letters that she had received from her grandmother had simply been sweet and cheerful until the last one, and then, they stopped.

As soon as the early morning train pulled in and she got off, she almost ran to the Idaho Falls Bank. Struggling to catch her breath, she managed to tell the front teller that she needed to see Mr. Grainer.

To her surprise, when she gave her name, the usual rather reticent teller snapped to and ran up the stairs to fetch Mr. Grainer from a board meeting. Returning quickly, completely out of breath himself, he motioned for Kayleigh to sit at the front desk until Mr. Grainer could come down.

Mr. Grainer was moving faster down the old winding stairs than she or anyone else had ever seen him move. He had also told those in the meeting, when they questioned him about excusing himself, that they would simply have to wait. Accustomed to him bowing to their every desire, they were shocked.

Mr. Grainer smiled at Kayleigh, his face flushed and his mustache twitching about. "Miss O'Brien," he said, offering his hand, "thank you for coming so quickly."

She smiled in return and thanked him for his wire. Then, when she had gained enough composure to ask, she said, "Mr. Grainer, what is this all about, and why would there be danger to my mother or myself?"

"My dear, how old are you?" he queried.

"I just turned twenty-four. Why, Mr. Grainer?" she asked expectantly.

"You are a year away from becoming a very wealthy young woman. In the meantime, you are still the proverbial 'church mouse,' but, knowing you, you will work your way through that."

"What are you talking about, Mr. Grainer? Is there some kind of inheritance?"

"Some kind," he grinned and chuckled, "some kind, indeed! You, my dear, have inherited from one, Kate O'Brien, one million dollars. Here," he reached inside his coat pocket, "this is the letter that accompanied the Boston Bank inspector, Mr. Everett. The money originated in Ireland, then London, then Boston. We could make neither heads nor tails of the letter, but perhaps you can. Someone said that they thought it is in old Irish."

Fighting off a feeling of shock and dream-like disbelief, Kayleigh read her grandmother's dear rounded handwriting silently:

My Beloved,

I will be gone when you read this, but you must know that I have fulfilled my pledge to you. The money that your blessed grandfather left me was fair. I invested a portion of it in a London shipping business and placed the rest in a London Bank and Trust. (Mind, I did keep enough to live out my days comfortably.) The sale of the china shop went well also, so your sum of inheritance is impressive.

I searched for the proper and "God help us" honest barrister to carry out my final wishes, and, in so doing, have hopefully arranged for you to be "well set" by your twenty-fifth year.

Do not let Kathleen, nor that, no doubt, bullying, "lay about" which she married, have anything to do with the transactions.

Find a secure bank and do not talk about your fortune. I'm hoping that you will be married and established by your twenty-fifth birthday, but if not, all the more reason to keep mum. You don't need someone marrying you for your money.

Walk with the Lord, stay busy with good work, and be faithful to the love of your life. If it's as good of a match as your grandfather and I, then you will be happy and enriched.

I've had a vision of your future, and I think all of these things are possible. It came to me once when I had a panicked feeling that you had been hurt. (Lord help me. I've had that feeling more than once about you. I wish I could have been there to help and protect you.) I think that this man in your future may be somehow damaged, but very good and protective.

I love you. My soul will continue with you.

Grandmother

P.S. Stay away from "the drink."

Mr. Grainer noticed the subtle changes in Kayleigh's facial expressions as she read the letter.

"Suffice it to say, Mr. Grainer," Kayleigh said, looking up, "you are correct about my inheritance. Now, how do I proceed? Just how much money is there, really, and when will it be available?" she asked, trying to affect some degree of calm and sophistication.

Mr. Grainer smiled, leaned back, and stretched in his rolling desk chair. "One million and approximately a year from today," he replied.

Kayleigh's freckles stood out as her face blanched white. She grabbed the edge of the desk. "Mr. Grainer, I do not appreciate such jokes," she said shakily. "I've been through enough."

"I assure you, Miss O'Brien, this is no joke. You will be a wealthy young woman," Mr. Grainer's solemn expression now assured her.

"This is your decision, dear lady," Mr. Grainer said softly. "Naturally, I would like for you to entrust your money here, but the choice will be yours. The bank inspector informed us that this was your last known residence, so naturally, they first came to us, but the funds can be delivered to any bank you choose. It may be best to split the money between, say…here, in Idaho Falls, and in, perhaps, Boise."

Kayleigh mused for only a brief moment, "Mr. Grainer, for the time being, please keep it here. Can you get the proper work going on it, sir, and stay in touch with me?"

"Of course, dear," he said and nodded, "but in the meantime, your stepfather is a concern. Do you know where he is? Your mother needs to be warned, but I would not reveal the full amount of your inheritance should she raise the topic.

"I and other members of the mayor's town council have had a serious talk with the sheriff's office. They seem to have a better understanding of what a public nuisance this man is."

"I will," she said, rising. "This is all a bit to take in, though. I must tell you that Mr. Herd and Mr. Asher and myself plan on taking teaching positions in Oregon. I will, of course, wire you when we are settled."

Mr. Grainer walked her to the door. "I would also advise you, Miss O'Brien, to make a will and set up a trust for your mother and little sister."

"Yes," she nodded, a bit in a daze, "I must do that."

She began to walk to her mother's cottage. This was not to be a clear walk to her later. Still in a daze, she thought that she saw Mr. Langley crossing the street but was not sure. She continued walking with urgency and overwhelming fear.

Reaching the cottage door, she called out, "Mama, it's Kayleigh."

Later, she would remember Mr. Langley walking her to Mitch and Rosemary's home and Mitch, Rosemary, Zach, and Caroline walking with her to the depot, telling her again and again, "Your mother simply met with a tragic accident. Cassie is safe. You will be alright. We must go now." She was going again. She was running again, and this time, the train and the tracks seemed to echo her fleeing: "Better run, girl, better run."

PART II: JACOB'S STORY

INTRODUCTION: THE 1919 MEETING OF THE FAITHFUL LADIES READING CIRCLE

It was a morning of snow flurries and women who reminded me of whirling snow and the remaining leaves of fall as they entered Mary Alice's home. The home itself was more of a cottage, very prettily appointed and arranged, with only a few furnishings that reminded one that a man also resided there.

We were settled and warm when the door flew open, banging the side of the frame and admitting cold air. There stood Beatrice Atwood, her hair somewhat disheveled under her fur bonnet, her chubby cheeks red from the cold, and her skirt protruding at her generous midline.

"Well, Lands Sake, ladies! You might tell a lady when plans have changed," Beatrice scolded. "Both Maddie and Mrs. Margaret Ruth made a great show of telling me not to meet at Mary Alice's because of illness. So, there I was, banging away at the door of Jennifer Ann's house."

"Oh, so sorry," Aunt Maddie said, barely suppressing a smile." "How absent-minded that was of me!"

"Well, no harm, no foul," Beatrice said both good-naturedly and suspiciously as she settled herself into the circle. "I'll just start out the discussion of this Jane Eyre book since I'm the somewhat wronged party." She paused then, giving a sidelong glance at the hearth and the dog lying there.

"Oh goodness! Is that horrible Sawyer dog still alive? Why in the world did you bring him, Kayleigh?" she asked in mock horror.

"He just followed me, and Mary Alice was kind enough to let him come in, and no, Beatrice," my Miss O'Brien said wearily, "it's not the original dog. After all, it's been thirty years since I took him in. This is one that he would be a great, great grandfather sire to. Or, at least, that's what we think." She shrugged and laughed a bit.

Beatrice's eyes rolled, but Mary Alice offered her some of the warm tea punch she had made.

"First of all," she said, after two rather hefty slurps of the tea punch, "I've never read anyone's writing that expressed such self-pity. So, the girl was orphaned and put in a home. At least she had somewhere to go, and at least someone then took her in. On top of that, she found a job and a vocation.

"I truly doubt that most orphanages are that bad. It sounds a bit exaggerated to me, and besides, she's rescued by a man. What was her problem?"

My Miss O'Brien began, very forcefully, to our surprise, "I assure you many orphanages are that bad and even worse, and the family that did take her in abused her. As for her job, teaching, whether private or public, is not an easy vocation.

"It often involves children as well as parents who look down on the teacher and the vocation. The story is illustrating class distinctions, as well as abandonment, and the courage that must be shown to simply survive."

"Well, I think," Beatrice began, but to my surprise, my mother intervened.

"I agree, and what's more, although the idea of being rescued by a man is a point of exaggeration, Mr. Rochester was quite flawed and burdened and actually unable to even rescue himself. What they ultimately had was more of a partnership, which is how most good marriages do begin and end," she concluded.

"Here, here!" our Mrs. Margaret Ruth said, setting her tea aside while her tidy dark bun bobbed a bit as she turned her head toward each member in the group. "Most men are encumbered in some way, and even the strongest of them are usually looking for the help of a good woman."

"Very well put," Mrs. Mary Alice agreed as she gracefully smoothed her skirts and opened her copy of the book slightly. Leaning down over the book, her white hair showed in the beautiful upswept and pinned style that she wore it in.

"Mr. Rodchester's past had to be burned away, while Jane's had to be confronted. With that confrontation, she sorted out who would be trusted and loved and who would simply have to be forgiven."

Aunt Maddie began speaking, her crystal blue eyes twinkling with the fireplace and her still beautiful blond hair hanging at her shoulders. "Two things pulled at my heart the most: the death of dear Helen, Jane's sweet companion in the orphanage, and Mr. Rodchester's blindness. I took both occurrences as a nod to the unfairness of life but noted the relief and help that can sometimes come from a higher power."

We all sat silently for a time before I ventured an observation, "Jane's strength is what captured my attention," I commented. "This was a story of beautiful inspiration."

"Indeed!" Penny agreed, smiling. "Although, in her situation, I believe my temper might have prevailed! A few blows might have been struck! I also believe it should be noted that although it was difficult and sometimes dangerous, she survived without Mr. Rodchester before returning. She was self-reliant against great obstacles."

Mary laughed and agreed, "Yes, sister of mine, I can certainly see that, and I have to say that I seethed over the behavior of several characters."

Again, I thought of my Ned, and I thought of what we had all endured in one way or another.

After helping with the clean-up, my Miss O'Brien asked me to walk with her. She said that she had something to give me when we reached her house. We talked along the way about Jane Eyre and our book circle, and she reminded me that several had said that Beatrice Atwood was often belittled by her own mother, who always thought that her thoughts and opinions were superior to all others. So, again, there was an example of someone shaped by their past.

When we reached her home with its pretty blue shutters, white fence, and wide porch, she gave me two things without ceremony, only with a smile and a short explanation.

"This is your grandmother Jennifer's journal, and these are my letters from Margaret Ruth and Peaches. The journal is yours to keep, but the letters I will want returned. Also, when you're ready, I'll fill in a few more details that I've learned through the years. Talking to you will give me something to look forward to, especially now that Jack is gone. Come by after school sometime, and we'll have some tea or coffee."

She smiled and walked me to the door. I left knowing what she wanted, the second part, the rest of the story.

CHAPTER 18: THE GOOD OLDEST SON

If there was one thing that the good citizens of Faithful, Oregon, had agreed upon, it was that Jacob McVale was a good son to his parents. He worked with his father after school to help him with the fishing boats and went on fishing trips with him as he could. He respected his mother, Jennifer, and helped with all of the usual chores around their home, and he kept a good cheerful attitude.

He was also a good older brother to his younger brother, Daniel, and his younger sister, Maddie. However, the younger twins, Samuel and Sarah, were the two that tugged at his heart and the two that he loved to come home and see.

It was not unusual to see him up at 4:00 a.m. and to bed well after 11:00 p.m. when his studies were completed. In fact, his intellect could have been directed into a different profession, but his father, Joshua McVale, was determined to make him a part of the fishing and shipping business, and he considered reading and studying to be a kind of hobby. He wanted his son to be educated, but not overly so. After all, he was not raising a lawyer or a professor. He was raising a son to take over his legacy. This was fine with Jacob at the time. He admired his father greatly and longed to please him and be a part of expanding the business.

His father, Joshua McVale, was a large man, six foot four in height, with curling brown hair intertwined with grey. At forty-five years of age, he was still a handsome man, with a look that might have made others think of him as fierce or intimidating until they considered his blue eyes, which seemed to twinkle with an inner secret joke that he might or might not make others privy to. He was a man to be reckoned with, and he expected a lot from Jacob.

At fifteen, Jacob was all legs and arms, yet handsome and more manly than many his age. Looking at Joshua gave others close to him a glimpse of who Jacob would become.

There were times with Joshua McVale that Jacob would hold in his heart. There were sunrise walks when the two would watch the sun's appearance while readying the boats and men for the day. Occasionally, Joshua would wink, lean over, and whisper to Jacob, "Well, God just outdid Himself today. Look at the sheer beauty of that sunrise."

So, Jacob delivered the work and service that his father expected until he was seventeen. Prior to this age, he had not considered any other way of living his life, but then the rebellion set in. It set in, at the start, in little ways. Jacob would propose an idea that his father would dismiss. Jacob was naturally somewhat frustrated but did not show any form of pushback or disrespect. This situation, however, blossomed into a full-out argument over purchasing warehouses from Neb Darius' father.

"Dad, I'm telling you," Jacob asserted, "approach Old Man Darius about selling you a warehouse. Renting space is already costing us, and I think you could get a fair and low cost right now. Who knows what might happen in a few years?"

"First of all, you don't tell me anything, lad," Joshua said while wagging his finger in Jacob's face. "Second, we don't have that kind of money on hand, and we need two more small boats first. The day I die is the day I'll approach Reuben Darius about anything else."

"But the shipping business is going better than fishing right now. Why not expand that?" Jacob questioned in a more heated manner.

"The answer is no!" Joshua shouted. "There will be no warehouse now. If we have to let our rented space go, we will unload on the dock and have the cargo guarded, as we have done. Or, we'll keep the cargo in the boat until it can be unloaded. That is the end of it!"

The two stared at each other in anger, frustration, and the anxiety of knowing that their relationship was changing.

At the same time, Jacob was dealing with Neb Darius, the son of Reuben. He fancied himself a scholar, a young businessman, and a lady's man. Jacob often mentally recounted how things had started between them years before and how much he would love to set the record straight, but he stayed contained and in control.

CHAPTER 19: A TOUCH OF BLUE

Jacob fell in love with Kelly Simon very quickly. She was his young love. After the argument with his father and the fact that he could not present even the slightest independent idea to him, Jacob was ready and susceptible to anyone offering a new job. So, much like the next act in a play, Nabal Simon entered.

Recently arrived from Boston, he brought his wife, daughter, and entourage with him. A short, rather stout man, bald and well into his fifties, he flashed money, a fancy suit, a large signet ring, and a knowing smile.

In complete contrast, his wife, Amanda, and daughter, Kelly, were beautiful. When they arrived in town, Joshua and Jacob were loading supplies into their wagon. Joshua paused and said, "Let's lend a hand to these people."

Kelly peaked shyly out of the carriage. Jacob literally felt his heart leap as he smiled at her and carefully reached for her waist to help her down. He took her all in, from her blonde hair to her clear blue eyes and perfect features. "Perfect" was the word that came to him.

She was slim but beautifully shaped, and Jacob was completely smitten. Kelly very quickly became his world, and he became hers. Standing and politely talking to Nabal and Amanda Simon, Joshua saw it happening, and he felt in his heart what many fathers have felt through the years when they've witnessed their sons falling in love; he hoped that she did not hurt him, and he hoped that he did not hurt her. He never dreamed, though, that Nabal Simon would hurt both him and his son.

The romance developed quickly, and Kelly lit Jacob's world as he lit Kelly's. For the most part, the romance was allowed, although Joshua and Jennifer counseled him to go slowly, and Amanda Simon was hoping it would simply end. Nabal, however, saw it as something that he could use.

The love between the two was not nearly as surprising or concerning to Joshua as the fact that Nabal was now his competition, for this new man in town had come to begin his own fishing and shipping business. There was no talk of collaboration or respecting territories. Joshua recognized very quickly that this man was ruthless and dishonest, and he wondered what had driven him from Boston to the West.

It was not long before Joshua began to witness another romance, the romance of Nabal tempting his son to come into business with him. The offer was more than almost any young man could resist, the promise of his beautiful daughter and his own business, but Joshua had met his share of "Nabals." They were full of promises but left behind a den of dishonesty and broken dreams.

"Jacob," he said one Friday while they unloaded the large sailboat together, "don't go in with this Nabal Simon on anything. He is all talk and bluster. I doubt that he even knows the fishing business or the shipping enterprises. He will make a big splash with many in town, especially the younger ones, and then they will begin to see the real man, the sham that he is."

"I can't work with you any longer, Dad," Jacob said as the two pierced each other with their looks and unspoken feelings. "You will not, or cannot, listen to me. I am a man. I know that seventeen is still young, but I've carried a man's share for some time, and you know it."

He walked away from Joshua then and did not return until all that his father had foreseen happened and more. Jacob would indeed surprise his father, though, and his father's heart would ache for him.

Working for Nabal Simon was not a great deal better than working for his own father, but at least Simon did seem to listen to him and take a few suggestions under consideration. He did not particularly like or trust the man, but he was making a point with Joshua, and he was aware in his own heart and counsel that this was the case. He would, however, never admit this to anyone else.

One sunny and windy afternoon, Jacob suggested that Nabal split his boats up into shifts instead of sending them all out at one time each day, often in the heat of the day or the worst of weather.

Nabal looked Jacob up and down, chewed on the tip of a cigar, and spoke with a bit of a sneer. "I'll tell you what. You can have all of my small blue fishing boats, and I'll keep the white if you can outfish me with the blue ones. As you can see, the blue ones are far newer than the white. Also, you and Kelly can go on and get married.

"However, if you don't win this competition, you'd better work with me a few more years to better learn the trade. When I decide you are ready, you will be allowed to marry my daughter."

Jacob's blue eyes blazed as the sun lit them, and his mind burned with the stinging offer of this man who dangled his daughter like a carnival prize. How dare this blowhard imply that he didn't know the fishing business. Joshua McVale had taught him and taught him well. He knew enough to recognize damaged boats with a brighter coat of paint.

With restraint, Jacob answered, "I'll think on it, sir."

"Don't think on it too long," Nabal answered. "You have until I return from the bank in Portland. There are a few things I have to attend to, and then I'll want your answer."

It was then that Pete Jamison, Jacob's best friend, thundered over, having overheard the conversation. A bear of a man who often spoke first and thought later, his long, straight dark hair streamed back from the wind, and his dark brown eyes seemed to snap with life. Only a few years older than Jacob, his face was already beginning to be weather-worn and brown.

"You know I worked for old Nabal for a few weeks before we came to words," he reminded Jacob, "and I have some information that you might like to know. Nabal was planning on selling those blue boats to unsuspecting men, and there's still a lot of that blue and white paint left," he said with a slight raise of the eyebrows. "Also, old Nabal doesn't see so well."

By now, the two thought so much alike that Jacob instantly knew what he had in mind. The two enlisted a few other men, who hated Nabal and knew how to keep their mouths shut, to help drag the boats behind trees and paint the white ones blue and the blue ones white.

Nabal proclaimed a fishing contest upon his return after Jacob agreed to his terms. When Nabal's white boats either failed to float at a good pace or out and out sank, Jacob's load of fish and his clear, wide smile told the outcome. He and his men were declared the winners, while an explosion of cheers took place at the docks.

Nabal's face flamed red as he glared at Jacob, and his fists clenched and unclenched. "I know what you did," he spat the words in complete hatred.

"I know what you did, too." Jacob snarled

At that, Nabal turned, casting his eyes back long enough to tell Jacob, "You will never marry my daughter."

How much Jacob wanted to say, "Ah, but I already have."

CHAPTER 20: A FRIENDSHIP, A GRUDGE, AND A SEARCH FOR PEACE

Neb Darius and Jacob shared a singular bond. Both of them had been born and raised in Faithful. There was no transplanting or search for sanctuary in their pasts. This, of course, did not ultimately bond them in friendship. Neb was no Pete Jamison, and Jacob had long ago ceased to think of him as anything more than an acquaintance.

Neb's full name was Nebraska Darius. The Darius family was large and had been moved about a good bit. Reuben Darius had taken to naming his children after the states in which they were born. In Jacob's mind, it always reminded him of Nebuchadnezzar from the Bible. Even with all of his shortcomings, Neb tended to think that he was a cut above the rest of the town.

Jacob was a year older than Neb, but they often wound up in the same grade levels while in school. Of course, Neb received expensive tutoring after his graduation from eighth grade and went on to college afterward.

Jacob, on the other hand, went to work on the docks and fishing boats and came to know the business almost as well as his father.

Reuben was a land speculator and had made many a shrewd deal, turning unused land into business and housing tracts. As Joshua McVale put it, "Aye, he'll speculate you right into the poor house if you let him."

Neb and Jacob could have become fast enemies, and, in fact, there was some tension between the two of them, but there were also shared secrets of earlier struggles with young manhood between the two of them. Neb knew the reason for Jacob often going to San Francisco, besides helping his father on fishing trips, and Jacob knew that Neb had been bullied on a regular basis. The two were more like portals of possible humiliation for each other rather than harbingers of earth-shaking information. Nonetheless, neither young man cared to have their secrets revealed to everyone.

Neb had not been a healthy child. He could very well have died on several occasions. Small, with spindly legs and a tendency to tire easily at any exertion, he had somehow survived several illnesses unscathed, protected by both his mother and summoned doctors.

When he did return to school, he was bullied and tormented by larger boys who had never known a sick day in their lives, with the exception of Jacob McVale, who did not bully.

Jacob took Neb under his wing and taught him some of the intricacies of being a young man. Neb was a fast study and caught on quickly to outthinking and out-talking many of those who had brute force but little mental power.

The fighting and self-defense, however, were harder for Neb to acquire. He lacked the build and agility of Jacob, but he did come to realize that he could at least survive a fistfight.

With his confidence increased and his body no longer bone-thin, he was becoming a handsome young man. Gone were the times of being plunged face down into manure or having his pants and shoes taken by the end of the school day, as he was forced to walk home in that state. He now had the appearance of a young gentleman and the attention of several young ladies.

Jacob shrugged mentally. Their friendship had never been anything to write home about, but he had helped the boy out. He expected the same fair treatment, but Neb, among other faults, was developing loose lips. He fancied himself a ladies' man with a fast way of talking and getting next to young girls.

So, when Neb also fancied Kelly Simon, the same girl that Jacob loved, he thought it fair play to let her know about how Jacob had outsmarted and cheated her father. (Of course, he left out the detail of how Nabal had originally painted the boats.)

It so happened that neither Joshua nor Nabal were aware that Jacob and Kelly had been married in the neighboring county weeks before the fishing contest. Mr. and Mrs. Simon kept putting off Jacob from marrying their daughter, so the two decided to elope.

Now, it was unclear, even years later, whether Neb knew that the two were secretly married, waiting for a good opportunity to tell Kelly's mother and father before starting their lives together, or not. Only Pete and Maddie knew of the marriage and traveled with them to witness.

However, one sunny day, as Neb saw the beautiful Kelly walking and smiling at others as she made her way through town, he remembered his own longing for her. Approaching her, gliding like a shining snake, he flashed his smile and greeted her before cunningly revealing his own carefully obtained story.

"Ah, Kelly," he said, approaching and kissing her hand, "you become more beautiful each day. Are things well between you and Jacob?" he asked.

"Yes, why wouldn't they be?" she countered cautiously.

"Well, I just know how kind and honest you are, Kelly, and I would hate to see you hurt by someone as deceptive as our Jacob. After all, he did cheat your very own father out of his win in the fishing contest by sabotaging the boats," he explained.

Kelly's lips opened slightly in surprise, but she knew better than to give any indication of her feelings. "I'm sure that I don't know what you mean," she said innocently. "Now, if you'll excuse me," I just need to get home and see if my mother needs anything," she said while gingerly walking toward their home.

That evening, Jacob came by to call on Kelly as he usually did, but he met with Kelly's mother, explaining that Kelly did not care to see him. After continual questioning by Jacob, Kelly's mother finally relented and called for her to come downstairs.

One look at her usually pretty and cheerful face told Jacob that something was terribly wrong. When he sat down with her in the parlor and her mother had gone into the other room, the story finally spilled out.

"Jacob, how could you have cheated my father?" Kelly choked out through tears and sobs.

"It was he who first tried to cheat me," he told her, gradually coming closer to her until she allowed him to hold her.

He explained to Kelly that he knew it was deceptive, but it was no more than what her father had planned to do to him. He pleaded with her to know that he would never deliberately hurt her.

Although Kelly believed him, the damage was done to her mother, who went into a true rage when Kelly blurted out that the two were already married. The rage continued into the next day when she gave Kelly the ultimatum of annulment or never seeing her or her father again. When Kelly refused the annulment, Mrs. Simon then began arrangements for a trip back to Boston and her family.

Oregon seemed to be a good escape when she and Nabal were in danger of losing everything back east, with Nabal headed to jail. Now, Nabal had made another fortune, and she was more afraid of young Jacob outsmarting him again and causing the fortune to be lost.

She was a calculating woman, and she really didn't care that Jacob and Kelly were married, but it did complicate things. Even with Mr. and Mrs. McVale pleading with her to reconsider, Amanda Simon's mind was made up, and plans were being made to return to the East.

Joshua then helped Jacob with his own plans for helping him run the family business. The truth was that he had missed Jacob sorely. He felt that Jacob knew the fishing business, the ocean, and San Francisco well enough to make a real go of things with him, and this time, he would not make the mistake of not listening to his son.

Kelly moved in with the McVales, and although things were rather cramped, she enjoyed the feeling of having a true family. As an only child with an over protective mother and a domineering father, she was truly enjoying having laughter and children around her.

She and Maddie could be seen shopping together in town, and she loved helping out with meals and Samuel and Sarah.

"Oh, I have more help than I've ever had!" Jennifer McVale would laugh and smile. "I've two grown daughters now."

As for Jacob, the next time that he saw Neb down at the docks, sneering and speaking arrogantly to him, he beat him bloody. "Jacob," he finally screamed, "just stop! I'm sorry. I didn't know you were married."

"Don't worry," Jacob yelled. "Your pretty face will be fine. Don't ever look to me for help again," he continued. "You're nothing to me. I should have let the bullies at school kill you years ago."

The two, and everyone else in town, assumed that these feelings would stay the same forever with the pain they had caused each other. No one could have foreseen the changes that would come to the town.

First, Jennifer McVale became ill. She had known for some time that she had a tumor of some sort but hoped and prayed that it would go away. As the pain developed and her breathing grew more labored, Joshua insisted that she see a doctor. He confirmed what she already knew. She had developed cancer, and all that could be offered was a relief of some of the pain through the use of morphine and laudanum. She put as much in order as she could with her family and died, as her life had been, quietly and sweetly in their home.

Neb, who, of course, never spoke to Jacob, approached him quietly at church, his new young wife at his side, and offered his hand, "I'm sorry, Jacob, your mother was such a dear lady."

"Thank you," Jacob managed before Kelly patted his arm, and he helped gather up his brothers and sisters.

It would soon, however, be Jacob's turn to approach Neb. The influenza epidemic hit with a fury. Most town folk quarantined, a few stubbornly keeping shops open while wearing bandannas over their faces, but the scourge of the virus hit both young and old, mainly taking the old and those weakened physically. Joshua was adamant that his youngest children be secured in the upper attic loft and that all be careful not to eat or drink after each other or go into town. Sarah and Samuel were spared, as were Jacob and Kelly, for some unknown reason.

Joshua, Daniel, and Maddie were stricken; however, for the most part, Daniel and Maddie took care of themselves, but Joshua was not to recover.

Jacob and Kelly nursed Joshua to the best of their abilities, and Joshua knew that they were doing all that they could. One evening, he pulled Jacob's sleeve and told him it was time to talk.

"Son, you will have much on you in a very short time. First, there are Sarah and Samuel to take care of. Then there will be the upkeep of the cabin and our land, but the boats, the fishermen, and all of our workers will be the biggest burden."

Mind the handling of Daniel and Maddie. Maddie is a bit wild, but a good man will tame her. Daniel, on the other hand, has shy and inscrutable ways. I hope a good woman will understand him. See that both of them work and carry their share."

"Dad," Jacob began, "Please try to rally. There's much left for you to do. Together, we can make a great success of the business and keep the family together."

"Nay, Jacob," he answered. "My courage and my strength died with Jennifer. I am bound to leave this world. Remember what I have taught you, and be a man of your word. I am sorry for the disagreement that we had. I love you, and I'm proud of you."

They buried him next to his wife and their mother. The twins were having a hard time understanding why both had been taken from them, but they were all, under Jacob's guidance, gradually recovering. In fact, this time, it was Jacob's turn to speak to Neb since his young bride had succumbed to the influenza.

He approached Neb carefully in church and offered his hand. "I was very sorry to hear about your wife and baby, Neb."

"Thank you, Jacob," Neb said, barely suppressing tears. He, like Jacob, had fallen hard for a lovely and devoted young woman new to Faithful. "I was sorry to hear about your father. He will be sorely missed."

Jacob nodded, "Things will work their way out."

Indeed, they did for most of the families in Faithful. Kelly and Jacob comforted each other and the family. In fact, most people were returning to work and each other. Then, the next wave of misfortune came. A measles epidemic came in with as much force as the influenza had. This time, however, it was affecting more of the children.

Jacob, Daniel, and Maddie had all experienced mild cases when they were much younger, and Jacob tried to keep the twins inside, with as little contact with anyone as possible; however, his efforts were too late. Sarah came down with the sickness when all the other children in Faithful did. Maddie tended to her and tried to keep Samuel separated.

Although her fever and rash subsided, Sarah could not return to her former health. She remained weakened and sick. In desperation, Kelly insisted that she and Jacob take her to a Portland doctor, specializing in children's maladies, while Daniel worked and Maddie stayed with Sammy.

The doctor's conclusion was that her heart had been damaged, and he recommended that Jacob return home with her so that her loved ones could be around her.

When they returned, they found that Sammy, as they most often called Samuel, was now stricken as well and showing no signs of reviving. Maddie was exhausted and near hysteria, and Jacob, in silent acceptance but still hoping for a miracle, lay Sarah down in bed with Sammy.

"It's alright, Jacob," Sarah smiled weakly. Her blonde hair was fanned out around her, and her little face was translucent in the winter light. "Sammy and I have each other now." She turned then, and the two looked at each other with wide blue eyes, smiled, and held hands. They were still in that pose when they died the following morning.

Daniel hit his fist into the front wall of the cabin. Maddie, through a single tear, quietly said, "They gave us seven years of pure sweetness and joy." Jacob made the burial arrangements, told Kelly to find their Sunday outfits, and spoke with Reverend McKendree.

Again, things began to return to normal, but the town was not so young now. It had been through one crisis upon another, and there was weariness present. A need for everyday joys was evident, but Jacob and Kelly had hope. They were expecting a baby in the summer.

This also gave hope and joy to Maddie, who, at seventeen, was already seeing herself as a protective aunt. Daniel was also taking heart and carved a beautiful and decorative new cradle for the baby.

Jacob doted on his bride and mother-to-be, protective of her health and safety. Many of the townspeople were made happy by simply seeing the couple together, and the ladies made plans to knit and sew for the new child. Others began to gather to make baby quilts. This would be the first baby to be born in at least two years, and the town had warmed to the idea of this being "their baby."

They were all a family again, but both Daniel and Maddie knew that they would need to find their own way soon. They both seemed restless and yet cherished their times together, waiting on the birth of the baby.

It was a stormy night when Kelly went into labor, and it was difficult for Beatrice Atwood and her mother, the town midwives, to get to the McVale cabin. Jacob was not overly fond of these two ladies because of their "gossipy ways," as his mother had phrased it.

However, they were knowledgeable, experienced, and they loved babies. (Jacob had always felt a bit sorry for Beatrice. She was so demure and dominated by her mother.)

They both bustled in with an air of happiness and anticipation. Their little round faces and equally round tummies bounced through the room with greetings and their bags. Maddie assured them that she had boiled water and led them to Jacob and Kelly's bedroom. That's when she noticed that Kelly was suddenly sweating and clutching at the sheets while screaming and shaking uncontrollably.

This was frightening enough, but she expected the Atwood ladies to merely inform her that this was "part of the labor process," but instead, their faces betrayed a bit of panic. They began to examine Kelly while soothing her, and Maddie held her hand.

"I want Jacob, Maddie," Kelly moaned. "I need him now," she insisted. Maddie looked at the older Mrs. Atwood, and she nodded.

"Go ahead, Maddie," she said in a low voice. "I need to talk to him now."

Jacob, of course, had heard the screaming and did not know whether to enter the room or not, but was beginning to approach when Maddie came out. "Kelly wants to see you," she told Jacob with a look of fear in her eyes.

He brushed past her into the room and saw Kelly in agony. He knew that women went through a lot in childbirth from his own mother's experiences, but he didn't really know what was normal and what was not. This did not seem right. This was more than just the hard endurance of continual pain. This was a woman in trouble.

He went to her side and took her hand, and she tried to look at him clearly. "Jacob," she gasped, "try to save the baby. Let the ladies do that," she begged.

He vaguely noticed Beatrice as she desperately tried to stop the bleeding, but it was too much too soon. Kelly was losing her battle.

"What, darling, what…I don't understand. Make this right, Mrs. Atwood," he shouted, but Mrs. Atwood was working with Beatrice now.

"Do you see the head, Beatrice?" she asked loudly.

"It's crowning, but Mama, it's in trouble," Beatrice answered.

"I love you, Jacob," Kelly said one last time, and she was gone, as was the baby. She was a beautiful stillborn baby, and Jacob would never forget her or his beautiful Kelly.

For three years, he went through every emotion, from gut-wrenching grief to anger and envy for the families that his brother and sister managed to form. Memories of the night Kelly died and daily mental beatings of "If only I had…" assaulted him.

He walked like a shadow or someone in a bad dream, and his speech was often vague and dismissive or angry. He ran the business, he watched out for his brother and sister, and he existed, but he did not truly live. Jacob sometimes longed for a fiery force from heaven to burn away his grief and reforge him into the man he was.

However, as time has a way of doing, he was gradually, if not healed, at least able to cope with life more fully. People were now able to glimpse an ember of "the old Jacob."

CHAPTER 21: MARY ALICE ENTERS

Four years after Kelly died, a young woman entered the Faithful Mission House who had witnessed an "Indian attack" on the wagon train that she and her parents had joined. So it was that Mary Alice Kingston saw her parents killed and, later in life, was thankful that they were gunned down by the rifles that the "Indians" brandished rather than being killed by tomahawks and scalping. She, herself, had been grazed by a bullet at the base of her neck.

Up until the final push of their journey to Oregon and the attack, the Native Americans had traded with them and watched after them. However, after being warned several times, members of the wagon train disturbed a burial ground and took some things buried with tribe members.

A surviving family took her as far as the Mission House in Faithful, where the Reverend William McKendree's wife, Reba, took her in and helped settle her. In fact, Mrs. McKendree looked on her as another daughter and had much concern for the young woman. She also marveled that the young woman had lived.

"I don't think that I'm the same person anymore," Mary Alice confessed to Mrs. McKendree.

"Sure, you're not, love," Reba McKendree answered her with a bit of a Scottish brogue. "You've had a brush with death."

Mary Alice was lovely and beautiful, though, with light chestnut-colored hair and light brown eyes. Her nose and features were dainty, and she dimpled when she smiled. Somewhat tall for her age, she intimidated some young men with her height and bearing, but she seemed unaware of her beauty and, quite frankly, was uninterested in "would-be" suitors.

 Mrs. McKendree, though, had noticed Jacob's interest in the young woman and hoped that this would become something more for him. Since Jennifer McVale had been her dearest friend, and she thought of Jacob as the son she had never had, she was delighted when, indeed, it did look as though something could develop.

She was beautiful, charming, hard-working, and soft-spoken. Respect was also present when the townspeople thought of Mary Alice. After all, she had survived a horrific experience and still managed to be a sweet and kind individual. None of them would have suspected the kind of rage that she harbored.

"That girl is just a beautiful breath of fresh air," more than one person had commented in a similar way.

Eventually, though, this restless fear and resentment flamed into an obsessive hatred. What had her family done? They weren't directly on Indian land. They didn't harm any of the tribes. Why were they so brutally attacked? So, she also nursed a rather large grudge against all Native Americans because of what had happened to her family and the wagon train. Although she was gifted in sewing, cooking, and organizing social events and was kind-hearted to most, she was icy toward the young man named Nathan Ryan, believing him to simply be one more "lying and thieving Indian."

Although the McVales and McKendrees knew that Nathan was part Irish and part Chinook, they also knew that he was a gentle soul who helped others. Mary Alice, however, felt that she knew better than anyone in town and thought that he was probably just waiting for his chance to kill everyone.

Nathan shrugged or raised his shoulders sometimes when she stared daggers at him. He simply continued making his way to the Mission, where he, too, had found himself after Mary Alice had moved out.

Mary Alice now rented a small room from Miss Griggs, the town spinster who owned a good deal of land in and around Faithful. She also worked in both the diner and as a maid in the boarding house, which would become The Tavern Inn. Her only breaks from continual work seemed to come when Jacob could see her.

Nathan Ryan was trying to settle in during his time at the Mission along with a young woman named Lydia. Ironically, the new Reverend and Mrs. McKendree were also trying to settle into the town.

William McKendree had suffered a heart attack one Sunday after a good sermon and a good restful day. Reba McKendree died soon after. The cause was never really determined. Some called it a broken heart, but whatever the cause, the dear lady simply "fell out" one day while cooking a meal for a sick neighbor and was discovered dead.

Now, the task of preaching and chaperoning the mission fell to Reverend Mckendree's son and his wife, who had mysteriously come to town only a few months before the Reverend's death. The rumor was that this previously unknown son was the result of an earlier union in the elder Reverend's life. Only Eugenia Campbell, his daughter who was born and raised in Faithful, along with her husband, Virgil Campbell, knew the real truth. It was apparent, though, that neither was especially happy with the half-brother.

However, since a young man and woman were currently being housed in The Mission, one upstairs and one downstairs, the new Reverend McKendree would often take the young man to the small home that he and his wife shared to spend the evening. Mrs. McKendree stayed with Lydia.

In this way, the two young people did not spend the night in the same house, and gossip could not ensue. (However, Reverend McKendree hoped the situation would soon be resolved, and he would have his wife back.) He knew that he would be the next preacher, but he had not counted on overseeing The Mission.

Although Nathan had accepted this situation, as soon as he could, he moved into a room at the small boarding house destined to become part of Lucy's Inn and Diner. He was never an anxious or reckless person, but he was adrift like most who came to stay there. He needed a job, better and cleaner clothes, good meals, and a girlfriend. Even more, though, than any of these things that dominate a young man's heart and brain, he needed to forget. He wanted to forget, and he wanted to be set free from the sights, sounds, and smells of fire and charred flesh and his mother screaming. He wanted none of this embedded in his mind.

Both Mary Alice and Nathan were in these states of mind when they went about their days. Nathan, thankfully, had been hired by Jacob McVale.

Leaving the docks for the day, Nathan planned on having a meal at the inn and a good night's rest. He did not have much more than this on his mind while he was walking there and saw Mary Alice.

Jacob left a few minutes later, in time to see Neb Darius riding his new stallion wildly toward the town. His first thought was of the fortune that it must have cost. His next was that the horse was completely out of control. "Are you crazy, Darius?" he called out. "It's too much horse for you," he added.

Nathan continued walking toward the inn on the boardwalk. He reflected on how the whole town knew what had happened to Mary Alice, and he had not been unaware of the hateful and menacing looks that she directed toward him.

She looked at him and looked away. "Where was Jacob anyway," she thought. He was supposed to meet her and take her to dinner. This was just like him to run completely late and then shrug it off. She turned toward the docks. Her coral dress, which she had recently made, flowed behind her, showing her figure to perfection. She wondered if she should walk to the docks to hasten Jacob along. She began to hesitantly cross the street and walk back.

She was a gloriously beautiful woman, Nathan thought before he continued to the inn. It was too bad that she had some kind of a grudge against one group of humanity.

They both heard the thundering hooves at the same time as Darius struggled to get the stallion under control. Nathan had almost reached the inn. Mary Alice was halfway across.

Seeing the wild beast plunging toward Mary Alice, Nathan ran swiftly, his strong, lean legs moving as though timed to perfection. He quickly encircled Mary Alice in his arms and pulled her out of the way.

"You're safe now," he said, and she knew that she was.

Beginning to see the scene unfold, Jacob started running also. He then saw Nathan rescue Mary Alice. It was a mixed emotion as he was relieved of the sickening fear that had gripped him and then squeezed by the frustrating feelings of losing.

At the edge of the boardwalk, Mary Alice was still in Nathan's arms. They both looked at one another in shock but with a touch of curiosity. It did not feel threatening to be held by Nathan. In fact, it felt safe. It did not feel awkward to hold Mary Alice. In fact, it felt natural.

"You saved me," Mary Alice whispered with awe and disbelief so that it was more of a question.

Jacob approached with a glare of disbelief. "Well, thank you, Nathan. I owe you a debt for saving her," he managed to say.

Sounding both dazed and confused, Nathan answered, "Well, of course. I was glad to help her."

The shouting then ensued as Neb Darius approached.

"Is she alright?" Darius yelled after managing to tether the wild horse.

"If you can't control him, don't ride him," Jacob shouted, realizing that he suddenly sounded a great deal like his father. "You could have killed Mary Alice, you idiot!" I'm reporting you to the sheriff."

"She looks fine," Darius observed calmly.

Nathan released Mary Alice as Jacob approached the pair. "Are you alright?" Jacob asked as he helped Mary Alice to her feet.

"I'm alright," she managed to say, "thanks to Nathan."

Again, the two exchanged glances, and it jolted Jacob. It was the same kind of look he and Kelly had given each other when he first helped her from her father's carriage. Mary Alice would not be seeing him much longer, and he knew it before she did.

Then, a gradual yet rather quick transition began. It started when Mary Alice baked a loaf of bread and shyly took it to Nathan in gratitude.

"I'm sorry for how I've treated you," Mary Alice started.

She shrugged, with the bread basket still in her hands, "I just, well, wanted to explain and bring you this." She placed the bread basket on his small bureau and pushed back her chestnut hair.

"It's alright," he said. "We've all been through something. I know that the Sioux tribe killed your parents and others in the wagon train. It was bound to have affected how you look at natives in this part of the country."

"What happened to you, Nathan?" she asked.

"My father was a big, kind-hearted Irishman who married a very young Chinook squaw. Yet, somehow, it worked for them. She truly loved him.

"They faced their share of cruelty along the way but were always able to deal with it, and we moved a lot from one town to another. (My father was a logger in Washington.)

"Then, one town was particularly unaccepting, and they torched the small hotel where we were staying. My father managed to get Mother and me out, but he was burned too badly. My mother lived another week but died of breathing in the smoke.

"The next thing I knew, I had somehow found Faithful. I don't even remember how. Here I am," he smiled and raised his hands.

"And yet, you've managed not to become bitter," she said and smiled back.

"What would it help?" he asked.

There was a bond, then. It was a bond of persecution for the circumstances of birth and the brutality of ancestors. They found each other in that bond. Nathan had already taken note of Mary Alice's beauty, and she was beginning to notice his combined qualities of high cheekbones, dark way hair, and watchful dark blue eyes. They were a beautiful couple, ready to take on anyone who thought otherwise.

When Nathan began work at McVale's Fishing and Shipping Company, he worked hard as both a fisherman and an overseer of the boats. He was one of the best fishermen that Jacob had, and he was always capable of repairs on the boats, with a ready ear listening to the saddest tales that most men could tell and, ironically, Jacob came to rely on Nathan as the business progressed.

Daniel was extremely organized and hard-working, while Pete was all strength like a charging bull, and Jacob was a bit of a salesman. Somehow, Nathan tempered all of these characteristics. He was soft-spoken and of good humor. He could be firm with the other men, but he understood when to bend.

There were many times when Jacob backed away and considered how far his father's venture had come. As much as they had clashed, he missed his father fiercely, and he missed the old Mission as it was no longer so essential to the town. Life was a different road now. Faithful was not young now, and it was gradually being redefined.

As for Mary Alice, her only regret was Jacob. She would always have love and appreciation for him. She could not explain or help how things had turned out and could not possibly see how they would end.

As for Jacob, it hurt. There was no denying that, but not as deeply or completely as losing Kelly had. In truth, he had always thought of Kelly, even in his more romantic moments with Mary Alice. He had not stopped thinking of her and longing for her.

So, his words to Mary Alice were simply, "If this is what you want, sweetheart, I won't stand in the way, but remember, I'm not hard to find if things don't work out with him."

CHAPTER 22: THE OLD MISSION

There was a good bit of pioneer and settler history associated with the "Old Mission." It sat in the center of town and had once been just that, the center of town. The Mission House was built to take in those who were visiting town or trying to get back on their feet or were ready to make a life in Faithful but hadn't built their home yet.

The structure was two stories and square, similar to what Lucy, the inn and diner owner, would later refer to as a "cracker box." Even when first built, it looked rough-hewn and, somehow, never received a good coat of paint. Still, it was functional and welcoming, and its residents were often heard to say that finding the small town of Faithful had been difficult, but it had rescued them from death.

To be sure, it housed those in need, often those who had survived the Oregon Trail, but it also served as the church for the first ten years of the town. So even with the kitchen, sitting area, and three rooms downstairs, as well as the three upstairs, it was often cramped.

Between the Reverend and his family and those seeking sanctuary, it was never empty. However, fights broke out between settlers and drifters finding their way to a new home in Oregon or Washington, even as the Oregon Trail began to be a thing of the past. As a result, the interior of the Mission had been "shot up," and furniture and windows broken several times.

Jacob's father was set to board it up and close it when the two young people wandered into town, Lydia and Nathan. They had no connection with one another other than both being orphaned and in need of shelter. So, the decision was made to leave the mission open for a time longer until places could be found for the two.

It stayed full until 1883, about the time when Nathan left and found Mary Alice. Then, of course, the two predators came that no one in the town of Faithful had expected: influenza and measles. Influenza took both of young Lydia's parents.

It sometimes seemed to Jacob that everything concerning the mission had become entrapped in a complicated mess, but he did admire the last two young people who stayed in the mission. Both Nathan and Lydia had been hard-working and eager to get along with the other residents of the town.

Both of them had cleaned, cooked, and gone to church. The mission had served many people in need, but now it was almost empty, and its fate, along with the fate of the remaining orphan, Lydia, was in question.

There was one more thing Jacob had to deal with. He had helped bury his mother two years before he buried his father. Then, he watched his beloved baby sister and brother pass away. Next, his wife and baby had died before his eyes. Now, at twenty-seven years of age, the future of the mission and a young orphaned life were in his hands, along with the family business.

He thought the best thing was to close the mission, and so he went to talk to Reverend McKendree and Lydia. Then, an idea came to him, one that would change and expand his family forever.

"Lydia," he began, trying to weigh his words very carefully, "The town can only afford to keep the mission open for a few more months. We'll have to find, well, a different situation for you with Mrs. McKendree's help. She's been very good about staying here, as has Reverend McKendree, but we still need to make decisions."

Mrs. McKendree smiled and turned to Lydia. "Lydia, we'll figure out something," she assured her.

Lydia looked crestfallen but held her chin up, "I don't mind working at just about anything," she asserted while trying not to cry. "I'm good with weaving and selling. I also cook well, and I don't mind taking care of the sick and shut-ins," she added.

Jacob had another idea then, and when Jacob had an idea, he usually acted on it. He needed to talk seriously to Daniel, and soon. Lydia was too dear of a girl to be sent away or to be thrown to some of the wolfish men that occupied the town. He had seen Daniel cast a few shy looks at Lydia, so that might well be the answer.

"Daniel, I'd like a word with you," Jacob called out that evening after he knew that his younger brother was back from work and getting settled for the evening.

"Alright, what is it, brother?" Daniel answered quietly, already in the room. His dark brown hair was thick and sometimes a bit shaggy, falling gently to the right, often just barely brushing over his right eye. His eyes, in contrast, were a crystal blue and seemed to take in every part of a person's soul, and his chin had a slight cleft, making him look both mature and childlike at the same time.

He was thin and not quite as tall as Jacob, but he had been known to best men bigger than himself in fights. Daniel did not seek out any type of fighting, but he had been trained by Joshua and Jacob to handle it quickly should it arise. Jacob always found his silent approaches a bit unnerving, and their father had always said that Daniel must be an old Irish soul based on how silently he could move into a room or disappear in the shadows.

"I thought that you might be interested in knowing that The Mission will be closing. I'm concerned about what will happen to Lydia. It won't be immediate, but unless she finds a way to support herself (which is hard for a woman in this town) or marries, she'll need to find relatives," Jacob waited, and Daniel was silent. Perhaps he had misjudged his brother's feelings. It was always hard to tell with him.

Then, Daniel spoke slowly and with few words, as was his way, "I'll call on her tomorrow," he said. "Good night."

Jacob could only hope that this would settle the matter. The rest was up to Lydia.

The next day, Lydia was deep in thought. She swept the front steps of the mission and began to gather firewood. Her coal-dark hair was tied back in a bow at the crown. Her green eyes squinted against the sun, which also lit the shape of her petite figure as she stooped.

"Let me help you," Daniel offered.

"Where had he come from?" Lydia wondered. This man had a way of simply appearing.

"Alright," Lydia agreed and gave a slight smile, "thank you." Lately, Daniel McVale seemed to be about more often, always quiet, always ready to help.

He gathered the firewood and carried it in for her. "I'm glad I caught you," he said. "I was wondering if we could go for a walk." He looked at her and smiled and then looked quickly away.

"Well, it's not like I'm in big demand," Lydia laughed a little too nervously. "I mean, well, sure."

They walked toward the docks silently, but it did not seem awkward. Lydia recognized that Daniel was simply a quiet person, and she was generally not. She enjoyed talking and talking a lot. It was what kept her both from despair and boredom. The problem was that she had few people to talk with at all lately.

"You should tell me about the business that you and your brother run sometime," she started. "I think you can learn a lot from simply listening to people. Don't you? It's pleasant out tonight, isn't it? Do you walk a good bit at night?" She drew a breath and was getting ready to continue when Daniel suddenly stopped, took her by the waist, and drew her to him. He kissed her slowly and tenderly, then released her.

"Well, we'd better get you home before it gets too dark," he smiled.

She slowly closed her mouth and allowed him to lead her back to the mission.

She stopped and looked at him. Who was this man? She had always considered him a quiet man in the background of his brother's presence, but he was much more than that. He embraced her again before she went in the door and kissed her again.

In the course of a week, they walked, talked, had a picnic, had dinner together, and discussed their mutual likes and dislikes. He was both amused and relieved that she could talk as much as she did.

He smiled at her and took her hand, "Would you like to get married this spring?" he asked.

"Do you love me?" she questioned incredulously.

He hesitated, and she was shocked that there was a tear in his eye. "Very much," he answered. "This is forever with me, and if you don't love me yet, that's alright. I'll do my best to win you over."

"I love you already, and this spring is just fine," she said.

This left Maddie to be settled with her own life. "You've been through six men now!" Jacob shouted at her one evening after dinner. "Do you want to be known as the town bad girl? People are talking!"

Anger and pain burned in Maddie's blue eyes. Gregarious and very fair-haired, Maddie was also considered tall for a woman. She had enjoyed her pick of suitors, and, similar to Jacob, with her bright blue eyes and large winning smile, she could be very charming when she chose to be. As one scholarly young man had gushed, "She's like a perfect Norse goddess."

Maddie had no idea what a Norse goddess looked like, but she assumed it was good and made the most of it, simply flirting with men as a tonic for the sadness of losing her parents and little sister and brother.

"Don't you think I'd like to find a truly good man?" she shouted back at him. "I haven't done anything wrong. I just like to talk to men. At least the ones I've been around have taken my mind off of Daddy and the twins."

Then, the same spring that Daniel found Lydia, Maddie finally began to take an interest in Pete, who, for all his bravado, had always admired her from a distance. Now, it was she who was quite obviously in love. The sensitivity that his sister showed was a surprise to Jacob, considering the men that she had casually dismissed since the deaths of her father and little brother and sister.

Called a wild child and orphaned at nine, Pete's life had been anything but easy; however, somehow, he retained a sweetness and goodness that was now going straight to Maddie's heart. He was also undeniably handsome. His hair, dark, with just a hint of red, and his features, set off by remarkably large, dark brown eyes, had captured the attention of several ladies. His tall, strong build also made him one of Jacob's best workers at the docks and earned him respect among the other men. It had also drawn looks from the females who passed by the docks.

The main thing, though, was that he loved Maddie deeply, and he cared about Faithful. In his own time and way, he, too, had become a part of the town.

Seeing the difference in his sister touched Jacob. He had almost given up on her, and seeing how she finally realized the feelings that Pete had always had for her and returning them meant that he could now stop endlessly trying to protect her.

Jacob remembered these events as he, Noah Thomas (the town banker and accountant), Neb Darius, Daniel, Nathan, and other townsmen who volunteered to empty and shutter the Old Mission walked through town. It marked the beginning of a different time, and the town was not quite as young and welcoming to strangers anymore.

Daniel, who was always a man of his word, sometimes created a problem for Jacob, as he did on this particular day of closing the mission up indefinitely, and, although Daniel was usually quiet and unassuming, he was beginning to surprise more than one person with his personal strength and expectations. He had taken more than a few beatings for his beliefs as a schoolboy, and he had given back a few as well.

When it came time that morning to shut the Mission down, it didn't surprise Jacob that Daniel objected and stood in front of the Old Mission, daring anyone to touch it. Declaring that the men would have to come through him to begin the boarding up and shuttering, he visualized his parents and those seeking refuge through the years. To him, it represented the soul of the town.

A crowd began to gather when Jacob finally hit upon a solution. "What if this is only temporary, Daniel?" he reasoned. "What if we reopen it after repairs and such can be made, and another noble cause presents itself?" He yelled out to his stalwart brother, whose arms were raised as if protecting a child.

"What kind of noble cause, Jacob?" he demanded.

"Well, I don't know," Jacob started. Then, as if hit by a bolt of lightning, he raised his hand as though he was inspired and ventured a possibility, "Well, why not for a school? With just a bit more growth, the town will need another building for an upper school."

At this, Daniel smiled. "Yes," he said. "That would be a good purpose. Let's do that."

Now, Jacob had no clue at the time that this idea would become a reality. Perhaps, there would be such a use for the one-time sanctuary at some other point in time, but no one wanted to deal with its original purpose now. Little did they know that it would one day provide sanctuary for two school teachers in need of a final home for themselves and their wives.

Jacob, Noah Thomas, and Neb Darius became the leaders of the town. They were, each in their own way, three men who had known great promise and were now nursing great pain.

Jacob would throw himself into his work and retain his natural ability to read the intentions of people and help where he could. Noah would remain a bit of a loner, seen as a bit of a harbinger of bad news, but respected for his honesty and abilities with money. And Neb would hide behind the facade of a desirable widow and man about town, running the warehouses that he owned and which Jacob eventually rented. (It seemed they might never be free of one another.)

So, one sunny morning, at 5:00 a.m., seven years later, he met Daniel, and they began unboarding and repairing the Old Mission to become a school. Jacob remembered the events and thoughts of seven years past as he helped Noah Thomas, Neb Darius, Daniel, Pete, and other townsmen who now volunteered to renovate the old mission and make an upper school—an entirely different but equally important mission.

CHAPTER 23: A YOUNG MAN
NAMED CALEB SPIVY

In Caleb Spivy's younger days, he had found himself orphaned, evicted, and penniless at the tender age of sixteen. After a few days of living in the woods, he gathered his courage together, tried to groom himself as best he could, and went to seek work at the docks from someone that his father had called "McVale."

"If anything ever happens to me, boy, and you need a job, go see McVale at the docks and beg for a job. Get the mess out of your head about being a bounty hunter or a detective, and tell him you'll work and work hard," his father concluded.

There was no particular family or friend connection for Caleb's father and Jacob, but he had witnessed Joshua offer jobs to some that others considered non-hireable. He had sometimes thought of going to him, himself.

So Caleb took his father's advice and appealed to Jacob McVale for a job, any job. Something in Jacob's gut told him that Caleb would be a good worker, but first, he sat him down to eat with the men and suggested that he get a bath at the inn and have his clothes laundered. Caleb went as instructed and requested that Lucy put the bath, lodging and laundering on Jacob's credit. She was familiar with Jacob's techniques with new hires, so she did, and Jacob took it out of the boy's first pay.

"Listen," Jacob told the boy, "I'm taking a chance on you, and I expect an honest day's work in return. If I don't get that, then you're gone, and word gets around when a young man is not willing to work. Do we understand each other?"

Jacob knew but managed not to admit, even to himself, that the boy was somewhat of a project. With the mission now boarded up for over five years and his brother and sister both on their own, he was interested in seeing what might be made of this young man. He eyed Caleb again and waited for his answer.

"Oh, yes, sir," Caleb replied. "I'll always do my share. I have a lot of goals, and I'm always willing to work toward them."

"Well, see to it that two of your goals are loading and unloading boats or going out fishing with the men if I ask you to. Are we clear on that?" Jacob finished.

He worked Caleb hard with loading and unloading all summer and into the next year. In between times, as was his custom, he and Daniel, or Nathan, would take their noon meal with the men working for them. Generally, the men were a little more careful about their conversations if Jacob or his brother wound up at their weathered table on the dock or if they were eating in the warehouse with them; however, Caleb Spivy was not your typical worker.

A bit on the stocky side, with dark hair and a rather swarthy complexion, Jacob guessed that he might have been part of the Prussian group that had settled outside of Faithful, and he found it amusing that the boy assumed everyone liked to talk about different topics that he found interesting. Not being shy, he spoke his mind about the world rather freely. Jacob was generally interested and looked upon him somewhat as he would one of his siblings.

He had to admit, though, that detective work sounded like an interesting vocation, and occasionally, he would read some of the literature that Caleb collected concerning this "Exciting Profession for the Clever and Adventurous Young Man," as described in the posters and fliers. (Jacob generally had a good laugh from that description, yet he had a touch of envy over the choices that Caleb still had.)

So when Caleb completed a correspondence course to become a detective and came to Jacob five years later, earnestly sorry to be leaving but excited that he had saved enough money to travel to San Francisco, take the exam, and apply for his license as a detective, Jacob smiled and gave him his blessings.

"Maybe I can pay you back somehow, Mr. McVale," Caleb offered. "You know, you might need my services someday," he explained.

"Well, let's hope not," Jacob laughed, "but you never know. You can at least drop back through town if you're ever this way," he said.

Caleb had one day of work left, and Jacob had put him on unloading and storing in the warehouse. He was there when the fire broke out. In fact, he had cautioned one of the other workers to be careful how he stored the kerosene, and he was there when Jacob ran in and methodically pulled him, Nathan, and three others out before Daniel and Pete pulled the nearly unconscious Jacob out.

Jacob would not learn of Nathan's death for nearly two more weeks. At first, he thought it was part of his fevered dream, but then he heard the whispering between Lydia and Maddie about Mary Alice. He began to realize that Nathan had not made it.

He would ask Maddie later if it was true that Mary Alice had lost the baby that she and Nathan were expecting and that she had to be watched to make sure that she did not harm herself afterward. Maddie looked shocked that he had heard and retained this from his morphine-induced sleep, but she confirmed his fears. It was then that he vowed to watch over her when he was well.

Caleb stayed those two weeks to make sure that Jacob would live. Then, he wrote to Daniel several times to check on Jacob's progress. That was the last that anyone in Faithful heard of him until a little over three years later.

CHAPTER 24: THE VIEW

Well, she was lost. Of course, this was brilliant. Kayleigh had never had any sense of direction. She simply, as Mitch put it, "walked by faith," which reminded her of how angry she was with both Mitch and Zach for leaving Lucy's Tavern and Inn without her. She raised her hands in resignation and said aloud to herself, "Well, Kayleigh, you've lost your way again. You're almost twenty-five years old, and you've traveled all around, but you still manage to get turned about."

She had not been in Faithful more than one night, but she knew that the first board meeting was imperative. Her trunks were still at the inn, and she was unsure of what to do about that. She decided to worry about that later. The board meeting itself was to take place at the lower school. She did not want to be late, but not too early, either.

She had a restless night in the inn, but the lady, Lucy, who ran both it and the diner, had been very kind and told her several things about the town that she would not have known (mainly to beware of Miss Griggs); and, so, she set out to reach the lower school and meet with what were considered the school board members.

It was a confusing and strange fog that shrouded her memory of leaving Idaho Falls and coming into Faithful. In fact, she was having trouble clearly remembering her previous teaching assignments. *What was wrong with her?* she wondered in panic. Had the trauma of seeing her mother hung wiped out her past?

So, on her way, she stopped at an old, closed well (trying to get her bearings), and she could not help but notice the most spectacular view of both the landscape and the sun's rays streaming through the evergreen trees. It was as though the heaven's spectrum had been split by thousands of light points filtered through the prisms of pines and balsams.

Mountains were at a distance, and she paused to take it in and pray one last time that this job would be granted to her with as few difficulties as possible when she was suddenly aware that someone was standing directly next to her. She turned and looked up into blue eyes belonging to a tall, well-built man. He smiled while she tried to compose herself.

"Hello," he said softly, "can I help you?"

Jacob McVale stood six foot four inches tall. He was broad-chested but slim at the waist, with strong, long legs. His brown hair waved gently to the side, and he often wore a beard but was clean-shaven today. The forehead was generous and somewhat more weathered and furrowed, but his smile was still quick and charming. His nose was large, with a bit of a hook, but it now looked suited for a forceful man, and it enhanced his features. His jaw was strong, and his cheekbones were somewhat high, and his Scottish ancestry shone through. Indeed, he looked a good deal like his father.

"Oh," was all she was able to say until she forced herself to continue, "I'm sorry. This is your property. Isn't it? I didn't know. I just stopped to look at the view on my way. It won't happen again." (She didn't know who he was, but it didn't matter. She needed to get away.)

"It's quite alright," he reassured her. "The view, as you call it, doesn't really belong to anyone. Where are you trying to go?"

"I need to be at the school board meeting," she explained. "I think it's this way," she said and pointed to the right.

He hesitated for a moment before saying, "It is. That's where I'm headed. Could I walk you there?"

Her first reactive thought was, *Oh great, he's on the board*, and her second was her usual warning of caution. *Don't trust anyone, especially a male.*

However, under the circumstances, the polite thing was to accept the invitation, so she did. "Well, thank you. I am a little turned about."

"I'm Jacob McVale, by the way," he explained as he began to lead her toward the little, overcrowded elementary school.

He looked at her expectantly until it finally sunk in that he was waiting for her to introduce herself.

"I'm Miss O'Brien. I'm applying for the lower school position," she explained, and she suddenly realized that she did not really remember how she even came to Faithful. There was a vague memory of the train and a horrible memory of her poor mother, but nothing in between. She was even unsure of how she had come to this picturesque spot with its view of mountains and trees. Now, here she was, preparing to walk into a school board meeting.

Jacob's brother, Daniel, was somewhat surprised when Jacob walked in with her, but only somewhat. Jacob had a way of attracting in, and ushering about, any young woman, although this was different. She was singularly focused on the task at hand, and that was facing and speaking to the school board. He was more surprised, though, when Lydia entered, making it clear that she planned to stay and planned to stay affixed to his side.

Daniel loved his wife, perhaps more than anything. Lydia had done more to push him along and build his self-confidence than anyone had previously done or cared to attempt, except, of course, for Jacob. However, there were times when he wished that she would either leave things to him or leave them alone completely. He recognized, though, that she did often understand both people and situations very quickly, and somehow, he knew that she would apply that ability to this new young woman.

CHAPTER 25: FACING A NEW LIFE

Seven years previous to helping Miss O'Brien find her way, Jacob would not have dreamed of serving on a board of education. His shipping and fishing business were his life and identity, along with being considered a lady's man and a respected man of the town. He clung to all of these elements because that was what he had, and it seemed enough.

He had not been a man subject to bouts of melancholy or introversion, but the last three years had been different for him. His masculine pride made him expect to be the lead male in most situations, but there were doubts and questions that had never been in his mind before. One night, he awakened from a disturbing sleep, ran his hand through his hair, and found himself saying, "Jacob, it may be time to start giving back."

Most of this was due to the fire and his injury. He was, as several had reminded him to be, thankful that the injury had not been more extensive or scarring than it had been. As his sister-in-law, Lydia, had said, "Why, Jacob, you can't even see the scarring unless your shirt is off. Just let it be a reminder of how heroically you rescued three men." She then immediately looked stricken, remembering that Nathan had not survived and that Daniel had rescued Jacob.

He supposed that his behavior could be seen as brave, but the pain and fevered dreams he had suffered afterward were catalysts for shaping and re-sculpting his world and the things that he had thought of as so set and important. He also began to suppose that being a widower had chosen him. He and Mary Alice were good friends, and he sometimes escorted her, but there was nothing else there.

So, he had fallen into the role of brother-in-law and uncle, slowly but firmly; however, at the age of thirty-four, he didn't feel any restless need for a wife.

Mary Alice was his favorite companion, though. Years before, when they had both been interested in each other, it seemed that his life path might become more settled. Then, she married Nathan. It was a disappointment, but it was years ago, and somehow, she had known that he was still in mourning for Kelly.

Then, when Nathan passed away, they gradually began to accompany each other to church and different gatherings. He knew her sadness from losing Nathan and the child that the two were expecting.

Many assumed that they would one day marry, considering how well they got on. Neither of them, though, seemed to be in any hurry.

He still ran the shipping business, although his brother and brother-in-law had begun to take on more and more responsibilities. The truth was that they had run it completely while he was recovering from his injuries and had done quite a good job. It had not been expanded to different states and territories, as he had hoped, but they had kept it going and turned a profit.

The memories of the night of the fire remained a jigsaw puzzle that he could sometimes put together and sometimes not. Of course, he knew the facts about it. One of the warehouses that he rented had caught fire from a cargo of kerosene and oil that it was holding.

Three of his men were there, ready to start the unloading. Suddenly, a sphere of fire blew up like a geyser into the night air. He pulled out three of the men before the explosion and before collapsing and having Daniel pull him out. The fire was snaking itself in through the collapsing building, with a fog of smoke and soot following.

It was then that he suffered a burn that ran from his right shoulder and arm down his side to just above his hip. Nathan, who he had pulled out along with Caleb Spivy and a newly hired man, had apparently been overcome by inhaling the smoke. He would later learn that even Neb had tried to help, but it was all doubly sad and devastating since Nathan's mother had died in much the same way.

The pain, for the first three weeks, was almost unbearable, and the morphine caused him to have hallucinations and crazed dreams. For a man who had always been in control, this was a difficult thing to later learn from those who attended him most closely.

He knew that his mother appeared to him several times, and he began to remember childhood scenes, things he had not thought of in many years. However, being his mother's first and only child for seven years, he had been very close to her, so much so that they thought alike and were in sync with each other's feelings.

So, in one way, he was not overly surprised within himself by seeing her or talking to her. In another portion of his still conscious mind, he knew this was not a logical possibility. Somehow, he chose the illogical, longing to talk to her after years of never allowing himself the luxury of mourning her.

She evoked memories of his boyhood, from biscuits she baked just for him to watching her hang the laundry in the morning sun. She was youthful again, and he had incredulously realized that she was young. After all, she was Mama. She had always been an indefinable maternal age, but this woman was young and well, with long blonde hair, which she wore down, framing her crystal blue eyes.

"I'm bringing you someone, Jacob, my handsome lad," she smiled over her shoulder at him as she pinned the laundry to the line. She is somewhat damaged. "Be patient with her," she warned. She's tough and brave but very fragile and damaged. Be patient," she had warned again.

Then, in one vision, he saw her sitting in front of the fire, rocking gently. Her small hands gingerly snapped beans into a pan and were always busy and engaged.

Her hair was gently swept up, and her delicate features and dimpled chin were highlighted by the fire as she motioned for him to stand in front of her and give his lesson recitations. She gently corrected him and encouraged him, and it then occurred to his half-awake mind how intelligent a woman she was and how much more she might have been; but, then, in his childlike mind, women had always worked in the home. Where else would they have been?

"It's your turn now, my sweet lad," she had smiled, stopping her work and touching his hand. "It's your turn now. You need your own family."

In other visions, he was surrounded by his younger brothers and sisters. He was going off to work with his father, who was desperately trying to buy a large sailing ship for the fishing and shipping business he had started.

His mother was busy with Daniel and Maddie and the babies but managed to give him a slight smile before he stole out the door with his "larger than life" father.

"You are my pride," she had said quietly.

He was sixteen and a bit embarrassed, and then he was standing by her bedside before she passed away, finally, at the end of this fevered dream.

"Take care of them," she had nodded to his brothers and sisters, "and then of her. She will, in turn, make you very happy. Just be patient, very patient," she finished.

He puzzled over these visions sometimes in the evening. He had more time to reflect now that his brother had taken on more and more responsibilities with the business. He had too much time now, he sometimes thought.

His mother's description matched Mary Alice in many ways, but "damaged" was not really an adjective that he would ever apply to her. She had been through her share of tragedies, but fragile didn't quite fit, or did it? To be truthful, he didn't know.

In his last vision, when his mother began to gently fade and take her leave, he grabbed her hand. Surprise followed by acceptance spread across her face.

"Tell me who she is, Mama," he demanded.

"She will find you," is all that she replied.

With time, the visions, themselves, began to fade, and he had more and more trouble remembering them.

After the last vision, Jacob was stronger and, within a week, was able to ride out to the ledge, which looked over the town. Daniel, seeing the big Bay horse that Jacob often rode, rode out also. Once they were both there, Jacob explained the dreams to Daniel, and Daniel voiced his own conjectures about the visions.

Jacob began by saying, "I think she's trying to tell me to make my mind up and make my intentions known to Mary Alice," he told Daniel, and, being Jacob, he assumed that his interpretation was correct.

They sat on horsebacks, side by side. Daniel's dark hair fanned out like his horse's dark mane as the wind blew gently. He turned to the side, looking Jacob fully in the eyes. "I don't think so," he answered. "I think this is someone completely different. I think this is someone who will be broken on the inside and has never healed.

"Mary Alice has healed twice," he continued. "The first healing was over losing her family. The second healing was over Nathan and her unborn baby. She is still sad at times but whole."

Jacob shifted in the saddle a bit, scratched at the dark brown beard that had grown on his face, and said, "Then again, it could just be a dream resulting from pain, a fever, and morphine."

Daniel grinned. "It could be, brother. It could be."

CHAPTER 26: THE BOARD MEETING

Daniel had never really wanted to be on the school board, but considering the abysmal school year that everyone's child had suffered last term with Miss Craddock, especially his own daughter, he supposed that Lydia had done well to insert him on the board and in the choosing of the new lower school teacher.

Always quiet and unassuming, Daniel had come a long way since his painfully shy years of youth. Still, though, public speaking and formal meetings were not his best arenas.

Of course, truthfully, his older brother, Jacob, had played the biggest role in bringing in this new teacher for the lower school and her co-harts for the upper school. It was, after all, he who had corresponded with all three after searching through the various advertisements for teachers seeking re-locations and employment.

These three new hires had identified as "circuit teachers," with the two married couples seeking "more permanent" positions and Miss O'Brien stating that her contract might "be renewed at the end of the term if it so suited the board." Jacob was no fool, and he recognized that this also meant that she could bow out if she so chose.

However, there was something about these letters out of all of the candidates who wrote in. All three had a certain flair for the English language and a descriptive narrative of their past positions and abilities. Also, their references were good, complimentary, and confirmed.

He had enjoyed reading Miss O'Brien's letters the most, though. She had a lyrical way of describing the "strategies, methods, and pedagogy" that she used with her students. (That word, "pedagogy," intrigued Jacob, and he set about discovering just what it meant.)

He also knew, though, just how trying the last year had been for Daniel and Lydia. First, they discovered their daughter, Jennifer Anne's hearing loss, then Lydia lost the baby that she was carrying, and finally, Jennifer Anne refused to go to school.

When they finally got to the bottom of the situation, they found that her teacher, Miss Craddock, had humiliated Jennifer Anne in class, calling her "a foolish girl who didn't listen." They had learned this from Mary, Maddie's older daughter. Maddie generally said whatever she wanted, and her demand for a new lower-school teacher was clear. Thankfully, Miss Craddock chose to depart before she was asked to leave.

So, when Jacob saw from Miss O'Brien's credentials that she had experience in working with the deaf, he saw that as a bonus and possibly the answer to a prayer. Realistically, he viewed it as a "good hire."

As Daniel sat and turned the year's events over in his mind, Maddie entered with Pete. Daniel smiled to himself. So his sister's husband would have his say also. That made sense. Maddie's daughter,

Mary, had never refused to go to school, but she was not happy about going, and a feeling of dread and sickness seemed to come over her each morning.

Now, neither Daniel nor Maddie were lacking in a belief in discipline and a firm hand, but they also had loving hearts for their daughters, and to see them so sad and nervous over school was something that neither had counted on.

So, it appeared that half the town was beginning to slowly drift in, filling in chairs, normally used by children, or standing, while Miss O'Brien, Dave, and Zach sat in chairs on the front platform, facing the crowd.

Superintendent Strickland, who usually resided in Portland, Mr. McVale, Neb Darius, and Noah Thomas sat behind a large table in front of the prospective teachers. They would rise and face the parents and townspeople who had come, giving their addresses, and then turn back to the teachers to address their questions.

Superintendent Strickland did not speak; however, it was clear that he was taking the whole scene in. He was a tall, lean man, sitting uncomfortably in a chair designed for a child of ten, but his discomfort was set off by his interest in this new group of teachers.

Of course, the place of honor was saved for Miss Griggs, who reigned supreme over this function and often over many others for one simple reason: She owned a good bit of land and, thus, a good chunk of the town.

She sat like a queen, separately, directly in front of the platform, while Jacob and his brother quietly cringed from their different positions in the school. Miss Griggs was always in her element when she was allowed to grill a new victim.

Miss Griggs made it clear to the three gentlemen seated at the table next to her that she would begin. It also became clear, though, that Jacob, who had purposely seated himself next to her, held some degree of charm over her. Before she could start her questioning, Jacob interceded, flashing a large smile at her.

"If we could have everyone's attention," he said, rising and facing the full school room. "I'm sure that we would all like an introduction of our new teachers. If they would stand as I introduce them, I'll draw from their own letters of introduction."

Jacob was usually a plain-spoken man, but he could charm a crowd and change his speech to persuasiveness at a moment's notice.

He looked around quickly, hoping that Mary Alice had come. This was partly because she was respected, and he liked to hear her opinions after the meetings, and, of course, it was partly because he enjoyed showing off for her.

Wonderful, Kayleigh thought. She hated this part more than the very first day of school. *Don't fidget*, she reminded herself. *Irish charm*, her mind muttered to itself, *professionalism laced with Irish charm.*

She looked up cautiously and caught a glimpse of Daniel McVale. She looked back at Mitch and Zach quickly, conscious that anyone seeing her look at any man might make something of it. In truth, he simply and somewhat eerily reminded her of the Indian Brave that she had sometimes seen and wondered about.

Jacob motioned to Mitch. *Of course, he would start with Mitch*, she thought. *Of course, he would start with the men.* She wouldn't be allowed to get this over with.

"Mitch Herd comes to us from his latest position in Idaho Falls, where he was the school master for students from the seventh to eighth levels. He brings those skills and abilities to our children and young men and women," Jacob finished.

Mitch stood amiably, his tall, lanky frame always accentuated by the length of his long legs. He wore his usually dark suit, but somehow, Mitch was never somber in his appearance. He also had hat dark hair and those dark brown eyes, but, oh, what a huge and engaging smile. So, just as some were ready to compare him yet again to Ichabod Crane, the smile took that imagery away.

Even with his angular features and large nose, there was something still handsome and charming about him. He still presented his self-effacing and humorous personality, so he was liked but somewhat underestimated until he was seen as the classroom disciplinarian that he could also be.

For her part, Kayleigh noticed that he did not have his cane today, and so she also noticed how careful he was being in his stance, something that only a close friend would notice. She also mentally noted that Mitch and Mr. McVale had the smile and gift of gab in common.

Interesting, she thought. *Physically, they couldn't be more contrasted, but personality-wise, they were somewhat alike.*

"Why thank you, Mr. McVale," Mitch grinned. "I do have the majority of my experiences within the age group of thirteen to fifteen years old, but I also provide tutoring and lessons for those adults wishing to improve their reading, math, and language skills. You have a lovely, thriving town, and I look forward to meeting all of you," he finished.

Clever boy, Kayleigh thought. *You just charmed the town and made a bid for your second income.*

"Then," Jacob continued, "next, we have Mr. Zach Asher. He has been the lead teacher for grades four to six. He is widely supported for his 'unique methods,' and he and Mr. Herd will sometimes work together with these groups."

Zach again grinned as he stood. His build was still short and stocky, and his face was continually that of a little boy planning his next misadventure. "Well," Zach began, "it's easy to have 'unique' methods when you think like a ten-year-old yourself." The attendees laughed.

I could never get away with that, thought Kayleigh. *But he can say one thing with those expressions and that grin, and everyone is ready to laugh.*

"Now, that doesn't mean that we don't work," Zach continued. "I'll expect a lot of your students, and they'll know it, but we'll manage to have a bit of fun, too," he gave the grin again as he sat.

"And we saved the best till last," Jacob motioned to Kayleigh.

He's really good, Kayleigh thought. *He could have played the game and been a top con.* She then silently berated herself for her thoughts. She had promised herself that she would no longer think of that chapter of her life, and here it was at the most inopportune time.

Miss O'Brien is very highly recommended for her work with young children," Jacob motioned for her to stand. "She has done excellent work with children aged five to nine. Indeed, they did not want to release her from her last position. We are lucky to have her."

More like I was desperate to get away from the man in that town and get back to Cassie, Kayleigh thought, closely followed by, *Pull it together, Kayleigh.*

"My life's work is teaching children," Kayleigh started and smiled quietly. "I will give this teaching position all of my time and skills, and I look forward to working with each parent. Thank you for this opportunity."

"Okay, O'Brien," she reflected as she sat. "That wasn't bad. That should do it."

"I have a question for Miss O'Brien," Neb Darius, who was seated next to Jacob, ventured before Miss Griggs could begin her interrogation. Jacob sat down and waited for the questions.

Darius was now rakishly handsome with a well-groomed dark mustache, dark, slicked-back hair, and a trim, impeccably dressed physique. "What's your first name?" he asked, smiling.

"My full name is Kayleigh Naomi-Rebecca O'Brien," she replied. "I'm called Kayleigh or, of course, Miss O'Brien." The small crowd showed expressions that were amused, surprised, and perplexed, and there was a bit of murmuring.

"I have a question too," a young man, Cal Lindstrom, from the audience, called out. "Are you married, and how old are you?"

Don't blush, she told herself. After all she had been through and all of the situations she had been in, she was still prone to blushing.

"No, I am not, and I am twenty-four years old," she said quietly after the crowd had stopped laughing in as matter-of-fact and pleasant way as possible.

"Would you like to be married?" he asked.

The small crowd laughed again, and she gave a slight shrug. Mitch and Zach exchanged knowing side glances and smiled.

"Enough of this," Miss Griggs suddenly snapped. "Let's get to the important questions. Mrs. Mary Louise Lindstrom, as well as Joshua and Jennifer McVale, did not sacrifice most of their lives to this town to have it be a point of mere amusement." With that comment, she cast steely looks at both Jacob and Cal.

At the sound of his parents' names, Jacob began to listen even more carefully, while Cal's smile diminished at the remembrance of his beloved mother.

Miss Griggs was bird-like. From her tiny, frail body to her small, ever-alert dark eyes and rather pronounced sharp nose, she had often reminded others of a crow or a hawk.

Her manner of dress was always somewhat severe, with solid black dresses and cameos or a solid, plain white shirt, black shawl, and black skirt. She perpetually looked as though she was in mourning.

In truth, Kayleigh herself often wore black and white, yet, somehow, it didn't look as severe on her. Miss Griggs, though, even with her small frame and severe clothes, looked like a force to be reckoned with, and she was.

"I'll start with Miss O'Brien," Miss Griggs intoned. "Young woman, what are your discipline policies?" she demanded.

Jacob rolled his eyes, as did Darius and half of the crowd.

"Could you be a bit more specific?" Kayleigh inquired.

"It's a simple enough question," Miss Griggs countered. "How do you discipline children?"

"Well, it depends on the child and the offense, Miss Griggs," Kayleigh countered.

"Do you paddle, use the strap, or the ruler, Miss O'Brien? Answer the question."

"I have never used any of those methods," Kayleigh returned. "There are other forms of discipline."

"What then, Miss O'Brien, the dunce hat, the nose in the corner of the blackboard?"

Parents were beginning to lean in because, after all, this could be their child.

"I have occasionally used standing or sitting in the corner if the child was blatantly disrespectful or staying after school or write-offs on the board or a parent contact; but, I think that the other two methods of the dunce cap or the nose in a ring are overly humiliating."

"So you just let the children run wild?" Miss Griggs inferred with a slight curled smiled.

"No, I assure you that I do not let the children run wild," Kayleigh answered, trying to keep her voice calm and controlled. "We are in order and busy in my classroom. There is very little time or desire for misbehavior."

"You don't look old enough to have taught for very long, young woman, so how do you know that these methods work?"

By this time, Mitch and Zach were bobbing their heads back and forth like witnesses at a good prize fight.

"Well, as my resumé details, Miss Griggs, I've taught for nine years," Kayleigh answered.

"Nine years!" Miss Griggs responded as though she had just heard the most shocking news possible. "How old were you when you began?"

"Sixteen," Kayleigh responded, and several in the audience looked surprised as well. Although it was not unheard of for a young woman to begin teaching at sixteen, the usual age was eighteen or older.

"What religion are you?" Miss Griggs asked, taking on a new tactic. "Are you a Catholic? I find that Catholics often interject their own religious views into the classroom."

Having noticed the "All Saints" sign on the local church, Kayleigh weighed her words carefully. "I am a non-denominational follower of Christ and embrace the belief that we are all God's children."

"That's right," Zach agreed. "We're all saints."

Laughter erupted again, and Mitch kept his eyes downward so as not to betray both his exasperation with Zach and his humorous take on the whole situation.

"I'm sure that you'd like to direct some questions to Mr. Herd and Mr. Asher as well, Miss Griggs," Kayleigh concluded.

("I like her already," Lydia beamed and whispered to Daniel.)

"Actually, I have a few statements I'd like to make rather than a question," Mr. Noah Thomas, the final member of the panel of four, said.

Noah Thomas was a good, no-nonsense man who usually saw the greatest needs of a situation. He and Jacob typically made a good team since he could cut right to the practicalities, while Jacob could put a more poetic and positive spin on the situation.

He stood, himself also a tall figure, with dark hair, matter-of-fact brown eyes, and a handlebar mustache over a straight, determined mouth. He was not exactly handsome, but he was striking.

"Just a few housekeeping details need to be addressed. First of all, the old Mission has been converted into the Upper School House for the two male teachers and their wives, and it is in good condition. The first floor is both the school house and the quarters for one family. The second floor is somewhat smaller but can serve as the quarters for another family. So," he concluded, "I think that you two will be fine, although it may need a few minor repairs here and there.

"However," he continued, "the elementary school house is still in need of quite a few repairs, as is the school itself, as you can probably see. I think that all of the repairs can be made in time for the start of school; however, I wouldn't recommend trying to live in the house before then. Also, there was talk of a room addition to the school itself. I think this could be done while school is in session or at the end of the day," he concluded in his usual all-business, serious, and somewhat deadpan fashion.

Miss O'Brien was becoming somewhat visibly nervous when Jacob stood. "I'd like to volunteer my brother, my brother-in-law, and myself to make the repairs," he smiled. "I'm sure that Mr. Darius and Mr. Thomas will be glad to volunteer their services also."

The two men nodded, but Thomas continued with his litany of bad tidings. "Miss O'Brien, I'm afraid you'll need to stay at Lucy's Inn for another week, at least, or with some other accommodations."

"Oh, wonderful," Kayleigh fought back disappointment. She certainly did not need to show it in her face, or any other emotion for that matter, but how was she going to afford that?

Mitch and Zach gave her sympathetic side glances. There was nothing that they could do, and it wouldn't be appropriate to suggest that she stay in the other school house with them.

"I have a solution," Lydia announced. All heads turned toward her. "Miss O'Brien can stay at our home. We can, in turn, introduce her about town."

Kayleigh opened her mouth to politely say that this was a very generous offer, but she could not impose in this way when Miss Griggs loudly announced, "Then it's settled. Count yourself as a fortunate young woman," Miss Griggs warned.

Kayleigh smiled weakly at Lydia. What had she gotten herself into with this town?

CHAPTER 27: THE UNSPOKEN TEST

Jennifer Anne was two when her parents began to notice that she was not hearing well or learning as fast as many other children. A year later, they took her to a doctor in Portland who confirmed that she was deaf in her left ear. Her right seemed to have only a slight loss.

So, in Lydia's mind, Miss O'Brien might well be the answer to luring Jennifer Anne back to school and watching over her once she was there. This might well be the answer to her prayer.

In fact, when Beatrice Atwood had the audacity to ask Lydia if it didn't bother her having a woman like Miss O'Brien under the same roof as her husband, Lydia glared at her and asked, "Are you inferring that my husband has a wandering eye, or can't be trusted? Has he ever given any indication of that?"

"Well, no," Beatrice answered haltingly while looking down at her feet and shuffling her rather robust figure about, "I just meant that it, uh…"

"Kindly keep your advice, Beatrice," Lydia answered tersely. "I plan to sponsor this lady, and I suggest you help her also. She's a good woman, and she may well be the answer to how terribly last year's school year went.

"Of course, it doesn't hurt that the school board has finally addressed a need for teachers of ten to sixteen-year-olds, either. I suggest that you support all three teachers for the sake of your own four children. We all know just how wild a good many of the older children were behaving.

"The town is growing rapidly," she added, "and so is the student population. We need good teachers," she finished and turned abruptly.

Beatrice left, slightly abashed and huffing, as her little bun and hat jostled about. Moreover, she still did not completely approve of Lydia's stand, and she would let others know.

Kayleigh was canny, though, and she knew that Lydia had an ulterior motive attached to the generous offering of her home. She wanted Kayleigh to get to know Jennifer Anne and charm her into coming to school. This was further emphasized by the fact that she was to share a room with the child.

Kayleigh had offered to simply take the Victorian couch in the front room/parlor, but Lydia had insisted that she share the room with Jennifer Anne, and, in truth, it would provide some degree of comfort and privacy.

Jennifer scowled at Miss O'Brien as she entered the door with her Uncle Jacob carrying the valise. Her dark hair was a bit disarrayed, with part of it falling in her dark blue eyes. There was an untamed quality about the child that did not escape the teacher.

"Well, you must be Jennifer Anne!" Kayleigh said, smiling at the tiny six-year-old.

"Yes," she replied and turned away, busying herself with her rag doll and blocks spread out on the large, round, braided rug.

Kayleigh smiled as Daniel and Lydia watched hopefully. Slowly, she approached Jennifer Anne, lowering herself on the carpet opposite of her.

"I like your dolly," she said. "What's her name?"

Jennifer Anne looked up and shrugged.

Like a child cautiously approaching a cat, she settled in next to Jennifer Anne. She then spoke quietly into her right ear. "What's your dolly's name, Jennifer Anne?"

"Sissy," she responded cautiously, a slight speech impediment evident, her large blue eyes gazing into Kayleigh's.

"Well, she's lovely," Kayleigh replied, and Jennifer Anne smiled slightly.

Lydia's heart gave a small leap. "Please, God, let this work," she prayed silently.

Kayleigh slipped to Jennifer Anne's left side and asked, "What are you building with your blocks?" There was no answer this time, and the child did not look up from her building. Kayleigh slid to Jennifer Anne's other side and repeated the question.

"A tower," she responded.

"Does a princess live there?" Kayleigh inquired.

"Yes," Jennifer Anne answered, this time with a smile, revealing a missing front tooth.

"Oh dear. She isn't trapped, is she?" Kayleigh pursued.

"She is," Jennifer Anne smiled again, "but the prince will get her."

"How brave he must be," Kayleigh nodded approvingly. "May I play?"

"Okay," Jennifer Anne answered and grinned.

As she and Jacob watched, another thought occurred to Lydia after looking over at her brother-in-law and his admiring gaze. Jacob and Miss O'Brien would be good together. However, he was also good with Mary Alice and, from all accounts, his lady friend in San Francisco.

The week went swiftly, and true to her word, Lydia introduced Kayleigh to many of the town's mothers, fathers, grandmothers, grandfathers, aunts, uncles, siblings, and church workers. The latter was included with an introduction to the minister and his wife, and all of this was done through a series of teas and dinners.

Kayleigh found it all a bit dizzying but had to admit it would help greatly with her first few weeks at the school.

She had only been in the school once, accompanied by Lydia, Maddie, and the McVale brothers. The brothers had put a crew together and were working hard to make repairs both in the school and the schoolhouse before the children returned. Pete ran their business while they were at the school.

There were things that Kayleigh would have liked to do herself inside the school, but she could not, at this point, without being in the way. Even more than that, she would have loved to settle her few belongings in the schoolhouse also.

As grateful as she was for the hospitality, this inability to get herself settled was an anxious frustration. She did not feel that she could properly prepare. Plus, her trunk had not been moved from the inn. She was limited in her materials for school preparation until she could get the trunk moved.

As these thoughts continued to flood her mind, Lydia and Maddie made a special Sunday dinner after church to mark the end of Miss O'Brien's stay. Kayleigh was both relieved and grateful.

She had been introduced and introduced and introduced, but the highlight of the whole church service was when she was leaving and old Mr. Capor picked her up, swung her around, and shouted, "Well, welcome to town, little cutie baby doll!"

As those leaving the church stifled grins and laughter, Daniel and Jacob swiftly intervened, with Daniel cautioning, "Mr. Capor, that's not appropriate. We've told you before not to do that."

"Well, she's just so cute," Mr. Capor said defensively.

Neb Darius found it especially funny. "Well, she is at that, Mr. Capor, but we don't want to lose her before she even starts," he laughed.

Jacob smiled and shrugged at the now blushing and mortified Kayleigh. "He's harmless. His mind and self-control aren't what they used to be," but, privately, he thought, *He's not wrong.*

However, in Kayleigh's mind, she was already feeling awkward and strange enough without the added effect of being lifted up in front of the departing congregation.

It had already been noticeable to her that after she was seated on the McVale pew, she was also maneuvered next to Jacob. Lydia's thinking was that since Mary Alice was out of town, visiting a surviving friend from the wagon train attack who had stayed in touch with her, and since she would be in Portland for a week, Jacob might as well sit next to another eligible woman.

Jacob offered her his arm as they began the short trek to Daniel and Lydia's home, which she would be leaving that evening. She was anxious to be settled in the schoolhouse, and that was her main thought as she politely took his arm.

The Sunday dinner company only included the McVale families this time. Maddie and Pete and their two daughters, Mary and Penny, and, of course, Daniel, Lydia, Jennifer Anne, and Jacob were all present.

Lydia and Daniel would not allow Kayleigh to help with dinner. She was accustomed to working for everything, so this bothered her also. Again, she felt an awkward mix of gratitude and anxiety, but it was also clear that she was to spend time with the children.

While she was on the rug talking and playing with the three girls, the two brothers and Pete gathered at the hearth and discussed their business and the business of the town. However, Kayleigh was also aware of their glances in her direction as she interacted with the girls. Whether they were approving or disapproving glances, she was unsure.

Mary was a very pretty seven-year-old with long dark curls and brilliant brown eyes. One could only wonder at how beautiful she would be as a young woman. Quiet but self-assured, she organized her pretend tea party with Jennifer Anne like an experienced entertainer. Penny, on the other hand, was a ball of energy who rolled to and fro on the carpet, demanding, "Look at what I can do!"

She and Mary could not have been more opposite in their appearance and demeanor. Penny was blonde and blue-eyed like her mother and full of raw energy. She was also very smart for a four-year-old, already reading parts of a picture book and declaring, "I'll be going to school too!"

"No, you won't, Mary said in a matter-of-fact voice, barely sparing Penny a glance. "You're too young and little. You'll be at home with Mama."

"I'm a big girl too," Penny shouted, and Maddie thought that she would be needed to intervene, but Miss O'Brien leaned over and patted Penny's arm.

"Oh, love, it won't be long at all before you are coming to school also, and," she gently held up a finger to signal that Penny should listen rather than talk, "I need little visitors and helpers. Perhaps your mama could bring you by the school ever so often (not every day, mind) to do big girl things."

While Penny beamed, Kayleigh held up one index finger again and cautioned, "But you really would have to be a big girl and behave."

"I will!" Penny promised while Mary rolled her eyes, and Kayleigh silently thought, *You may be the one to watch as you grow up*, as she smiled.

Jacob looked at Kayleigh, careful not to linger too long with his gaze. He thought, with relief, that he'd made the right decision and hire, and he hoped that for the children's sake and Miss O'Brien's that he had, but he also had the peaceful feeling that accompanies a task well done.

"Dinner is ready," Lydia announced as all began to gather at the table. The girls were gravitating toward sitting with Miss O'Brien when Lydia and Maddie ushered them over to their fathers, leaving two seats at the end of the table for Jacob and Kayleigh.

Kayleigh wasn't sure whether this was pure coincidence or a bit of a plan, but she was tired and hungry and decided that it didn't really matter.

Jacob, on the other hand, was simply grateful.

"Tell us about where you've lived," Mary said after the prayer had been said.

"Mary, let Miss O'Brien eat her dinner," Maddie chastised. (But, in reality, she and the others at the table wondered just what those destinations were.)

"It's alright," Kayleigh answered. "I'll be glad to tell you a bit about my adventures.

"I started, of course, in Ireland, and my mom and I came to New York on a huge boat. It was both for passengers and for hauling things such as livestock. I remember seeing the Statue of Liberty for the first time. We then lived in New York for three years, and my brother, Luke, and I rode street cars and explored the city when he wasn't working and I wasn't in school. Or, sometimes, I would meet him at the restaurant where he worked clearing tables, and the manager would give us a free fancy dessert.

"Then we began to travel because of my stepfather's business. He began to help run carnivals from the mid-west to the west. We were in various states, from Minnesota to South Dakota. Later, I went to Teachers College in South Dakota before teaching in Wyoming and Idaho, and now I'm here," she said, turning her hands upward with a slight shrug.

Mary and Jennifer Anne were beginning to talk at the same time, "What was the carnival like? How cold is it really in South Dakota?" Then, Maddie and Lydia both called a polite ending to the questioning so that Miss O'Brien could, indeed, eat her dinner, but they all wondered in their own silent reverie.

Daniel wondered who had hurt her and what she kept moving away from. Pete wondered who was probably still after her. Lydia wondered how her mother could let her "explore" New York on her own, a mere child, and Maddie wondered why she was still unmarried.

As for Jacob, he wondered if she would ever tell him just what her "true adventures" really were. There was a story within the story there, and he imagined it was not so fun and simplistic.

CHAPTER 28: GETTING SETTLED

That evening, after Maddie, Pete, and their girls had departed, Jacob and Lydia accompanied Kayleigh to the schoolhouse while Daniel watched over Jennifer Anne. Kayleigh's trunk had been delivered from the inn, and Kayleigh was anxious to get a good look at the small schoolhouse connected to the school, hoping, more than anything, that it had a good bed.

Kayleigh had officially claimed the carnival trunk before getting to South Dakota. As Peaches explained it, "Well, of course, it's yours, sweetheart. It always has been. We don't know what we're going into in Colorado. What would we do with a trunk? Sometimes, less is better."

It had been painted a "carnival red," and at one point or another, it had experienced many functions. From storage to a table to a footrest, and even as a door stop, it had proved useful and strong. There was something comforting about it.

Peaches had called it Kayleigh's treasure chest. In fact, now, it contained the treasures of teaching that Kayleigh had collected along the way, such as art supplies, paint, pencils, canvasses, books, sweet letters from a few students and parents, slates, school play costumes, an abacus for arithmetic practice, a model skeleton that she had agreed to store for Zach's science classes, and her beloved fiddle which was donated by Peaches and Pop.

The trunk was a faithful companion, reminding her of where she had been and where she was going. It had seen her through three teaching assignments and would see her through one more. Others might not understand, but to her, it was a constant in a continually changing world, and it reminded her of people she had met along the way, battered on the outside but, oh, so full of beauty and goodness inwardly.

"May I place your trunk and your valise for you?" Jacob asked politely as he and Pete hauled the trunk and Lydia and Maddie carried Kayleigh's valise and other items that they had gathered for her.

"Well, the trunk is quite heavy," she explained. "It contains school materials. So, perhaps you could just carefully slide it into the large hall or...closet that connects the house and the school. The valise," she said, smiling and motioning to the two women, "is just my clothes. You can just throw it in the bedroom."

They followed her instructions, minus the throwing. Jacob had a smile and one eyebrow slightly raised. Most women would approach it the opposite way, with the clothes being carefully protected.

He also had the sense that Miss O'Brien watched him as he picked up and moved the trunk when he noticed she turned away suddenly when he turned back around. Perhaps she admired strength. He was wondering about this when she began to express her thanks to both him and Lydia. When she paused, she noted that there was a back porch with a small fenced-in yard and clothesline.

"Oh, how wonderful!" she exclaimed. "There's a small back porch and a fence about the yard."

"Well, about that," Jacob grinned slightly. "It will need some carpentry work. My brother and I noticed that the fence was a little unstable. So, I'll work on that in addition to the things that are left to correct in the school."

"Oh well, okay," Miss O'Brien nodded a little absently.

"We'll get out of your way now," Lydia concluded and begged Kayleigh to get some rest and let them know if she needed anything.

"It's hard to believe that school starts in two days!" Maddie added and hugged Kayleigh.

As Lydia, Maddie, Pete, and Jacob made their way back, Lydia turned to Jacob, "The back fence needs carpentry? It looks fine," she said, smiling slyly at Jacob and winking at Maddie.

"Have you been out there lately?" he asked.

"No, she admitted.

"Well, then, you have no cause to question a carpentry repair," he said gruffly.

"No, I guess not," she smiled again, and even Pete and Maddie smiled to themselves. Neither had ever seen Jacob "smitten" since his marriage to Kelly.

There was just one thing that bothered Jacob. He had seen something in the trunk when he placed it in the connecting hall. The old trunk's latch had popped open, revealing a slit through which he saw gleaming, quite innocently, a pistol.

CHAPTER 29: SCHOOL DAYS

To say the first days of school went well would be a fair statement, but given the circumstances of the previous year, the town felt that the first few days were well-ordered and great. There were no publicly voiced complaints and quite a few compliments for all three teachers

Miss O'Brien had made special desk tags for each child using her calligraphy pens. She had then stacked each student's books neatly on their desks and had her globe and abacus out and ready. Her board work for the older students was also ready, and she had made sure that each desk had a slate, using her own spare ones where needed. While she was working with this, she noticed a plaque next to the doorway reading, "In Honor of the Efforts of Joshua and Jennifer McVale and the Dedication of Mary Louise Lindstrom." She assumed these were the same individuals referred to by Miss Griggs and that Mary Louise was somehow related to the outspoken Cal.

Jacob McVale, his brother and brother-in-law, and the rest of the board were finding out, rather quickly, that these were practiced, experienced teachers. Still, he felt a continued protectiveness toward Miss O'Brien, different from his usual instinctive feelings of protection toward females.

Most of the work that was done on the elementary/lower school room was in the afternoon after the children were dismissed. In this way, any noise of hammering, sawing, or boards being moved about would not interfere with lessons.

Occasionally, though, work was done during the regular school day, such as hanging windows, cleaning up sawdust, or bringing in new desks. The school board had made good on their promise of an addition and repairs. Miss O'Brien had hung several quilts between the regular schoolroom and the addition for a little added privacy.

She was excited that she could move her third and fourth graders to the addition instead of having them overcrowded in the back of the room. The current situation made it difficult for her to get to them for help and to see exactly what was going on with them while attending to the younger students.

So, the McVales, Mr. Thomas, and any others who happened to be working and helping out couldn't help but hear lessons being taught, discipline being given, or children's answers and comments. Even recess play made its way to their ears.

If any of the workers had experienced doubts or misgivings about Miss O'Brien, they were being quickly replaced by a better understanding of the teacher/student dynamic and even admiration of her and her methods. Of course, each man had his own "take" on what was heard and seen.

For example, Daniel was completely grateful for the extra attention Miss O'Brien showed to Jennifer Anne, building her confidence by calling on her carefully and waiting patiently for her responses. Also, their after-school sessions with speech and lip reading exercises did not escape his attention.

When he heard Miss O'Brien say such things as "Watch how I say this when I read, and then you say it the same way," he said a silent prayer of thanksgiving that his stubborn little daughter was actually doing what she was asked.

As a result, Jennifer Anne's reading and communication improved greatly, and she even began to politely ask people to repeat what they had said "toward her other ear." Her frustration was lessening, and her confidence was increasing.

Jacob appreciated the way that she kept the boys under control. She seemed to anticipate moments of restlessness with them and the need to sometimes "stretch their legs."

Indeed, she had partnered with Mitch and Zach to form the "Noble Knights" club for the fourth-level boys, allowing her third-level students to associate with the older boys from time to time.

Jacob loved to hear Miss O'Brien call out, "Noble Knights, assemble for your time with Head Knight, Mr. Mitch!"

He also felt sorry for boys who had not earned their "Noble Knights" time due to missing homework or misbehavior during the week. However, he had to admit that the three teachers had engineered an ingenious method for offering incentives.

Jacob noticed everything, from the way Kayleigh handled delicate situations, such as little Dottie Eastwood's wetting accident, to the older Eastwood sister's (Linda) lack of hygiene and clean clothes. He noted how kind and efficient she was.

He equally admired how she interacted with Ned Manning, who he long suspected was mistreated by his father. She made sure that he had a sandwich to eat for lunch, which he also suspected was actually hers, and made a point to talk with him at recess. Jacob had a feeling that more needed to be done for Ned, but it wasn't in his nature to go into people's home lives. Of course, his mother, Jennifer McVale, would have made it her business, but he didn't have that touch. For that matter, many women didn't either.

Jacob also appreciated how Miss O'Brien tried to make each student feel special about him or herself but didn't play favorites. She had a real sense of fair play and occasionally a bit of temper, as was the case with Teddy Measer, who frequently spoke out of turn or passed gas for attention.

However, she stood her ground with students such as Teddy Measer, the class clown and showout, and many the time that he would be leaving from repair work to see Teddy attempting to finish a board write-off, such as "I will not share what I consider witticisms with the rest of the class while my teacher is speaking." Jacob was torn between pity and laughter after reading some of Teddy's assigned writings.

Her punishments for his behavior varied from denial for Noble Knights attendance to truly creative and longboard write-offs to instructing him to "go outside until you are in control of your physical faculties. By the way, I've invited your mother to come observe your difficulties so that she can arrange a doctor's visit. Also, anyone who laughs at Teddy's antics can forget about being a Noble Knight or going out at recess."

So it was that Jacob found himself finding repairs and additions to be made to both the school and the adjoining house, which, in truth, could have been delayed or put off completely.

Also, he had never thought of himself as an interloper or eavesdropper. He did a good job, most of the time, of minding his own business, but for reasons that he couldn't explain, he couldn't help but listen to some of the after-school conversations that happened between Miss O'Brien and students and parents.

He admired her quiet but determined ways while he wondered about her reclusiveness after school and on Saturdays and Sundays. She seemed to slip in and out of the school and into the connected house as quietly as a shy child.

Recess was his favorite for casual observation, especially on Fridays when Miss O'Brien would play Red Rover with the class, turn the jump rope with the girls, or invite Mr. Mitch's and Mr. Zach's class over for a baseball game. In truth, all four of the men, and any other helpers who were around, loved to see the baseball games. It was not a game that they had grown up with, but they could see themselves playing it and enjoyed watching it.

Mr. Thomas, in contrast, appreciated the fact that Miss O'Brien was not a demanding person. As the treasurer for the school board, he noted that she rarely asked for anything, and when she did, it was truly needed, such as chalk or ink. However, he also showed true emotion, an oddity for him, when Miss O'Brien led the class in singing.

"Why, Thomas, is that a tear in your eye?" Jacob asked teasingly one day.

"Mind your own business, McVale," he warned. "She just reminds me of someone special to me when she sang around the house. She had an Irish accent, too. When they're all singing together, it sounds a little like angels. That's all. Mind your own business," he finished while dabbing at his nose.

Then there were the parents who came by at the end of the day to collect children, get an update on their child's behavior and progress, and, frankly, just to look at Miss O'Brien for purposes of praise or just plain gossip. (Why was she unmarried anyway, etc.) In this way, Miss O'Brien's skills were noticed and talked of throughout the town.

A few afternoons a week, Jacob came through the schoolroom and spoke to Kayleigh, although he always addressed her as Miss O'Brien since it was her workplace, and mainly since she still always addressed him as Mr. McVale. It was on one such afternoon that he came through, only to find her in a rather compromising position. Namely, she was bent down, head behind the bookcase, and fanny in the air.

Jacob cleared his throat, and she nearly bumped her head, moving out and away from the bookcase. "Anything that I can help with?" Jacob asked while trying not to smile or possibly break out with laughter.

"Um…no, uh, no, I keep hearing a noise from behind the bookcase, and well, I was just…" She knew that she was blushing and that her hair was gradually coming undone.

"Well, let's just have a look," Jacob said while he pushed the bookcase, books and all, away from the wall. "Oh, here's the culprit," he said as he reached down and grabbed a large mouse by the tail.

He observed that Miss O'Brien's eyes were as large as saucers as he lifted them in front of her. "What shall I do with him?" he asked as seriously as possible. "Or, would you like to do the honors?"

"No!" she half screamed before she even realized it. "I mean, I'm sorry, but I really don't like them. I mean, don't hurt him or anything of that sort. Maybe just toss him out."

"Alright," he laughed. "Here he goes," he said, tossing him out the door. Then, his smile faded as he noticed that Miss O'Brien was shaking.

"I'm sorry," he said, approaching her desk, which she was now sitting behind. "I wasn't trying to scare you."

She turned a bit in the chair to face him. "It's alright," she said. "It's just that I had a bad experience as a child with a mouse. Well, never mind. Thank you for…relocating him," she finished.

"You're welcome," he said, wondering what that bad experience might be. "I just wanted to let you know that we're about finished. We'll need maybe one more day at the most," he explained. "Then, we'll be out of your way," he smiled, and he was secretly pleased to see just a hint of disappointment in Miss O'Brien's returned smile.

"You know, though," he continued. "I never did get to the back steps at the schoolhouse. I can follow up on that next week if it's okay with you," he finished.

"Well, sure, I mean whatever you think about them, Mr. McVale," she answered.

By this time, Teddy was beginning to grin to himself and cast sidelong glances at the two of them.

"Turn around, Teddy, and finish!" Kayleigh warned loudly.

"Oh, you've misspelled 'ignorant,'" Jacob advised Teddy. "In your sentence, 'I will cease behaving in an ignorant manner so as to gain personal attention,' it's *or* not *er*."

Kayleigh smiled. Teddy shrugged and started erasing.

Then, one warm fall day, outdoor play, or "recess," ran late. Several parents had assembled outside the schoolhouse and upper school, watching a round of baseball as they waited for their children. Generally, these were the parents of the elementary students, always concerned about what went on at school and how their children behaved with this new school teacher.

Today, however, they had combined the elementary and upper school for a baseball game led by "Mr. Mitch" and "Mr. Zach." The smaller children sat watching while the older children played, learning the "ins and outs" of New York baseball, or "street ball," as some called it. Mitch's goal was to order some bats and proper baseballs to teach young men how to play the game and then form a team.

"Do you remember what the upper-level students in this town were like only a few months back?" Daniel asked as he came up the hill and stood next to Lydia. It was unusual for him to pose questions.

"Indeed, I do," she replied. "Most of them quit going to school, and some just tried to see what trouble they could cause or who they could bedevil."

Zach, seeing an opportunity to have some fun at Kayleigh's expense, called out, "Batter, batter, we need a new batter! Batter up, Miss O'Brien."

"Yay! Go, Miss O'Brien," her students urged her.

Kayleigh could have smacked Zach, but what choice did she have but to go to the makeshift mound, which consisted of a big rock on top of a sheet of paper that one of the upper school girls had voluntarily given?

It was at this time that Jacob strolled up the hill behind the schools to the flat area of land usually reserved for recess, games, and gatherings. Maddie, seeing her brother, motioned him over.

"Why are you here, dear brother?" Maddie asked innocently.

"I heard the loud voices and wondered what was going on. Also, I'm supposed to give the new addition a final going-over inspection to satisfy Noah Thomas before we let the children continue to meet in that part of the schoolhouse," he explained.

Maddie shrugged. "Noah needs to take up drinking," she said quietly.

Lydia laughed and leaned around Maddie to Jacob. "Guess who's up to hit at the ball?"

Jacob grinned as he saw Kayleigh going to the mound. "This is good," he said. "The older children need sports and exercise to divert all that energy." Maddie smirked a little and rolled her eyes.

Zach now began his act. "Let's watch the lady bat,' he said while prissing about the field like a girl holding up her skirts. (Most of the mothers laughed, despite themselves.)

"Get out of the way, Zach, or I'll send it right at your head," Kayleigh called out. "Shouldn't hurt your hard head, though," she added.

Since it was Friday, she had her usual outfit on: her striped shirt, blue skirt, belted at the waist, and wide-brimmed hat. She crouched a bit into the bat, waiting for the pitch.

Mitch pitched the ball hard and fast to her, knowing that she could handle it. Nonetheless, he watched to make sure she was up to the game as she connected and hit the ball across the green, running the sad little bases as fast as she could and holding on to her hat.

"Go, Miss O'Brien, go!" many of the children yelled. She ran all of them, partly because the out-fielder was not very fast and partly because the players weren't trying very hard to get her out.

"Well, that is just a disgrace," Beatrice Atwood murmured. "Her skirts are flying up, and she's going to jiggle right out of that corset. She does the same thing when she jumps rope with the little girls."

Some of the mothers nodded in agreement, while others ignored Beatrice.

"You just wish you could jiggle like that," Maddie said under her breath.

Jacob had finally stopped being completely overcome with grief and panic every time he saw Beatrice, and, for a moment, Jacob reflected on how outspoken Beatrice had become. He decided that he liked her better when she had been a quiet young woman.

Jacob grinned again, for various reasons, and Lydia leaned around Maddie again. "When she's out here like this, she doesn't look much older than some of the students. It just makes you want to scoop her up and take her home. Wouldn't you like to, Jacob?"

Jacob looked momentarily shocked before answering calmly, "Mind your own business, Lydia. You'll live longer."

Sadly, though, word got back to Kayleigh about Beatrice's comments, and she never jumped rope with the little girls or played baseball with the older children again.

Maybe that was just how the whole town thought of her, as some tart trying to show off her body, she thought. *Or maybe, more likely, they just thought her to be one more old maid school teacher*, she reasoned. Either way, she was a misfit yet again.

CHAPTER 30: ON A SATURDAY AND A SUNDAY

Kayleigh was beginning to feel settled in Faithful and was developing a routine. She often did her letter-writing on Friday nights. This was also when she missed people like Peaches and Pop, who had been so good to her when she was younger. Or she sometimes corresponded with her friend, Margaret Ruth.

August 1890

Dear Peaches and Pop,

You have urged me to write each time that I am settled. I have left Idaho, and my life is progressing in this new little hamlet that I have settled in. I am enjoying my teaching assignment as well as the children. Most of the town's people have been quite kind to me.

You may or may not be saddened to know that both Pa and Mama have passed away. I have boarded Cassie with a Morman couple (the Langleys) in Idaho, and she seems to be doing well.

In truth, Faithful is a fine, aspiring young town. I have, as I usually do, established a daily routine. I arise at 4:45, ready myself, and have my tea and perhaps a biscuit, light the fire in the school stove, if needed, and make sure that my board work is prepared. By this time, my third-level students arrive, followed a half hour later by my first and second-level pupils.

On a Saturday, I, like most of the town, go to the mercantile (The Campbell Mercantile) to purchase supplies for the coming week. I have become especially fond of the couple who run it. Mr. and Mrs. Campbell have been extremely kind to me, allowing me to run a balance until I am paid. They also keep me immediately informed of any letter. In addition to yours, I also receive letters from the Langleys, Professor Gallant, my old friend, Margaret Ruth, who is still working at a school in Boise, and sometimes Dr. Healthful and Mr. Leonardo.

They also inform me of telegrams, which are not of such an informative and pleasant nature. In fact, generally, they are from Matthew or Marcus. Those messages are typically an embarrassment both in tone and meaning. (Will I ever be free of them?)

On a Sunday, of course, I go to church. A non-denominational faith seems to prevail here, which is fine since I simply identify most often as a Christian. The McKendrees run the church. Reverend McKendree is a good preacher and an excellent pastor to the congregation. Mrs. Mckendree seems to be an equal partner with him and the church's planned activities. I admire that greatly. It's so seldom that a woman is allowed in any part of a man's vocation. It also seems that the Campbells are related to the Mckendrees.

To give a brief history of the town, apparently, everything leads back to Mrs. McVale, who passed away over ten years ago. Jacob McVale, her son, and his brother and sister are members of the school board and have also treated me with kindness and respect. It seems that Mrs. Campbell's mother, the first Mrs. McKendree was quite close with Mrs. McVale. She was like a mother figure to the young Mrs. McVale. In turn, her husband, Joshua McVale, and the father of the board members I mentioned helped the original Reverend and Mrs. McKendree build the church. There was also a mission built next to the church, which now serves as the Upper School and housing for Mitch and Zach.

Mrs. Campbell (often called Eugenia by the older members of Faithful) was the daughter of the first Reverend and Mrs. Mckendree. When she was young, she didn't even know that her half-brother, the current Reverend, existed. So, they were not particularly thrilled with each other in the beginning when he began to preach here. Time, though, apparently healed all wounds, and they now seem to be a closely bound family. (Indeed, the whole town seems closely bound by one secret or another.)

As usual, my payment for the wonderful things you did for me is enclosed. I miss you and Pop and will love you forever.

Love, Kayleigh

Dear Kayleigh,

Reading your letter is like reading a good penny novel. I just look forward to them like you wouldn't believe.

'Course Pop can't read, never could, even before his eyes went, but I always read them to him. He wouldn't have it no other way, and Lord knows I wouldn't write this good if Professor Gallant had not helped me.

We is traveling again, so after this week I'm gonna write you so you'll know where we are, Baby Girl. You will be in our prayers. Who knows? Maybe Dream Town will come your way.

Love, Peaches and Pop

P.S. You know you don't have to send us no money. Thank you, though. We put it to good use.

CHAPTER 31: WHO DOES GOD WANT?

Kayleigh was sitting in her regular back pew that she had adopted. She sat in between her third-grade student, Ned (who most often knew that he was expected by his father to go to church but also knew that his father would never be seen in a church, himself) and Mrs. Hemshaw, whose husband had "run off," for "parts unknown," as the town folk related.

She thought that this pew was for the best when Mary Alice returned from visiting her friend in Portland. Her friend, from the days that the two were both in a wagon train, was recently widowed. She had asked Mary Alice to come and live in Portland, but Mary Alice considered Faithful her home. So, she promised to visit her from time to time. However, it had made her think. What was holding her to Faithful?

Kayleigh had to admit that Mary Alice was a very beautiful lady, and Mr. McVale would be foolish not to choose the lady now sitting next to him. She seemed so composed, beautiful, and intelligent. How could he not have marriage plans with her?

When she wasn't observing the other church members from her back seat view, she did make an attempt to listen to the sermon, but Mr. Campbell, filling in for the new Reverend McKendree while he fulfilled a circuit preaching obligation, was often a soft-spoken man and, several times, she had actually nodded off or placed a copy of *Ivanhoe* inside the hymnal and read during the sermon. (No one had noticed, with the possible exception of Jacob McVale, who again looked as though he was about to break out in laughter.)

So, when Reverend McKendree returned and announced from the pulpit that the topic of his sermon was "Who Does God Want?" Kayleigh's first thought was, *I don't know. Who? It couldn't possibly be me.* He had her attention.

"I think it is natural to think that our Lord wants the very best people who have led the very best lives, but who are the best people?" the new Reverend asked in an intense manner.

"Does the Lord find these people among the wealthy, the greatly talented, the medical profession, or simply among those who are recognized for their extreme kindness and loving souls?"

That sounds about right, Kayleigh thought.

"I would suggest to you," he continued, "that, yes, the Lord does look to these people to do His work, if they have the heart for it, but He also looks to the weak, to the adulterers, to murderers, to thieves and liars, and to the sick of mind and body."

The good Reverend was beginning to garner quite a few looks. People were starting to wonder just where Reverend McKendree was going with this particular sermon.

"I would propose that Peter was so weak he denied Christ. The woman to be stoned was an adulteress. Saul was a continual murderer, and the thief on the cross was promised paradise.

"Abraham lied about Sarah, David committed adultery, and Jesus drove demons out of the possessed. He also healed lepers and cripples, only to then use their testimonies.

"Also remember, the return of the prodigal son," and at this point, he gave a meaningful look to Eugenia Campbell (who had hoped that her husband, Virgil, might have an opportunity to take over her father's pulpit in addition to running the mercantile). "Remember that his father welcomed him, but his own brother could not accept him."

Jacob, listening to the sermon as well, thought, *I'm not sure why some of the townfolk have doubts about him. He seems like a good preacher to me.*

Way to air our family laundry, Mrs. Campbell thought as she sat with an unassuming and unflinching look, smoothing her proper little brown gingham dress over her plump waist and then patting her proper gray bun at the base of her neck. However, if one had looked more closely, they would have seen her deep-set blue eyes a bit ablaze. *How do you think I felt when you suddenly appeared as my father's illegitimate son?* flashed through her mind and soul.

"My point is: He wants us all. He needs us all. There is something within you that no one else has, something that you, specifically, can give. I would urge you to dedicate what you have as an offering to the Lord.

"One way of doing this is through baptism, an outward showing of one's faith in Christ, and indeed, this should be the first step of dedication. However, the simple living of one's life in the most excellent way possible demonstrates a dependable form of dedication."

Well, he's good, Kayleigh thought as her mind worked. *The sermon is good, but it's no Sinners in the Hands of an Angry God by Jonathan Edwards.*

Then, Reverend McKendree made a statement that penetrated into her attention, her insecurities, and her shame. "Perhaps you have been the victim of deception, or betrayal, or thievery, or violence. Perhaps you were left to bear the shame and humiliation that someone else inflicted upon you. Let me assure you that the Lord still wants to love you, longs to heal you. The question is, 'Will you let Him?' Please do. You're far too valuable to lose.

"If you wish to make your confession or ask the congregation for prayers, won't you come? Please be a part of our body and the body of Christ," the Reverend concluded.

Kayleigh dug her nails into her joined hands. He could not have reached her more if he had pointed at her and said, "I know you were deeply hurt, but you still have to serve God."

Didn't she serve the Lord every day? she wondered. *What more did he want?* Perhaps, though, she should think about baptism for both Cassie and herself.

As for Reverend McKendree, he hoped he had not pushed his last point too far. He knew the signs of abuse and deep insecurities, though. This dear, new young woman was good at an outward show of confidence, but she was running, and he feared that she always would.

CHAPTER 32: SAVING NED AND MEETING HER PAST AT THE FAIR

On many days, Kayleigh could be seen working diligently after school with Ned Manning. As she attempted to improve his reading and math skills, she also advised him that he did not have to be like his father or mother.

This was not their usual help day, and as she smiled and looked at him in the doorway, his head was tucked downward. Light from the afternoon streamed in, and she noticed the bruise under his eye.

"Ned!" Kayleigh called out. "Wait just a moment."

He paused at the doorway with the same sad and hopeless look on his face.

Kayleigh got up from her desk and approached the door. "Ned, come with me," she said, taking his hand, and they made their way to the docks.

When they arrived, Kayleigh demanded to see "Mr. McVale." Daniel nodded and went to find Jacob. Men were gathering, partly to look at Miss O'Brien and partly to look at the scene that was about to unfold.

Jacob approached the group slowly, analyzing the scene. He gave his usual wide grin and asked the obvious question, "May I help you, Miss O'Brien?"

"No, but we could all possibly help this boy," she responded.

She gently lifted his chin so that the crowd saw his face. Most were silent, but there were a few comments, such as, "His daddy is at it again."

"What do all of you plan on doing about this?" she asked, her eyes and cheeks burning.

"Well, what do you think we can do, little lady?" Neb Darius smirked. "Harlan Manning's always been this way."

"This is one of the children of this town," Kayleigh continued, unaffected. "Is this how you want your schoolchildren treated?"

"She's right," Jacob said. "First, we need to get him out of that house. Then, we need to let Harlan know that he won't be taking him home, and that may take several of us to several locations. Do you understand me?" Jacob glared.

"Miss O'Brien," he continued, "let's see if Lucy can't accommodate him for a while." He motioned to the two of them, and they walked toward Lucy's together.

"My mama might come back to me," Ned said sadly.

"I doubt it, sweetie," Kayleigh said softly. "Let's go with Mr. McVale. We have the beginning of a plan now."

As for Lucy and Kayleigh, they formed a bond based on their agreement. Kayleigh knew that she had a rather powerful ally, and Lucy simply knew that she liked this girl, but she had to admit Kayleigh reminded her of someone, and she wondered if Jacob had noticed yet. For every time she looked at the young woman, the image of Jennifer McVale came to her.

Jacob turned to Kayleigh, offered his arm, and quietly walked her home.

Kayleigh turned at the door and offered a handshake. "Thank you, Mr. McVale. Maybe we saved him."

But still, Kayleigh did not participate in any socializing town activities other than church, and her participation there was limited to attendance. This meant that she usually slipped into the back pew with Lucy, Mrs. Hemshaw, and Ned and left as fast as possible. Mrs. Mckendree had tried to talk Kayleigh into attending choir practice and church functions, but she always explained that she was very busy with school.

She could, however, be seen out and about in town on Saturdays, buying dry goods and groceries, and occasionally, on weekdays, she made her way to the post and telegraph office, both housed within the town Mercantile.

The Campbells, who ran the offices, had befriended her also and helped her send through her telegrams to the Langleys to check on her little sister and advised her on the best way to send funds. (In truth, they wondered why she did not keep an account in the small bank run by Noah Thomas but respected her decision to stay with the bank in Boise.)

They also alerted her to any letters that they could tell were from her little sister. Mrs. Campbell was especially fond of her and secretly reflected on the fact that Kayleigh reminded her of her own mother's dear friend, Jennifer McVale.

There were a few times that Jacob had caught a glimpse of Kayleigh outside of the school, walking down the street with her long, curly, reddish blonde hair streaming out, released from its usual bun.

On one such day, he decided to casually catch up to her at the Campbell's Mercantile and Dry Goods Store. He noticed that she was reaching for a small bolt of muslin, slightly out of her reach. Slowly coming up next to her, he put his hand up, taking the material down and presenting it with his usual wide grin as though it were a rare present. "For you, madame," he gave a slight bow of his head.

"Oh, Mr. McVale," she said, somewhat shocked. "I guess, I," she stammered. "I guess they shouldn't put these items up so high. Thank you for your assistance," she managed to finish.

Jacob noticed that she was somewhat flushed and disconcerted. On the one hand, he hoped that he hadn't upset her. On the other hand, he was glad that he had gotten a reaction from her. He noticed that she blushed very prettily.

"Of course, any time," he replied. "There's a fair in town this evening. He pointed at the square, where various booths and venues were being set up. It benefits the people who run it and the town. I'd be glad to escort you around it."

She looked out the window to see the banner labeled "Your Town Fair." "I don't know she said, headed toward the counter to pay. "I have a lot to do."

"It's Saturday," he observed and smiled. "There shouldn't be quite as much to do. Even teachers deserve a day off."

She managed a smile and thought quickly of how kind he had been, and, again, she had trouble understanding her own feelings. She did not take to men except as considering them not much higher than children, who could be collected and adopted. Jacob was not childish, needy, or overly hurt by life, though. These feelings toward him were a curiosity to her.

"Well, alright then," she agreed. "As long as we're not out very long," she smiled.

"I will respect your wishes, My Lady," Jacob regally intoned and gave a half-bow before offering his arm.

Despite herself, she grinned and took his arm. It occurred to her briefly that she was breaking every rule she'd ever made, but somehow, it finally seemed alright. It also occurred to her that this was somewhat like the time that Joey had walked her about the carnival.

She told Mrs. Campbell that she'd return for her purchase later. Mrs. Campbell smiled and said, "Of course, dear, don't worry about it."

As they walked, she suddenly felt more like herself than she had in years. There was some kind of balance between the child and the young woman that she had become. It was honestly more freeing than she had felt in a long while.

"Let's start over here," Jacob said as he led her over to the "Game of Chance" booth.

Kayleigh smiled to herself. This looked a lot like one of the booths that she had often seen and sometimes been a part of back when she had "played the game."

Kayleigh noticed that Ned had also wandered up to the same booth, looking curiously at the game.

"Look here, look here," the young man near the booth barked out. "Take a chance. Guess where the dice will be found – under which cup? Take a chance. Win a prize."

"How much, Mister?" Ned asked.

Kayleigh hated to see Ned depart with any of his small wages that Lucy had begun to give him.

"Listen, Ned," she said, pulling him to her side. "This is not an honest game. Even if you are quick enough of eye to track it, you still may lose your money."

"Then you help me," Ned said pleadingly. "I want that little stuffed bear for my sister whenever she and Mama come back for me."

Kayleigh closed her eyes. The boy was still clinging to the notion that his mother would return for him. "Alright," she said, sighing softly. "Alright, but don't be disappointed if you lose. Just take it as a life lesson."

The young man began the game, and Jacob, taking notice of how intently Kayleigh watched, was intrigued.

"Alright, Ned," she whispered. "It's under the second cup. Tell him that and don't let him talk you out of your pick."

"But I saw it under the cup that's first. That should be where it is," he whispered.

She shook her head and whispered with her eyes still on the cups, "Two."

Ned pointed and said, as instructed by Kayleigh, that he thought the dice were under the second cup.

Before the man could begin to speak, Jacob said, "Let's have a look then under the second."

The dice were there, and Ned was awarded the bear while the man glared at Kayleigh.

"I believe you've played the game before," he sneered.

"So I have," she replied. "So I have."

"How did you know it was the second cup?" Jacob questioned as they walked away.

"As he slid the cups, he palmed the dice out," she explained. "He knows better than to simply hold onto them, which some con men would do, but more and more customers are on to this and insist on seeing the man's hands, so he makes it look as though it will definitely be under one cup while he moves the dice to another. It's an old and short-shell con. He just happened to get caught. Anyway, we'll be a good advertisement for his business. Others will try for a prize."

"I see," Jacob replied. It wasn't as though he had never witnessed a shell game before, but he wondered even more about Miss O'Brien.

As they went down the fairway set up by the workers, the booths looked more and more familiar to Kayleigh, as though she was stepping back in a warped mirror. *They couldn't be the same*, she thought. What were the chances that the booths would look the same and be set in the same way?

A crowd was beginning to develop, with men coming in from the docks and mothers and wives coming out for a change of pace. The streets were becoming lively and animated.

As they progressed, music began to fill the air. Kayleigh was recognizing more and more of the tunes, and she began to feel a slow sense of panic. The panic was fully realized when a young man playing the banjo called out to her, "Kayleigh, hey girl, over here! Look, Peaches, it's Kayleigh! Pop, it's Kayleigh!"

"You know the musicians?" Jacob asked with a grin and a quizzical look on his face.

The fall evening was setting in, the last of the crickets chirping and a cool breeze blowing. It was a beautiful evening, but, again, Kayleigh was feeling the panic.

"Well, yes, some of the…I…" she began when the older gentleman playing the fiddle called out, "Is that really you, Kayleigh?"

"It sure is!" assured the striking woman, readying herself to sing. "Kayleigh, you get on up here and play the fiddle with Pop. Nobody can put a bow to a fiddle like you," she finished in a distinct southern twang.

A crowd was gathering around the platform where the performers stood, and many were looking on at Miss O'Brien with unabashed curiosity and wonder.

"Why don't you go on up and play?" Jacob asked, still smiling. "It's great that you have that kind of a gift."

Kayleigh thought that she should have felt cornered, but given the encouragement and the press of the crowd, she surprisingly felt that she would like the feel of a fiddle and the applause of a crowd again. Jacob then suddenly gave her a slight lift onto the first step going up to the stage, and she could hear several children saying, "Look, it's Miss O'Brien!"

She quietly approached Pop and touched his hand. He beamed and handed her a fiddle. Part of the crowd was now beginning to realize that Pop was blind. As Peaches announced that the crowd was "in for a treat" with "two of the finest fiddle players God ever put on earth," Kayleigh readied the bow and herself.

As they played and wove their music through renditions of "Soldiers Joy," "Sally Goodin," and "Cotton Eyed Joe," the audience was both mesmerized and enthused. The initial shock that the school teacher could play the fiddle was replaced by admiration. Jacob smiled and wondered just who this girl really was and what she had been through. This was not the typical school teacher.

Later that evening, after he had said his goodbyes to Miss O'Brien, Jacob was having a beer with some of the men from the dock when he saw Kayleigh enter the inn.

The surprise that he felt also registered on Lucy's face as they both watched Kayleigh go directly to the table where the older gentleman from the fair was sitting.

"Well, he said that he was meeting a 'young lady,'" Lucy whispered to Jacob. "I just never dreamed that it would be Miss O'Brien."

Like reading a novelette as a guilty pleasure, the two watched and listened as Kayleigh conversed with the man she called "Pop."

The older gentleman's face came alive, but his hands shook as he began to talk with Kayleigh. She took note of his hands. She also noticed her friend reach shakily into his pocket. She then reached over and withdrew his tobacco pouch and cigarette papers and rather expertly rolled a near-perfect cigarette. Removing his matches from the other shirt pocket, she struck one on the heel of her shoe and lit the cigarette for him.

Lucy and Jacob watched in fascination while some of the other men, waiting on their meals or casually eating their dinner, were caught with their mouths open.

"I wish I was that old man," one drawled.

"She's probably a cold fish," Neb Darius said, sneering. The truth was that Darius had made several overtures to Kayleigh, which she had simply ignored.

Jacob gave them all a disgusted sidelong glance and said, "I doubt that." Inwardly, though, he had to admit that she was, on the one hand, a buttoned-up little school teacher, but, on the other hand, she knew a little more of the world than the average school teacher.

Kayleigh and "Pop" talked for quite a while before he and Peaches left. She told him that he needed to stop smoking, and he smiled and told her that he was too old to give up his one final vice.

She took his arm and walked him down the street before walking back to her own small home at the schoolhouse. Jacob watched curiously as she made her way home until a woman's voice interrupted his reverie.

"Mr. McVale?" she questioned as she approached. It was the same twanging southern accent that he had previously detected in the woman called "Peaches, the woman with the vibrant red hair who had sung while Kayleigh played.

"Mr. McVale, I just wanted to have a talk with you about my girl, Kayleigh," she said, raising her chin just a trifle as though not unaccustomed to confrontation when needed. "I noticed you walking with her earlier, and you seem like a good sort. Could I walk with you for a bit?"

"Certainly," Jacob replied, now even more curious as to the bond that these three seemed to share.

He motioned for Peaches to walk with him, and they began to keep in step as they strode back toward the tent near the musicians' stage, which is where he assumed she was headed.

"Kayleigh is really special to Pop and me," she began. "She wasn't much more than thirteen when she came to us. Her stepfather and step-brothers were working the games with us, and they had their own con on the side. They used Kayleigh like bait and then had her do some of their thieving and pick-pocketing. I didn't say anything at first because you have to be careful in my line of work. I wasn't sure what was going on, but then, when I could tell that she was frightened for her life, Pop and I got involved.

"I'd been watching her anyway. Her mama and baby sister traveled with them, and she was always around the baby, taking care of it and helping.

"Then, one day, she just wasn't around. So, when Pop and I began to ask about her, we found out that the sheriff had gotten hold of her and taken her to jail.

"Of course, we went and bailed her out. There she was, pretty as a picture, tears streaking those rosy cheeks, sitting in between two women who were no strangers to being in jail.

"We told her that our condition was that she would stay with us and learn to sing and play in our show. She agreed but also begged to still see her little sister. Of course, we agreed to that.

"Our biggest shock was how talented she already was. She could play the piano and fiddle almost instantly, and I tell you, Mr. McVale, the girl has a voice that could make an angel weep. (Getting her to sing, though, is a different matter.)

"She is the closest thing Pop and I ever had to a daughter. Her mother just didn't have much of a connection to her, and we did.

"Now, I'm not saying that we were the best thing for her, and I knew how smart she was, how much she loved books, and how badly she wanted to go to school.

"So, no one was happier than I was when she took her tests for eighth grade and passed with high marks, but no one was sadder either. It about killed poor Pop. She was his pet, and she didn't mind 'being his eyes' for him."

Peaches leaned in more closely, "Pop got hold of bad whiskey back years ago before he found Jesus, and he lost his eyesight," she explained. "Mr. McVale," she continued, "I'm telling you these things because I don't think you're the type to run and blab to the whole town, and I think maybe you have the same protective-type instinct as Pop. I guess I'm just telling you because I'd like to know that you're keeping an eye on her," she finished.

Jacob turned to her as they reached her tent. "I already am," he said with a quiet smile.

The next evening, as the assorted workers and musicians packed to leave, Kayleigh could be seen bidding Pop and Peaches goodbye. Jacob noticed that Kayleigh leaned in as Pop whispered to her that she could go with them.

As Jacob, busy with helping other members of the fair, approached, he could hear her say, "Pop, you saved me once, and it was one of the greatest moments of my life, but I don't need to be saved anymore, not from the trap I was in at that time, anyway."

As Jacob, busy with helping other members of the fair, approached, he could hear her say, "Pop, you saved me once, and it was one of the greatest moments of my life, but I don't need to be saved anymore, not from the trap I was in at that time, anyway."

She kissed him on the cheek and helped him, along with a strong arm from Jacob, board the wagon that Peaches would drive. She blew Peaches a kiss and made her way back to the schoolhouse alone.

Kayleigh would never stop missing them, but she knew that they could not settle in one place, and she did not yet know where she might settle. She would hold them in her heart forever.

CHAPTER 33: THE MARGARET RUTH LETTERS

One thing that Kayleigh always looked forward to was her letters from Margaret Ruth. Margaret Ruth was still a force to be reckoned with, but also a true loyal champion to those she cared about, and she cared about Kayleigh. Margaret Ruth continued to give the impression that she had arrived to ignite a scene, direct it, and finish it as she saw fit.

August 1890

Dearest Kayleigh,

Well, it's been the "same old, same old" here in Boise, that is, until I met a certain "Professor Gallant," who claims to know you!

We have, if you can believe it, "been keeping company" with each other. Now, you know me. I can be a bit brazen or bold with men, but it generally means nothing. Well, "Katie bar the door," it means something this time! We're a bit unsuited to each other at first glance, but once we got past those first glances, we were more alike than we were different.

Frankly, this could not have come at a better time. My situation with Boise is not necessarily the best. I don't have any real problems with the children (Oh, there are always a few little "wise crackers"), but mainly, I don't agree with any of the choices or mandates that the school board makes.

For example, I requested a few badly needed supplies, such as slates, chalk, books, etc., and I was told that "a real teacher could make do with whatever she had." Well, of course, that's true, but it's not as though this school board can't afford supplies. (They have more than enough for their fancy little dinners.) So, I've been a bit on the downside and holding my tongue since I need the job, but Professor Gallant has me dreaming of better things in life.

What about you, little friend? Have you found anyone? You do know that it's time for you to do so, don't you? A true man will understand about Cassie. A true man will understand about anything if he loves you. Remember that!

Well, I've got to go. Gallant is here at the door, and I'm one foot out the door.

Love, Margaret Ruth

***

August 1890

Dear Margaret Ruth,

Yes, I did meet Professor Gallant when I worked with the Dream Town Carnivals. I believe he was a full-time teacher at some point. He was very charming and knowledgeable.

I understand your situation with the school board. Fortunately, I've been hired by a group that tries to meet all school supply needs. In fact, they even added an addition to the lower school house.

Also, Mitch and Zach seem to be in teacher heaven with a complete teaching and living facility for the fifth through tenth levels.

It's wonderful that you have met someone, and it seems to be going well; however, marriage may never be a possibility for me.

It is my wish, though, that somehow we could be together in one school. With you, Mitch, Zach, and possibly Professor Gallant, I would have my family about me each day.

Love, Kayleigh

***

September 1890

Dear Kayleigh,

Did you know that a new program or system is being developed for schools so that instead of just one school master, principals are being appointed at each school level?

Of course, primarily, men are being appointed to these positions, but they are considering women for elementary principal positions. I think this is the modern trend for women and educators.

Professor Gallant currently teaches at the upper school, and what a spell-binder he can be with his lessons.

Take note, little friend, please don't count yourself out on marriage. If you'll just look around, there are probably three or four men looking right back at you. They always did.

I really don't hear anything about Faithful. One old timer in town told me that he had known a man who once went there for some type of sanctuary, but he also indicated that it was hard to find. Oh well, who knows? I may try to find it myself someday.

Say, listen, do you ever do any of the old comedy bits you used to tell me about? You could raise money for your new schools there in Faithful. That could be a hoot.

Hope to hear from you soon.

Love, Margaret Ruth

P.S. Regale me with a story. Surely, you've had some sort of adventure!

***

September 1890

Dear Margaret Ruth,

Truth be told, I've had several adventures already. However, I think I'll "regale" you with my "horse adventure." That's right, I said "horse adventure."

As you know, I'm terrified of the creatures, but I keep it as covered up as I can. Several have suspected my fear, though, including my students.

One of the board members (Mr. Jacob McVale) offered the use of a horse and wagon to make things easier on me when I make home visits, but, of course, I made excuses and declined. (I may be wrong, but I felt that I caught a glimmer of discernment in his eyes. He always seems to know things.)

Back to my story, though, one of my little first-level students took suddenly ill with a fever. I felt it imperative to get her to her mother and the doctor, so I borrowed a horse from one of my older students, Teddy Measer, who often keeps the animal tethered outside the schoolhouse.

Somehow, I managed to appoint students to watch the younger children and sound the school bell while I mounted the beast and had one of the bigger boys hand little Karin (the child in distress) into my arms.

When I tried to get her mother to the door of their house by shouting, I was unsuccessful. One of the neighbors appeared and said that Karin's mother was at the Mercantile, and she agreed to have her meet me at the doctor's office.

The doctor praised me for getting the child there as quickly as I did, and he was able to decrease her fever and begin on her medicine. Her poor mother was both frightened and grateful.

Then, oddly enough, Mr. McVale was there, smiling at me. I know that he is a busy man with a business to run, so I was surprised at his presence. He offered to take me back to the schoolhouse, but I requested that he return the horse to Teddy Measer's home. (By then, it was time for school to be dismissed, and many of the children had already walked home.)

So, there is my "adventure" for the week, dear Margaret Ruth. I can't wait to hear from you.

Love, Kayleigh

***

October 1890

Dear Kayleigh,

For the "Love of Mike!" Catch a clue and be friendly to Mr. McVale. He sounds like a nice man to me. Does he have some type of impediment? Is he really short or ugly? Well, even so, it couldn't hurt to be nice to him.

I'm really proud of you, though, and how you took on the situation. Your confidence should be increasing. You seem to have put behind you the incident in which your brutal brothers threw a mouse on you and pushed you in front of that horse in New York.

As for me, I'm having doubts about Professor Gallant. Word has spread to Boise that he was dismissed in disgrace from his last teaching assignment in Detroit. Also, he was in charge of the exotic dancing act at the carnival. Did you know that?

The truth is, he is neither a professor nor a gallant man. He is, instead, a well-educated phony. Therefore, I have decided to confront him on all of these points. I can stand a person with a past, but not one who has concealed so much and presented himself as a much different character.

Your Hurt and Betrayed Friend,

Margaret Ruth

***

October 1890

Dearest Margaret Ruth,

I suspect that Professor Gallant (or whoever he really is) adopted the most protective identity that he could imagine for himself, as we all do at one time or another.

He was most kind to me when I was in need of tutoring for my school examinations. He has also helped others dear to me (You remember me speaking of Peaches.) when they needed help with their reading and writing.

I guess that I'm trying to tell you that the Professor has a good heart if a misplaced sense of grandeur, and, of course, you, dear Margaret Ruth, are a strong enough match for any man. That is to say, I believe you could more than "take him in hand."

As for me, I hardly think that someone in the position of town leadership that Mr. McVale is in would ever be interested in the likes of me. No, my life and future is Cassie, and I will have her soon. Then, life will fall into place, and my heart will be light.

All My Love, Kayleigh

***

October 1890

My Sweet Friend,

I have heard a good bit about little Cassie through Gallant.

I know that you love her so much, dear, but you must also make a good life for yourself. Although I've never been to Faithful, I feel somehow that I know the town and know that the town has taken you in.

I may well be trying to find Faithful myself one day. I told Gallant straight out that I had decided to keep him, but he must "come clean" with me and be who he truly is.

So, I have now met Torrence William Blachett (no wonder he changed his name, besides his fear of the law). It seems he encouraged young men and women whom he had in class in Detroit to express themselves through poetry.

Two of the young people expressed their love for each other through this communication. It was not meant to be read aloud, but, as students will do, two boys took hold of their poems and read them.

Gallant was then beaten and driven out of town by the fathers of the young man and woman. He was accused of both corruption of youth and of being an encourager of fornication. It is only by God's grace that he escaped with his life or avoided a trial and hanging. (He said that at one point during the beating, he actually thought that he was dead.)

So, we have agreed on a more honest but genteel name. His middle name is William, so I will be calling him Will from now on, as will everyone, and our married name will be Gallant—Margaret Ruth Gallant, oh my! In the meantime, I plan on keeping him in check. I love a good fantasy myself, but I am, at heart, a realist.

You take heart, my sweet girl. I pray continuously for you and that God will lead the right one to you.

Your Forever Friend, Margaret Ruth

CHAPTER 34: A DOLL, A BID, A DINNER

A month after school began, the town had begun to buzz with the talk of the fair, the church bazaar, and the auction. The fair had not turned out to be the disaster that Kayleigh had feared, but she wasn't about to take any more chances. She had basically decided not to become any more involved in the town events than necessary, but plans often take different turns. As the bazaar and auction approached, Kayleigh was beginning to realize that she might be expected to make an appearance.

After saying her goodbyes to Peaches and Pop on Saturday morning, Kayleigh could see the comings and goings of people from the church to the inn. She knew that people could buy things at the bazaar, silently bid on odds and ends at the auction, and then witness the traditional old "bid on the girl's homemade pie and win a dinner with her."

Kayleigh was familiar with the process and had managed to avoid it in several other towns. However, she was never quite sure whether she avoided it for fear of not being bid on or for fear of actually being bid upon.

She was contemplating whether to get a jump on her lessons for Monday or take a bath when there was a knock on the door.

Lydia and Maddie stood on the small front porch and smiled widely as she opened the door.

"Hi, Kayleigh," Lydia began. "We were just headed over to Lucy's, where the auction is being held, and we thought that you might like to go along."

Before she could answer, Maddie began. "Mary would love to see her teacher there, and, well, I'm sure that Jennifer Anne would too," she said, looking over at Lydia. "You know it's important for children to see their teachers in different settings."

They've rehearsed this, Kayleigh thought, somewhat amused.

"Well, I'm not really dressed," Kayleigh started her excuse.

"That's fine," Lydia assured her. We'll wait," and with that, they quietly slipped past Kayleigh and into the house.

Kayleigh did the only thing that she could. She raised her hands and shoulders in a shrug of surrender, headed into the bedroom, shut the door, and put on her one good school outfit. After all, they had both been wonderful friends to her.

She could vaguely hear the two of them whispering as she changed from her blue skirt and striped shirt. There was a plot afoot, and she was not sure just who it involved yet, other than herself.

As they made their way down the street to Lucy's, Lydia and Maddie chatted about how they had seen her at the fair the day before but missed her at the church bazaar that morning.

They continued by detailing the silent auction rules that prevailed at Lucy's and hinted at another "mystery" event.

Mystery, my eye, Kayleigh thought. *There will be some kind of woman-meat auction.*

However, she felt oddly excited about actually going to a town event. It had felt good to get out and about the night before, and she had to admit to herself that it felt good now, too.

Lydia and Maddie excused themselves when they entered so that they could help with the different preparations, leaving Kayleigh to browse the various "silent auction" items. Both women had cautioned Kayleigh that some of the items were new and "quite nice while others were "pure junk" or leftovers from the bizarre. However, arranged in neat, long rows, the inn had been transformed into a "Shop of Wonders," according to the sign.

It was fun for Kayleigh, though. She loved browsing and thinking about how each item could be used, and then she saw it. It caught her eye and captivated her heart.

It was a doll, but not just any doll. The hair looked genuine, a mass of blonde curls. The blue glass eyes were so realistic that they caused her to stop for a moment, reassuring herself that they were not real. Her face was beautiful, with high cheekbones and pouty lips. Her dress was actual lace with a silk sash.

She was a beauty, and for once, Kayleigh desperately wanted something that served no practical purpose, not for herself but rather for her little sister. The child had never had a doll (even a rag one), and in reality, she never would have a doll if Kayleigh did not provide it.

The bids were written on folded pieces of paper in front of the beauty, and the bidders were continually warned not to "peek" at the "secret" bids. However, Kayleigh didn't need to see the bids to know that it was unlikely that she could ever afford her.

There was also a line of mothers and little girls building in the back of Kayleigh with excited chatter over the doll. She hastily wrote out a bid, hoping it was slightly higher than the last on the list, and signed it. She both hoped and dreaded that she might have the highest bid. She could not afford the little work of art, and judging by the line behind her, she would not even be in the running.

Kayleigh was completely unaware that Jacob was watching her at a distance. He took in the look in her eyes, the touch of her hand on the doll's blonde curls, and her skeptical, frustrated look when she wrote in her bid. He motioned to Lydia, and together, they concocted a plan.

As the night progressed, Kayleigh enjoyed chatting with students and parents, and, just as she expected, there was beginning to be talk of a pie auction, connected with a dinner for two, per each gentleman with the highest bid and lady who had her pie bid upon.

Kayleigh also did not notice that Lydia purposely waited out the others in line at the Silent Auction. Making sure that she was the very last in line before Maddie called, "Time's up for the silent auction," she peeked at each bid while Maddie began asking for "everyone's attention" and then placed the highest bid and signed "Anonymous."

The final piece of this well-meant conspiracy was Maddie placing Kayleigh's name on the apple crumb pie that she had made. Kayleigh's unawareness continued, however, as she became preoccupied with talking to Mitch, Zach, and their wives before the announcement of the pie and dinner auction began.

Lucy stood on a chair and began to review the crowd on the rules, "Now, gentlemen, remember, this is a bid on a lady's pie and dinner with her on whatever evening you both agree to. Of course, the highest bid wins, but let's avoid any name-calling or sore losers. After all, it's in good fun, and the money will help our building fund for both the school and the church. We'll announce the silent auction bid winners after this."

Kayleigh rolled her eyes as Mr. Darius began the bid announcements. Well, at least she wouldn't have to endure this since she didn't have a pie entered. In fact, she watched in amusement as, one by one, the young and still unmarried women of the town had their pies and attentions bid upon.

Kayleigh had already begun to make her way to the door. She'd much rather get ready for bed and read a book than endure this. Then, in shock, she heard her name called. She hadn't made a pie!

Mr. Darius continued, "Now our own school teacher has an apple crumb pie to offer," Neb continued. What is my bid for this wonderful confection?"

The crowd grew very still and quiet, just as her worst dreams had always conveyed.

"Is she allowed to court?" a woman whispered a bit too loudly.

"Well, I'll just start then," Mr. Darius offered, smiling widely. Neb Darius was, of course, a widower and confirmed bachelor who enjoyed the company of women, and although he was respected to some degree, it was well-known that he liked himself more than anyone else. "One dollar," he bid.

"Three dollars!" Cal Lindstrom called out. There was shock and murmuring, but a large grin from Cal. Kayleigh, herself, was barely breathing, sure that she would awaken, and she was silently containing the nagging feeling that some young girl would say at any moment that Cal was not for her. This feeling was confirmed by the dagger stare several young ladies were giving her.

Kayleigh could literally hear her heart beating out of her chest when Darius began the chant of "going once, going twice…"

"Five dollars!" came a clear and resonant voice. "I bid five dollars," said Jacob McVale.

"Why, Jacob!" Miss Griggs chastised amid quiet laughter.

"Oh, come now, people," Jacob reasoned. "It's for our building fund, and part of that will go toward the school and what our teachers need. I'm just thinking of it that way."

So that was it, Kayleigh thought. Well, that made sense. She was a charity object.

"Going once, going twice, gone to Jacob McVale," Neb Darius announced. "We have a highly valued little school teacher, don't we?" Darius concluded among laughter. "Maybe we can improve a paycheck or two," he said, laughing at his own joke.

She knew that her cheeks were on fire, but she tried to smile as she quietly backed her way to the door and walked around to the path in the back of the inn. That path would take her straight to the back of the school house and safety.

Her hands shook as she unlocked the back door and made a bee-line to lock the front door. She sat down in the old rocker in front of the fireplace and hugged herself. "It's all over now," she told herself. "You can find a way to pay Mr. McVale back, and you'll be gone from this town in May."

She had a piece of bread and a cup of tea for dinner, and she was almost beginning to be calm enough to prepare for bed when there was a knock.

"Kayleigh," Lydia called. "Could we talk for a few moments?"

She opened the door to find Lydia standing with a box, "Could I come in?" She motioned with a head bob to the passing town's people making their way to their homes for the evening.

"All right," Kayleigh stepped back and waved her in. "Please have a seat."

"Thank you," Lydia said as she sat on the small settee. "Please sit with me," Lydia pleaded.

Kayleigh sat down, and Lydia began to talk, her eyes a bit anxious but determined.

"Kayleigh," she started, "I'm sorry if Maddie and I overstepped our friendship, but sometimes you just see something that needs to happen with just a bit of a push."

"What do you mean?" Kayleigh asked. "What do you think you're seeing?"

"Well," Lydia began and hesitated, "you and Jacob—I think you'd be good for each other."

"Is that what all of that was about?" Kayleigh questioned in disbelief. "I don't think Mr. McVale has that kind of interest in me."

"Well, why do you think that he bid that high, Kayleigh?" Lydia asked in disbelief.

"I think he explained it," Kayleigh returned. "He was trying to help the funding for the school and the church.

"He could have done that privately, Kayleigh," Lydia reminded her. "Naturally, he wasn't going to just shout out, 'I like Miss O'Brien.' Men have their pride. He's very interested in you, just like several other men in this town are, but in a less, well, obvious way.

"You can't tell me that men haven't been interested in you before, Kayleigh," Lydia was not going to let go of the topic. "Is there a reason why you're not interested? Can you tell me what has happened?"

"Let it go, Lydia," Kayleigh cautioned. "Maybe I will go with Mr. McVale if he's really serious about it and asks me. Otherwise, I guess he can consider it a contribution."

"Alright," Lydia conceded. "That's fair enough. This is yours, by the way," she said, handing the box to Kayleigh.

"What is this?" Kayleigh asked suspiciously.

"I'll tell you what. I'll get out of your way and let you take a look," Lydia smiled. "Now, are we alright? I'd hate to lose your friendship, Kayleigh. I really would. You've meant the world to Jennifer Anne and our family." Lydia was close to tears.

"Oh my goodness, of course, Lydia," Kayleigh answered. "You're one of the dearest ladies I've ever met," and in her private thoughts, she thought that she might one day open up to Lydia, but then again, probably not.

After they said their goodbyes, she sat down and opened the box, and a small note fell out. "I hope that you enjoy the doll," it read, and it was signed "One of your admirers."

Days went by, and Kayleigh recognized couples from the auction coming and going into Lucy's Diner for their dinners. Most looked more than pleased to be with each other or romantically in love. Then again, a few looked like they were just having a good time. Only one couple that she had observed looked completely awkward, but she was the only woman who was bid upon that had not been to dinner.

Mr. McVale had not been to the school of late, but then she had always taken it for granted that no one would ever ask her out, so why should this be different?

In the meantime, though, there was more than enough to do with her students. Four levels of instruction were not easy to prepare for. Then, there were also requisitions for student supplies, school district reports, for which she always seemed to be responsible, rather than Mitch and Zach, meetings with parents, and the cleaning and maintenance of the school house itself.

There were also her responsibilities to her younger sister and the small amount of shopping she did for herself. Mr. and Mrs. Campbell, who ran the mercantile, post, and telegraph office, had already commented to Mr. McVale that they "Didn't know how she made it with the little money she had left after wiring most of it to her sister's guardians."

Of course, some of the ladies in town were not as kind, with comments such as, "Her wardrobe seems to be rather limited," and no one was more aware of this than Kayleigh herself.

She had one complete outfit for church, one skirt and two shirtwaists for the school week, and one blue skirt for Fridays and shopping on Saturdays; and, of course, there was her round brim hat with the lariat style tie that she also wore on Fridays for recess.

However, having traveled a good bit, Kayleigh was also aware that this was much more than many women had in this part of the country. So, for the most part, she was thankful, but occasionally, she did wish for more.

One Friday, fatigued from the school day and week, she reflected on some of those wishes after leaving the telegraph office. Her lower back felt as though it would break in two, and hot pain shot through her unmercifully. This was always a sure sign that her back would ache and hurt her for several days. It was also a time when she was reminded of her continual pain and loneliness.

She was then reminded, by the growling in her stomach, that she was intensely hungry. She had started to buy an apple but then realized that with paying for the telegraph service and her postal fee, she would not have any change left. She had deftly replaced the apple, unaware that the action had been seen. She planned to go straight to the schoolhouse, open her post, which should contain her mail-order medicine for Dr. Healthful's Back Pain Elixir, and go to bed.

To add to her dismay, it was at this point that Mrs. Campbell pulled her aside and whispered, "It's alright to ask for help, sweetie. In fact, it's downright normal. Let us run a tab for you," she pleaded with her eyes and continued.

"You don't have to keep putting items back," she whispered.

Jacob had returned to town earlier in the day, met with his brother, inspected the new boat that they had bought, and talked with him about the bank terms of the loan he had taken.

After seeing his brother and brother-in-law, Jacob met Lucy, who had just finished her shopping and was headed back to the inn. They chatted about his trip and the Inn and Diner's profit for the year when they saw Kayleigh through the window at the Campbell's.

"Speaking of the Inn and Diner, you dear man, there's a very hungry young lady there that you owe a dinner to," she nodded her head in the direction of the mercantile and continued, "Why don't you ask her tonight?" Lucy asked, and she waved as she made her way to Mademoiselle Jeanette's Dress Shop.

McVale shrugged. According to Lydia, he had misspoken at the auction, although he wasn't sure how. Oh well, he wanted to see her, and this seemed to be the best way.

She looked extremely fatigued, and he knew that he needed to approach her carefully. He didn't want to startle her, but he also didn't want to miss his opportunity.

"Miss O'Brien," he said gently, moving up closer to her as she emerged from the storefront with her few purchases. "How are you?"

"Oh, hello, Mr. McVale," she responded, and he noticed the dark circles under her eyes and the slightly disconnected response.

"You seem to receive a good bit of post," Jacob commented while wondering if any of the letters were from a man.

Kayleigh clutched her letter from Margaret Ruth. "I have a teaching friend in Idaho. She was, and is, a wonderful friend to me. Her name is Margaret Ruth, and I really look forward to her letters," she explained.

"Ah," Jacob said, somewhat relieved. "The friends from our past are sometimes the very best."

Kayleigh nodded in agreement.

"Would you like to have our dinner tonight?" he asked, hoping that the request appeared very casual. "Have you already eaten?"

"Actually, I think I've forgotten to eat today, if that's possible. I was headed home to eat a bite of something," she smiled.

"Well, why not just cross the street with me and eat now?" he asked, somewhat aware of the enthusiasm charging into his voice.

"It's just…I'm not really dressed for it," she struggled to explain as she removed her hat, causing her hair, which she often wore down on Fridays, to spill out about her face.

"Why, you look fine!" he assured her, wishing that she would always wear her hair down. "I would really be appreciative if you'd accompany me." He leaned over confidentially and said, "I really hate eating alone," and with that, he held out his arm.

Once again, hesitantly, she took it, and he escorted her down the street to the diner that Lucy ran next door to the tavern. Lucy, herself, was inspecting the tables and instructing the two young women who worked there on how to set another table.

When she looked up, Lucy smiled very brightly, with a bit of a gleam in her eye. She had hoped that this would happen because it was beginning to look as though it wouldn't.

"Well, here's a lovely couple!" Lucy greeted them. "Come to take advantage of your dinner, I take it?" Lucy continued and motioned for them to sit. Other people and obvious couples were beginning to enter for the dinner hour, but Lucy put them at what she considered her best table.

Kayleigh was more than a bit embarrassed and beginning to feel her cheeks flush as people in the diner began to give knowing glances and whisper. One older woman, eating with her daughter's family, patted Kayleigh's hair and gave her an intense look as she passed by. Lucy simply gave them two hand-printed menus and directed one of the young women to wait on them.

As Lucy walked away, she reflected on how pretty Kayleigh was and wished that the young teacher had the clothes to match. She thought about how she and her husband had once been and how she had enjoyed dressing up for him, but that had vanished a long time ago, with too many years passing after his death.

"Well," Kayleigh began, trying to put a good and normal spin on the situation. "What is good to eat here? What do you usually get?" she asked as sweetly as she could.

Jacob leaned over to her, putting his arm across the back of her chair. "I usually have the ham with potatoes and whatever vegetable they have for the day. Does that suit you?"

Kayleigh was aware of his nearness yet again, but she also felt as though she could have eaten the entire pig itself, along with a healthy dose of her pain medicine and some warm tea. She managed, however, to say, "Oh, of course. That would be perfect."

"Sally," he motioned to the young woman setting another table, "I think we're ready."

Sally, young, with her brown hair neatly pulled back and braided, smiled widely. She liked Jacob. He was one of her favorites. He was patient, never difficult, and usually tipped a bit.

Jacob gave the order and turned to Kayleigh. "Do you drink coffee?"

"I'd prefer a cup of tea if you have it and it's not trouble," she spoke to Sally.

"Oh, I think that can be done, don't you, Sally?" Jacob asked.

"Of course, Mr. McVale," Sally smiled.

"And please, sweetheart," Jacob reminded, "bring us the sugar and cream as well."

"Sure," Sally nodded and made her way to the kitchen.

"I just assumed you might want sugar or cream," Jacob explained. "Personally, I take my coffee black."

"Yes," Kayleigh said reflectively. "You're exactly right. I like to have both."

The meal progressed normally, and Kayleigh ate well, trying to hold back and conceal how hungry she was. Still, Jacob leaned over and let her know that she could have "seconds" and that Lucy was "quite generous about that."

Realizing that she must have eaten like a famished child, Kayleigh scooted the plate away from herself, dabbed at her mouth with her napkin, and said, "No, thank you, I'm finished. In fact, thank you for the dinner. You've been very generous."

"Well, it's not over," Jacob said, somewhat taken aback. He smiled warmly and reminded her, "We still have dessert and another coffee and tea. By the way, the apple pie was quite good."

Kayleigh rolled her eyes and sat back a bit in her chair, "Yes, Maddie did a great job," she smiled. "I think a conspiracy was afoot."

Jacob smiled and laughed.

"Why are you being so nice to me, Mr. McVale?" Kayleigh asked suddenly. "Is it a pity thing? Or do you feel a responsibility to the school board to keep an eye on me, the crazy little Irish woman? Did you lose a bet?"

He looked surprised for a moment but answered quickly. "I assure you that I do not pity you, and if I'm keeping an eye on you, it's because I like to look at you, but mainly, it's because I like you and what you've been able to do with the school, and, well, I just like talking to you."

"Speaking of talking," he continued as though no rather blunt question had been asked, "what do you think of the town?"

Kayleigh hesitated for a time, considering his answer, before giving hers. "I like the town very much," she said. "It has great potential for growth, and most people have been very kind to me."

"So, you don't think that Faithful is destined to be a small town forever?"

"Oh no," Kayleigh answered in a very decided way that amused Jacob, "it will be a large city one day. It has everything that it needs except a bridge and a railway station. Here, let me show you," and with that, she began to dig through her small cloth handbag for a spare scrap of paper and a crayon, which she often carried for the school children. She produced the paper but couldn't quite find the crayon. Jacob looked on, amused and in anticipation.

Finally, she stopped, blushed furiously, and felt in her hair. There, she discovered the crayon that she had quickly stashed after helping a child with a drawing.

She smiled, "And you said that I looked fine."

"You do," he smiled in return. "I don't think I noticed until now."

They both laughed as she smoothed out the paper. She then began to sketch the town, adding in the railway station and the bridge in the distance, which would transverse the bay.

Jacob watched in fascination as her sketching produced the town in the future. It was a work of art.

"Well, I mean, I'm just messin' about," Kayleigh said when she finished, "but I think it would look something like this." She slipped it over to him. "Of course," she continued, "I do warn you that it won't quite be Faithful anymore. I suspect it will take on a new identity and life."

"You know, you'll probably think I'm just saying this, but this is pretty much how I've pictured it, too," he looked up at her and smiled.

"Oh well," she said softly, and she reached to take it back at the same time that he put his hand on it to keep it. She drew her hand back quickly and managed to stammer out, "I was just…I can throw it away for you."

"No, please," he said. "I'd like to keep it if you don't mind. In fact, I'd like to show it to an engineer friend that I have."

"Oh, well, I can do it better, more to scale, you know," she answered.

He smiled widely, "I don't think you realize how good this is. Please, let me keep it."

"Well, alright," she conceded and then added, "I guess we should be going."

"Oh no, not yet, remember? We still have the pie coming. We can't leave before that," he grinned.

She grinned, despite herself, and they enjoyed the end of the dinner. As they rose to leave, poor Sally was trying to balance two glasses of water and a plate of fried chicken when she lost her footing and tripped into Kayleigh.

The other customers began to gasp, and poor Sally was mortified to tears. Jacob simply froze, but to his surprise, Kayleigh began to laugh. While remnants of the beer splashed on his jacket, she picked up a napkin and began to dab at her shirt and skirt.

She was still laughing when Sally tried to help.

By this time, Lucy both heard and saw the commotion. She sent word to get two more glasses of water and more fried chicken ready. "I'm so sorry," Sally managed to say.

"So am I," Lucy said, producing another clean napkin to dab away at Kayleigh's skirt.

"Don't worry about it," Kayleigh said, smiling. "I'll just be a little damp; however, I will give you a tip, Sally. Next time, carry the water and plate on a round tray. I've seen several around, so you don't have to carry everything directly in your hands." Lucy shook her head in agreement.

Sally looked a little dazed and confused but nodded. "Oh, and by the way, Miss O'Brien, I meant to tell you how cute the two of you look together," she said, motioning to both Kayleigh and Jacob. With that, Sally made her way to the kitchen as Kayleigh, once again, blushed.

Jacob looked on in surprise. He decided that he would never understand women. So many small details seemed to bother Miss O'Brien, but a small catastrophe like this with the water, she found funny.

Still, that was good. A major embarrassment and humiliation would have been a bad ending to an otherwise great evening. It was curious, though, how she had known the best way to carry drinks.

As they walked back to the schoolhouse, Jacob offered his jacket to Kayleigh, and, to his quiet delight, she took it. She was, after all, a bit chilly, and the water on her shirt was somewhat visible.

"Thank you," she replied as she took the jacket. He ventured to put his arm around her shoulders and help her with putting on the jacket. She stiffened a bit but then seemed to still see the humor.

As they walked, Jacob realized that at some point, Miss O'Brien had acquired a dog. It was the same dog that had frightened Miss Craddock into near hysterics. She was sure, based on what she described as his "maniacal" growl, that he had "mad dog" disease and should be "put down." He had followed her about for days with what she described as a "menacing and evil look."

Part sheepdog and part "who knows?" he always looked a little lopsided and lost. However, several of the upper school boys were determined to keep him around. In fact, two of them had kept him hidden and secretly fed him, but he was out and about again after Miss Craddock left.

When he first approached Miss O'Brien with the "menacing" growl, she stopped, put her hands on her hips, and told him with a good bit of authority, "Now, none of that. You're just out of sorts from hunger and thirst. Come along home now."

Within a few weeks, she had his fur brushed out, his paws treated for sores, and taught him to sit, stand on his hind legs, lie down, and roll over to both sides. He quickly became "Sawyer" in honor of Tom Sawyer because of his "misadventures" and "charm."

In the mornings, he obediently followed by Miss O'Brien's side and waited outside the schoolhouse for her or the children. In the evenings, he sat on the back porch waiting for Kayleigh's company or a chance at the fireplace hearth if the weather was chilly. Sawyer quickly became a good companion.

She found herself far more attached to the shaggy old beast than she had meant to be, but he helped with her loneliness, which she was trying to keep well hidden from humans. Sawyer, however, could have availability to all of her secrets.

So it was that Jacob had first discovered that he could see the back of Miss O'Brien's little house from his own home. He thought that he had heard a barking one morning and took his coffee to the back window of his cabin, which overlooked a ledge and the woods below, leading into the town.

From there, he saw Kayleigh and Sawyer. Sawyer was running about while Kayleigh hung laundry on the line just off her back porch. He laughed before he caught himself, feeling, again, a little like an interloper. However, now that he had made that discovery, he found himself drawn more and more to the back window before he went into work or town.

He learned that Miss O'Brien washed her hair outside on Saturdays, that she read the Bible and prayed before going to church on Sunday, that she fed, chastised, and petted Sawyer before heading to school each morning, and that she sometimes looked very sad and forlorn as she sat and read and wrote during the afternoons.

He had never been this interested in and fascinated by a woman on a regular day-to-day basis before. It continually caused him to think that there must be some way to break the ice with her.

So, as Kayleigh and Jacob approached the schoolhouse after their dinner, Sawyer appeared and began to growl at Jacob as though he knew what Jacob had been thinking.

"Sawyer, go home and be still, now!" Kayleigh commanded. The dog then lopped off, giving a few backward glances at Jacob.

"I'm impressed," Jacob said. "You definitely have charge of him, but I'm also wondering, why the name Sawyer? What's the significance of the name?"

"Don't tell me that you haven't heard of Mark Twain?" Kayleigh asked in wonder. "Why, I think his story of Tom Sawyer will be famous."

"Tom is a little boy and a bit of a scoundrel, always looking for a way into adventure. However, he has a good heart. You know, come to think of it, I think that you would enjoy the book very much. I can lend it to you," she offered.

"Well, how can I turn down great literature from a dear friend?" he questioned.

They laughed again as they approached the little house attached to the school, and when they made their way to the front porch, Jacob hesitated. He knew that a kiss with this lady might be inappropriate and might scare her away for good, yet he wondered about the approach and the possibility.

"Have you ever heard the story of the pilot dolphin?" he asked as they drew near to the front door.

"No, I can't say that I have," she answered. *Surely, this isn't a dirty story*, she thought. *He's always been such a gentleman.*

"The sailors of long ago sometimes followed the dolphins in addition to, or instead of, their compasses," Jacob began. "They were often as good as a map or sextant since they knew the currents.

"So, the sailors took to calling them 'pilot dolphins' and regarded them as friends. More than one time, they depended on them to lead them away from the shallows or out of the reefs.

"Of course, the pilot dolphins never stayed with just one boat. They loved to visit different ships and sailors, but then, one day, a dolphin seemed to be in distress. She stayed with one boat most of the day, making more noise than any of the sailors had heard from a dolphin before that day.

"Yet, she wasn't leading the sailors forward. They knew that she was leading them backward rather than forward and then in a circle.

"Finally, the captain told the crew, 'Boys, we won't know what she needs until we follow her,' and so they did.

"Now, in their minds, she might be leading them to a fellow dolphin in distress, but they didn't quite expect what they found."

By this time, Kayleigh was completely enthralled and didn't even notice that Jacob had circled directly in front of her while he held her hands gently in his.

"There was a calf, a baby dolphin, her baby, entwined in coiled rope that some other ship had discarded. The baby could not free itself. It had already turned completely on its side, and its breathing was slowing.

"The sailors immediately cut the ropes, freeing the calf. It, of course, returned immediately to its mama, and she nudged him and swam with him, making sure he was alright."

Jacob tilted his head slightly and leaned in even closer, and without even realizing it, Kayleigh mirrored him and did the same.

"After that, the mama dolphin was never far from the sailors and their boat, even after her baby grew up and left.

"They named her their 'Dearest Pilot,' and she never left them; and, when the sailors leaned out to her, she would come up and press her mouth toward their cheeks."

Jacob leaned in yet further, as did Kayleigh, when a shrill little girl's voice pierced the evening, "Hi, Miss O'Brien! What is Mr. McVale doing on your porch?"

Kayleigh shook her head briefly as if clearing her thoughts and reverie. "Hello, dear," she called out. "I'll see you in school tomorrow."

"For goodness sake, Abigail," her mother said, pulling the little girl along. "Let Miss O'Brien have a moment."

Oh, good Lord, Kayleigh thought. *What am I doing?*

"Well, good evening, Mr. McVale," she managed. "Thank you again for the lovely dinner, and, um, I'll clean your jacket for you and get it back to you if that's okay."

Jacob had been transfixed by her soft gaze, but she had now turned away. Whatever had been in her heart and mind for a few precious seconds was now gone. Kayleigh simply felt that she had danced this dance before, but she also knew that she had been completely enthralled for the time that Jacob told his story.

She reached for the door handle and realized it was on the other side of the door. What was wrong with her? she wondered.

Jacob smiled and said that he hoped to see her the next day.

"Hi, Mr. McVale!" Abigail shouted as he left the porch.

"Hello, dear," he returned through clenched teeth.

And so it was that although Jacob was somewhat disappointed about missing out on a kiss, Kayleigh had a glimpse of genuine romance for perhaps the first time in her life.

In fact, later that week, Kayleigh had Ned deliver a full-scale, water-colored rendering of the future town of Faithful to Jacob's office at the docks. It was an impulse, and she knew that she might regret it, but she couldn't seem to help herself.

Jacob endured a little teasing about being the teacher's pet, which he took very good-naturedly. Later, he framed the sketch and hung it over the fireplace of his cabin. He was touched and wondered when he would see her again.

Then, once again, she could not help herself, and she hit upon a plan of returning his jacket and bringing him her copy of *Tom Sawyer*. It seemed a good plan, and she couldn't believe that she had hatched it.

She had never planned how to see a man in her life. So, with cautious excitement, the following evening, she took his jacket, which she had carefully cleaned, and her copy of Tom Sawyer as she headed toward his home.

She greeted several students on the way and glanced in shops as she walked, and this was when she saw it. Jacob was entwined with Mademoiselle Jeanette Marteen, who owned and ran the dress shop.

It did look a bit one-sided, as though Jeanette had grabbed him, and the encounter had progressed from there, but then, who could say?

Again, though, Lucy, who had witnessed the whole thing from across the street, made a note to let Jacob know that Kayleigh had seen his encounter, and, come to think of it, she was curious also.

As she turned back toward the schoolhouse, Jacob seemed to be trying to extract himself from the embrace, but that didn't do anything to alleviate the pain in her gut. She was foolish, and she should have known better.

After seeing the scene as she walked back to the inn from her shopping, Lucy sighed. Mademoiselle Jeanette Marteen was an opportunist. She saw a handsome, confident, prosperous man, and she wanted him. It was that simple.

Lucy knew what it was like to love, lose, and keep going with an illusion of happiness and contentment. She hoped Jacob would find real love this time.

CHAPTER 35: A CONVERSATION WITH "MR. MITCH"

After observing Jacob at the town fair and the auction, Mitch decided to wait for an opportune moment for a talk with him. He had two motives: wanting a report of how he and Zach were perceived as teachers and how Jacob felt about Kayleigh. Of course, he didn't plan on just out and out asking about either topic. Mitch was as good as Jacob when it came to the art of talk.

So, when one afternoon Mitch spotted Jacob coming out of the Campbell's Mercantile as he was dismissing his students from the upper school, he seized the moment and flagged him down. He opened with, "Hello, Mr. McVale," and a big wave, followed closely with, "Just wondered if I could have a brief talk with you."

"Of course, Mitch," Jacob answered. "How can I help you?"

Mitch motioned to one of the rockers on the front porch of the upper school, and Jacob settled his large frame into one while Mitch folded his long, thin legs into a seated position in another. They could not have been more different, Mitch with his tall, thin frame and angular face with a perpetual smile, and Jacob with his tall, broad-shouldered frame and sometimes a rather serious expression.

"I just wanted to approach you about your view of my performance to this point, as well as Zach's," Mitch explained and began to prepare to listen attentively.

"Well, just based on what I've heard, both the board and parents seem happy with what you and Zach are teaching and your methods. A few have said that you were both a bit unconventional, but most are happy with everything from your discipline to your subject matter. I think that you're off to a good start," he concluded and smiled.

"That's great, Mr. McVale, just great! That's the kind of review that Zach and I live for. So, everything is good with Kayleigh too, I presume," he was digging now.

"Why, yes," Jacob answered. "She seems to have settled quite well and won the trust of both the children and the parents. Why do you ask?" Jacob pursued.

"Well, I guess it's just a brotherly kind of thing," Mitch answered with an air of concern. "You see, she tends to withdraw socially. Please don't repeat this and let it stay between the two of us," he pleaded.

"It will go no further," Jacob guaranteed with a look of concern. "What do you mean by 'withdraw'?" he asked.

"I mean that once she has her school year started and the children in good order, she no longer joins in with town events or visits unless they directly concern the children. She is a bit of a hermit. It takes a lot of encouragement to break her out of her shell," he concluded.

"Why would that be, Mitch?" Jacob countered. "She's a lovely young lady and seems fairly confident. Why would she shun social events?"

"She doesn't want the attention of men, or most men, that is. I mean, I think that she could be encouraged or persuaded by the right type of man, but most men just put her off because of their behavior." He was grasping now for the right wording. The last thing he wanted was to make Kayleigh seem like a strange old maid.

"Has she had a bad experience?" Jacob questioned.

"She's had several bad experiences, none due to her behavior or anything that she said," Mitch continued. "You see, I know that she comes off as rather brash with Zach and myself, but she's actually rather retiring around most men. We are more like her brothers.

"I'm sure that you've heard the expression that 'hurting people find hurting people,' and that's pretty much exactly what happened to all three of us."

Mitch motioned to his right leg, "I most often tell people that I walk with a cane due to an accident in my youth, and, for the most part, that's true, except that it was no accident on my father's part. He threw me down the stairs of our New York flat in hopes that he could kill me.

"You see, I always looked out for my brothers and sisters. We were a large family, and I felt it was my responsibility to make sure they were safe and well each day, especially since my old man was not usually around.

"However, he didn't like that, or he was somehow jealous of it.

"Zach, on the other hand, is deaf in one ear," he continued as Jacob's face betrayed surprise. "That's because his mother grabbed him by it in order to slam him against the wall. (He jokes that his half-hearing matches his half-wit.)

"He was a very quiet and shy child and wouldn't speak up in class. One day, his teacher visited and said that she felt he was not bright enough to attend school. I guess, somehow, his mother felt that hard punishment would improve his abilities. Anyway, after the state orphanage took him, he became the comic and the clown. We met there and became like brothers.

"I'm not sure what has happened to Kayleigh, but I have a pretty good idea. She should have had a much better life. It's a wonder that she has survived and maintained her dignity and brightness.

"So, we formed our own family when we met at the State Teacher College. She sized us up and began treating us as her naive brothers. We had a lot of fun and even worked up an act that we used at the local inn. She had been waiting tables there and fending off men, but when they found out that we could all sing and Kayleigh and I could play the piano, they let us entertain for money put in my hat that we passed around.

"She knew that I was falling for her, so, in classic Kayleigh style, she found a woman for me. She'd been working part-time at the School for the Deaf, and she kept telling me about this very beautiful young woman who she was teaching to sign. Of course, that was my Rosemary, and Kayleigh was right. I adored her, and she lowered her standards to love me," Mitch gave a nervous laugh.

"She also found Caroline for Zach. She worked with Caroline also, and dear Caroline worked as a char woman at the school in order to make her expenses. As Kayleigh described her, 'She always has a smile on her face.'

"Kayleigh joked as she talked about matching both Zach and me with deaf ladies. 'This is perfect. They won't have to listen to either one of you,' she said. She's a good matchmaker. She just doesn't use that ability for herself," Mitch explained.

"You seem to be your own man, Mr. McVale," Mitch continued. "Could you watch out a bit for my friend? We're hoping that she'll stay for more than a year, but she'll have to feel safe. Would you be willing to help with that?" Mitch asked, his eyes pleading into Jacob's. "She seems to trust you."

"I'll tell you, as I already have another person who was concerned about her, 'I already am,'" Jacob replied, and with that, he stood, offered his hand to Mitch, and then quietly walked away.

CHAPTER 36: CASSIE'S VISIT

It was not uncommon that fall for Jacob to continue his visits to the schoolhouse in the afternoons, usually with a small crew of men, such as Mr. Thomas or Daniel. Together, they would work on repairing the school or finishing the new attached classroom. Parents (again, mainly curious mothers) would also drift in and out to collect children, chat with Miss O'Brien, or observe the new building.

Often, though, if Kayleigh was not working with a student one-to-one, Jacob would stay just a bit longer to ask if Miss O'Brien needed help with anything or to inquire how her teaching job was progressing.

Of course, usually, the answer was, "Everything's just fine, thank you." Today, however, she surprised him by shyly saying, "Well, I do have a small question for you."

"Of course," he replied, thankful to have an opening, "what is it?"

"I'm sorry. I just don't know who else to ask," she prefaced the question.

"It's fine," Jacob assured. "What is it?"

"My little sister will be coming through town with Mr. and Mrs. Langley, the people I board her with, next week. They need to go on further north to purchase seeds and supplies, and they'd like to leave her with me while they go. It would only be for three or four days," she finished hastily.

"Anyway, I need a Friday and a Monday off to be with her before they return. Would this be alright? I think that Lydia could take over. She has offered."

Jacob was touched by how hopeful she looked and that she had felt confident enough to ask him. "Of course," he answered. "I can't see any problem with that."

"Well, Mr. McVale, she is a bit different," Kayleigh said, leaning forward in the chair behind the desk and lowering her voice. "She is twelve years old, but she's very childlike, more like a six-year-old, in fact."

"I don't think that you have anything to worry about. People may say a few things, but most will have the manners to just be politely concerned. She'll be fine," he assured.

"Well, let's hope you're right," she answered while her own doubts fought with her intense desire to see her Cassie.

When the Langley couple pulled into town that next week, Kayleigh had already been waiting for an hour, pacing to and fro outside the mercantile and the telegraph office. Daniel McVale, aware of the little girl's impending arrival since his wife was teaching for the day, watched with curiosity as the two ran to each other.

In town, to check for any telegrams or letters directed to the business that he and his brother and Pete ran, he felt a bit like an interloper himself, who was witnessing Kayleigh and her little sister embrace. They were both oblivious, though, to him, and he, in fact, did need to get on with other errands before returning to work.

Still, he did notice that the little girl seemed to have a bit of a disability, and his heart went out to her. Having been through so much with Jennifer Anne, he knew that children and life were not always kind to anyone with a difference.

The Langleys exchanged polite conversation with Kayleigh, along with news of how Cassie had been. Then, after making sure that Cassie's little valise was unloaded, they made their way onward.

Kayleigh took the valise in one hand and Cassie's own hand in the other. Together, they made their way to the small house attached to the school, perfectly content with one another.

The next day, Kayleigh took Cassie on a small picnic beside a stream that she had noticed on a walk she took once after school. Cassie took great delight in wading into the stream and splashing. She would make up childish songs and kick the water about.

Kayleigh, in turn, delighted in seeing her happy. They had missed each other desperately, and she knew that the Langleys, although kind people, had very little idea of what constituted fun for a child.

As Kayleigh put away their picnic food and continued to sit and watch Cassie, she began to notice that other people had had the same thought for this beautiful Saturday afternoon.

She had bought Cassie a picture book that they had thoroughly read the night before and yet again at their picnic. Also scattered about were pictures that Cassie had drawn and etchings of a beautiful little house, which Kayleigh had done.

"Hi, Miss O'Brien!" Mary and Jennifer Anne called out. "We missed you Thursday and Friday."

"I missed you two girls," Kayleigh responded and waved.

Cassie suddenly walked back up the bank, emerging in front of Kayleigh like a little wet puppy. Although Kayleigh had tucked up the girl's skirt and tied it to the side, Cassie had still managed to soak a good bit of her dress.

The child was so happy that Kayleigh had a wild thought that maybe, just maybe, she could move Cassie to this town, and perhaps they could finally settle down together. In fact, so lost was she in this thought that she almost did not hear Mr. McVale when he greeted her. Startled, she turned to see him standing above her.

"Hello, Miss O'Brien. I'm glad to see that you are enjoying the day…and who is this young lady?"

Cassie turned her head into Kayleigh's shoulder and began sucking her thumb. "Cassie," Kayleigh whispered, "be a big girl and smile at Mr. McVale."

"This is my little sister, Cassie O'Connor," Kayleigh answered.

Jacob noted the difference in last names but simply asked, "Do you mind if I join you?" "I found a tiny frog, and I thought you might be interested in seeing him."

Cassie's eyes grew big as Kayleigh motioned for Jacob to sit with them.

He showed Cassie the tiny frog in the palm of his hand, and she was fascinated. She shyly moved over closer to him.

"I like frogs," she said quietly. "They hop a lot."

"Yes, they do," Jacob agreed. "I think it's time to let this one go ahead and hop away," he said as he freed the tiny frog.

They all laughed as they saw the small creature hop sideways along the bank of the stream.

"Look at my sissy's drawings," Cassie said, holding up an etching to Jacob.

"Cassie," Kayleigh cautioned, "Mr. McVale doesn't want to see our drawings…"

"Well, of course I do," Jacob protested. "Why wouldn't I?" He took the sketch and studied it as Cassie explained that it was a picture of the house that she and Kayleigh would one day have.

He noted the cottage style, the white fence around the front, the blue shutters, a blue bench in front of a white fence, and mountains in the background. There was a lot of detail, similar to the drawing she had done of the town with a bridge in the distance, the night that they had shared a dinner.

"We're going to live in Canada, in an artist and teachin' colny," Cassie continued. "Sissy almost has enough money."

"Colony," Kayleigh corrected quietly. She shrugged toward Jacob, "It's just one possibility," she said.

"Why not let Faithful be a possibility?" Jacob asked. "You're well-liked here. You could have a home here."

"Well, I'll think about it," Kayleigh said noncommittally, biting her lip.

"I like you, Mr. McVale," Cassie declared.

"Thank you, Cassie. I like you too," Jacob returned.

"You could marry him," Cassie turned to Kayleigh and said in a serious tone.

"Cassie, please!" Kayleigh exclaimed while blushing furiously.

Jacob smiled, partly because of Cassie's bluntness, partly because of the pretty way that Kayleigh blushed, and partly because he liked the idea.

"Well, you said maybe if you ever found someone who didn't have one foot in the grave and had good sense." Cassie reminded her of Kayleigh's own words once spoken to her mother.

"Do you ever stop talking?" Kayleigh asked, exasperated.

"No," Cassie grinned, and with that, Kayleigh began to tickle her while she exploded into giggles.

Jacob began to laugh, too. It was, in many ways, just a classic scene of a younger sibling embarrassing an older one, a scene he'd lived through several times with his own brother and sister. Yet, he wondered about their relationship. Somehow, they seemed even more than just sisters.

While Cassie began to recover from her onslaught of laughter, Mary, Penny, and Jennifer Anne approached Kayleigh. "Miss O'Brien," Mary began, "would your little sister like to play with us?"

Cassie smiled shyly at the girls before turning to Kayleigh. Please, Sissy," she begged. "Please!"

"I don't know," Kayleigh hesitated. Jacob put his hand very lightly on Kayleigh's shoulder. "Why not let her?" he asked. "They'll watch out for her."

Kayleigh looked over to see Daniel and Lydia sitting on a blanket in the distance, and they waved to her.

"Well, alright," she conceded. "Go ahead," but don't get too hot or tired. Remember what we talked about."

"She's a very dear little girl," Jacob observed as she joined hands and skipped away with the little girls.

"Yes, but she's not your typical twelve-year-old," Kayleigh said, studying Jacob's face and reactions.

"No, she's not," he agreed, "but none of us are really 'typical,'" he smiled.

"No, I guess not," she smiled in return.

They watched as Cassie played with the other younger girls. They giggled and played chase and ring around the rosies until they were tired.

Mary and Jennifer Anne walked Cassie back.

"We had fun, Sissy!" the little girl beamed.

"I saw!" Kayleigh said. "It looked like great fun!"

Cassie giggled and whispered, "But they don't believe I'm twelve," she said, motioning to Mary and Jennifer Anne as they walked back to Lydia. "They think I'm seven or eight."

Jacob could see the shadow of pain come over Kayleigh's face.

"Oh well," Kayleigh managed to say and smile.

"We'd best be getting back," Kayleigh said quietly while gathering up the basket and blanket.

"Here, let me help and walk the two of you back," Jacob offered.

"Thank you, Mr. McVale, but we'll be fine."

"Please, Sissy," Cassie took her hand with begging eyes.

"It would be fun for me to see two pretty ladies home," he smiled with that smile that could convince most women of anything.

"Let Mr. McVale have fun with us two pretty ladies," Cassie pleaded, and, despite herself, Kayleigh laughed and said, "Well, alright, yes. I can't argue with both of you."

As they walked, Cassie chatted away about playing with the girls, the little frog, and the Langleys, something that even Kayleigh had trouble getting her to share; however, with Jacob, the child was sharing tidbits about the farm, her chores, and Mr. Langley's funny beard. It was unlike the little girl to become close to a male adult so easily.

"Well, here we are," Kayleigh said as they approached the door of the schoolhouse. "Thank you, Mr. McVale, for your help."

"Please don't go," Cassie cried, hugging Jacob about the middle.

"Cassie, honestly," Kayleigh blushed and pulled the little girl away.

"I'll tell you what," Jacob said, kneeling down on the porch, "Why don't I come by tomorrow morning and walk you two to church?"

"Yes!" Cassie squealed. "Let Mr. McVale walk us to church, Sissy!"

"Alright," Kayleigh agreed slowly, knowing that she was beaten yet again.

As he walked away, he could hear Kayleigh patiently lecturing Cassie. "What did I tell you about talking to men that we don't know that well? He has other lady friends."

What had she been through? Jacob wondered as he walked away.

That Sunday, when Jacob arrived at Kayleigh's doorway, Cassie was waiting, beaming at him, and anxious to tell him that she was wearing a new dress as she twirled and demonstrated.

"Well, it's quite beautiful," Jacob told her. "Your sister looks very pretty also," he added.

Cassie leaned in and whispered to him, "It's the same black dress she had since I was little, but she says that she may get a new one when we buy our house."

"Thank you, Miss Busy-Body," Kayleigh said, rolling her eyes. "Now tell Mr. McVale 'thank you' for walking us to church."

"We'll be sitting in the back, Mr. McVale," Kayleigh said as Cassie took his hand. He offered his arm to Kayleigh, and she hesitated, looked at Cassie, and then took it.

"Why don't you sit with me and the rest of the family?" he questioned. "That way, the girls can all be together."

"Well, I…I don't want to disturb your and Mary Alice's seating arrangement," Kayleigh managed to say.

"Mary Alice is a friend, Kayleigh. We've known each other quite a while, and when her husband passed (also a good friend of mine), we decided to sometimes keep company. In short, she is fine with not sitting with me."

"Well, if you say so, Mr. McVale, but we would be fine sitting in the back," Kayleigh assured.

He smiled at them both and walked them to his pew. Cassie joyfully sat with Mary, Penny, and Jennifer Anne, leaving Kayleigh again next to Jacob. Several women noticed Cassie's dress and commented on how expensive it must have been. As Beatrice put it, "No wonder she has a limited wardrobe. She spends it all on the child."

Lydia and Maddie leaned over and smiled at Kayleigh. She returned the smiles, which seemed to be reading a little more into her sitting next to Jacob than was the case.

Still, despite herself, she was aware of him next to her, aware of his warmth and strength. *Stop it!* she told herself. *The man's simply being nice to you. Besides, there's no telling what he's really like. He is a man, after all.*

Jacob was a self-disciplined, moral man, and he respected the fact that he was in church, but he had felt the nearness of her for some time.

He knew instinctively that she had been hurt and that she was hiding another life. He also knew that anything other than kindness and friendship would be completely misinterpreted or perhaps rightly interpreted as a desire for something more. He smiled at her and began to sing as the hymn began. It was good to have her next to him, whatever the circumstances.

Lydia, of course, asked Kayleigh and Cassie to dinner after church, along with her brother-in-law, Jacob, and, again, Kayleigh felt some guilt that she was not contributing to the meal, but, oh, it was a wonderful dinner. It was almost like being a part of a family.

After eating, Cassie played with Jennifer Anne, and then Mary and Penny came over and joined in.

Kayleigh, Jacob, Daniel, and Lydia sat on the front porch with their coffee and conversation, and it was the most content Kayleigh had felt in a long time. There was a cool breeze that ruffled her hair and smelled of the fall, beginning to surrender.

Pete and Maddie came by, and they all played cards, with Jacob and Kayleigh winning a round. "Just don't tell the Reverend that we've been playing cards," Maddie said confidentially but with a wide smile.

For a moment, Kayleigh forgot herself and exclaimed, "Oh, I love winning, don't you?" as she turned to Jacob.

"Yes, I do, very much," Jacob said with a smile, and he took in her pretty face and hair. He smelled the light scent that she had used that morning. She was a picture. The moment was not lost on the group, though, as small, quiet smiles were exchanged.

By the time they were ready to go home, though, Kayleigh was back to her private self and her private thoughts. Cassie would be leaving in the morning, and she needed to get her prepared.

As Jacob walked the two home, he and Kayleigh both noticed how fatigued Cassie was. She had had a great day of fun and friendship, but she seemed to barely be walking.

"I can carry her if you want," Jacob offered, a worried tone in his voice, and to his surprise, Kayleigh agreed, her forehead furrowed in worry also.

Jacob carried the now limp child into the schoolhouse, looking to Kayleigh for help or explanation.

"Lay her down on the floor," Kayleigh directed as Jacob looked at her in shock.

"Don't you want her in her bed," he asked disbelievingly.

"She's about to have a seizure," she answered calmly. "Lay her down and I'll get a cushion for her head and a spoon for her mouth. Please just do what I ask."

Jacob felt the child beginning to stiffen as he laid her down as gently as he could, and Kayleigh placed a rolled-up shawl under her head.

Then, the attack began. "Please get me the sheet off my bed, Mr. McVale," Kayleigh directed as she held the little girl in her arms and placed the wooden spoon at her mouth.

Jacob stripped the sheet off the bed and took it back into the main room.

"Please place it over her waist to her legs," Kayleigh requested. Jacob watched as the poor child thrashed uncontrollably, and Kayleigh spoke soothingly to her.

"What can I do?" Jacob asked helplessly.

"Hold her legs down, please," Kayleigh directed.

Slowly, Cassie's small body subsided from its jerking and thrashing. She was then very still, her eyes glazed, not aware of her surroundings.

"Cassie, you're here with Sissy and Mr. McVale. Everything is alright. I love you," she said, stroking her hair. "Everything will be alright."

Kayleigh removed the spoon, and Jacob let go of her legs. Gradually, she became more aware of where she was and who she was at the moment. Then, she began to cry softly, "I had an accident. I don't want him to see."

"It's alright. You're covered up," Kayleigh exclaimed, also in a whisper.

Jacob felt pain for the child's embarrassment and loss of control. She was such a sweet little girl. He felt the injustice of the whole scene, and, for the first time in quite a while, he thought of his own little sister, Sarah.

"Thank you, Mr. McVale," Kayleigh spoke to him in a tone that he recognized as telling him that his part was done.

"You know, the Langleys will be back tomorrow morning. Perhaps you could come by before noon and tell Cassie goodbye." Still crouched down next to the child, she turned to face Cassie, "Would you like that, love?"

"Yes," she whispered and gave a shy smile to Jacob.

The next morning, Jacob saw Langley's plain but functional buckboard outside the schoolhouse.

"Plain but functional," he turned that phrase over in his mind. That pretty much described the Langleys as well.

Before he could even knock on the door, Cassie ran and flung open the door. "Mr. McVale!" she beamed and hugged him tightly.

He smiled and patted her back. "I'm so glad to see you feeling well, Cassie," he said.

The Langleys, sitting at the small kitchen table, raised their eyebrows in unison. Jacob wasn't sure if they were registering surprise, disapproval, or both.

"Mavis, Josiah, this is Mr. McVale," Kayleigh explained. "Mr. McVale is on our school board."

Mr. Langley rose slowly and took Jacob's hand. "I'm pleased to meet you," Jacob said.

"We are pleased to meet you as well," Josiah returned. "We are pleased that Kayleigh has found a good location."

Kayleigh looked somewhat uncomfortable before speaking, "Mr. McVale was very helpful to us when we had our picnic and attended church."

"I see," Mr. Langley returned cautiously. "Well," he said while withdrawing a pocket watch from his overalls, "we had best be going while we have the light."

"Yes," Mavis agreed. "We best get on our way. Come, Cassidy. Let go of Mr. McVale. It is unseemly."

"No!" Cassie suddenly screamed. "I don't want to go! Why can't I stay?" she demanded, crying.

"Cassidy, child, contain yourself," Mavis cautioned. "You have already had an episode. We will take you to the special doctor when we return."

"Mrs. Langley, please," Kayleigh put her hand up in a stop motion. "Let me talk with her."

Cassie threw herself into Kayleigh's arms, sobbing, while Jacob looked somewhat helpless and confused. (This was not a look that he usually wore for any reason.)

"Cassie, look at me, darling," Kayleigh said. "I have a surprise for you if you can be a good girl and go with the Langleys. I meant to save it until Christmas, but you may have it now if you can go back to the farm for a while. Then, now look at me and listen, love," Kayleigh said, trying not to cry, "we'll be together at Thanksgiving, and Sissy will find a way to keep you here with me. I promise that I just need a bit more time to think and plan. Alright, darling?" she asked.

Cassie wiped at her eyes. "May I see the surprise now, Sissy?"

"Wait right here. I'll just be a moment," Kayleigh said. She went into the bedroom and reemerged with the doll that Jacob had "anonymously" bought for her. Jacob smiled quietly at the sight of the doll.

"Oh, Sissy, she's beautiful," Cassie said, holding out her arms for the doll.

"Alright, let's carry her to the wagon then. You can tell her all about the farm on the way home," Kayleigh smiled.

Mavis Langley clicked her tongue and gave Kayleigh a look that spoke of the guilt that she felt Kayleigh should have weighing upon her.

"Really, Kayleigh, you have bought such an extravagant and frivolous gift. Betwixt her clothes and this, she will be completely spoiled," Mavis half-whispered and half-hissed to Kayleigh.

"I love the child too, but God does not intend for women to grow accustomed to such things, and you are promising the child foolish things about living with you," Mavis continued until Josiah held up his hand.

"Be still, Mavis. You will keep your opinions to yourself."

Kayleigh's blue eyes had grown cold and intense. "I don't promise what I cannot give. I will bring her here at Thanksgiving," she finished.

Jacob looked approvingly at her as they stepped out to the street and up to the wagon. Cassie was clinging to Kayleigh and the doll when she suddenly turned to Jacob and took his hand. "I'll see you at Thanksgiving, Mr. McVale," and just as suddenly, she pulled his hand over to Kayleigh's and joined them. "You two," she said, "you two together."

"Cassie!" Kayleigh said, trying to jerk her hand away. "I'm sorry," she said to Jacob. "She just doesn't know…"

"Yes, I do!" the little girl cried out. "Yes, I do."

Kayleigh embraced her fiercely, and they kissed goodbye. She watched as the wagon began to disappear, fighting an overwhelming need to cry. Jacob put his arm around her shoulders and walked her back to the schoolhouse.

CHAPTER 37: ROSEMARY AND CAROLINE SAVE THE SING-ALONG

Kayleigh had told Mitch and Zach repeatedly that she did not want to be a part of the "Sing-Along." As she explained to them, the Sing-Alongs in towns where she had no attachment or possibility of staying was one thing, but in a town where she had not yet decided about staying, respectability was still important. She had not yet told her two friends that she was bringing Cassie to Faithful, but it was foremost in her mind.

She was in her small home, singing a song to Sawyer after feeding him and before putting him out, when there was a pounding at the door. It was so hard and persisted so long that she guessed it to be a large male. Instead, upon opening it, she found the beautiful and petite Rosemary and the stout, usually grinning, Caroline.

They both looked agitated and confused. She motioned for them to come in and began to sign and question them about what was wrong. It was then that they revealed, in a hasty and urgent manner, that Mitch and Zach had begun the Sing-Along without much success and that they were, in fact, losing their audience and any hopes of passing the hat for money. The act was meant to be for three and to include a woman.

Then, Rosemary, knowing exactly what she was doing, signed that Mitch was "completely humiliated" and feared being disrespected and fired. She well knew that Kayleigh could not abide by any unnecessary hurt or embarrassment to befall her adopted brothers.

Kayleigh signed, "Just a moment," grabbed her shawl, and smoothed her loose hair, hoping that she looked satisfactory. The three walked quickly to Lucy's, and a look of relief swept over the faces of the two men as they entered the large main room of the inn. They were dying a slow death in front of a half-full house, and they knew it. Kayleigh was the needed link.

Kayleigh had scarcely taken off her wrap and drawn a breath before Mitch began, "Well, ladies and gentlemen, the lovely third part of our act has finally arrived, always one for a grand entrance!"

"Why, Professor Iknowmore and his assistant, Imalittledaft," Kayleigh intoned dramatically, "I came as quickly as I could when I heard of your impending doom," and with that, she put her hand to her brow as if close to fainting away. The crowd was beginning to chuckle when Mitch hunched slightly and put an old top hat on his head.

"Yeah," he said, adopting a German accent, "I nearly expired of boredom myself before your entrance. My great learning could not even save me!"

"Nor could I," moaned Zach, limping about as though injured, "although I tried to loan him my vast intelligence." The crowd laughed while Caroline slipped Kayleigh a long slender stick, which she used to lightly strike both of them before ordering, "To your places, both of you before the games begin! And now to the rules, good people," and she turned to the crowd and recited:

Lend an ear to our game,

Pass the hat is its name.

Should we know the song you say,

The hat shall pass and money paid.

But should we know not the song you choose,

One of us to you will lose.

That one will wear the hat until,

A song we know,

Frees us of woe.

As you gather 'round with coins in hand,

Listening to the School Teacher band.

"I wanna hear 'Beautiful Dreamer,'" Cal Lindstrom shouted. His angular face was alight, with a large grin, and he had slicked back his thick blond hair, "and I want Miss O'Brien to sing it." He leaned back, both elbows resting on the bar and his long legs angled in front.

"Well, let's see," Kayleigh said with her index finger to her chin. "Do I know that one?"

Out of the corner of her eye, she could see Lucy smiling and leaning over to whisper to Jacob.

"I think it goes like this," Zach said, doing a silly jig and singing falsetto, "Beautiful dreamer, do you want to dream of me?"

After some raucous laughter, Kayleigh rolled her eyes at Zach and said, "I think it goes like this," at which point she began to play the piano and sing while Mitch silently placed the hat on Kayleigh's head.

The audience was transfixed by her voice and the beauty of the song, and at the far end of the room, talking to Mary Alice, Jacob was as enamored as the other males who were listening attentively. *This is how happy she should always be*, he thought. *Now, she is in her element.*

Some were listening as though smitten, and others (such as Daniel and Pete) listened with musical admiration. The ladies, such as Maddie and Lydia, were enjoying the whole event now that it had been saved, and it did not escape the attention of both the younger women…

…and more mature ladies, as more people began to fill the inn, that Kayleigh had her share of admirers. This was something that she did not seem to notice.

As she finished, Mitch removed the hat as those present applauded, and he passed it about the audience for coins. "Next request!" Zach called out.

"I'd like to hear Clementine," an old timer from the back tables called out. Lucy smiled, remembering that her own father had actually liked that tune as well.

"Well, now, I seem to remember that tune," Mitch said, stretching his long frame and scratching his head.

"Is she that girl you kept company with back in South Dakota?" Zach questioned earnestly. "You know the one who could shimmy and shake?" and with that, he gave his best impression of a dancer.

As the crowd laughed at Zach's antics, Mitch blushed, assured the audience that he had never had such a girlfriend, and sat down to the piano with the hat now on his head. Again, the crowd was impressed by his vocalization, and when Mitch sang "Oh my darling," it was directed straight at his beautiful Rosemary, which the crowd found most charming and dear.

And, so, the hat was passed again. Of course, some could give more than others, especially as the night wore on, but all wanted to participate and give to the supplies and upkeep of the schools.

One of the final tunes fell to Zach and Kayleigh, Reuben and Rachel. The two kept somewhat true to the tune and also improvised.

When Zach took the hat and shared the piano bench with Kayleigh, the inn was treated to a saucy duet:

Reuben, Reuben, I've been thinking

What a world this would be

If the men were all transported

Far beyond the Northern Sea!

Rachel, Rachel, I've been thinking

What a world this would be

If the girls were all transported

Far beyond the northern Sea!

Chorus: Too-ral-loo-ral-loo, Too-ral-loo-ral,

Too-ral-loo-ral-loo, Too-ral-lee

Far beyond the Northern Sea!

Reuben, Reuben, I've been thinking

Life would be so easy then;

What a lovely world this would be

If there were no tiresome men!

Rachel, Rachel, I've been thinking

Life would be so easy then;

What a lovely world this would be

If you'd leave it to the men!

Reuben, Reuben, I've been thinking

If we went beyond the seas,

All the men would follow after

Like a swarm of bumble-bees!

Rachel, Rachel, I've been thinking

If we went beyond the seas,

All the girls would follow after

Like a swarm of honey-bees!

"Sing with us on the chorus now," Zach motioned with his hand, and the tavern group sang with them.

"Too-ral-loo-ral-loo, Too-ral-lee."

Then, Maddie, never one to be shy or stand on ceremony, grabbed Pete, and they began to dance to the tune while other couples followed suit. The crowd actually stumped them on one song request but still insisted that the hat be passed.

In the final moments, the crowd was shocked when Noah Thomas requested a final Irish ballad, Maggie.

"Mr. Thomas," Kayleigh began, "we will be glad to honor that beautiful request, but we do sing it just a little differently, with the typical male tenor," and she motioned to Mitch," and with a bit of a responding female voice," and she pointed to herself.

"That's fine," Noah answered, and the two began the ballad.

Mitch and Kayleigh stood side by side while Zach played accompaniment. Jacob felt a surprising pang of jealousy, knowing it was ridiculous.

Mitch started the whimsical song:

"I wandered today, through the hills, Maggie

To watch the scene below

The creek and the creaking old mill, Maggie

As we used to long long ago."

Kayleigh responded in their amended version:

"The green growth is gone from the hills

Where first the daisies sprung.

The creaking old mill is still, My Love.

It's different from when we were young."

As the song continued, there were tears and touched hearts as Mitch closed with, "Thank you so much for attending our Sing-Along and supporting our schools. We love you, and we love your children."

Applause and handshaking followed, and Cal asked Kaleigh to go walking with him sometime. She responded in a low voice, "I've never been so flattered, but you're a bit too young, my dear."

Cal responded even lower, "I'm twenty-one, Miss O'Brien. That ain't too young."

To his surprise, Jacob watched as Mary Alice waved and left with Noah. The two were talking very amiably, and he had the feeling that she was asking him about his song selection. Then, from the corner of his eye, he saw Miss O'Brien slipping out alone. He made his way to the door and left also.

He caught up to her as Neb Darius became louder and louder while following behind her. "How about a kiss, sweetie? I saw how prettily you sang those love songs. You need a man."

"Neb, go home," Jacob said while putting a hand on Darius' shoulder. "The lady's trying to get home. Leave her be. She doesn't need you. You need to get some sleep before you head to work in the morning."

Darius shuffled on his way, still somewhat intimidated by Jacob, even after all the years that had passed. Jacob then came side by side with Kayleigh. He ignored the bright red that her face had turned and began complimenting her on the Sing-Along.

"I didn't realize how lovely your voice is," he smiled. "Who came up with that act?"

"Um, well, I guess we all did, in a way," Kayleigh said quietly, "I'm glad you enjoyed it."

"Well, we're here," she said, pointing to the schoolhouse. "Thank you for walking with me."

"You're very welcome," Jacob said. "I'll be glad to any time. You know that," he said quietly.

"Yes, I know. You've been very kind," she said while beginning to open the door. *And you enjoy other ladies as well*, she thought, remembering the scene with Jeanette.

"It's not just kindness, Kayleigh," he replied. "I think we should start seeing each other. Think it over," he said and kissed her hand before smiling and walking away.

Kayleigh stood in mystified silence. Was he serious or not?

Jacob had never agreed with Neb Darius about anything except that last comment he had made. In his view, Kayleigh needed a man—him.

On the other side of the now-crowded street, Mary Alice finally caught up to Noah Thomas. She came up quietly to him and touched him on the arm as the rest of those attending the Sing-Along spilled out of Lucy's Inn and Diner.

"Noah, that was a beautiful ballad you chose," Mary Alice said softly. "How did you come to know it?"

"Oh, it's a long story," he smiled shyly.

"I have time," Mary Alice smiled in return.

It was becoming more and more obvious to Mary Alice that Jacob was falling in love with Miss O'Brien. She knew him well enough to see it, even if others did not, and she did not want to seem "standing in the way." Noah could prove the distraction needed and a friend as well. After all, she had always been curious about him, and now she had a leading question for him.

"I had a young wife once," he began, "and she loved Irish songs. She was part Irish herself, and she often sang Maggie."

"Noah," Mary Alice said with soft surprise in her voice, "I never even knew you were married. Do others know?"

"No, I don't think so," he admitted. "I guess some things are just too painful to share with others."

She sent her arm through his and began to step in time with him. The evening was beautiful. A quarter moon was beginning to appear as they walked, and other couples nodded quietly to them, some with a slight look of surprise. Others laughed and talked in their own private world as they made their way down the street.

"Yes, Noah, they are," she replied. "I think we all have our own private loneliness that we carry inside," she said quietly.

"Are you Irish, Noah?" Mary Alice asked, taking his arm.

He blushed a bit before answering, "No, I'm mainly German, but part Indian also."

Mary Alice stopped walking and looked a bit shocked.

"Well, I know I don't look it, but my great-grandmother was Cherokee," he explained. "Most of my parentage is German, but she was my great-grandmother and quite a fierce little character."

"So you came to Faithful before I did," Mary Alice said quietly, as though putting a puzzle together, "and you may have come a little after Lucy did. Now there's a character, but she really has a good heart and an understanding of people," Mary Alice observed.

"Yes," Noah agreed, "I've often wondered about her." (In truth, he had often wondered about Mary Alice's life too. Most who were newer in Faithful did not know the full story of Nathan and his death. However, somehow Noah now knew that he could trust this soul and, in so trusting, find a loving companion.)

He walked her home, and, to her surprise and gladness, he asked to walk with her again, and in this way, they began. Initially, there was little more than walking and talking, and that was enough; for, in knowing each other's stories, they formed a bond of empathy, and although empathy may not be the most romantic of emotions, it can be a beginning.

As for Noah, it was as though a wall of secrets and pain had been torn down so that he was free to love again. He felt that there might finally be a remedy to his steely loneliness.

No one took notice at first, but then, people such as Beatrice Atwood began to note that Noah Thomas was actually smiling as he walked down the street, sometimes whistling. The silent companion of grief that usually ushered him along each day had departed.

CHAPTER 38: FROM LUCIA TO LUCY

Lucy was born in San Diego, California, as Lucia Valdez. She quickly learned that she could get along better, and fit in better, if she was fluent in both Spanish and English. In this way, she could communicate with and interpret for her family and get along with the wealthier landowners' families.

Few people knew, and no one thought to ask Lucia what she wanted from life. Her family, who lived on the continual edge of poverty, assumed she wanted a husband and a good place to live. Outsiders either assumed the same or didn't really care.

In truth, she wasn't sure either, except that she knew that she wanted something to call her own. The ranches and rancheros that she saw were symbols of power to her. So were the businesses that ranchers owned, such as shops, banks, cafes and diners, and saloons.

All of this, however, meant nothing to her father. His plan, like those of most men at that time, was to marry her off to the best provider. He was not without a heart, nor were her brothers and mother, but being the only girl in a family of five brothers, her voice was seldom recognized, even by her mother.

She enjoyed school, but she was not allowed to go after she was nine and needed at home. It was no surprise to anyone but her when her father arranged her marriage when she was fourteen. She was a month shy of her fifteenth birthday and considered more than mature enough for marriage.

Lucia might have been able to accept the marriage if the man had been in his twenties or thirties, or even forties. However, when sixty-year-old Harve' Martinez appeared, with his belly preceding him along with his body odor and shiny bald head, Lucia tried to run, and the man that she wanted to run to was Braden Keith.

Braden's family lived on the conjoining farm. They did not socialize. In fact, there were no neighborly interactions between his parents and Lucia's. However, the two saw each other when they rode out to the fences that made the border for the Valdez's cattle and the Keiths' horses. Lucia loved to spy Braden breaking a wild horse.

Tall and slender, his mother's Spanish coloring in his hair and eyes made more than one woman take a second look, while his father's Scottish smile and high cheekbones gave him an alert and canny persona. He was taken with Lucia immediately, but he knew that she was a bit too young.

Still, the two were in love almost before they ever spoke to each other. At eighteen, Braden was still a bit shy, but he knew his own mind. At fourteen, Lucia had the maturity of a young woman ready to start life with her love. It was a true Romeo and Juliet scenario, with much plotting between the two about waiting until Lucia's fifteenth birthday and how much money Braden could hide away.

Lucia's parents were not blind to this blossoming romance, and their mental wheels were also turning. Harve' Martinez seemed to be the answer.

One day, Lucia's parents sat her down in the small sitting room of their hacienda. Her mother spoke first in rapid Spanish. "You will never be with Braden Keith, so get that out of your head. He is half Scottish, and his family, and all like them, want the land that we should rightfully have. He will have his way with you but never marry you, and his father will take our land."

"We have given you everything!" her father screamed at her. "This marriage is the least that you can do for our family. It will make our business ties and holdings solid. You will marry Harve'," he finished by slamming his fist down on the table.

Lucia had always loved her parents dearly, so she was confused and hurt by their words. They were breaking her heart, and she knew that they would not relent.

She saw her only chance as running, which she tried that very night when she thought that her parents and brothers were fully asleep. Running into the night, not sure of her path, but knowing that she wanted nothing more than to get to Braden, she ran barefoot in her white nightgown with her long dark hair streaming out behind he

Sadly, her brothers caught her and brought her back. Locking her in her room until the wedding. For Lucia, it was like a death sentence. Her mother chastised her to stop crying, and her father told her to be grateful a wealthy man wanted her.

"Wealthy" was a relative term where this man was concerned. He owned a prosperous inn and a small house. He had never had any children to carry on what he saw as a burgeoning dynasty, and he viewed Lucia as his channel to that goal.

Then, the night before the wedding, Braden climbed to her window, and she silently followed him back down into the night. This began their running and the knowledge that if they were caught, Braden would probably be killed. They ran hand in hand to the fence post where Braden had tied two of the family's best horses. Still, silently, they mounted them and began their long ride.

Lucy's father put together a search party the next morning, vowing to kill Braden, while Harve' demanded that he still be given Lucia's dowry. It seemed that all involved were more concerned about the money that might be lost as opposed to the loss of Lucia.

Braden quickly bought supplies in the next town, including a dress for Lucia. The two were then able to camp anywhere that offered shelter and braved both the torrential rain and the heat of desert terrain. The day offered little cover or protection, and they were nearly captured at the border of California and Oregon.

As they came close to a high embankment, rain pouring in sideways, they had no choice but to urge the horses down the tall, slick embankment toward the swelling river. Almost miraculously, the animals made it down the bank and into the water before Lucia's horse threw her.

She went under with the current, gasped, and went down again before Braden pulled her up and onto his horse while her mount ran wildly out into the surrounding woods. Lucia looked at Braden in shock as his horse carefully swam its way to the other side.

"Lucia, I thought you were dead," he gasped. "Are you alright?"

"Yes, she said, but you are bleeding," she said with her breath coming in gasps. He looked at his side where his shirt had torn, saw the blood, and on inspection, saw that part of a tree branch had wedged into him below his ribcage.

"My love, we must get you to a doctor," Lucia cried as they came up the bank with Braden now leading the horse.

"Now, darling, how do you think that we can manage that? We don't know where we are, and we don't have any money. I'll be alright," he assured her.

After tethering the horse, facing the fact that the other horse was gone, and taking off his belt and biting down on it, he pulled the branch out and collapsed. He lay so still, and his pulse was so weak that, for a time, Lucia was afraid that he would die. Nonetheless, she diligently made a bandage out of her battered nightgown. He began to revive as she had him sip water.

Once in Oregon, they both felt more secure and began to discuss a plan for carrying on with their lives. It was then that Braden revealed his hope for refuge.

"I've heard of a town called Faithful, somewhere in the Oregon territory," told her. "They have a mission. They might take us in. Word is they don't ask too many questions," he said with hope in his voice.

As they traveled, they began to change their identities. Braden became Jeff just because he liked the name, and Lucia became Lucy. It just seemed to fit. They would keep Keith as a last name and marry as soon as possible along the way.

When they finally found and pulled into the mission in Faithful, they were battered and exhausted, but they had their story straight. They had been General Store owners in California, but bandits had robbed them and burned the store. They were now looking to start another business of some type or help with one already established.

Joshua McVale quietly and kindly told them that they already had a mercantile, but he was more than willing to work Jeff on one of his fishing boats or on the docks.

Of course, neither McVale nor Jeff knew that Lucy had taken her father's bankroll, which he kept in his safe for her dowry. She would bide her time, find a plot of land, make the connections, and begin an inn.

While Jeff worked on the docks, Lucy located the land near the edge of town and a small abandoned inn. After she approached Neb Darius, who owned the property, it became clear what her plan was. A startled town wanted answers, and a town hall was called to meet in the church. Although not invited, Lucy appeared.

She stood, a strikingly beautiful woman with hair as black as crow feathers cascading thickly down her back. Her black eyes took in everything, and her sensuous mouth took on a whole different look as she smiled.

As several townspeople began to shout and speak out against her, Joshua McVale silently stood and raised one hand. In the Scottish brogue that often gained him both attention and respect, he announced, "Let's allow Mrs. Keith to have her say, but before she does, I'd like to have mine.

I've watched men who have worked a long, hard day, for me, desire something in the way of drink. This never came to any good, as we learned with the last inn that Larita tried to run with the offer of alcohol.

Now, it seems to me that a good establishment, looking out for its patrons, will not serve alcohol. Instead, the proprietors will provide a meeting place, which is usually larger than what a church, schoolhouse, or even a mission can provide. Sometimes, they even serve a good dinner or have a sing-along.

Such establishments also give back to their towns by generously supporting local churches or missions and by dutifully paying their share of taxes. Isn't that so?" Joshua looked quizzically and knowingly at Lucy.

She smiled and nodded. She knew exactly what Mr. McVale was telling her, and she understood completely how he expected her to conduct herself.

"As Mr. McVale has said," Lucy began, "the inn will be a warm place of talk, music, and friendship. We will help support the town, particularly the church, and we will also serve as a boarding house or hotel and a warm meal for weary travelers. Jeff and I want to serve the town of Faithful," she finished with a sincere smile.

"Well, I suppose we'll take a vote now," Darius said. "All in favor of allowing the inn, say aye." Everyone but a few stalwart mothers said aye.

As the crowd began to leave, Lucy noticed Jacob in the back of the church, wearing a sly grin. She took note that he was a handsome young man with probably the same canny business sense as his father. She turned to find Jeff and saw Mr. McVale smiling and coming straight toward her.

"Do we understand each other, Young Miss?" he asked.

"Yes, sir," she answered, "completely."

"Good," he smiled. "Remind me, and one day, I'll tell you about the time I was running from the law," he whispered.

Lucy's eyes went wide. "That's right, Missy," Joshua continued. "I often know more than I let on, and I'm not asking questions about your particular situation, but you best be careful about how you proceed and run your establishment."

With that, he tipped his cap and returned his voice to its regular volume. "Welcome to Faithful, Mrs. Keith. I hope this will be your home for a long time," Jacob smiled.

Jeff gave Lucy a furtive look, wondering just what had transpired between the two but not really wanting to know, and that arrangement was fine. He was the bookkeeper. He knew the clientele, paid the bills and taxes, and made sure that the church and mission were well supported.

Lucy sometimes played the piano and sang. Of course, in addition, Lucy made good on her promise to make sure that the door was opened to town meetings whenever needed.

She was happier than she had ever been, and Jeff was living a dream. Yes, it was just an inn in a small unknown town, but it was their home, their family, and, most importantly, it was theirs. Even through the times of illness in the town, they were thankful for their own good fortune.

It was a beautiful spring night after things had settled in the town yet again. She had just finished playing the piano, and some of their regulars had been dancing. Lucy smiled at Jeff across the room. He smiled back, fell, and his heart stopped.

After that, Lucy went through the motions of life for a year. Sometimes, she had a smile, especially when Joshua and Jacob McVale came in. Somehow, she knew that she and Jacob were both in a state of grief, not quite the same state of mourning, but pain nonetheless.

However, when she was most immersed in her loss of Braden and Jeff or resentful of what her parents had caused in her life, she remembered that she had found a home where she belonged and that she had true love for a time. Now, at twenty-four years of age, she was better off than many, and she remained with her adopted family in Faithful.

CHAPTER 39: THE FALL FESTIVAL

It was in mid-October that Mrs. Campbell began to secretly alert Jacob about Kayleigh's telegraphs. She had never done this before and felt completely "immoral," as she confided in Jacob. She further confessed that "Even Mr. Campbell doesn't know."

Mrs. Campbell looked almost exactly as her mother had, the original Mrs. McKendree, who had comforted Mary Alice in the old mission. She was barely five foot one, and her once curvaceous figure was now a bit plump due to childbirth and life. She looked like everyone's mother or grandmother. Her long braided gray hair was worn up, wrapped about the crown of her head or in a tight little bun at the base of her neck, and her features were almost completely empathetic and motherly, from her bright blue eyes to her cherub mouth and rounded chin.

Mr. Campbell looked to be just as affable and easy-going as he naturally was. He usually wore a shopkeeper's apron and sometimes a visor. He had a continual smile and a look of kindness. The couple was well-loved by the town.

Jacob was torn between amusement and irritation with the two. He had already told the dear lady several times that he did not want to hear about or read someone's private telegraphs, but she was insistent that it was a matter of personal safety for "dear little Miss O'Brien."

So, she gradually revealed to Jacob that Kayleigh received telegraphs informing her that "I know where she is."

Or "I know where you are and what you did."

And, the most frightening, according to Mrs. Campbell, "We'll make you pay."

Even Jacob, who'd had his share of threats and dirty dealings from others, thought these to be severe intimidation tactics toward a woman alone in the world.

"And," Mrs. Campbell continued, "You should see the looks on her sweet face when she reads these. Why would anyone say these things to her?"

"I don't know, Mrs. Campbell," he replied and shrugged, but a look of worry and concern was on his face, and, privately, he wondered why anyone would threaten her.

He had kept his distance from her for the last few weeks because she had kept hers from him. He was not sure what had happened, but Lucy seemed to think that it had something to do with the kiss that Jeanette had impulsively planted on him while he was walking past her shop. So, he and Mary Alice began to have dinner together again, although he was often preoccupied.

However, as the fall and school days drifted by, he was reminded of his own boyhood and was again impressed by how well Miss O'Brien and her colleagues organized school events. He had hopes that he could see her at the Fall Festival, which she and Mitch and Zach had put together.

On the Saturday of the festival, the children displayed their different scarecrows, dressed in different costumes to represent different nations. Jacob particularly liked "McTavish, Laird of the Scared!"

Mitch and Zach went with a more historical theme, displaying scarecrows that their students had made representing Columbus, Native Americans, George Washington, and other Revolutionary War figures. The children were showing off their works of art to their parents in between bobbing for apples and games of chase.

Mitch led people through the scarecrow display for a penny, while Zach took pennies to sell or help carve faces on pumpkins. Kayleigh enjoyed running the apple bobbing contest inside the school room and assured "customers" that the pennies collected would go to the small library that they were starting in each school. Of course, Miss Griggs did not approve of the whole process, but she did not reprove it either since it would bring in money for books.

Kayleigh began to close down the contest as she laughed at the final contestants and gave out prizes when Jacob entered. She had dejectedly given up on him and was trying not to show how happy she was that he had come.

"Oh, am I too late to bob for apples?" he called out while he laughed.

"Well, it depends," Kayleigh answered, somewhat startled. "Do you have a penny?"

"Actually, I have a nickel since it's for a good cause," Jacob smiled.

"Oh well, in that case," she said in a businesslike manner, "you are welcome to try."

"Let's just call it a donation," he smiled and said as he struggled a bit to sit in one of the student desks. (Considering his size and height, it was a bit difficult.)

"Well, that's it. I need to pack up," she motioned to the tubs of water with apples floating about. "Also, your jacket is draped over that first student desk. I think you'll find it clean. I meant to get it back sooner, but with Cassie's visit and all, I'm afraid I forgot. I'm sorry."

"Wait a moment," Jacob said, holding up his hand. "What's changed? It almost seems as though you're mad at me."

"No, Mr. McVale, I'm not mad," she replied.

"Well, something is different," he remarked. "You were much friendlier a few weeks ago. What happened?"

"Nothing," she answered, "I just don't care to be one more woman on your list. That's all."

"What?" he asked with a mix of clueless and confused shock.

"I have eyes and ears, Mr. McVale. I can tell when someone is involved with several ladies. I don't want or need to be one of those ladies," she explained.

"Could we go outside and talk?" he asked.

"What's wrong with here?" she asked as she began to scoop out apples from the tubs and place them on a towel spread on her desk.

"Well, it's a school, and people…" he lowered his voice as a child ran through, picked up a treat he had left on his desk, and ran back out.

"People are coming and going," he finished.

"Alright," she agreed, "but there's nothing to really talk about. It's none of my business."

"Please," he said and motioned to the door.

They walked a short distance until they reached an elm tree with a rounded wooden bench built for the school children. It was a bit of a comical moment: a big, tall man sitting on a small bench, and it was not lost on Jacob, but he sat down, sighed, and looked directly into Kayleigh's blue eyes.

"I'm not a perfect man. There are no perfect men, which you well know. I'm thirty-four years old, and I have been married. She was the light of my life, and she died trying to have our child.

"I blamed myself for years, and sometimes, I still do. I don't even remember much of the time after her death. I know I worked and lived, but I felt as though I was dead. I did not particularly want a woman in my life, but I did care about the welfare of Mary Alice, who had been through much the same experience.

"Now, though, I think I'm ready to try again. I want the one who will light my life and stay with me. I'm looking for just her, and I think I'm close to finding her," he finished with a half smile.

There were tears in Kayleigh's eyes when she spoke. "Well, I guess I just thought that Miss Jeanette Marteen meant something to you."

"Miss Marteen wants someone who she perceives as having money or position or both," Jacob concluded. "I want someone who wants me," he continued. "I want someone who sees me for who I am yet still wants me, and, so you'll know, I would never just put you on a list of some sort. You would be the entire list. So, could we please just spend time together? You know, just because I'm thirty-four and I know a little more about life than I once did doesn't make this any easier."

She smiled slowly. "No, I guess it never gets any easier."

"It does not," he smiled in return, "but sometimes it's worth it. Now, let's clean up the schoolroom."

Later that evening, as he hung his jacket in the chiffonier, he noticed something in the large inside pocket: a copy of *Tom Sawyer*.

CHAPTER 40: HE WALKED IN BEAUTY

It was a beautiful October day when Joseph O'Dell walked into town. From the viewpoint of casual observers, it would have been hard to tell which was more beautiful, Joseph or the day.

He wore a nonchalant but forceful look. He was now a man who knew his own mind and place in life. If others did not approve, that was simply their opinion and possible problem.

His gait was long, matching his height, and there was sometimes almost a child-like innocence about him. However, he was obviously intelligent and more worldly than his appearance told.

His hair was still dark in loose waves toward his shoulders. It still matched his dark honey-brown eyes and the tan in his cheeks. His nose was the kind of straight perfection that women often long for, and his full lips and ideal teeth were standards of classic good looks. His beard was roughing its way through and now had a bit of grey peppered in. He also still used his six foot three frame to its full effect—broad shoulders back, back straight, slim waist, long legs and arms, all perfectly proportioned.

His facial features remained accented with a dimpled chin and a welcoming smile. His mouth was now almost woman-like in its beauty and intensity.

Young women stopped in their tracks to view him, and older women wished they were young. He seemed unaware, but then he was practiced at appearing that way. Some men stared, caught themselves, and then, embarrassed, walked away. Others looked at him scornfully as though to say, "Look at the pretty boy," but then they had never dealt with Joseph O'Dell.

He smiled and nodded at individuals as he walked through, making sure that the outward appearance didn't betray the inward apprehension. *Let me find her in this town*, he thought. *Let us settle the unsettled.*

He stopped at Lucy's, and, even she had to admit to herself that he was a Greek statue come to life. Daniel McVale was a good-looking man, and Jacob McVale was nice-looking and pure masculinity, but this man was in a class all his own.

He stood at the bar after ordering a beer, smiled at Lucy, and casually asked, "Ma'am, would you know of a young woman named Kayleigh O'Brien?"

Lucy smiled back, and the looks of the man were not lost on her. "Well, yes," she said. "She is our new school teacher. Do you know each other?"

"Yes," he smiled, and even Lucy, as immune as she was to the charms of men, hesitated a moment, trying to remember if her hair was still in order before smiling in return.

"We were friends a few years back," he said. "I would just like to see her again and talk."

"Well," she began, "she would be at the school. So, that means that she'll be leaving the school and probably headed to the attached house in about an hour. I would offer to walk you there, but as you can see, I have a full house." Lucy made a sweeping gesture toward the full tavern as if to illustrate her point.

"I'll be glad to walk you in that direction," Jacob seemed to appear and speak suddenly from out of the blue, and Lucy's mouth was just a bit ajar.

"Let me buy you a beer first," he grinned amiably, "and welcome to Faithful." He offered his hand then, "I'm Jacob McVale. My brother and I own the fishing and shipping business down the way." He motioned toward the docks.

What is he up to? Lucy wondered. She already knew that Jacob was falling for Kayleigh. She could not tell whether others knew yet or not. What she hadn't counted on, as many did not, was the shrewdness and astuteness of Joseph O'Dell. He sensed that there was about to be a subtle inquisition.

In juxtaposition, the two could not have looked more different. With his curling brown hair and bright, twinkling blue eyes, Jacob was broad about the shoulders and chest.

Joseph was still tall and thin but well-built. His coal-dark hair was now streaked with a few strands of grey, and his dark eyes told of sadness, but he still had the sparkle of a man who loved life and was interested in others. Most found his southern drawl charming, and others simply envied him.

Jacob sized Joseph up as he did any man. He deemed that he would be a good, strong worker but that it might be hard to keep the women from distracting him, or vice versa. When he spoke, though, he betrayed none of that musing.

After a bit of small talk, Jacob skillfully led the conversation around to Kayleigh and how she and Joseph knew one another.

Joseph knew the thinking of both men and women, and he knew that Jacob was playing a bit of a game to find out if he wanted to start seeing Kayleigh. Of course, the truth was that he did, and he had come a long way to find out if she felt the same. Joseph carefully chose his words.

"Kayleigh was my friend about nine years ago. I felt that she was far too young for anything serious, and I married another woman. I loved my wife, and we were as happy as life would allow for seven years. She passed away almost two years ago."

That answered Jacob's unspoken question. This man had mourned and still felt grief, but he was also ready to find someone. He also knew that Joseph wanted to know about him when he asked, "And how do you and Kayleigh know each other? Just from her being the town's school teacher?"

"Well, mainly," Jacob admitted, "but we've shared a meal and a few walks to church." He realized how generic and pristine that sounded, but at least the man knew that he knew Kayleigh socially.

"No man in town has a chance with the woman of his heart with this one around." Jacob thought. He then caught himself and realized that this time that might also apply to him.

Lucy watched the exchange and mentally compared it with two prize fighters sitting down, sizing each other up, and verbally sparring. She had never seen Jacob so evenly matched before.

After a time of beer and talking, it became clear that there was not anything left to be done but direct Joseph to the school or walk him. Jacob elected to walk him. After all, that way, he could see Miss O'Brien's reaction.

Joseph walked in his own aura of splendor, and after a time of walking next to him, Jacob ventured another question. "Do you have business dealings in Oregon or Washington?"

I was stricken with an illness shortly after my wife died, and it was believed that I might not survive either, but I had a vision that I would expand my dry goods stores throughout the United States, and that helped to pull me out of my sick bed; and, now that I'm here, I'd like to locate my dear little friend," he ended with a slightly wistful smile.

"Well, we're here," Jacob said and motioned quietly to the school, "and it appears that school is letting out. I suppose we can put our heads in the door and see if Kayleigh is available."

"Kayleigh was beginning to tidy up her desk and talk with Ned about his arithmetic work. She had gathered two books up into her hands as Ned made his way out the door. She glanced after him as he approached the door, and a curious look crossed her face—a mix of confusion and shock, which caused her to drop both books. It couldn't be, could it? Why would he be here?

He approached her smiling while Jacob hung back, a curious, challenging, and somewhat sad look on his own face. Then, suddenly, she flung her arms around Joseph, and he returned the embrace.

"Joey," she whispered. "Where is Fancy?"

"She passed, Little Bit," he said, barely above a whisper. "I'm in Oregon on business, and I just wanted to look in on you. I go by Joseph now. It matches my more mature gray hair," he said and laughed.

Jacob turned and left. He walked to the docks without a word, feeling as though he had been hit in the gut, hit hard. He hadn't felt this sensation since the loss of Kelly.

He stayed away from Kayleigh but watched respectfully from a distance. *After all*, he mused, *the young woman deserved to be happy, and if this was the man to help that happen, why not?* Then, on a Friday afternoon, Joseph tipped his hat to Jacob as they both crossed the street, and Jacob held up his hand in a half wave before beginning to turn away, "Be good to her, McVale. She is strong but still somewhat different and so dear," Joseph said, catching up to Jacob and shaking his hand before turning back to get his horse.

Kayleigh and Joseph had been seen out walking and talking throughout the town, and one of the older ladies in town even speculated on "what a beautiful baby they would make!" Then, on a Saturday morning, a week after he had entered town, several of the townspeople saw Kayleigh kiss him gently on the cheek, and he returned the kiss in the same manner before he spoke to Jacob and rode away.

Of course, word had already gotten back to Jacob, and he decided to make sure that Kayleigh saw him in town. "Well, what became of your friend, Mr. O'Dell?" Jacob asked as nonchalantly as possible with a slight smile and a gleam in his eye."

Kayleigh was aware of the situation enough to realize the undercurrent of the question. "I didn't feel the same towards him as I did when I was a girl. It's really as simple as that. By the way, Mr. McVale," she said hesitantly, "I've…I've missed seeing you about town." She looked down, wondering if she had said far too much.

Jacob beamed, "Well…I've certainly missed our talks." With that, he offered his arm, and they walked back toward the schoolhouse together.

CHAPTER 41: A PREVAILING SADNESS

As the fall days wove themselves into a daily pattern colored by the town, the school children, and the falling leaves themselves, Jacob and Kayleigh went into a pattern of going to church together, taking walks, and shopping in town on Saturdays. The end of October and the beginning of November were very beautiful, and they made a beautiful couple.

Daniel, Lydia, Maddie, and Pete were as happy for Jacob as Mitch, Rosemary, Zach, and Caroline were for Kayleigh. In fact, much of the town who had always known Jacob, or the parents who had come to appreciate Miss O'Brien, were happy with the match, but, in the forefront of Kayleigh's mind was the continual obsessive question, "What if he finds out?"

So, for three weeks of courtship that were unfolding, all was sweet, fun, and, to Jacob's disappointment, very platonic. Not even a kiss had been exchanged. Somehow, his instincts were telling him to be very careful, lest she skitter away like a deer he had once observed, who came no closer than the water that she was seeking. He knew also that she was lonely, but he also knew that she would never admit or reveal that fact or why.

Still, for a man accustomed to being pursued, or at least responded to very quickly, this was a different situation and none too easy on his pride and ego. Lately, his mother's words from his fevered dreams were returning to him, and he knew that patience was the key. It also touched him when Kayleigh spoke of Thanksgiving and having Cassie there in town with her. A woman who cared that much about a child could be worth the wait.

Then, on a beautiful Tuesday morning, the word came. Daniel had been dispatched by Jacob to check on telegraphs and bids. When he showed up at the mercantile, what he saw were the Campbells in a combination of shock and sadness.

Seeing one of the men who worked on the docks gathering supplies for work, he asked him to get Jacob as quickly as he could and bring him to the Campbell's Mercantile. He further instructed him to tell Jacob to wait there until he returned.

Daniel himself went home to get Lydia. Fortunately, Maddie was also there with Lydia, helping with the weekly baking. He took both of them to the mercantile, explaining along the way what he had learned.

Kayleigh was in the middle of a geography lesson with her older students while the younger students finished their arithmetic lessons on their slates when she saw the four approaching.

She quickly gave the group a reading assignment and approached the door. "Well, to what do I owe this wonderful visit?" she asked, smiling.

"Could you step out with us?" Lydia asked, trying not to alarm Kayleigh. "Maddie can watch the students for a while. We have a telegram for you."

Kayleigh nodded as Maddie slipped by her and into the school. She felt her throat go dry and her legs weakening. This was not good.

She opened the telegram with trembling hands:

To Kayleigh O'Brien:

Come quickly.

Cassie has died.

Come now! Will meet you at station.

Matthew

The trees were spinning about her, and she could not make herself speak. There was something caught in her throat, and then she realized, as did everyone, that it was a low scream mixed with a cry.

"But this is impossible," she finally managed to say. "This is a mistake. You all saw her just a few weeks ago," she appealed desperately.

Pete came up then in a wagon, tethered the horses to a tree, and made his way over to Daniel. He knew that something was wrong and had been informed by the Campbells of the message. He felt that he might best serve by bringing a means of getting Miss O'Brien to the nearest railway station.

Jacob had taken Kayleigh's arm to steady her while Lydia patted her shoulder gently. "Kayleigh," she started softly, "let me help you get your things together, and Jacob can get you to the railway station."

"No," she stated somewhat wildly, "no, that's not a good idea."

"Kayleigh," Lydia said softly, "someone has to go with you. Someone has to help you to the station. Please let us help you."

She nodded slowly, realizing through her fog that Lydia was, as usual, right. This time, she had to have help. There was no way around it. This couldn't be real, though. Somehow, she had to wake up.

Lydia led her into the schoolhouse to gather a few items of clothing and her purse. Lydia was talking softly to her, but she had no idea what she was saying.

Jacob helped her up into the seat of the wagon, but she wasn't aware of him touching her. Nothing was real. Maybe she wasn't real.

Very little was said on the way to the station. At some point, he told her to take his arm because there would be many bumps along the way. She didn't remember doing it, yet she obediently did, as though in a trance.

When they pulled into the station depot, Matthew spotted her rather quickly and made his way through the crowd to the wagon.

"Well, Colleen (He disrespectfully sneered the Irish term for "girl"). It took you long enough." His accent was thicker and far rougher than hers. Of a stocky build, with dark hair and brows, he looked as though the permanent mean scowl had been plastered on his face.

"Matthew, this is Mr. McVale. He is on the school board. Mr. McVale, this is my step-brother, Matthew." She introduced them mechanically.

Matthew smirked at them both. "What do you think I care, Colleen? Get down so we can get on the train back to Idaho Falls and get the child buried. She was a problem in life, and now she's one in death."

"Listen, man," Jacob began, anger burning through his eyes and his hands clenching.

Kayleigh held her hand up and faced Jacob. "It's alright, Mr. McVale. Don't worry about it. I'll be back in town as soon as I have her settled. I should be taking the Monday train from Idaho Falls, so I'll teach on Tuesday. I can arrange for a ride."

With that, she jumped down from the wagon, indicating to Matthew where her valise was. He smirked and rolled his eyes, taking it wordlessly before ushering her toward the train.

McVale felt helpless again, and he hated the feeling. He had not felt this frustrated by a lack of action since his illness. He watched as the two made their way to the train.

He had wanted to tell her that he would be back to meet her, but that was not something she had the presence of mind and heart…

…to be concerned about, and he understood. So, instead, he glanced at his pocket watch, marked the time, and remembered that she had said she would come back in on Monday to teach on Tuesday. He would be back here on Monday, and, hopefully, so would she, without her stepbrother.

The week passed slowly. He was intensely worried about her and had debated over going and finding her. He had not realized how he had looked forward to talking to her each day or how she had gradually become a large part of his day-to-day life.

One evening, while he and Mary Alice were eating dinner together at Lucy's Diner, she leaned forward and took his hand. "Jacob, where are you? You're definitely not here," she smiled. "You'd better find a way to marry that girl, Jacob. She's in your heart and mind now."

Jacob looked at her in a bit of shock. How did women always know these things? Most often, they knew even before men. However, he managed to come back with, "So, you and Noah, eh? Now that's something I would never have put money on."

Mary Alice grinned like a schoolgirl and shrugged. "I can't explain it. We just have a connection. He was even a little jealous that I was meeting you for dinner tonight. I guess we'd better make this our last, my dear Jacob."

Jacob nodded. "We don't want old Noah jealous," he smiled. "I'll miss you, though."

Mary Alice then became aware that several other couples and patrons were watching them and smiling. "I knew they'd finally get together," Miss Griggs whispered to her friend, Loretta Lynch. (The two always ate together on Fridays before Loretta returned to her nephew's home and Miss Griggs returned to her cats and religious books.) "He's better off with her than with that smarty little trashy Irish teacher," she proclaimed with a quiet hiss.

"Well, of course," Miss Loretta agreed. "I told my nephew, Melvin. I said, 'Melvin, I don't care who you court in this town, but don't let it be that piece of Irish baggage. She just puts on a show of goodness.' For all we know, she may be robbing the board of precious dollars marked for education." She ended with a satisfied nod.

"Besides that," Miss Griggs leaned forward in an even more confidential manner, "big-bosomed women like her most often have designs on unsuspecting men."

"That's right. I fully agree," Miss Loretta closed the conversation.

Never mind that Melvin was the homeliest man in town and would have loved attention from anyone or that Miss Loretta's father had spent the majority of her youthful years in jail for manslaughter or even that Miss Griggs was so flat-chested she'd never needed a corset. They self-righteously maintained that they knew best.

As Jacob walked Mary Alice out the door, she took his arm. "I want to talk to you, Jacob," she said. "Maybe we could walk out toward the docks?" He nodded silently.

"Jacob," she began and sighed, trying to fit the words together, "this girl, Kayleigh, has been hurt, and very badly, but she has her pride, and that's about all. She's starved for love, but she'll never admit it, and she goes from job to job to avoid commitment. She may never trust any man, plus she's just lost the only real love she ever had, her little sister, who, I seriously doubt, was her sister."

Jacob's eyes widened, but he said nothing. Someone had voiced what he had privately thought.

"You know, when I first came here, I was bitter, and my heart was broken. You and Nathan were the only two men that I thought would understand, and I loved you both for it. I did love Nathan completely, and he was ready for marriage and a family. I didn't think that you were, but you are now."

She squeezed his arm gently, "Find a way to rescue her, Jacob. If you can, she'll give you more love than you ever imagined. Your biggest problem will be her Irish jealousy for you. Once she finally lets you in, you'll have all of her."

"Now, I'm not going to lie," she said, smiling. "I'll miss you too, but I'll get over it. I'll be fine now," she smiled, "but I don't think you will be if you don't find a way to make Miss O'Brien yours."

Jacob smiled. "Well, we'll see, won't we," he said. "We'll see."

CHAPTER 42: FETCHING KAYLEIGH

Jacob looked at his watch again. It was 1:00, just as it had been a week before when he had brought Kayleigh to the station. He scanned the crowd nervously, fearing that he would miss her when his eyes came back to the depot itself.

She was standing with Matthew, and they appeared to be arguing. Jacob got down, tied the horses, and headed toward the two while the argument grew more heated. *Why didn't Matthew just stay in Idaho Falls?* he wondered. He could understand meeting her the first time, but why come back with her?

As he came closer, he saw Matthew roughly take her arm, and he heard Kayleigh yell, "Just stop it!" Jacob was running now without even realizing that he had begun the sprint.

Then, as he ran and weaved through the crowd, he saw Matthew hit her hard in the side of the face, upward into her cheekbone, so hard that she fell backward into the depot wall. Later, Jacob would better understand the expression, "He saw red," but for now, he was only concerned with one thing: killing Matthew.

Without an awareness of time, direction, or self-control, he found himself on top of the cruel, stocky man, beating him with his fists in the face and about the head.

Jacob was not naturally a violent man, but he wanted to see blood on this man. He wanted to hurt him, and the idea of death did not bother him, but just as suddenly, he felt a small, delicate hand on his forearm. "Jacob, please stop. They'll take you to jail, not him. He is in with the sheriff."

Somewhere in the outer realms of his mind, the fact that she had finally called him by his first name brought him out of his trance and back to the bloody mess that he was making.

"Please, Jacob," she said, her voice low and hoarse, "he's worthless."

He held Matthew's head upward by the shirt collar, and his other hand was in a fist, raised in the air as he crouched over the brute. For a moment, he caught sight of Kayleigh's face and the purplish bruise that was already forming. He did not want to let this piece of filth live, but he felt himself loosening his grip.

"Let's just go, please, Mr. McVale," she pleaded.

He shoved Matthew's limp body against the wall of the depot and got to his feet. Turning, he put his arm around Kayleigh's waist and led her to the wagon. As he lifted her to the seat, he noticed how thin and limp she was. The area around her eye was beginning to swell also.

She was carrying the same valise and a long, narrow box, both of which she had put down in order to get in the wagon seat. He placed the valise in the back, and she touched his arm, asking him to lay the box in her lap. "It's her doll," she explained softly.

His heart gave a slight lurch as he remembered buying it anonymously and having Lydia take it to Kayleigh. He also remembered Kayleigh giving it to Cassie with promises of seeing her at Thanksgiving.

He reminded her again to take his arm, and they rode on in silence. The feelings of helpless frustration were returning, and he could not offer her comfort.

When they returned, he awoke her from the numb state that had embodied her and gently helped her down. That morning, he had asked Lydia and Maddie not to come until he sent for them.

"Kayleigh, we're back," he told her. "Let me help you in."

"That's not necessary," she said in a dull voice.

"Listen to me," he said, putting both hands on her shoulders. "No one should ever hit you."

She looked at him with a dull scoff of disbelief. "I've been hit at a lot, Mr. McVale. I just didn't get out of the way this time."

He looked at her, and the pain in his eyes matched the pain in hers. "Can you tell me what the argument was about?" he asked.

"Money," she said with anger and the beginning of tears. "What else? Everything is money and control with him and my other step-brother, Marcus, as well."

"Why do they want money from you?" he asked quietly and evenly."

"Because I have it!" she said. "I have money that I earned, and well," she hesitated, unsure of how much to reveal, "but they think they should have it," her voice was raising with anger and emotion now, as though every unfair ugliness was in danger of spilling out.

"I just wanted to properly bury her!" she was coming close to hysteria now. "But no, they couldn't even let me have that—my own child—and…I mean, my…" she stopped, grasping for words, a scream rising to her throat.

Jacob took her by the waist and drew her to him, her head resting on his chest, and, to his surprise, she wrapped her arms about his back, hanging on for dear life. He held her as she sobbed quietly, deep convulses of grief.

Suddenly, she stopped and pulled back, placing her hands against his chest before pulling completely away. "I'm sorry," she said. "That won't happen again. I've messed up the front of your shirt. I'm sorry."

"I have other shirts," Jacob assured her, "and there's nothing to be sorry about."

"Why not take a few more days off from work?" he asked quietly.

"That's all I have," she said, looking at him in shock. He was not sure whether the shock was coming from his suggestion or from the fact that she was just now realizing this herself.

"I don't know what I'm doing anymore," she said, running her hand through her hair. "I've lived over half of my life for that child, and now she's gone. I have nothing. I am nothing."

"Kayleigh, listen to me," he began. Then, slowly, Caroline and Rosemary came around the corner, between the schoolhouse and the back pathway leading to the upper school and home, signing to Kayleigh.

"They want me to go with them," Kayleigh said and signed back. "They say that they're my family, and they're right," she wiped tears out of her eyes and picked up the valise. Caroline hurried over and picked up the box containing the doll. Rosemary, big with child, took Kayleigh's arm and began to lead her to the upper schoolhouse, where they would look after her until they felt she was ready to be on her own.

Jacob turned to go, now facing the task of telling Lydia and Maddie that they wouldn't be needed and nursing his own feeling of not being needed.

CHAPTER 43: BEFORE HIDING

At first, after her return from Cassie's burial and service, Kayleigh tried to go on as though things were still normal with her. She tried to do her shopping and go to church. However, she caught herself finding fault with everything or losing her temper and composure.

The first incident occurred one Friday evening when she went to pick up her Dr. Healthful medicine that was now labeled: "Medicine for Back Pain and Other Lady Maladies." The Campbells were always kind about holding it for her and very discreet. However, this time, the box and wrapping looked different. Her brow was wrinkled as she paused and undid the package to check the bottle within. The bottle was labeled differently. The design had been changed, and the title now boasted in small print, "Greatly Improved Relief for Women's Maladies." The print for the ingredients was even smaller.

Kayleigh paused before she went out the door from the mercantile. "This isn't right," she said loudly.

"What isn't right, dear?" Mrs. Campbell asked.

"This medicine!" Kayleigh answered. "It's different. You would think a company could get things right. No one tries to get anything right!" Her voice was rising in near hysteria again.

Mr. Campbell came over from behind the counter and touched Kayleigh's shoulder. "Sweetheart, Mrs. Campbell and I will write the company and try to straighten it out. Let us look into it."

"No, I'm sorry," Kayleigh said. "It certainly isn't your fault. I'll write them."

"Well, let us walk you home, dear," Mrs. Campbell offered.

"Yes," Mr. Campbell agreed.

"No, I'm alright," she said, holding up her hand. "I'll be alright."

But she wasn't. Had she read the contents of the bottle, she would have noticed, in very small print, that a substantial percent of laudanum had been added.

CHAPTER 44: BEST INTENTIONS

"It's a beautiful Saturday, and the dress shop is open! Nothing makes me feel better than a new dress, so let's go!" Lydia made this animated announcement after Kayleigh opened the door to her and Maddie.

She had to admit even to herself that she did need some new clothes, and now that she no longer had some of her other expenses, she could afford a new dress or two.

"Well, I can see I'm outnumbered," she admitted. "Why not?"

And, indeed, the dress in the window of Mademoiselle Jeanette Marteen's Dress Shop did mesmerize Kayleigh and stop her in her tracks. It was possibly the most beautiful dress that Kayleigh had ever seen. It almost had the look of a wedding gown.

"Isn't it a beauty?" Maddie asked. "Let's go inside and see how much it would set you back," she finished with a grin.

Kayleigh grinned, too. Despite herself, she wanted to buy something pretty, something that felt good to wear.

Indeed, Mademoiselle Jeanette Marteen's Dress Shop definitely had a French feel. This was a shop somewhat out of place for a new and still primitive town. It was what Mademoiselle Jeanette referred to as "an oasis of chic."

This was not the shop where women went for everyday dresses. Most ladies went to the mercantile, the town seamstress, ordered out of the catalogs available, or made them themselves.

The front of the shop was like a French salon with dress forms and couture displays leading to the next room with racks of the displayed dresses and clothes in various sizes. It was rumored that Mademoiselle Jeanette was rich (an inheritance from her father).

It was also rumored that Jeanette had her eye on Jacob McVale. Kayleigh found that easy to believe also.

"Could I help you?" Miss Rainer, her diminutive assistant, asked cheerfully in her French Canadian accent.

Lydia turned to Kayleigh while Maddie busied herself looking at the little girl dresses. They, like the ladies' dresses, were rather luxurious. Kayleigh smiled and told Miss Rainer that she was interested in the dress in the window.

"Let me just find Mademoiselle," Miss Rainer said, looking about. "I don't believe she's hung any of the newly arrived dresses yet, or she can take your measurements and have our seamstress create one."

Lydia raised her eyebrows and smiled. "It sounds 'tres chic,'" she said. They both laughed but stopped when they saw Jeanette bustle into the room.

"I understand that you like the dress in the window," she said abruptly. "We simply do not carry it in your dimensions," she motioned toward Kayleigh's chest in a matter-of-fact way.

"Well, alright," Kayleigh answered. "What if your seamstress made it for me?"

"I'm afraid that we do not have any more of that fabric coming in," Jeanette said in a dismissive French accent.

"Could it be special ordered?" Kayleigh persisted.

"I have never known them to carry true couture gowns in your dimensions," Jeanette smirked.

Lydia and Kayleigh both stood a bit dumbfounded, and Maddie, startled, looked up from her browsing.

"Now listen, Jeanette," Lydia started, her voice low with anger, "you know good and well…"

Kayleigh said quietly, barely above a whisper, "It's okay, Lydia. I have something else in mind anyway,"

"Yes, the mercantile or the catalogs might have your style or measurements," Jeanette gave a small laugh.

"Well, it's too bad you can't order a new soul or personality through the catalogs," Lydia said furiously. "Let's go, Kayleigh," she said as she and Maddie glared at Jeanette and left.

After apologies and promises of other shopping excursions, Lydia and Maddie left reluctantly from the schoolhouse, sadly feeling that somehow they'd done more harm than good.

Kayleigh, however, had an idea in mind that would profit both her and Caroline and put Mademoiselle Jeanette in her place.

CHAPTER 45: A HAUNTING PIANO TUNE

On Christmas Eve, when Miss O'Brien seemed to have disappeared except for being seen in the school or the schoolyard, Jacob, Daniel, and Pete went to hear the town's Lady's Choir sing Christmas carols at Lucy's.

The fishermen and dock workers were merrily celebrating the small bonuses Jacob had doled out to each, and Daniel and Pete were looking forward to Christmas Eve and Christmas morning with their girls as they slipped out early with Jacob.

The three were about to part ways as they walked down Main Street when they heard the eerie echoing of the church organ and a forlorn but beautiful voice.

They looked at each other and, with silent agreement, headed toward the church. "Daniel," Jacob instructed, "stand at the door and don't let anyone come into the church. Tell them that the ladies are having a Christmas choir practice or whatever you come up with."

Daniel nodded as Jacob and Pete made their way into the church. As Jacob had suspected, Miss O'Brien was sitting at the organ playing a somewhat off-key version of 'Silent Night' and singing in a slurred voice. Yet, somehow, the prettiness of her voice still came through.

"Jacob, has she been…" Pete asked in a whisper, making a drinking motion.

Jacob shook his head and quietly said, "She wouldn't do that."

As they both made their way toward the back of the church, Kayleigh folded over the keyboard of the organ, head on her arms, like a flower wilting from the hint of a cold wind.

Jacob approached her slowly, "Kayleigh, it's time to go home now." He carefully placed his hand on her shoulder. "Let's go home now, love," he said softly.

Pete looked on with sympathy and a bit of surprise, given Jacob's tenderness toward Kayleigh. He knew, though, that this was a grieving woman, a woman with no one that she was certain she could turn to.

Daniel gently opened the door and looked into the small church. "Is she okay?" he mouthed, not wanting to startle her or his brother.

"Yes," Jacob said in a low voice. "Just keep watching. We'll go out the back way."

Suddenly, Kayleigh raised her head and, through hazy eyes, looked at Pete and asked, "And where is home? We don't all have one," she said with halting and slurred speech.

"Well," Pete began softly and gently, "right now, yours is the schoolhouse."

"Oh yes," she agreed, "my assigned abode."

"Come along, dear," Jacob said as he helped her rise to her feet. "We'll go out the back way to the schoolhouse," he said quietly to Pete.

With Pete on one side and Jacob on the other, they each took an arm and helped her carefully down the path along the back of the church to the schoolhouse. Daniel peaked around the church in time to see them quietly slipping past him.

He waved to let them know that he was going home, but he would definitely have a talk with them tomorrow. He wanted to tell them anyway that he had taken it upon himself to have a quiet conversation with Miss Griggs and Mademoiselle Jeanette concerning their treatment of Miss O'Brien and her current situation. In his mind, Kayleigh O'Brien was not to be hurt, and they needed to know it.

"Kayleigh," Jacob began carefully, "can you tell me what you've had to drink?"

"What are you…What are you tryin' to say?" she said with all the offense and dignity that her present condition would allow. "I just had some of my medicine," she said, swaying between Pete and Jacob. "As you may know, I have back troubles."

"Yes, dear, we know," Jacob soothed, "but it could be that it's too strong for you, or you need to cut the dose back. Try not to take it anymore."

"So, what are you, Mr. MaVale?" She slurred, "*A doctour*? Oh, alright, I'll try not to take it!"

Pete laughed quietly despite himself.

"And what about that school board, anyway?" she continued, veering to a completely different topic, "I mean, what flew up Miss Griggs' skirt, or never did, and what about that Mr. Thomas? One day, he's gonna smile, and we'll declare a holiday. Then there's you," she said pointing to Jacob. "You knows what?" she said, pointing to Jacob. "You are one of those *perfeck peeple*, are not you?" she said, still weaving, "Just plain *perfeck*."

Pete looked at Jacob and smiled. Then, just as suddenly as her humorous litany, she switched to sadness. "Why did she have to die?" she cried. She was coming here. We were going to have Thanksgiving and Christmas together. I was going to play 'Silent Night' for her. We were going to have a house… somewhere, maybe in Canada. I just wanted my lil' girl. Why does God take everythin' just when it looks like you might get it?"

Pete looked at Jacob questioningly. Was she saying what he thought? This dear lady had been through even more than anyone knew except maybe Jacob. Gradually, they made it to the back door of the schoolhouse and helped her up the steps.

"Pete, I want you to go now," Jacob said, "and make sure that you don't tell anyone about this, even Maddie. I'll help her get settled and be on my way."

Kayleigh was swaying like a limp rag doll as Jacob picked her up. "Jacob, I've got to tell you that won't look good if anyone finds out," Pete said with a mix of worry and doubt.

"No one will know, will they?" Jacob returned defensively. "I'm going to get her settled for sleep and leave. That's it," Jacob finished, the usual authority back in his voice.

Pete nodded and opened the door as Jacob made his way in. Pete made his way back onto Main Street, and once in, Jacob did just what he had said. He laid her gently on her bed and noticed that she was already going into sleep. He removed her shoes and turned to leave before taking in the contents of the room. The doll that he had bought her and that she had given to Cassie lay on the opposite pillow as if waiting for her.

On her side dresser, she had an old daguerreotype picture of herself as a little girl, along with her mother, grandmother, and possibly her father. There was also a hand-sketched picture of a young man. He thought that this might be her stepbrother, Luke. He was handsome but looked rather childlike.

Then, of course, there was her sketch of Cassie, and there seemed to be another sketch that she was working on. He lifted it quietly and, to his surprise, saw himself.

In tiny handwriting at the bottom of the paper, he saw "My Love" written in her correct curved writing. His face was lit with surprise and joy as he smiled softly to himself.

Then, to his shock, he felt a small hand on his, and the grip was very firm before she went completely limp into sleep. He smiled again and gently kissed the top of her head before slipping into the cold night air. In his hand, he held the small bottle that contained her Dr. Healthful elixir, which he had quietly lifted from her bureau. He could not see the contents in the darkness, but he knew that it was not something she needed as he silently poured it out.

Noah Thomas made his way slowly down the street. Mary Alice had asked him to come by the inn for the choir's performance. He had a small gift for her. He hoped a lady's handkerchief would be fine. He was smiling to himself when he saw what looked like a shadow slipping out the back door of the schoolhouse. He was almost certain that it was Jacob McVale, but he was not a man to carry tales, and he trusted Jacob.

The next morning, Jacob went by and knocked on the schoolhouse door. He had thought that he would offer to get her a cup of coffee to help with what was probably an aching. However, there was no one home. Miss O'Brien had already left for Mitch and Zach's house.

CHAPTER 46: A SECOND CONVERSATION WITH MITCH

Then, the real reclusive behavior began. Kayleigh completed her teaching duties each day, went out the back door to the upper schoolhouse, and was later walked back to her little house by Zach and Caroline.

She no longer did her after school tutoring, and if she needed items from the mercantile, Caroline and Zach, or Mitch and Rosemary, handled it for her.

She no longer answered her door either, and church was no longer a part of her Sundays. Parents and town acquaintances were beginning to question why she was no longer being seen in the usual settings. They understood needing a few weeks, but this was stretching into two months.

She spent most evenings with Mitch, Zach, and their wives. They were glad to have her, but their concern was growing as well. So, when Jacob came to the upper school door one evening after trying to get Miss O'Brien to her own door, Mitch appeared and quietly came out on the porch with Jacob.

"Well, Mitch, I've been sent on a mission to find our Miss O'Brien and see if we can get her out and about rather than just to school and back," Jacob disclosed.

"And just who sent you on that mission, Mr. McVale?" Mitch smiled.

"Well, let's see, that would be Lydia, Maddie, Jennifer Anne, Mary, Penny, my brother, Pete, Lucy, the Campbells, the Reverend and his wife, and half the town," Jacob replied, as he took a deep breath and laughed.

"And what about you?" Mitch asked, still smiling in a kind way.

"What about me, Mitch?" Jacob asked.

"Well, Jacob, I know that you care about her. You're not going to deny it, are you?" he asked.

"No," he said. "I want to know when she'll be out and about again."

"Could you sit down for a bit, Jacob?" Mitch motioned to the two rockers on the front porch.

"All right," Jacob agreed.

"Part of her hiding," Mitch began quietly, "is pure mourning and probably some anger. Part of it is embarrassment."

"Embarrassment?" Jacob questioned. "Why should she be embarrassed?"

"Well, think about it, Jacob," Mitch said as though instructing one of his adolescent pupils.

"You've seen the wreck of a family that she comes from, the abuse heaped on her, and pure, raw grief. The persona that she has so carefully constructed just fell apart in front of you.

"Zach and I, well, we already knew how things were. It's not like we come from any better. It's not like a lot of people come from any better, but Kayleigh looks up to you, Jacob. In her mind, you and your family are on higher moral ground, beacons of the community and that sort of thing."

Jacob was visibly touched by Mitch's view of the situation. He hesitated before asking, "Mitch, as one man to another, do you honestly think I'm that kind of a paradigm of virtue?"

"No, Jacob," Mitch laughed. "I think you're a good man with some living under your belt, but it doesn't really matter what I think. It's Kayleigh that we're concerned with here. Also, I've got to tell you. I've never seen her really infatuated with, or in love with, any man—until now."

"You think that she's in love with me?" Jacob asked, leaning forward, a look of incredulous disbelief and hope on his face.

"Oh, I know it," Mitch answered. "However, that doesn't mean that you'll ever see her show it, and you know that she doesn't plan on staying past this year, although she'd die before she revealed that particular information to anyone. No, in her mind, she's not romantic material for anyone like you. You'll have to go after her and don't ask me how. I certainly never knew how.

"However, I can tell you that she goes home each evening and sits out on that little back porch in the evening. That's where she could be found, but you run the risk of startling her."

Mitch paused and looked very directly at Jacob in that somewhat primitive way that even men like Mitch used on other men. "Do you love her, Jacob?"

"Yes," and Jacob took his time answering, "but if you go about making that everyone's business, including Zach's and your wife's, I'll beat you like a drum, Mitch," Jacob concluded in a matter-of-fact way. "Do we understand each other, Mitch?"

"I believe we do, Jacob," Mitch answered. "I believe we do."

CHAPTER 47: KAYLEIGH'S VISIT WITH MISS GRIGGS

Kayleigh was helping Rosemary arrange a little nursery for the baby one Saturday afternoon. With permission from the board, Mitch had walled off a small area in his and Rosemary's bedroom. It would serve as a small room for the baby.

Rosemary signed with Kayleigh about the plans she and Mitch had for having the baby and staying on at the upper school. Rosemary felt that they had finally found a home. Kayleigh assured her that she was happy for both of them but did not reveal her own plans.

Kayleigh thanked the couple for a lovely day and decided to walk back the front way. The town was practically deserted, and she could use the exercise of walking about the square before turning toward home.

As she walked, she saw a small figure in the middle of the street between the mercantile and the tavern. As she approached, she saw that it was Miss Griggs, and she seemed to have fallen while clutching some sort of album or scrapbook. Her little body was curled into a fetal position, and she was obviously in some sort of shock.

Kayleigh kneeled down next to Miss Griggs. "Can you move, Miss Griggs?" she asked.

"I'm not sure," she answered. "I seem to have tripped somehow."

"May I help you up, or do I need to get someone to carry you?" Kayleigh asked soothingly.

"No man will ever have to carry me until my time is at an end," Regina Griggs declared. "You may help me up," she concluded.

Kayleigh helped her into a sitting position and then helped her all the way up. "Are you steady, Miss Griggs?" she asked.

"I seem to be," she responded. "Would you help me get home?"

Kayleigh began walking her toward her home when she ventured the obvious question. "Miss Griggs, where were you going?"

"Actually, I was coming to see you," she answered.

Kayleigh shook her head as if to clear it of an annoying fog. "Given our history together, might I ask why?" she said.

Miss Griggs sighed, "Get me home, and I'll explain."

Miss Griggs' home looked much like Miss Griggs. From the subdued colors in the drapery and carpets to the austere furnishings, her only bow to color was her red velvet sofa.

"Sit down," she said abruptly. "I have something to show you."

Kayleigh sat down next to Miss Griggs in the parlor. Less than an hour before, she had just finished looking at baby quilts with Rosemary. "What was she doing here with this fiendish little woman?" she wondered.

Miss Griggs had removed her cape and urged Kayleigh to hand her the wrap that she wore. She laid them both to the side on the opulent sofa before opening the album that she carried.

"I want to show you something," Miss Griggs said, motioning Kayleigh to look at her album. The album itself was a mixture of a few daguerreotype pictures and mementos from a young man's life—a very handsome young man.

"I'll be telling you a few things that I am beseeching you not to tell another," Miss Griggs seemed to beg with her eyes.

"Alright," Kayleigh agreed. "I don't disclose private information, and I don't breach a trust."

"Well, you may have wondered why I have been so hard on you," Miss Griggs continued.

Kayleigh laughed, "Well, that's putting it mildly."

"Well, this is it," Miss Griggs said, pounding the album with her small index finger.

"I came here twenty-four years ago to live with my uncle, Reginald. He is still known as the first man of wealth to live in this town and this territory. Most assumed that I came because my parents were deceased, and I suppose that may be partly true, but mainly, I came for him," and she softly touched the picture in her lap.

"This is my son," Miss O'Brien," she said, drawing a breath, "but most people who remember him would identify him as my nephew.

"You know, Daniel McVale came to see me a few days ago. He and Rory (that was my son's name) were friends. Daniel was always like a conscience to Rory and some of the other boys in town. I don't think dishonesty or cruelty know Daniel McVale. They're just not a part of him.

"Anyway, he informed me of the loss you had just experienced with your little sister and the grief that you were trying to find your way through. I understand that kind of grief, Miss O'Brien, and I know that I have done you a disservice by questioning your every motive.

"You see, years ago, I lived with my parents in Kansas City, far past the time that most girls live with their parents. I did what I could to help them and take care of them, but then, when I was about thirty years old, it hit me hard that I was not much more than an isolated and trapped old maid.

"An Irish man and his sister came to town. They presented themselves as a handyman and a maid. My father had passed away, and my mother's sickness was a long and suffering one, so, after a time, I hired them. Their names were Colin and Shannon O'Leary. They began to live in our small guest house. I had divided the room with a curtain so that they could have privacy, although I offered to let Shannon stay in the smaller bedroom inside the house.

"Colin was beautiful to look at, and, believe me, I had never thought of calling a man beautiful, but he was not unlike that young man who just recently walked into town, except that Colin had dark blond wavy hair and piercing blue eyes. His sister was a redhead with gorgeous green eyes and a figure to match.

"They were both so affable, so agreeable, so soothing, and a bit of fun as well. I was smitten with him and enchanted by her. My loneliness became more evident and demanded to be recognized and taken away.

"When Mother died, rather than the extreme grief that I should have felt, I felt fear, fear that Colin and Shannon would now leave.

"One evening, after the funeral and the visitors for my mother, I set about trying to find out if they would stay or leave. I walked over to the guest house and knocked on the door. Colin answered the door, and Shannon excused herself, claiming that she needed to complete her food shopping for the week.

"I sat down at the small table with Colin and began to ask about his plans when he took my hand in his and said, "I don't want to leave you, Regina, but I need a commitment. I need to know that you trust me. I want to marry you."

"I was overcome with joy, so much so that I began to cry, and things seemed to be going well in the next few weeks. We were married in the spring.

"He said that he needed some money to start a farm for us. He claimed that he couldn't be a 'kept man' from the funds that my parents had left me from their dairies. The dairies had been sold long before Colin came along. So, I foolishly allowed him access to my bank voucher book, which gave him access to my inheritance.

"Then, one morning, I awoke, and he and Shannon were both gone. A few days later, a Pinkerton man came by and told me that Colin and Shannon Murphy were a husband and wife con team. They preyed on unmarried women and widows. Colin was a bigamist.

"I had the house and a hundred dollars left, and by this time, I knew that I was pregnant. I wired my aunt in Topeka that I needed a place to stay, and she agreed to take me in.

"After selling the house and taking my hundred dollars, I arrived in Topeka. Of course, she was scandalized by my condition but still allowed me to stay. She told me that I nearly died in childbirth, but thankfully, I don't remember. Rory was born, and he thrived. We lived with Aunt Sadie for four years.

"We had told people that I was widowed, and most believed that without question. Then, a couple from Kansas City came to town and, after seeing me, felt it their mission to let many of the town folk know what had really happened.

"Aunt Sadie and I agreed that I needed a new identity and a new home. After wiring my uncle Reginald, we traveled here to Faithful. It was a difficult trip and rather hard to find the town.

"By this time, Rory was five years old. Between the three of us, we decided that Rory was an orphaned cousin that we were taking in, and I was his spinster aunt. This made me Uncle Reginald's sister. This also made me next in line to both his and Aunt Sadie's fortunes.

"The town bought it, and because it is a more remote territory, we didn't worry about any more Kansas visitors. I also had instant status and respect, or possibly fear, from the town folk. At any rate, I am a wealthy woman of influence in this town. I am also, quite often, a lonely woman, a woman who could not grieve properly for her own son."

"How did Rory die?" Kayleigh ventured since Miss Griggs seemed to be at a stopping point in her story.

"When he was twelve, he ran a high fever and seemed to be swelling in his legs. I took him to a doctor in Portland, who diagnosed it as rheumatic fever. His heart was gradually shutting down. He lingered a few more years, and all of his friends came. We buried him on what would have been his fifteenth birthday.

"Daniel was a poll bearer. Those two were close friends with boyish schemes and memories of carefree school days. It's strange, but somehow, I always felt that Daniel knew how things would go."

That was also strange because Kayleigh had always felt that Daniel knew her situation, too. He had that kind of sensitivity.

"Miss Griggs," she asked, "what exactly did Daniel tell you?"

"Only that your little sister had passed and that you were especially close to her and responsible for her," Miss Griggs answered.

Then, slowly, Miss Regina Griggs took Kayleigh's hand and said what Kayleigh never thought she would hear from her or anyone, "I'm sorry," Miss Griggs said.

"It's alright," Miss Griggs," Kayleigh said. "It's alright, and so are we."

CHAPTER 48: A ONE-TO-ONE ON A BACK PORCH AND A TRIP TO CHURCH

"Miss O'Brien," a male voice called out.

Despite herself, a hearty cry of "Saints preserve us!" spilled out as she clutched her nighttime wrapper about herself.

She could now distinguish Jacob McVale as he came closer toward the lantern that she had placed on the porch step next to her.

"I'm so sorry. I didn't mean to startle you," he said.

"Well, after all, Mr. McVale," it is pitch dark, and I am on my own back steps in a night wrapper," she said defensively.

"Oh, I've seen ladies in their night clothes before," he said, grinning.

"Well, good for you. I'm sure you have," she said, frowning.

For a moment, he took her in. With her hair down, the little spectacles off that she sometimes worked in, her sketches scattered about her, and clutching at her wrapper, she looked very childlike.

The lantern cast a lovely light on Jacob's features and caused her to mentally outline the shadow of his strong jaw, and there, in the passing flash of an instant, she saw what they could be together, what their future could be, and how they could age together; but, then she had felt these feelings before. Could he ever understand?

"Why are you here, Mr. McVale?" she asked suspiciously.

"Well, I've been somewhat 'appointed' to make sure you're well and alive at night and to try to coax you into getting out and about again," he finished.

"Well, as you can see, I'm fine," she said, her hand still on the collar of the wrapper.

His first thought was, "Not really," but he settled for saying, "I'm glad. Could I ask what you're drawing?"

She slowly handed him a sketch, which he held up to the lantern. He smiled as he took it, but then the smile changed to a look of sadness mixed with care.

"This is a very good likeness of her, Kayleigh, and it looks as though we're all at our little picnic," he said, looking up at her.

"Yes," she said and held out her hand to take it back. She then picked up her second sketch and handed it to him. His eyes showed his surprise and pleasure immediately as he studied this second sketch.

"It's your view," Kayleigh said shyly. "I've always thought it was so pretty, and I haven't had a chance to properly thank you for helping Cassie and me. I hope you like it," she finished.

"This is beautiful, Kayleigh," he said quietly. "Thank you. You have a true gift. In fact, you have several: art, music, and teaching. You're very talented."

Kayleigh shrugged, but she smiled. "The teaching keeps me grounded and makes my living. The art and music help me to live."

Jacob returned the smile. They were beginning to be a little more comfortable with each other now. He pointed toward her other drawing and asked about it.

She looked a bit embarrassed but turned the sketch toward him.

"Well, that's a very pretty dress," he commented. "Are you thinking of buying one or having one made?"

"I'm having one made," she said, looking down. "I'm not sure about this one yet."

"Will you consider getting out to a few places this week?" he asked hopefully.

"Well, I have been thinking of going back to church," she said.

Jacob beamed and slapped his knee. "Wonderful! I'll be 'round for you at quarter to 8:00," he said as he began rising to go.

"W…Wait," she stammered. "I didn't say anything about…" and then she caught the look in his eye. Maybe she was wrong, but it almost looked as though he could be very hurt, and she had never thought of that as a possibility for a big, strong man like Jacob McVale.

"Well, I think that would be very good," she said. "I'll see you then."

He rose, kissed her hand, and smiled. "I'll see you then."

As he went out the gate, Sawyer gave a low growl and began his way in.

"Yeah, I know you don't like me," Jacob said under his breath, "but you'd better get used to me."

Jacob had never really been nervous about asking to escort a woman to any event, including church. He wasn't typically the nervous type. Even if a woman refused, which didn't happen very often, he just shrugged and moved on, but this time was different.

This time, he tied and retied his tie three times. This time, he re-combed his hair twice. This time, he re-polished his boots and rehearsed his greeting. This time was different, and he knew why.

Kayleigh had decided on her dress, yet she kept fidgeting with her hair in the mirror. It was the first time she had felt confident to wear it up since the bruise had finally faded.

When he reached the door, he took a deep breath and stretched his shoulders and arms a bit before knocking. Then, he pulled his breath back in, full force, when he saw Kayleigh open the door.

The light blue dress she wore had a background of small rose florets in the pattern, and it showed her figure to its full advantage. Her hair was swept up and pinned in the back and shone like gold.

Speak, he told himself, and he managed to say, "Well, good morning! You look very lovely."

She smiled and studied his face. "Do you think the dress is alright? Because I can change it if you don't think it appropriate."

"You're very beautiful," he told her earnestly, "and I wouldn't change anything. I don't think I've ever seen you in such a beautiful color."

No, Kayleigh thought, *that's because I only have the two good outfits, and they're both black*, but aloud, she only said, "Thank you, Mr. McVale."

He studied her from head to toe and noted her hair, her little lace gloves, and her new high-heeled shoes. "Shall we go?" he was finally able to say as he offered his arm.

They walked slowly up the main way to the small white church along with other couples and families. The fact that Miss O'Brien was out and about was not lost on the others also walking to church, nor was her appearance, nor was the fact that she was on Jacob McVale's arm.

She leaned slightly toward him and told him very quietly, "You can just drop me off in the back pew. I'll just sit with Ned and Mrs. Hemshaw."

"Well, I don't think that will work," Jacob said as he smiled. "You see, Ned has taken to sitting with us at the invitation of the girls, and Mrs. Hemshaw's husband finally saw the error of his ways and came home."

"What about Mary Alice?" she asked, realizing a little too late how desperate that sounded.

Jacob simply smiled again, "Mary Alice has taken to sitting with Mr. Thomas now."

"Oh," she said quietly.

As they walked in, more than a few heads turned, and Jacob held her arm a little more tightly for reassurance. Most knew about her little sister's death now, and several had been shamed into silence, including Mademoiselle Jeanette, who sat sulking in the back.

The initial shock of simply seeing Miss O'Brien out and about was quickly replaced by her beauty. Many in town already knew that she was pretty, but it was kept so subdued by her manner of style and dress that this was a total and lovely surprise for those who cared about her.

Jacob seated her next to him as he sat on the aisle. Their pew was truly full with family and friends. The girls leaned over and smiled, as did Ned and Maddie and Lydia.

Somewhere, mid-sermon, she began to notice that Jacob had taken hold of her hand, but perhaps it was a good thing since the Reverend McKendree had decided to talk about loss and grief.

"Maybe," she thought, "it was a good thing to sometimes have a hand to hold."

As they left, several women commented on how pretty her dress was, and more than one asked where she had bought it. One young woman commented that "it looks like the dress in Mademoiselle Jeanette's front window, but prettier."

Kayleigh was glad to tell them that Caroline had made the dress and one more in the same style but a different fabric.

She also advised the ladies that Caroline was an excellent seamstress who could make any dress, of any design, at a much less expensive cost than Mademoiselle Jeanette's shop. She advised them to simply write out the type of dress that they would like and show her a picture from a catalog if one was available.

"Caroline is also able to read lips," she informed them.

Thus began the decline in Mademoiselle Jeanette's monopoly on fine dresses and the rise in Caroline's business, which thrilled both her and Zach. Of course, it also thrilled Kayleigh, but for a much different reason.

CHAPTER 49: THE SPRING STORM

By late March, Jacob and Kayleigh's romance had progressed to hands held in church, quick kisses on the cheek, walks, dinners, and long talks. It was a slow progression for Jacob, but it seemed to suit Kayleigh and make her comfortable, and they had discussed stopping her "medicine" because of the effect it had on her.

However, it was time. In fact, it was more than time for the next step, and, at last, Kayleigh was beginning to know this too. Jacob wanted a commitment and marriage.

School would be out for the first week of April. Jacob planned to go to San Francisco to carry out some banking business as he usually did each spring. Kayleigh, meanwhile, missed Jacob while he was out of town, but she did not have time to miss him for very long.

On the second day that he was gone, she received a telegram informing her that Cassie's and her mother's tombstones were completed and the mortuary needed her to make final payments and sign off on them as soon as possible. They would then place them on the graves.

Noah Thomas agreed to take her to the station and would take no money for this. Her estimation of him, along with her opinions of Miss Griggs, were changing radically. There was something different about Mr. Thomas, although she was not quite sure what it was.

As they parted at the station, Mr. Thomas agreed to come back in two days to pick Kayleigh up and get her back. He wished her well, knowing the sadness of the reason for her visit, and he admonished her to be careful in her dealings.

In truth, Kayleigh would have asked Noah for financial advice. Or, she might have even set up an account in the small bank that he managed, but she was unsure how much of her situation to reveal.

Jacob had hoped that Kayleigh would meet him at the dock when he returned, but she was nowhere to be seen. When he knocked on the schoolhouse door, Noah called out to him and explained that Kayleigh had gone to Idaho Falls in order to have the tombstones placed. He also explained that he would pick her up the next day from the station.

Jacob would have liked to pick her up himself, but he had promised Daniel and Pete that they could have the day off in order to take their girls to the county fair. His main concern, though, was that Kayleigh did not run into the step-brothers. So, he spent a nerve-wracking day at work, fearing the worst for her.

Noah had thought that he would be back with Kayleigh by 4:00 p.m. or earlier; however, when Jacob looked out at the mercantile, which was generally where Noah Thomas stopped, there was no sight of the two of them. Plus, a spring storm was brewing, and it looked as though it would be a strong one.

At 4:30, he put on his rain gear and walked into town to Lucy's. He would wait there until he caught sight of them. By 5:00, a fully-fledged storm with driving wind and rain was underway. It was hard to tell now whether Noah had pulled in or not.

However, by 5:30, with Lucy's set of eyes helping, he could tell that they had. He fastened the rain slicker tighter about himself and made sure his hat was secure before making his way across the street.

Yelling to make himself heard over the wind, he made his way up to Kayleigh. "Put your arms around my neck," he ordered as he lifted her off of the wagon. "Thank you, Noah. I'll see her home. Be careful."

He grabbed her valise and opened his rain slicker on one side, wrapping her inward to his side. She was soaking wet and shaking. With her on one side and the valise on the other, he half-walked and half-carried her into the schoolhouse.

As he shoved the door shut, he noticed how shaky she was. "Go get your clothes changed and I'll make a fire," he said. He himself was about half-drenched but nothing that a good fire couldn't dry out. He lit her kerosene lamp and a lantern near the fireplace. He handed her the lantern as she made her way to her small bedroom.

After he made the fire and hung up his slicker and hat, he started a kettle for tea. He looked up to see her emerge from the bedroom, wearing her usual Friday and Saturday outfit of a blue skirt and shirt. Her hair was loose and wet, but not as wet as it had looked, pulled up into a tight bun. She looked small, frail, and pale.

He patted the second rocker as he took the first, warming his boots and feet at the edge of the hearth. "I've started the kettle for your tea," he said. It was then that he noticed she was limping a bit. He thought that she had been stepping differently as they made their way to the house, but, in the storm, it was hard to tell.

She smiled, "Thank you for meeting us and helping me."

He smiled before asking, "And what possessed you to go to Idaho Falls by yourself?"

"The tombstones were in for Mama's and Cassie's graves," she answered somewhat defensively. "I needed to make the final payments and see them placed. I also had some banking business to do," she finished.

"I didn't run into my step-brothers if that's what you're wondering," she said while eyeing him speculatively.

"Did you know that before you went?" he questioned.

"They rent themselves out in the spring," she explained. "They sign on to fish and work on one of the big boats. They call it 'living off of someone else's dime.' No one hurt me this time, Jacob. I swear it."

"What happened to your foot?" he asked skeptically, still not sure that she was being completely honest, but sure now that she had been limping a bit.

"I turned my ankle. I got off the train and decided to walk to the cemetery and the Langleys.

They wired for me to stay with them while I was in town. It's been quite a while since I walked to either place, and I became a bit confused. I turned around so quickly that I twisted my ankle," she motioned to her foot. "It was very foolish. Here, let me get the tea and pour," she said as she pushed herself up from the chair.

Jacob wasn't quite sure that this was the whole story, and Kayleigh was not ready to tell him that she saw Matthew lingering at the cemetery near a newly dug grave. She quickly began to run before he could see her and turned her ankle in the process. The Langleys were alarmed and bandaged it the best they could.

"I'll pour," Jacob said as he also got up. "Then let's sit for a while and give the storm a chance to pass."

She nodded, and they both felt the closeness of each other as they managed the tea. Actually, Jacob would have preferred a good cup of coffee, but he knew that she preferred tea.

They sat in front of the fire without saying much, and Kayleigh realized that she had never known a man who looked just as good in a rugged state as in "Sunday Go to Meetin'" dress suit attire.

Of course, he usually laughed and said, "Don't get too close to me," when he'd had a long day out on the boats. However, he cleaned up quickly and always looked the gentleman, whether in old dungarees and waders, a clean flannel shirt and regular pants, or his suit. Tonight, though, he looked rugged and just as wet from the rain as she did.

Kayleigh finished her cup of tea, and Jacob reached over and took her hand. "I have really missed you and been concerned for you," he said softly, gazing into the fire.

"I missed you too while you were gone to San Francisco." She knew now that he was serious about her, and that knowledge both elated and frightened her as they held hands and enjoyed the fire for a while longer. Then, they both noticed that the storm had subsided.

"Well, I think that I had best go while the storm is taking a rest," he said and stretched a bit. "I'll see you tomorrow, though. There's one more day of school being out, and we might as well take advantage of it," he grinned, and she nodded.

She went over to retrieve his slicker from where he had left it on the front peg. As he approached, she shook it out a bit and then stood on tiptoes to help him arrange it when she was taken by the humor of the situation. She laughed softly and looked up at him, and suddenly, she was in his arms, and he was gently kissing her lips.

He stepped back just a bit, still holding her, and looked very directly into her eyes. "You are very much a woman to me, so don't expect me not to be a man to you. Do you understand, darling?" he asked softly but firmly.

"Yes," she managed to reply before he held her in and kissed her again.

"I'll see you tomorrow," he said. "I'll stay in town at Lucy's for the night." He kissed her one last time and left her somewhat breathless. It was then that he realized that he had let go of Kelly, and he somehow felt that this was fine with her.

CHAPTER 50: DON'T DO THIS

For a short time, Kayleigh was so happy that she felt the world was brighter, more colorful, and lit just for her secret enjoyment. She wanted, more than anything, to spend as much time with Jacob as possible, stealing kisses and embraces.

They walked at the shore of the bay and held hands. She told him about the trip from Ireland, and he told her of sailing with his father. Jacob revealed a bit of what he went through with his brothers and sisters and told her about how deeply in love he had been with Kelly.

She was regaining hope and the possibility of a life with a truly good man. Then she went by the mercantile, and Mr. Campbell, with a worried look, let her know that he had a telegraph awaiting her. She knew from the look on his face that it was not just a mean message. This was something that had frightened even Mr. Campbell.

She took the message from him with a slight tremble, hoping it was just the general mean-spirited, threatening type of message that one of her step-brothers would send. It proved to be much more, and this one was from Marcus. If Matthew was brutal, Marcus was without a conscience, and his message was cruel.

We've given your name to the sheriff and the circuit judge.

We have made sure that all know the truth.

You will stand before a judge. You know what we want.

We can take care of anyone who tries to help you.

Indeed, she did know. How could she have ever thought that she would have a normal, good life with anyone? It was time to run. She managed to thank Mr. Campbell, although it was nothing to be thankful about, before going home.

Once again, she took out all of her literature about Canada and the teaching colony that had formed near Saskatchewan. She penned a letter to Mr. Leonardo informing him that she would be arriving in late May and thanking him again for the position. She also intended to wire her bank in Idaho Falls and ask if she could have her balance wired to the bank in Saskatchewan.

The next morning, before going to school, she stopped and left the letter with the Campbells. Mrs. Campbell's eyes grew wide at the post address, but she said nothing. Cal Lindstrom was also in the store, and he smiled at her and waved.

She returned the smile, but he knew that something was wrong, and he stole a look at the envelope. Cal might not have been well educated (his poor mother's biggest regret), but he was savvy about life. He knew when someone was getting ready to run.

Kayleigh made it through the day, but she avoided Jacob, and the next day, her mind was still racing and heavy with the message.

"You've been difficult to catch these last two days," Jacob said jovially as he came through the schoolhouse door, dodging the children who were beginning to leave. I thought we were going to see each other yesterday. "Have you started your after-school help again?"

"I have, sir. I just don't happen to have anyone today," she answered, and he noticed that a light had left her eyes. A sad determination had taken its place.

"Well, I'd like to talk to you a while," he said.

"I'm actually a good bit better, Mr. McVale," she answered. "My ankle is healed."

"Well, that's good to know," he returned the smile, and he wondered why she was back to "Mr. McVale. "I have your contract for the next school year," he told her and raised his hand to show her. "By the way, what will you be doing this Saturday after your famous 'Final Play' on Friday?"

"I'll be going to Canada with Mitch and Zach and their wives. Mitch and Zach's foster parents, who raised them, live there. I have met them before, and they've been very kind to all of us. Also, I have a job interview there, so it seems to be a good arrangement." She was careful not to meet his eyes.

"A job interview?" he asked quizzically.

"Yes, as I originally explained, I don't stay in one area for very long, so it's time to start looking for my next fall position. I'll need to have another place to go to," she explained.

"But you're well received and cared for here, Kayleigh," he said with a steady raise in his voice. "I don't understand this. You could stay here indefinitely. The whole town is in love with you. This is your home!"

"It's simply for the best," she tried to quietly reason.

He looked at her in frustration and with a tinge of anger. "I thought that we were in the beginning of something," he looked at her, but she looked away. Then he shrugged.

"Well, I suppose you would know best. Good day," he said as he turned and left. He knew that he was close to exploding in anger and thought it might be best to approach her again, a little calmer.

She gathered up her books with a look of sadness. As she walked to the schoolhouse, she felt that she had lost her best friend and the hope of anything more.

Superintendent Strickland sent a message the next day advising that he wanted to meet with all three teachers in the inn meeting room after school. Mitch let Kayleigh know that Rosemary was ill, and Zach simply didn't want to go, so it was just her and Strickland.

She explained the virtues of dividing schools into three separate levels, which was the information he had requested. Strickland then offered her a job at a school in Portland, which he said that he "frequently visited" while he eyed her rather obviously. (Somehow, she knew that he had only expected her to come.)

As she finally managed to leave Superintendent Strickland at Lucy's, sweet Cal asked once again to walk her home. (This was his third attempt.) This time, she just didn't feel like coming up with an excuse. So, he joyously walked alongside her down the main street. She was surprised, however, since lately he had been observed waiting on Mademoiselle Jeanette and walking her down the street.

At the back of the inn, Jacob McVale finished a cup of coffee before Lucy approached his table. "What are you doing, Jacob?

"Mind your own affairs, Lucy," Jacob replied.

"I am," she stated simply. "You are like my family, and I take care of my family. So, you saw her with Strickland and Cal? So what! She was strictly talking school with Strickland, and Cal means nothing to her romantically. Don't be foolish. Sleep on it and talk to her tomorrow," she warned.

Across the street, Cal made his own offer, "You know, Miss O'Brien," Cal began, "I wouldn't mind trying out a new town or a new country. Canada has always appealed to me."

She looked at him, a bit dumbstruck, wondering where he was going with this. "Why are you telling me this, Cal?" she asked rather bluntly, and from the corner of her eye, she could see the Mademoiselle Jeanette glaring at her.

I can see pretty clearly when someone is trying to run from one thing to another," he said with a smile. "I don't have any family left, so I don't think anyone would be looking for me. I'm also a good protector and listener, and I wouldn't expect anything from you.

Then, if you wanted marriage, we could make that happen. I'll support you in your work, and I'll find work," he said with a kind smile and a look of hope. "Would you at least think about it, Kayleigh?" he asked, and it was not lost on her that this was the first time that he had used her first name.

She glanced back at Mademoiselle Jeanette's Dress Shop to see Jacob grab Jeanette and kiss her fervently. A look of pure joy was spreading over Jeanette's face. Kayleigh felt a complete sickness that she had never felt before. It seemed to start in the center of her chest and extend to her stomach. It was an ache and a hurt beyond the physical, and suddenly, she felt as though she was choking or her clothes were strangling her.

After she assured Cal that she would think about his offer, she went in the door and unbuttoned her shirt a little further so that she could breathe. She tried to eat a quick and sparse dinner before reading her lessons for the next day, but she continued to shake and was fighting off tears.

It was a warm day in May, and she had opened the shutters above the little sink. She blew out the largest lamp and reflected that this was simply her life and always would be. She was about to go into the bedroom and ready herself for bed when she heard the hard knock at the front door. She opened it a crack to see Mr. McVale standing on the front porch.

"Mr. McVale, can I help you?" she asked.

"You can talk to me," he returned a little too loudly.

She glanced out the door and down the street. It seemed fairly empty, but people would be walking home soon. "Alright, come in," she said cautiously.

"I don't think I've ever seen you like this or looking angry and confused," she said, as though thinking aloud.

"I am angry and confused," he declared loudly. "I thought that we had the beginning of something, a friendship, or more, but this is...this is just like saying, 'I don't care anything about you. I never have.'"

"That's not what I'm sayin'. I'm...," she began.

"Then what?" he demanded. "Do we have something or not?"

"It's my fault," she said. "I should not have been so overly friendly," she said, struggling for her wording.

"What does that even mean?" he demanded, becoming increasingly more frustrated.

"I just shouldn't have encouraged a friendship," she said, as though giving a confession.

"Answer the question," he said, pounding his fist on her table. "Do we have something together or not?"

"Alright!" she shouted. "I'm having feelings for you that are not appropriate to the position. We don't need to see one another, and I need to move on before I humiliate both myself and you."

His face changed as his expression lightened. "Why don't you just let it happen?" he asked quietly. "You know that I care about you."

She held her hands up as if in defeat. "I'm not good enough for you!" she cried out.

"I can't offer you what the younger ladies in this town can. I lost that a long time ago, and I can't give you what the more mature ladies can, things like respectability, stability, and financial resources.

"When you picked me up from the train station, you saw just one part of my life, just one part, and, granted, it was one of the most painful parts, but you haven't seen it all, and I don't want you to see it," she finished.

"You don't need to protect me!" he exclaimed, with a trace of the anger back. "Whatever it is, tell me, and grant me the courtesy of making up my own mind."

"Oh, grant you the courtesy, is it?" she asked bitterly. "This isn't something to casually share at the dinner table."

"Don't you think I know that?" he shouted again. "I don't care what it is. Are you really trying to protect me or yourself? Are you that afraid of falling in love? I thought that you had more courage than to simply continue running."

"Then," he continued, "I see you with that womanizing Strickland and next Cal Lindstrom. Are you just going with any male that moves now?" he seemed to snarl the words out like an angry animal, and then he went in for the final blow.

"Or is it," he questioned with narrowed eyes, "simply that I'm not Mitch?"

This was too much. Kayleigh raised her arm to slap him and was just at his jaw when he captured her wrist hard in his own hand.

"You're hurting me," she said hoarsely, and he released her.

"What do you care?" she shouted at him. "I don't even know why you care. What does it matter? You have women around you all the time. Why don't you just reach out and take one?"

"Alright!" he yelled.

He moved quickly toward her and took her swiftly into his arms before kissing her hard and fervently. As though suddenly realizing what he had done, he backed away from her, as she did from him, both in a state of shock that it had happened and further shocked that it was as electric as it was. Perhaps he was wrong, but he thought that he had seen just the slightest smile on her lips before he backed away.

He took her back into a hard embrace and held her tightly against him. She felt as though she was melting into him.

Again, he stopped and held her out less tightly. "Kiss me," he whispered.

"I was kissing you," she whispered.

"No," he said in a low voice. "I kiss you, always. Now, you kiss me."

She took his face in her hands and slowly moved in and kissed him. He returned even more passionately. Then he held her out from him, searching her face.

She gave a slow smile and began to speak, "Jacob," she said quietly, "I really do…"

"Well, look there," Neb Darius shouted at the window and pointed while his newfound cronies laughed. "Little Miss O'Brien's really going at it. I guess you were right, Jacob. She's not so cold after all."

Jacob turned to the window while Neb and the other men ran like stupid adolescents.

Kayleigh stood in shock before she said in a low voice containing both rage and pain, "Get out."

"Kayleigh, I never said anything like that. I'm sorry," he said. "Please forgive me if I hurt you."

The feeling and the slight smile were gone as she said, "You have no idea of the twists and turns that my life has been forced to take. I am not a coward, Mr. McVale. Please just go. Go home. I have very little control over anything and never have, but I do have some control over the school and this schoolhouse, so please leave. I won't say anything about this, and neither should you."

"Kayleigh, please listen to me. Don't do this," he began.

"Get out!" she screamed. "Just get out."

"Alright, Kayleigh," he said, somewhat defeated, "but we need to talk again." He slipped out the back door, and she managed to get into bed before breaking into tears.

CHAPTER 51: THE FINAL PLAY

On the last day of school, both the upper and lower schools got together to stage a farewell play. Since the old mission/upper school was larger, it would be held there.

Zach had built a small make-shift stage that could be stored later, and the fixer-upper piano that Lucy had donated (when she bought a new one) was put to use. Parents, grandparents, brothers, sisters, aunts, and uncles all gathered. The theme was "Why We Love Faithful."

As everyone found a bench to sit on and the students began to prepare, the hum of conversation had a continual theme. Although the wording was different from person to person, the message was typically, "Can you believe what Jacob did to little Miss O'Brien?" or "I heard she just got desperate, invited him in, and nearly jumped him," and of course, "What kind of example does that set for our children?"

Other comments included, "Well, Miss O'Brien has a right to be a woman, like any other woman," and, "They're just doing what any other couple might do."

Lydia and Daniel exchanged looks, as did Maddie and Pete. "What are they talking about?" Maddie whispered to Lydia.

Mitch, Zach, and Kayleigh were settling the students in the back room. Mitch was readying himself to address the parents, and Zach was entertaining the older students with silly songs and games.

Amid the confusion, Jennifer Anne and Mary stood on a crate to look out the back window. When they saw Jacob, they hung out the window, calling to him, "Hi, Uncle Jacob," Jennifer Anne called out.

"Are you coming to the play?" Mary asked.

"No, sweethearts," he replied. "You can tell me about it later." He smiled as he noticed that Jennifer Anne had lost another tooth.

"Oh…" Mary whined, "please, Uncle Jacob. I'm an Indian princess, and Jennifer Anne has a little duet."

"Well, that is impressive," Jacob agreed, "but someone has to attend to business."

"Please, please," Jennifer Anne implored. "It only lasts about thirty-five minutes. Miss O'Brien timed it yesterday."

At the mention of Kayleigh's name, his chest tightened a bit. "Well, maybe," he said. It would give him a chance to talk to her afterward.

"Alright," he smiled.

"Goodie!" Mary shouted.

"Do your best," he said and headed into the school.

Seeing Lydia and Daniel, he went up to them and asked them to move down for him.

As he sat, he noticed that others were looking at him, some disapprovingly and some in sympathy.

"What in the world did you do to Kayleigh?" Lydia half-whispered and half-hissed.

"I didn't 'do' anything to her, and besides that, it's none of your business," he returned.

Lydia gave him a long, hard look before she turned to face "Mr. Mitch" along with the rest of the audience.

"Where is Kayleigh?" Jacob wondered. Mitch was standing in front of them, and Zach was peeking out from behind the curtain they had draped the back room with.

Kayleigh had actually positioned herself with the younger children, out of sight of the adults but close to the smaller students who needed reassurance and supervision. She was concerned that Linda, one of her eighth graders in the play, had not shown up yet to help with Jennifer Anne's singing, but there was nothing that she could do now.

With his characteristic charm, Mitch explained to the parents that they had combined to act and sing both separately and together and that their theme would be the Oregon Territory and "Why We Love Faithful." He further informed that he would be the Master of Ceremonies, while Mr. Zach would provide "other entertainment," and Miss O'Brien would play the piano.

Jacob noticed that the piano was turned toward the stage. Kayleigh would not even be facing the audience.

"So without further ado," Mitch stated, "let our play begin."

The upper school students started by acting out the trials and triumphs of the first Oregon Territory settlers, followed by singing renditions of "Old Dan Tucker" and "The Girl I Left Behind Me."

Middle students from the fourth to seventh levels gave a short play about the building of Faithful into a full township. This play also featured the mayor, played by Ned Manning. This left the lower elementary students to act out the influence of the Native tribes that had inhabited the land.

Miss O'Brien motioned to the children to come out, and Zach led them as the audience laughed at his Indian Brave costume. They laughed again when he made a motion at Kayleigh with his fake tomahawk, but she did not seem to react. She simply continued accompaniment on the piano while the play continued. It was, of course, hard to tell what she was feeling with her back to the audience.

The children gathered around Mary, who was the perfect Indian Princess, and together, the first through third levels acted out a scene in which the Indians met with the settlers, agreeing to share the land. (That had never really happened, but it made for a good story.)

As the mayor, Ned spoke up and said, "Let us live in peace and harmony."

Finally, the "head settler" added, "We all depend on each other."

The audience clapped, and Mitch came up on stage again. "And now, ladies and gentlemen," Mitch began, "we come to the singing portion of our presentation. We have three selections, and we're combining a student from the upper school with one from the lower school for each selection."

The first song combined one of the eight-level girl students with Teddy Measer, Miss O'Brien's favorite disciplinarian board writer. Together, they recited "Paddle Your Own Canoe," reflecting independence and responsibility. The audience laughed at Teddy's total animation, especially when he raised one arm like an opera singer.

Next, a fifth-level boy student dressed as a miner and a second-level girl student sang "Oh Susana," still a popular song with everyone. The miner was also flamboyant and finished with a flourishing bow. "You're such an old show off!" the little girl squealed and rolled her eyes while the audience exploded in laughter.

Finally, the plan was for Jennifer Anne to sing a closing ballad with an eighth-grade-level girl. Mitch explained that some of the eighth-grade level students would not be returning, and everyone agreed that it had been a very special year for the two schools.

The song, "Auld Lang Syne," was intended to be a poignant song for the end of school, but Linda was ill and did not come. Jennifer Anne's face was the picture of disappointment.

Seeing that, Kayleigh rose from the piano bench and went over and held Jennifer's hand.

"If it's alright with Jennifer Anne, I'll sing the final song with her since our eighth-grade student could not make it." With that, Jennifer Anne's face and spirits lifted. Mitch went to the piano and began their accompaniment while the two sang.

It was one of the sweetest interpretations of the song that Jacob had ever heard, and many in the audience had tears in their eyes. Again, the audience was impressed by Miss O'Brien's voice and surprised by the sweetness of Jennifer Anne's singing.

The whole cast came out and took another bow before the final applause. Mitch instructed the students to find their parents and thanked everyone. Mitch and Zach were beginning to move toward the door to tell both students and parents goodbye as Kayleigh quietly slipped out the back door and walked home.

This was not lost on Jacob, but he quietly made his way to the door along with all the others and congratulated Mitch and Zach on a good job. Why had she left so quickly? He understood if she didn't want to talk to him, but there were parents who really wanted to thank her for a good school year. Was she that upset?

CHAPTER 52: CALEB SPIVY RETURNS

Caleb came back into town on a rainy Friday morning. He went to the docks first and then to Jacob's house. When he couldn't find him in either place, he began to ask around town about him.

Finally, Mrs. Campbell was able to tell him where Jacob was. He, of course, had been attending the final school play, and it was the last day of school before the summer.

Mrs. Campbell was beginning to tell him how disappointed she was that she couldn't attend but instead had to watch over the mercantile when Caleb saw the school doors open and children and adults alike pouring out. For some reason, Jacob came out at the very end, looking somewhat confused. He then noticed that a crowd was gathering around Neb Darius.

"I saw them as clearly as a picture," he was loudly announcing, unaware that Jacob had attended the play and was nearby. "He was holding her, and she didn't have any objections," he declared loudly and informed the shocked crowd.

Then, Jacob was taking long strides toward Neb, and before anyone took notice, he had him by the collar. Spivy watched with avid curiosity.

"All we did was kiss," Jacob announced loudly. "Even teachers have a right to embrace and kiss."

With this, he shoved Darius into the front of the upper school porch and demanded that he tell the crowd all that he had really seen.

Darius, foolishly counting on Jacob's good nature and reluctance to fight, answered, "Well, I just told everyone, Jacob," he sneered.

With that, Jacob hit him with a closed fist across the face.

"Alright!" Neb yelled, like the true coward that he sometimes was. "Alright, Jacob's right. All I saw was the two of them kissing and holding each other, nothing more. It wasn't anything more than most courting people do," he concluded.

Jacob released him then, feeling that he was just as lowly a brute as Darius himself was a liar, but some things could not be tolerated, and he felt justified.

He took Neb Darius by the collar and told him in a low voice, "Get out of town for a few weeks or more."

The crowd began to disperse, and Caleb thought it a good time to catch up to Jacob and offer him a drink.

"Hey, Jacob," he called out. "How about a cup of coffee and lunch?"

Jacob turned around, still looking fierce from the fight, until he recognized Caleb. He raised a hand in recognition and yelled back, "Best offer I've had all day."

Mary and Penny turned to Pete, and Penny asked, "Daddy, did Uncle Jacob kiss Miss O'Brien?"

"It would seem so," Pete answered with a smile.

"What are you doing back in town?" Jacob asked Caleb as the two walked to the inn. "I never thought you'd come back to this small hamlet."

"I traced a young woman to this town, and I've heard that she's a friend of yours. I'd like to talk to you about her," he explained as they came up to the door of the inn, and with this, he looked very directly into Jacob's eyes.

As Jacob told Lucy that they'd like lunch and some coffee, they took a table, and Caleb spoke quietly. "I've got a lot to tell you, Jacob. I hope you like sad and desperate stories cause you're about to hear several."

Jacob surprised Spivy with his next words, "I don't think it matters anymore, Caleb. If it's the friend that I think it is, I may have ruined everything."

"Are you telling me that you don't want to hear the rest of a story that I just spent four months finding?" Caleb asked. "What's going on with you, Jacob? The Jacob I knew wanted the truth straight, and he went after whatever else he wanted as well."

"Of course, I want to hear about what you found out, Caleb. I just don't know if I can help her anymore," he said in a quiet hiss.

"Well, let's put it this way," Dan Caleb continued. "If you don't want to help her after this, you're not half the man I thought."

Lucy, herself, brought the coffees to the table, partly because she was short-handed and partly because she wanted to know what was going on.

"So, Caleb, out digging up dirt on someone?" she asked sweetly.

"Lucy, please go check on the lunch," Jacob advised.

"So, tell me, Caleb," he leaned forward and said once Lucy was out of earshot.

"Alright," Spivy said after taking a gulp of coffee, "here goes."

"I already knew that she was born in Ireland and lived for a time in New York. So, I called in a favor in Ireland. I've got a cousin there who I saved by sending him money for, let's say, a 'predicament' ten years ago, and believe me, it wasn't easy. He went to the Hall of Records in his county and decided to sleuth out the O'Briens.

"She was born to Kathleen O'Brien and Michael Flannigan, no record of a marriage, and, get this, Flannigan was hung for his 'political' views.

"So, she and her mother came to New York when Kayleigh was nine. You told me that she said she lived in Brooklyn, so again, I called in a favor, this time from my uncle Lenny. Uncle Lenny can barely read, but his wife is very educated, so I addressed the letter to both of them.

"My aunt went to the archives of the public library and City Hall and found the record of a marriage between Kathleen O'Brien and Nolan O'Connor. Nolan O'Connor had three sons from a previous marriage. Then, there's a record of the birth of a baby girl three years later. There are also various records of the old man being jailed.

"Then, this dear lady determines that she knew people from her childhood in the tenement building listed in the 'home birth' certificate. She actually goes to the tenement and asks if they remember Kayleigh.

"Most didn't, but one did, a little Jewish lady who says Kayleigh helped her sometimes on Sabbath. Her story is that Kayleigh, according to the family, became very sick when she was twelve and had to stay inside for months. One night, she heard her screaming and begging for help. A few days later, her mother appeared with a baby.

"Then, they disappeared, all of them, but she overheard the father telling Kayleigh that she was going to a Catholic Home for wayward girls in Quebec. According to this lady, the old man was as mean as a snake.

My trail almost grew cold from there, but I tracked down the church or home or whatever you want to call it. It had changed several times through the years, but some of the nuns had remained. I wrote to three of them, and only one replied.

"Her feelings for Kayleigh almost flowed through the paper. I think she loved the kid but didn't know how to help her. Kayleigh was there for almost two years and then disappeared, but the good sister seemed to think the youngest brother, Luke, came and got her. He was the only family member who ever came to look in on her. From there, even though she was in the States and getting closer to the Northwest, it was really difficult to trace her. It does appear, though, that Luke died.

"I've got a blank space until she enrolled in Teacher College in South Dakota. That was apparently the best and brightest part of her young life. That's where she met those two unusual schoolmasters you have in the old mission house.

"She made her own family and placed her mother and 'sister' in a little house with her and near to the Teacher College and the School for the Deaf where she taught. In the meantime, she and Mitch and Zach also worked and sang in an inn together.

"She had four different teaching positions before she came to Faithful. The last was in Boise. She apparently needed out of that one because the young minister had fallen in love with her and wanted to marry her. However, his mind was changed after he hired me, and I dug up a few of these same facts."

Jacob gave him a look of complete shock and bewilderment. "What do you mean that you dug up these same facts?"

"Look, I'm not proud of it, and that's the reason that I'm here. I want a man who knows the worth of a woman, despite her past, to know the truth. Somehow, I think it will exonerate me from that hypocrite who wound up simply propositioning her." Caleb raised his hands in defense.

"What can I say, Jacob? I needed the money, and he was willing to pay for information, but I felt like a dog when I realized who it was about. I would never intentionally hurt that good little woman," he finished.

"When she returned to the little farming area outside of Idaho Falls, where she had left her mother and 'little sister, her stepfather somehow appeared. I don't know what transpired, but suffice it to say, 'It wasn't pretty,' and here's the kicker, Jacob.

"The rumor was that she shot him. Now, here's where stories differ. Most in this Idaho Falls community said that she shot him in the arm, and he was later in town, headed for the local doctor.

"Others say that she may have killed him, but frankly, the true proponents of that story don't blame her. Others are speculating that the wife or one of the two remaining brothers killed him. The doctor said that the shot in the arm was basically a flesh wound caused by a derringer, but the shoulder was damaged.

"He didn't treat him for the other shot that people said had him bleeding out of the gut, but he examined him after he was dead. He thought the wound was caused by a rifle, not a derringer. (I had a lead on an eyewitness, but it turned out to be none other than one of the brothers, and I didn't pursue it for obvious reasons.) Then, to top it all off, the body mysteriously 'disappeared.'

"But we're not done, Jacob. She had returned to the house after living and teaching in Boise for a time, only to find her mother hanging from the rafters in the front room of the house.

"So, I suppose she saw your advertisement for three teachers, got her adopted brothers together, and raced to it. That's all I have on Kayleigh."

Jacob looked a bit stunned after that last bit of information concerning the mother. So, this meant only weeks before she came to the first school board meeting, she may have faced off with her stepfather and found her mother dead.

"Well, Caleb," Jacob offered, returning to his usual steely self, "at least let me pay you for your expenses."

"You know, I may take you up on that and ask for an endorsement from you. I'd like to set up an office in San Francisco," Caleb looked hopefully at Jacob.

"You have both, Caleb, the money and the endorsement. Just remember our agreement that you won't tell about any of this," Jacob reminded him.

"My lips are sealed, Jacob, but I do wonder. Will you be rescuing her?"

"We'll see, won't we?" With that, Jacob left.

CHAPTER 53: THE TURNING POINT

Jacob had intended to leave Caleb Spivy and go straight to the school house to try and talk with Kayleigh. However, there was some trouble at the docks. Two workers had gotten into a fight, and Pete had been hit while trying to break them up.

Then, there was a problem with one of the boats, and it seemed that he was the only person in the world who could deal with it. Sometimes, he still wondered if his brother and brother-in-law were fully capable of taking on added responsibility.

As he walked back into town, Mrs. Campbell walked quickly out of the mercantile and motioned for him to come inside. *What now?* he thought. *Did Daniel neglect to pay their monthly bill for supplies?*

"Jacob, I have to tell you," she said with quiet urgency. "I think that our young lady is in some type of trouble. She picked up her elixir, and do you know what she bought for her dinner?" Mrs. Campbell asked as if it were the most earth-shaking news available. "Well, not anything worth eating," she continued while Jacob silently shook his head.

"She bought a full box of candy. Now, at first, I thought it was some type of present for someone, but when I asked her, she said, 'No, this is just for me, just for tonight.'

"I commented on how sweet I heard that the play was, and she said, 'Thank you,' and then started out. So, I asked her again if she didn't want something else for dinner, and she came right up to the counter and said, 'With all due respect, Mrs. Campbell, who really cares?'

"So, I thought that perhaps you could go by, Jacob, and casually check in on her. What if she's sick, or some kind of harm comes to her from a fall? Could you just see about her?"

Jacob, of course, agreed to check in on Kayleigh, as he had planned to do. He had longed to see her every day and every evening, but he also knew that she did not want to see him.

He was a strong man, not dependent on ego or foolish assumptions about women, but even he was beginning to give up. Also, the fact that she was still receiving the elixir bothered him greatly.

So, as he walked toward the little house attached to the school, he wondered what would be the best approach when he heard what sounded like a crash and the distinct cry of "Oh, Bother!"

He sped up his walk as he approached the door to the schoolhouse. He knocked and waited for her to come. As she opened the screen door, what he saw was simultaneously a shock and a strike at his heart.

She looked so frail and unsteady as she opened the screen door.

"Yes?" she offered.

He answered, "I wanted to apologize for my previous remarks and actions yesterday. I shouldn't have said what I did, and I shouldn't have behaved as I did later." It seemed like an appropriate thing to say.

She looked at him through what appeared to be blurred eyes and answered, "Well, you weren't necessarily wrong. You just went about it the wrong way. I'm sorry if I said anything that hurt your feelings."

He looked at her and took in her appearance in her loosely wrapped robe with her long hair hanging disheveled, out of the usually tidy, swept-up hair. She was also wobbling back and forth, and he wanted nothing more than to take her in his arms and ask her what was wrong, but he knew better than to do that.

"Well, then, good evenin'," she said, and he noticed that her speech was very slurred. He also noticed that her left hand was bleeding.

She started to shut the door, but he stopped it gently with the toe of his boot. "What happened to your hand?" he asked.

"There's nothin' wrong with my hand," she started before looking down and noticing that it was bleeding. "Kindly get your boot out of my door."

"How did that happen?" he persisted and asked quietly.

"I don't know," she said confusedly. "I guess it was when I threw, I mean dropped, the plate."

"Here, let me help you," he said as he quietly slipped in the door.

"That's nice of you, but I really don't need your help, and you shouldn't be in here. People will talk," she finished.

"I don't think anyone will know," he assured her as he took her right hand and led her to the wash basin. "Besides that, they've already been talking, and I set them straight. Now, let's get your hand clean and look at it."

Thankfully, it was a small cut, but it had produced a good bit of blood. He picked up a clean tea towel and asked if he could use it to bind her hand until the bleeding stopped. She agreed, and he quickly and rather efficiently wrapped her hand.

"You know, Mr. McVale, you're a very good man," she said, gazing up at him while he smiled. "And you're so handsome," she continued. "You have the most beautiful hair and eyes." Now, it was official. He knew that she had taken the elixir.

"So, a few years from now, you'll be living the good life while I'll be a spinster old school teacher, fat and lice-infested, with twenty rabbits that I'm raisin'. The rabbits will probably chew me up when I die," she concluded.

"I don't think that rabbits do that," Jacob reasoned, torn, once again, between bewilderment and laughing out loud. "Now, a really big dog might, but rabbits, probably not. Well, I mean, they might eat off an ear or…"

"Could you stop talking about the rabbits!" she asked as she was becoming more agitated. "I'll officially be twenty-five in three months, and what do I have to show for it?"

"Have you had anything to eat or drink that has affected you?" he asked calmly.

"All I've had is the rest of my medicine. That's all," she finished.

"I was hoping that you weren't going to take any more of that," he said kindly.

"I hardly see what it matters," she began when he simply reached over and took the bottle, beginning to read the back of the bottle and smell of the contents.

"This has a good amount of laudanum in it," he said and pointed to the small print on the back.

Her eyes widened in horror before she began to cry. "I promised my grandmother that I would never drink," she lamented.

"It's not your fault," he reassured and tried to take her arm, but she jerked away. "Please, sit down. You're unsteady." It was then that he noticed the carnival red trunk had been pushed out of the bedroom and was completely opened as if waiting to devour whatever its owner deposited.

She allowed him to help her to the couch and began to stop crying before talking again. The Irish accent had thickened, and her grammar had slipped, but for being, she was doing remarkably well.

"My stepbrother was probably right, you know," she said while she was beginning to fight complete fatigue. "He told me that I was probably completely cold. I'd never even been really kissed by a man until you kissed me after the storm, and that was probably some pity thing.

"All these foolish men, who act like they've never seen a woman before, and all of their come on's. I feel nothin', just nothin', but you just walk by, and there's somethin' there, there's somethin'. It doesn't matter if you're dressed in your fishing garb complete with your slicker and waders or if you're dressed to go to Sunday meetin'."

Jacob smiled, and it did not nearly express what he felt. He had a chance with her, a real chance. "You're not cold," he said. "You're far from it, and I don't kiss women out of pity."

"Do you see my globe, Mr. McVale?" she asked abruptly, changing the subject as she stood and pointed to the globe in the corner of the room, which she sometimes kept in the school as well.

"Please sit down, Kayleigh," he pleaded.

"I'm trying to tell you some things," she yelled in frustration, "and it is not easy!"

"I know that, dear," he said in a quiet, calming voice, "but you'll be steadier if you just sit down."

"Do you see that long red line traced from Canada through Minnesota and all the way to Oregon? I tell people that it's a record of my travels, but actually, it's more a geographical reference to where we 'played the game' and stole.

"After I had Cassie, we went to Quebec City, where Ma and the monster that she married put me in a convent for bad girls, for bad girls!" she repeated. "How was I bad? That was the first time that

I ran. I ran with Luke. Luke, the youngest step-brother, who was like my brother, my protector, always gave me hope.

"But, of course, I didn't run until the priest had his chance to molest me. A priest, Mr. McVale, a man that you're supposed to entrust your very soul to! Why would he pick me?

"Anyway," she drew a breath, "Luke came back for me, and it wasn't hard to catch up to them and pick up the same con game that we'd played in New York. It was just with a carnival this time. So we played."

She leaned over and traced the line on the globe. "We played all the way from here to here. Of course, I knew that stealing was wrong, pickpocketing and conning and such, but I'll tell you, Mr. McVale, it's a lot better than being beaten or starving. So is jail. It's also a lot better than being locked in a closet or a trunk."

Now, Jacob was on the verge of tears, a man who had not cried since the deaths of Kelly, a man who did not cry in his own time of illness or during the monumental task of raising his brother and sister or starting and losing a business and then starting and losing again.

Miss O'Brien had slowly taken him from what could be compared to the comedies of Shakespeare and then to the tragedies of the same writer. Her life was indeed a heartbreaking combination of both.

"But," she continued, "my stepfather left me alone, and I could be with Ma and Cassie, and, finally, he and my stepbrothers took off so Ma and Cassie and I could be together. I got a regular job in an inn, waiting tables and sometimes playing the piano and singing and such. Ma took in sewing, and we were renting a little cottage. That's when I started Teacher's College and worked at the School for the Deaf. I met Mitch and Zach, Rosemary and Caroline, and I felt as though I had a family.

"Then I got back home one day after we moved to Idaho, and who's there? My stepfather stands there as bold as brass. 'Hand over your money,' says he. 'No,' says I, and that's when he pulls a knife and holds it to Cassie's neck. So, naturally, I turned over my hard-earned money.

"In the meantime, Mr. Langley showed me how to use a gun and, thankfully, never asked any questions. I worked in Boise for over a year. I always managed to make my way back to Ma and Cassie to see to them and make sure they were cared for.

"Then, sure enough, one day, when I was home, here comes my stepfather again, demanding money. This time, before he could pull a knife, I shot him in the arm, and his blood stained the wall that Ma and I had washed down before we moved in. Now, there's something, Mr. McVale, that you can't unsee.

"I remember that, at some point, my stepbrothers came wantin' to know if we'd seen 'Pa' and what I knew. Of course, Ma and I both told them that we hadn't seen him and knew nothing about his whereabouts.

"I left Cassie there with the Langleys because, frankly, Ma was not doing a good enough job of helping her and watching over her when she had her seizures. I paid for her board and food, and Ma lived in the little ramshackle house that we had found for cheap rent.

"So, I ran again. After all, I had a vocation to run to, a respectable one, and it earned honest money. But, yes, Mr. McVale, I run. I run continually. I ran here. I thought that I might finally find those who are faithful.

"There are still things that I just can't remember, though," she said, taking her small fist and hitting the side of her head.

He took her hand gently and said softly, "It seems to me that you've already found faithful people along the way. Your friends Mitch and Zach and their wives are good people who have stayed faithful in their friendships. I'd say that your writing friend is also the faithful sort, and, as for Peaches and Pop, they stood behind you, always, as though you were their daughter. Why, even that Joseph fellow thought of what could have been with you, and Luke was the most faithful of all.

"This is not a perfect town. It's a town of people who almost didn't live to reach this part of the world. It's a town of misfits and rejects and pretenders. It's also a town of people who usually take care of their own.

"My mother would poetically say that it was a 'patchwork quilt' with different stories of sadness and love. My father said that it was 'a collection of down and outs and a sanctuary for the half-dead and tortured.'

"Now, don't do that. Don't hurt yourself," he said as he took her hand away from her head and face. "So you don't remember some things. Don't worry about it. They'll either come back to you, or they won't. If they don't, then maybe they don't need to."

"That's easier said than done," she started as she shakily stood up from the couch. "You tell me, now, Mr. McVale, do you really want to take me on?" she asked as her voice broke with emotion and tears. "Is that really what you want in your life?"

Jacob stood up next to her and took her arm, "Yes, Kayleigh. That's what I want more than anything. That's all I've ever wanted since we met.

"I'm not some gentleman entrepreneur of the gentry. I've worked hard on docks and on the sea. I've cheated and tricked and told a lie or two to make ends meet, but I always try to pay people back.

"I am capable of being forever faithful, though, and, my love, I have never deliberately hurt anyone, with the exception of one man long ago who kept me from the girl that I loved.

"I am trying to change, Kayleigh. You have helped me to see what needs to be abandoned in my life and what needs to be improved. I love you."

A look of absolute surprise and shock registered on her face before he carefully took her into his arms. She stood rigid in his embrace before suddenly wrapping her own arms around him and pressing her head into his chest. She let out a sigh, and, once again, tears began to fall on the front of his shirt.

"I'm always messin' up your shirts," she said, and then she added, "You know, the first time that you held me like this, after you picked me up from the station, for just a split second, I thought, 'Kayleigh, you're finally home.' Then I thought, 'stupid, stupid, stupid,' and I pulled away."

"I love you, Kayleigh," he whispered. "And I've wanted to be with you and care for you from the start. I'm hoping that's what you want with me as well," he finished.

She looked up into his eyes and said softly, "I love you so much that I'm always afraid it shows."

"Well, let's just let it," he said. She leaned in then, and he kissed her.

She kissed him in return, and then harder and more passionately, wanting to continue, but he pulled away and quietly said, "No, Kayleigh. You need to stop."

She placed her hands to her face and cried, "I've shamed myself."

"No, no," he reassured her and pulled her back into the embrace.

"That's not it. It's just that I want you to really know what you're doing and to remember it. You're not yourself right now. I want you to promise me that you will never take that elixir again."

She nodded and pulled back to look at him. "I need to sleep. I'm exhausted. Could you…" she hesitated and looked down.

"Could I what? Sweetheart," he asked.

"It's inappropriate," she managed to say.

"It's what, darling?" Jacob took her hand and looked tenderly at her.

"Would you hold me while I sleep?"

Jacob considered the request for a moment before saying, "Put your arms around my neck." He leaned down to her and carried her to the larger rocking chair, sat down still holding her, and as he stretched out his long legs, he covered her with the blanket from the other chair. He slowly rocked her while she fell asleep.

The next morning, he awoke just before sunrise, stretched his stiff legs, gently awoke her to stand, and picked her up again, carrying her to her bed. As he was covering her, she took his hand and said, barely above a whisper, "Good night, sweet prince, whom I love."

He squeezed her hand in return and smiled, then silently slipped out the back door. Whether she knew it or not, she was now his, and he was hers. Nothing would stop him now, and she would not be running again.

The next morning, Jacob showed up at the door of the schoolhouse with a steaming cup of coffee that Lucy had provided. Kayleigh opened the door well dressed but with her hair in stubborn disarray, swollen eyes, and somewhat weak from throwing up seven times in a row.

Jacob stifled a laugh and put the coffee on the table, producing one of Lucy's blueberry muffins, wrapped in a handkerchief, from his pocket, "Eat a bite and drink some coffee," he laughed. "It really will help."

"Alright," she said obediently, "but if I start puking again, it's your fault. "Also," she said hesitantly and carefully, "I don't really care for coffee. Thank you, though," she added hastily, not wanting to sound ungrateful.

She sat and did as instructed and was shocked at the immediate help that both provided. "Mmm… This is good, Jacob. This coffee is tasty and acts like medicine. Thank you."

"You're very welcome. Lucy put a teaspoon of sugar in it," he said and sat down beside her. (Actually, she had put three teaspoons in it, but he decided to keep the details to himself.)

"What do you want to do today?" he asked.

"Oh well, I may actually feel better by lunch time, if you want to eat lunch." she offered. "Uh, a very small lunch," she added. "I don't know how much I'll want to eat."

"That's fine," Jacob agreed. "We could ride horseback up near my cabin and eat there."

"Uh, well, I don't really ride horses," she said, hoping that she was not disappointing him.

"Yes, I know. My nieces carry information about their teacher, but I'll be with you, riding with you," he explained.

"Well, yes, I know," she answered, "but even side by side, I don't think…" she wasn't sure how to finish.

"I don't mean side by side," he told her. "I mean, we'll be on the same horse. You'll ride in front of me. It'll get you used to the horse, and you'll have my help," but he was actually thinking that it would get her used to him.

"Well, alright, but don't get mad if I jump off," she said before she really thought that statement through.

He laughed. "You will feel hurt if you jump, but not at all if you stay on with me."

What she did feel was him, riding in front of him, with his arms around her and his hands on the reins. She felt the warmth, the scent, and the muscles of him. She was safe, but it was a bit risky at the same time.

When they arrived at the spot he had chosen, he got down and held his arms up for her to slide into, and slide she did, down the front of him until her feet touched the ground. She was pressed to him, and he to her. He kissed her long and sweetly and then held her out at arms' distance. As she looked up, she noticed that she was looking at the same beautiful view that she had seen her first day in Faithful.

"Oh, there's the well where we first spoke," she motioned toward it and studied his face.

"Yes, it's the strangest thing," he said. "It has come back to life. I thought that I heard a gurgling noise coming through it, so I removed the stone covering it. It's flowing with water again."

They spread a blanket and unpacked the basket that Jacob had a joyous Lydia pack. They enjoyed their lunch and each other when Jacob kissed her slowly and gently bent her down on the blanket. He could tell that she was a bit surprised. "Haven't you ever imagined this part before?" he asked softly.

"Yes, sometimes," she admitted, "but mainly, I just imagined some kind, nondescript man holding me while I slept."

"Well, we both know that part can happen too," he said and smiled, "though I hope that I'm not nondescript."

"Your house looks so picturesque from here. Is it as nice inside?" she asked, changing the subject and squinting from the sun, which seemed to be dancing back and forth.

"Well, I like to think it is," he said.

It began to rain and then pour. He put his jacket around her, and they ran into his cabin. She noticed, as they ran, two ladder-back chairs facing the direction of where the sunset was and a log rail fence painted white. Hung about the windows were blue shutters.

Jacob was soaked when they made it in, and his shirt clung to him. "Here," she said in her teacher tone, "let's get that off. You can put your jacket back on and tell me where to find a dry shirt," she finished.

She had never seen him shy before, didn't know it was possible, and she wondered why that would be; and, as she unbuttoned and peeled the wet shirt from him, she discovered the reason. He was very scarred from just below his left collar bone, down his left arm, and over half of his torso. She looked up at him, and he met her gaze steadily and calmly. Then, without speaking, she slowly kissed his neck, his arm, and his chest. He held her tightly to him.

She pulled back and unbuttoned the top button of her blouse. "No! Kayleigh, you don't have to…" and then he stopped short. A jagged scar ran to the top of her left arm.

"Who did this to you?" Jacob demanded.

"He did…that night," she answered. "He said that no man would want me. It was actually quite worse, but a kind doctor sutured it again. He did a much better job, of course, than my mother had."

Their eyes were locked together until they heard the banging on the door.

"Jacob! Jacob! Are you there?"

"I'll be right there, Daniel," he answered.

"Where are your shirts?" she asked.

He motioned with his head to the bedroom. "Top drawer of the bureau," he answered.

She draped his jacket on the chair at the fireplace and ran to get the shirt. She ran it back to him, and he immediately began to put it on. She went back to the bedroom out of the way of the door so she wouldn't be seen until Daniel left.

"Jacob, please, this is important," Daniel yelled.

He opened the door quickly, still buttoning his shirt. "What is it?" he asked impatiently.

"Why are you…What?" Daniel began.

"I got caught in the rain," Jacob answered. "Now, what is this about?"

"It's Kayleigh," Daniel said, regaining his breath. "There's a sheriff from Idaho in town with a warrant for her arrest. He claims that Kayleigh killed her stepfather. We don't know where she is, but we wanted to warn her."

"I'll find her and tell her," Jacob said, and Daniel was surprised at the lack of shock or disbelief in Jacob's answer.

"I said I'll find her, Daniel. Now go on," he gestured.

"Well, you don't really think…?"

"No, of course not, Daniel. Now, would you just…"

"I'm right here, Daniel," Kayleigh said in a flat, defeated voice as she came out of the bedroom, and seeing the look on Daniel's face, she quickly added, "Jacob and I had a picnic, and we were caught in the rain. He was just changing his shirt. That's all."

"Oh, well, I believe you, Kayleigh. I'm just sorry to let you know like this. I mean…" he fumbled for words.

"It's alright, Daniel," she said. "There is no good way to tell it. Suffice it to say, I'm not a murderer, and Jacob knows the story. Now I just have to let the story be told to twelve people that I don't know."

CHAPTER 54: A DREADED REUNION

Jacob and Kayleigh sat side-by-side, holding hands at a long table inside the front of the Idaho Falls courthouse. Attorney Jackson Armstrong sat on the end, with Kayleigh in the middle. *How had they even gotten here?* went through Kayleigh's mind again and again.

Jacob had met Armstrong once when the lawyer was called upon to settle a land dispute in Faithful. This was before Lucy had the tavern and inn built, so Armstrong had actually stayed with the McVales. This put fifteen-year-old Jacob out in the barn, and he was called upon to ride with Armstrong as he left town since several landowners were not happy with him. Usually, at this point in his life, the attorney kept to Fort Boise or Idaho Falls, so Jacob had played the "You owe me a little help" card.

A cold knife of afternoon air slit through the double oak doors of the courthouse. Kayleigh turned in her chair to see Matthew and Marcus enter. It had occurred to her several times in life that the brothers could have been twins. They both had limp dark hair in "bowl cut" styles. They were both red-faced with perpetual scowls, and they were both stocky and barrel-chested. Matthew was a few inches taller than Marcus with cold gray eyes, whereas Marcus had very dark brown eyes. However, both wore the same hateful looks of insolence. Today, they were both stuffed into navy blue suits, as was their burly attorney, and he wore an equally arrogant look on his face.

Judge Winfrey entered and called the courtroom to order. "Ladies and gentlemen," he intoned, "this is an unusual case. The defendant, Miss O'Brien, is being accused of the murder of her stepfather, Nolan O'Connor. She is countering that her step-brothers killed him. This leaves the court to play detective in determining who is responsible for the death of Mr. O'Connor. Therefore, in the course of this trial, we will also examine evidence concerning three different firearms, the location of the defendants at the time of the death, and the motives that might have prevailed.

"We will begin, of course, with opening statements from both attorneys before questioning and cross-examinations begin."

Caleb Spivy slipped through the courtroom doors quietly and sat in the back. He had contacted Armstrong earlier with the latest information from his investigation but also asked to remain anonymous since Jacob did not want it known that he had previously retained him.

Armstrong stood. He was a tall, thin, distinguished Lincoln type, even more so than Mr. Langley. He simply lacked the beard and the stove pipe hat. "Ladies and gentlemen of the jury, we have an innocent young lady here. The only crime she might be guilty of is caring too much. She defended her little sister (an impaired child prone to seizures) by shooting her stepfather in the shoulder as he threatened and held a knife to the child's throat.

"She was at a distance of approximately fifteen to twenty feet away from him. She entered and stood in the doorway. He stood across the front room in the small cottage. The gun was a small derringer that she was carrying in order to protect her mother and little sister.

"Through the progression of the trial, we will show that the defendant could not possibly have killed her stepfather based on three areas of evidence: the actual murder weapon, her location at the time of the crime, and motive.

"Ladies and gentlemen of the jury, this young lady, in the course of her life, has been bullied and brutalized by her stepfather and step-brothers." At this point, Armstrong pointed to Matthew and Marcus, "She, alone, supported her mother and sister, put herself through the South Dakota Normal School for Teachers, and became a highly respected teacher.

"I appeal to you, as a well-chosen jury of well-respected citizenry, to set her free from these evil men, once and for all. Allow her to live her life in safety and in the fulfillment of her profession."

Jacob squeezed Kayleigh's hand and smiled at her. He could not feel fully secure yet, but he wanted Kayleigh to feel as confident as possible. Of course, now it was the brothers' attorney who would have his say.

Kayleigh could feel Matthew's hateful eyes boring into her, but she did not turn to the opposite table. "Hold on to me," Jacob whispered, and Kayleigh took his arm. Thoughts were flashing through her mind so rapidly that she was having more and more trouble anchoring onto just one.

She did know that, less than a year ago, she wouldn't have counted on any man, much less held onto one. However, with Jacob, she felt that they were partners somehow. He felt what she felt, and she was beginning to feel what he felt as well.

The attorney for Marcus and Matthew stood and adjusted his too-tight jacket. He shoved his carrot bright red hair out of his eyes, and Douglas Andrews was ready to have his say. He started by saying, "Thank you so much, Your Honor." Kayleigh could recognize a New York accent anywhere, and she was recognizing it in him.

He faced the jury and began, "Now, what we have here, ladies and gentlemen of the jury, is a young woman who connives and manipulates her way into men's lives in order to control them and live off of their resources. Further, we propose that this young woman," he paused to point a finger at Kayleigh without even looking at her, "shot her own stepfather to death for what little cash he had from a hard-earned month of wages. She's that cold, ladies and gentlemen, and then she didn't even bother to stay around to see if he lived," and, with that last statement, he sat down.

Kayleigh was shaking with rage and could feel her face growing red. Jacob was containing his rage, something he had learned to master through the years. He leaned over and whispered to her, "Be strong. This is a game. We will win."

"This is my life, Jacob," she whispered in return, and as the back doors opened again, Jacob turned to see Jeremiah Langley enter.

A verse of scripture came to Langley's mind: "The eyes of the Lord keep watch over knowledge, but he frustrates the words of the unfaithful" (Proverbs 22:12, NIV).

CHAPTER 55: WINNING THE GAME

Caleb Spivy stole forward quickly and slipped a single note to Armstrong. He opened it to find, "You must call Mr. Langley," scrawled in Caleb's handwriting. Never one to betray emotion, Armstrong's face remained emotionless, and he merely nodded.

The first witness called was Doctor Randal. His sad blue eyes, shielded behind spectacles, gave witness to his years of service, along with his thick white hair, eyebrows, and mustache. He testified that he had been one of the two doctors in Idaho Falls when Kayleigh and her mother and sister lived there. He first testified that he had only observed Kayleigh coming and going quietly in town, with or without her mother and sister.

He then further confirmed that he was the first to examine Nolan O'Connor when his sons brought him in and shortly after he died. O'Connor actually had two gun wounds, one in his shoulder and one in the chest. The one in his shoulder was healed, but the one in his chest had just occurred. He removed the bullet lodged in Nolan's chest and kept it for further examination. The bullet in his chest came from a rifle, whereas the shoulder wound had been caused by a much smaller gun.

Upon cross-examination, Douglas Andrews asked if it was possible for one person to perpetrate both wounds. The doctor thought this a silly question but answered with a simple, "Yes, of course."

"Then it stands to reason that Miss O'Brien could have shot her stepfather twice, on two separate occasions. Doesn't it, Dr. Randal?" Anderson pursued.

"Objection, Your Honor!" Armstrong yelled. "He is leading the jury with a foolish line of questioning."

"I'll allow it this time," Judge Winfrey answered.

"Well, yes, but I don't think," Dr. Randal began.

"Thank you, Dr. Randal," he concluded.

"Call your next witness, Counselor Armstrong," Judge Winfrey instructed.

"Judge, I'd like to call someone that I did not previously submit," Armstrong said while Kayleigh and Jacob exchanged surprised glances. Andrews looked anxious as the brothers rolled their eyes and sneered.

"Who is this witness?" Judge Winfrey inquired.

"Josiah Langley, the guardian of Miss O'Brien's little sister," Jackson Armstrong replied in a very serious and measured tone.

"I'll allow it," the judge answered, "and if he is the gentleman that I think he is," he continued, "I imagine he will not be sworn in, as is the typical way."

"That's correct, Your Honor," Jackson Armstrong answered, " but he will give his word."

"So be it," the judge nodded.

Josiah Langley was called, his tall, long-legged figure and solemn face tucked into the witness box after giving his word to speak truthfully.

Jackson Armstrong stood tall and erect as he addressed the witness. He was a quick and good judge of character, and he knew an honest and tough man when he met one.

He took Langley through the paces of how he knew Kayleigh, her mother, and Cassie. He then asked the key questions of what had transpired the day that Kathleen O'Brien hanged herself.

Josiah Langley testified in his clear, deep voice that he and his wife had been neighbors of Kathleen, Kayleigh, and Cassie.

When it became clear that Kathleen was not up to the task of properly watching over Cassie, Kayleigh asked if they would provide the little girl with boarding. She suggested a payment, and they agreed. He was honest when he described their love for the child and the doctor visits that they took her to, but he also admitted that she died while in their care as she slept.

"You see," he said with genuine emotion, "my wife and I were not blessed by the Lord with children, so we loved having her about. She was much like a grandchild would have been, and we miss her sorely."

"We do not doubt that you gave her your best care, Mr. Langley," Armstrong reassured him. "My question is, now, why did you go to the home of Kathleen O'Connor, and what did you find?"

"I went to fetch the rest of Cassie's clothes and a few little books and toys that she treasured," Langley answered.

"When was this? What time was it?" Armstrong asked.

"By my pocket watch," Langley answered, "it was getting close to 10:00 in the morning."

"And what did you find?" Armstrong pressed on.

"I found that Kathleen had hung herself. There was a rifle on the floor and a letter placed on the one table in the room," Langley explained with tears forming in his eyes.

"Then what did you do?" Armstrong asked softly.

"I thought it best to go to the sheriff, so that's where I headed. I wanted to get Kathleen's body down, but I thought it best to leave everything as it was until the law was fetched."

"So, did you go to the law?" Armstrong asked and looked very directly at the jury.

"I did, sir," Langley answered in a short manner.

"What happened next?" Armstrong urged him on again.

"I saw Kayleigh as I came into town. She was walking toward the road which led to their house. I stopped her so she would be prepared for what she was about to see. We went to the sheriff together," he added.

"About what time was this, Mr. Langley?" Armstrong asked.

"It would have been getting close to 10:30," he answered.

"Then how long would it take to walk to the sheriff's office and then back to the house?"

"I suppose it was about noon when we arrived, sir," Langley answered.

"What did you find when you reached the home?" Armstrong urged him on.

"Well, Kathleen was in the same position, but the gun was gone, and so was the note," Langley concluded.

"So someone came in after you and removed these two items?" Armstrong questioned in a leading way.

"Objection, Your Honor!" Andrews called out. "The counselor is leading the witness to make conjectures and give opinions."

"This will be sustained," Judge Winfrey agreed, but he did not have the question removed from the record.

"I have no further questions, Your Honor," Armstrong said.

With that, Andrews began his cross-examination. "How did Miss O'Brien react upon seeing her mother hung?"

"She was, of course, upset and crying," Langley replied.

"Is it not true that Miss O'Brien hated her stepfather?" Douglas Andrews was now going for the point of weakness, the possible motive.

"Objection, Your Honor!" Armstrong countered. "This is hearsay, not hard evidence."

"Sustained," Judge Winfrey agreed.

"I'm sorry, Your Honor," Andrews replied. "I withdraw the question; however, is it not true that you supplied the derringer with which Miss O'Brien shot her stepfather in the shoulder?"

"It is," Langley answered shortly.

"Why?" Andrews countered.

"She was obviously frightened of the man and frightened for the child," Langley explained.

"Don't Mormons steer clear of weapons?" Andrews asked with almost genuine curiosity.

"Yes, but I was not always a Mormon," Langley revealed with a slight smile. "I still had a few weapons from my time in the army."

"How did you feel toward Nolan O'Connor, Mr. Langley?" Andrews asked shrewdly.

"Objection, Your Honor!" Armstrong roared. "This is irrelevant!"

"I'll allow it," Judge Winfrey conceded, partly in sheer curiosity himself.

"I did not like him," Langley answered. "He was a mean and low individual, as were his sons." The two glowered at him, but he barely noticed. It was beginning to be obvious to Jacob that Langley did not easily intimidate.

"Did you also supply the rifle for Mrs. O'Connor?" Anderson pressed.

"I did not," Langley answered, "but I had seen it in the house previously."

"When was this?" Andrews asked abruptly, seizing this moment.

"When my wife and I first went to collect Cassie," Langley answered.

"So there were two guns in that home," Andrews concluded and ended with, "I have no further questions, Your Honor."

"Mr. Langley," the judge stopped Josiah in his tracks. "May I see you a moment here at the bench?"

"Yes, sir," Josiah Langley answered and made his way to the judge while everyone else in the courtroom watched in a startled curiosity.

"I think I've finally placed you," the judge said in low tones that only Josiah could hear. "Did I not sentence you to a year in prison due to your military court marshal? Weren't you the one who refused to kill renegade Indians in the Nevada territory?"

"I was, sir," Langley admitted, "and I would do it again."

Judge Winfrey smiled, "Alright then, my searching mind is satisfied. I really thought they had killed you when I heard that you were stabbed in prison. I'm glad to hear that they didn't. I hope that you are at peace."

"I am, good sir," Josiah assured him before leaving.

After a recess, the sheriff, who came to the house after Kathleen's hanging, testified to what he had seen and how the body had been handled. He cast a sideways sneer at Kayleigh, and it was then time for her to take the stand. She pried her reluctant hand from Jacob's and took the stand.

"Miss O'Brien," Armstrong began, "what caused you to come back into town the day that your mother took her own life?"

"I had finished a teaching post and returned to see about my mother and sister, as I had promised," Kayleigh spoke clearly, if a little shakily.

"When was this?" he continued.

"May 20th," she answered.

"How did you feel upon discovering your mother had killed herself?" Armstrong was seeking to set up a field of sympathy between Kayleigh and the jury, and it was a fair question, if obvious.

"I was shocked and sickened," Kayleigh replied.

"Did you have any reason to believe she might do this before you left for your teaching position?" Armstrong pursued.

"No, she seemed fine," Kayleigh answered, clutching her hands together.

"Did you have knowledge of the rifle?" Armstrong was laying a foundation for truthful character, and Kayleigh knew it.

"I did," she answered quietly.

"Whose rifle was it?" Armstrong countered

"It was my stepfather's. Mama kept it from when they were still living together. It was always kept unloaded under the bed," she explained.

"But on this particular day, according to Mr. Langley, it was not. Isn't that right?" Armstrong was deftly leading but carefully.

"Objection!" Andrews called out. "This is pure hearsay for Miss O'Brien. It's already been established that the gun was gone when she arrived."

"Sustained," Judge Winfrey agreed.

"Alright, then, Miss O'Brien, I'll ask you this. Who else came and went in the home that you shared with your mother and, up to that point, your little sister?"

"My stepfather came by when he wanted money, and occasionally, he sent Matthew and Marcus," she revealed with a hushed and speculative response from the courtroom.

"Would your mother have become so frightened of these men that she would have taken the rifle out and loaded it?"

"Objection again, Your Honor," Andrews interrupted, "this would simply be opinion."

"I'll allow it," Winfrey pronounced. "Her daughter is as good of a source of gauging Mrs. O'Connor's temperament as any would be."

"Go ahead, Miss O'Brien," Armstrong urged.

"She was frightened to the point of terror," Kayleigh stated. "She may have felt the need for a rifle."

"What had your stepfather done to make her fear him so?" Jacob admired how Jackson Armstrong could verbally clear a trail and then travel if, for all it was worth.

"He threatened her and hit her continually. He also held a knife on her and my little sister," Kayleigh was trying to be stoic, but the emotion of remembering was hard to overcome.

"What happened on March 25th of last year, Miss O'Brien?" Armstrong was eager to set up a beginning time frame.

"I went to see Mama and my little sister, Cassie, while school was out. My stepfather held a knife to Cassie's neck and was harassing Mama and me for money."

"And, what did you do, Miss O'Brien?"

"I shot him in the shoulder," she answered while the courtroom filled with the buzz of speculation.

"What did he do?" Armstrong asked.

"He ran," Kayleigh answered.

"So let's put this scene together again," Armstrong paced a bit as though thinking aloud. "When you arrived with Mr. Langley and the sheriff, you did not see the gun or the letter."

"This has been established, Mr. Armstrong, please move on," Judge Winfrey warned.

"Yes, Your Honor," he complied. "Miss O'Brien, do you know of anyone with a reason to take these two items?" Considering the warning he had just received, Armstrong was taking a gamble to ask this.

"Objection, Your Honor. This is speculation. This whole line of questioning has been tenuous at best," Douglas Andrews stated as he went red in the face.

"I'll allow it," the judge said simply. "Please answer, Miss O'Brien."

She sighed and sat up straighter before answering. "I think that either Matthew or Marcus may have been by, looking for their father," Kayleigh answered, avoiding their stares.

"I have no further questions, Your Honor." Armstrong had finished with Kayleigh.

"Mr. Andrews, will you cross-examine now?" the judge was becoming restless as he motioned to Andrews.

"Yes, Your Honor," he answered, with a malicious stress on the word, "yes."

"Miss O'Brien," he began, "would it be safe to say that you disliked your stepfather?"

"Objection," Armstrong called. "we've already established the kind of man he was."

"I'll allow this line of questioning," Winfrey responded.

"Damn," Armstrong said very quietly under his breath.

"We did not like one another," Kayleigh answered carefully.

"Would it be safe to say that you hated him?" Andrews asked.

"Yes," Kayleigh said, barely above a whisper.

"Is this because of the treatment he gave your mother or the treatment that he gave you?" Andrews was opening a vein of testimony and began to bleed it.

"Both," she answered.

"Could you tell the court about the treatment you suffered from your stepfather?" Andrews was coming closer and closer to the witness stand until he was almost standing over it. He no longer cared how his clients were perceived if he could set up a motive for Kayleigh as the murderer.

With one hand, Armstrong pushed on Jacob's shoulder in order to return him to his seat, and with the other hand, he pushed himself up while gripping the table.

"Objection, Your Honor," Armstrong interjected in almost a yell, "the treatment of the witness has nothing to do with who did or didn't kill Mr. O'Connor."

"Oh, but I think it might," Winfrey replied and turned to Kayleigh.

"He abused me with his words and with his hands, as did his two older sons," she added.

"I see," Andrews intoned in a self-satisfied manner. "So you hate your step-brothers as well?"

"Oh God," Armstrong sucked in his breath, but Judge Winfrey warned Andrews quickly.

"You know better than this line of questioning, Mr. Andrews," Winfrey remarked dismissively.

"Excuse me, Your Honor, but we have only the word of Miss O'Brien that such 'abuse' ever really took place. Don't we?" Andrews strutted toward the jury box as he made this statement.

"Did you hate these three men enough to kill one or all of them?" Andrews asked through a cruel half-smile.

"Objection! Your Honor! This is enough. He's badgering her," Armstrong's deep voice was rising in a near rage.

"Sustained!" Judge Winfrey replied. "Ask a relevant question, Attorney Andrews. Stop leading the witness for your own purposes."

"Withdrawn, Your Honor," Andrews complied and continued.

"Mr. Langley testified that he saw you walking in town as he came into town. How long had you been there?"

"I'm not sure. I mean, I don't remember exactly. I know I had gotten off of the train and walked from the depot," Kayleigh replied.

"Really?" Andrews continued, "because Mr. Langley testified that you arrived together at your mother's home around noon, and the train arrived at 9:00 a.m."

"I know that…I…" Kayleigh began haltingly, "I don't remember everything."

"That's all," Andrews replied. "I have nothing more for the witness."

They adjourned for the day and had a quick dinner before Armstrong reviewed the day with Kayleigh and Jacob and planned for the following day.

Jacob walked Kayleigh to her room at the local inn before he would retire to his own room down the hall.

"Do you think that I killed him, Jacob?" she asked, crying.

"No, but please try to remember everything. We need a better time frame than we're presenting," he answered.

"I just can't remember, Jacob. I can't put it together," she cried.

"Kayleigh, you have to stay strong. We both do. You can't break down. That's what they want," Jacob said, and he held her and kissed her cheek before he turned to go.

The three walked silently to the courtroom the next morning. It was a beautiful day. Armstrong turned to Kayleigh before they entered the courtroom.

"Are you a praying woman, Miss O'Brien?" he asked.

"I am," she answered, "but I don't know if God hears me. I've never even been baptized."

"Do you believe that Jesus is your savior, Kayleigh?" he asked.

"I do," she said.

"Then pray," he directed.

CHAPTER 56: A TURN FOR JUSTICE

"Court is in session!" Judge Winfrey announced and lowered the gavel.

"Are you prepared, Counselor Armstrong?"

He answered that he was, and the judge asked the same of Andrews, who also affirmed that he was ready.

"Call your first witness, Mr. Armstrong," Judge Winfrey looked a bit weary but ready as he spoke.

"If it pleases the court, Your Honor, the Defense calls Marcus O'Connor." Armstrong appeared to speak with iron resolve. No one had to know that this moment had kept him up for the last two nights.

As Marcus swore to tell the truth, Kayleigh said under her breath, "I know just how much that means to you."

"What relation is the defendant, Kayleigh O'Brien, to you, Mr. O'Connor?" Armstrong began his questioning.

"She's my step-sister," he practically spat out.

"What kind of relationship do the two of you have?" he asked.

"Well, if you mean how we feel about each other, we don't care for one another. We never have," he said.

"And where were you on May 20th of last year?" Armstrong asked.

"I was working on repairs at our farmhouse when I heard a gunshot from my stepmother's house," he said methodically.

"And was your father in the house with you?" Armstrong questioned.

"He hadn't lived with Matthew and me for some time. Last we heard, he had started living somewhere in town, in Idaho Falls."

"So, your father and stepmother did not cohabit?" Armstrong pressed.

"No, I don't think they'd done none of that in a long time. They didn't live together either," he scowled.

A contained laughter rippled through the courtroom, and, in truth, Judge Winfrey came close to losing self-control as well before he glared and announced, "Order," and slammed the gavel. For his part, Marcus was lost to the cause of the laughter.

"So you heard the shot, Mr. O'Connor, then what did you do?"

"Matthew took the wagon down there to see what had happened," he said. "Then he came back and got me."

"Then, at what time were you both in the house together?" Armstrong was again setting the scene and time frame.

"I didn't time it, you know," Marcus barked, "but I guess around 11:30."

"And what did you find?" Armstrong was leaning in.

"What do you think? I found my father shot dead and Kathleen hangin' from the rafters," Marcus sneered."

"Watch your tone in answering questions, Mr. O'Connor," the judge warned.

"Well, anybody could have been in there before Matthew and killed him." With this, he gave a meaningful look at Kayleigh.

"That will be stricken from the record; however, the time reference will remain," Judge Winfrey ordered.

"Alright, Mr. O'Connor, what happened next then?" Armstrong continued.

"Matthew and me hauled Pa to the Doc. We knew he was dead, but we wanted the Doc to look at the wounds," Marcus explained. "He went in, and I went on to get the sheriff, but Langley had already gone by and led them to the house," he snarled.

"So, Kathleen had already hung herself?" Armstrong asked.

Marcus stole a look at Matthew before answering, "Of course!"

"And you left Kathleen still hanging?" Armstrong asked incredulously.

"Well, she wasn't goin' nowhere, now, was she?" Marcus asked, leaning forward toward Armstrong.

Kayleigh cringed as again laughter trickled through the room. Suddenly, she realized that she did love her mother, regardless of her weaknesses and her unwillingness to fight. She didn't deserve to be the butt of some joke.

Winfrey called for order again, and Marcus basked in his moment of glory.

"Do you know anything about the whereabouts of the rifle and the note?" Armstrong was not wasting any time.

"No," he hissed, "I seen both when we was there. Why don't you ask Kayleigh?"

"Move to strike," Armstrong said quickly.

"The jury will omit the last comment," Winfrey advised while staring at Marcus, "and sir, if you dishonor the courtroom with your surly remarks one more time, you will be removed."

"The Defense has no further questions for this witness," Armstrong concluded.

"Mr. Andrews," Winfrey asked, noting the look of triumph in his eyes, "do you wish to cross-examine?"

"No, Your Honor. We're satisfied with the testimony."

"We'll take a short recess and reconvene, Mr. Armstrong. There is a small room down the hall if you wish a conference with your client." The judge seemed to be giving more than just a suggestion.

After they found the room and were seated, Jackson Armstrong approached what he had been dreading. "Kayleigh, you may have to take the stand again."

She sat with her head lowered and then looked up at him. "Do you believe that I am innocent of this, Mr. Armstrong?" Jacob nodded his head and took her hand.

"The brutal truth is, Kayleigh, that it doesn't matter whether I believe that or not, although I do. My job is to defend you and take apart whatever comes from the prosecution, and believe me, I'm going to enjoy the latter. Your step-brothers are dung, and their lawyer is not much better. Right now, though, you need to be ready for more questioning. The wild card is your brother Matthew's testimony. That will determine whether we have to recall you, and we desperately need a time frame for your discovering your mother."

The court reconvened, and Matthew took the stand. Armstrong had decided to start by setting up his background with Kayleigh to gain sympathy. From there, he would lead up to her shooting of the stepfather again and reestablish a time frame.

"Mr. O'Connor," Armstrong began, "how old were you and your brothers when your father, Nolan O'Connor, married Kathleen, your stepmother?"

"I was eighteen," he said defiantly. "Marcus was sixteen, and Luke was fourteen."

"Were you happy with the marriage?" Armstrong asked skeptically.

"Objection!" Andrews stood and barked. "This has no real bearing on the case. He's leading the witness through speculation again."

"Sustained," the judge said wearily. "Mr. Armstrong, get to the issue."

"Would it be correct to say that the three of you, your father and Marcus, did not get along well with Kayleigh?" Armstrong tried a modified direction.

"Well, that was partly her, you know," Matthew spoke with distaste while he glared at Kayleigh. "She always thought she was better than us."

"How so?" he pressed.

"She just did. She didn't care for nobody but Luke, our younger brother," Matthew continued to glare at Kayleigh.

"Was that so bad?" Armstrong began his questioning.

"Objection! Your Honor!" Andrews looked as though he would burst out of his tight suit coat.

"Sustained," the judge said rather reluctantly. "Again, see to your point, Counselor Armstrong."

"Yes, Your Honor," he conceded.

"Did you help attend to your little sister?" Armstrong was now veering to another trek.

"Your Honor!" Andrews jumped up again. "Objection!"

"I'll allow it this time." Judge Winfrey said. "I think the little girl is pertinent to the issue at hand. Answer Mr. O'Connor."

"No, I didn't attend to some child!" he shouted. "That's women's work. What was she to me?"

"I don't know, Mr. O'Connor, what was she to you?" Armstrong pressed. "I mean, she was impaired, prone to seizures, and not very aware."

Kayleigh cringed as she listened, but she was smart enough to know what Armstrong was leading into.

"I didn't like the way that Pa treated her. That's all. She was scared of him. So, sometimes, I'd go by to see about her. Then, them religious people got hold of her, and I didn't see her no more," he trailed off in his speech.

"And did your father threaten her?" Armstrong had Matthew backed a little further toward the ropes of the ring.

"He'd say things, mainly to scare Cassie and Ma and get money out of them, but then he started holding a knife on her and saying he would kill her."

"And why did that bother you, Mr. O'Connor? I mean, she was little more than a nuisance to you and the family, a little cripple of sorts, and probably not very smart. She was probably just a by-product of your father and Kayleigh's coupling." Armstrong was beginning to deliver a blow, and Anderson was beginning to find his feet when Matthew flew into a rage.

"I don't know why!" Matthew shouted.

"Was she more than a little sister to you, Mr. O'Connor? Could that be possible?"

"Shut up, Matthew!" Marcus yelled out."

"Restrain your client, Mr. Andrews," the judge called out.

"She was mine!" Matthew screamed. "She was my child, by Kayleigh. Kayleigh should have been mine. I could have made her not tell," he yelled and slammed his fist on the rail.

Kayleigh had gone pale and was clutching at Jacob. "How could I have not known?" she whispered.

"Hold on, darling," Jacob whispered.

"Oh, how horrible," a woman was heard to say, and more than one gentleman commented, "Disgusting!" or "Animal!"

"Did you kill your father, Mr. O'Connor?" Armstrong had waited for the judge to call "order" and spoke very quietly.

"No! I didn't kill him. Either Kathleen or Kayleigh did!" he yelled.

Again, there was a need for the judge to call for order.

"And how do you know this?" Armstrong spoke very calmly.

Matthew, himself, was calm now in his speech, defeated, with his head hanging down. "I had given her the rifle to keep for protection some time back, and, that day, Pa had said he was going to her house to try and get money from her. He knew that Kayleigh sent her a little money now and then.

"Around what time did you discover your stepmother had hung herself and your father was dead, Mr. O'Connor?"

"I think around 9:30 by her clock. It looked to me like someone had already been in. "After Marcus and I pulled Pa out to the wagon, I went back in and took the rifle and letter."

"Where are the letter and rifle now?" The jury all seemed to lean in with this question.

"Objection! Andrews was making a last-ditch effort. "Your Honor, Counselor is leading the witness."

"I'll allow it," the judge looked as though he, too, was waiting anxiously for the answer.

"I gave them to Marcus for safekeeping. I don't know what he did with them," Matthew finished.

"Then here is my question to you, Mr. O'Connor, before we recall your brother to the stand. Why did you attempt to make it conclusively look as though Kayleigh O'Brien had killed your father?"

"Objection!" Andrews finally called after being inactive for an entire line of questioning. "Pure Speculation and fabrication!"

"Overruled!" the judge practically shouted. "We're past the point of you requesting anything. I'll allow this line of questioning. It's pertinent to motive. Answer, Mr. O'Connor."

"Marcus thought we could get money out of her. She's got a bank account that we can't touch. She's in tight with the Idaho Falls Bank and the tellers. Also, her grandmother left a trust to her that can't be touched until she's twenty-five. So, we thought we'd make a settlement with her directly, but she was gone, and for a while, we weren't sure where."

(*That's it!* Jacob thought. *She must have gone to the bank first. He would only wonder later about the trust and why she had not told him.*)

"You mean you decided to blackmail her and bleed her of whatever money you could get!" The courtroom, including the judge, was shocked that the controlled Mr. Armstrong could show such anger and that the young woman, sitting in such shock and defeat, had such resources.

"Mr. Armstrong!" Judge Winfrey shouted and slammed the gavel. "Get yourself under control. Approach the bench."

Armstrong approached the bench like a scolded child, which, given his height, was somewhat comical.

"Armstrong," the judge said in a low voice, "I understand how self-control is difficult when interviewing someone as low as this witness, but it has to be maintained. Am I clear?"

"Yes, Your Honor, of course," Armstrong replied.

"The jury is directed to disregard the last comments of Counselor Armstrong," Judge Winfrey announced.

"So," Armstrong said with his index finger at his chin. Kathleen's rifle was a Winchester. What type of rifle do you own, Matthew?"

"I carry a Remmington," he answered. "What of it?"

"Again, did you kill your father, Mr. O'Connor?" Armstrong continued.

"No!" Matthew yelled!"

Armstrong returned to the witness stand. "I have no further questions for this witness," he concluded."

"Do you want to cross-examine the witness, Mr. Andrews?" Judge Winfrey asked.

"No, Your Honor," he replied. In truth, he wouldn't have known where to start. Matthew had already completely incriminated himself. However, he still wanted to reexamine the time frame of Kayleigh walking from the depot. That might be the only straw of hope left for him and the brothers.

At this, Jackson Armstrong arose and declared, "Your Honor, the Defense would like to recall Marcus O'Connor to the stand," surprising himself and the rest of the courtroom.

Winfrey turned to Marcus. "Mr. O'Connor, take the stand."

Armstrong glanced at Kayleigh and the jury. He then eyed Matthew.

"I have only one question for you, Mr. O'Connor, and I'm sure that you know what it is. "Where are the rifle and letter, Marcus?"

"I put them under the floorboards of the farmhouse," he spat out while glaring at Armstrong.

"Your Honor, I'm requesting twenty-four hours for Mr. O'Connor to produce the weapon and the letter for the courtroom before closing arguments are made. He will, of course, need to be in custody while this is carried out.

"Mr. O'Connor, you will bring both the rifle and the letter to the courtroom tomorrow under supervision or be held in contempt in this court. I will also have you reprimanded to the courthouse jail.

Do you understand me?"

"Yes, sir," Marcus said, without respect but not as contemptuous as he had previously spoken.

CHAPTER 57: THREE LETTERS

Armstrong had prepped Kayleigh for the next day's proceedings, but she was still in a state of anxiety, and her stress had taken a toll. She was even thinner than she had been, and deep, dark circles were beneath her eyes. The rifle and letter had been placed on a small table in front of the judge's podium.

Kayleigh was not aware that Jacob, Armstrong, and Caleb Spivy had conferred the night before and located Mr. Grainer, who was more than willing to testify on Kayleigh's behalf. They had then hastily presented Grainer's name as a witness.

Since Grainer was well known as both a banker and man of his word, Winfrey accepted him for testimony.

"Your Honor," Armstrong began, "we would like to call our witness, J.T. Grainer."

Mr. Grainer entered in his portly tailored three-piece suit, perfectly parted hair, and groomed mustache. Most of those in the courtroom knew him and respected him.

After he was sworn in, Winfrey leaned over, grinned, and whispered in a voice only audible to Grainer, "Still keeping my money safe?"

Grainer stifled a laugh and nodded. Then, with his kind but no-nonsense demeanor, he confirmed that Kayleigh had been speaking to him around 9:15 a.m. to almost 10:00 when she left to go to her mother's home on the morning of May 20th.

Being a man of honor, he did not offer information about the trust but struck a blow for Kayleigh's defense.

Anderson declined to cross-examine Grainer, and it was again Kayleigh's turn.

"Your Honor," Armstrong stood once again on this last day of the trial, "I call for Counselor Andrews to present the letter in question to you for inspection."

Andrews approached as Judge Winfrey put on his reading glasses. Judge Winfrey took the letter and gently opened it, skimming it for details. He then returned it to Andrews, who replaced it on the table.

"You may open, Mr. Andrews." The judge informed him with raised eyebrows as if to say, "Don't try anything."

"Your Honor, the Defense rests, except, of course, for its closing statements." Andrews sat down.

"In that case, Counselor Armstrong, the ball has returned to you. Do you have any further testimonies?" he questioned, again with his eyebrows forming a distinctive arch.

"Yes, Your Honor," Armstrong affirmed, "and we would like the letter in order to proceed."

"I'll allow it," the judge said, almost triumphantly.

Armstrong picked up the letter and addressed the judge. "Your Honor, I would like to recall Kayleigh O'Brien to the stand," he said as he approached the stand with the letter.

Jacob helped her up from the chair, and Kayleigh shakily approached the stand.

"Miss O'Brien, as your attorney, I have watched your conduct with respect during this trial, and I know how difficult it must have been for you. Now, I'm calling on you to be courageous one more time. Please open the letter." He looked at Kayleigh and then at the jury, and Jacob thought again that Armstrong would have been a good actor.

Kayleigh opened the letter, and Armstrong asked, "Is this your mother's handwriting?"

"Objection!" Andrew shouted. "Of course, the witness would affirm it as her mother's."

"Overruled," Judge Winfrey replied. "I'll allow it."

"Yes," Kayleigh answered. "It's Mama's handwriting."

"Miss O'Brien," Armstrong requested, "would you give your own handwriting sample as a comparison?"

"Objection, Your Honor!" Andrews rose and called out again. "People can change their handwriting if needed."

"I'll allow it," Judge Winfrey ruled. Disgusted by Matthew, Marcus, and their lawyer, Winfrey was becoming more and more lenient toward the Defendant.

Armstrong produced a pen and paper from his suit coat pocket and instructed Kayleigh to copy the letter's salutation and first two sentences.

When she had finished, she handed it to Armstrong, along with the original letter.

"Your Honor, may I show these two samples both to you and the jury?"

"Yes," Judge Winfrey said, taking both samples, again putting on his reading glasses and examining both samples. He handed them back and instructed the jury to look at both writing samples carefully.

With this, Armstrong showed both samples to the jury, slyly also turning the letter and sample toward Jacob and allowing the jury to carefully pass both to one another for inspection.

Jacob noted that Kathleen's handwriting was rounded cursive, almost childish or "school girlish" in its appearance, whereas Kayleigh's handwriting was a bit more angular and sharp in its structure.

Armstrong returned to the stand. "Miss O'Brien, I think all would agree that the letter was not written in your hand. Would you please read the letter aloud?"

"Yes," she agreed and began.

My dearest Kayleigh,

I was not the best protector for you, and I will be eternally in regret and sadness for this.

I truly thought that marriage would be the best protection for both of us, but I misjudged Nolan O'Connor. He was upright and charming, just long enough to trick me into marriage. He soon turned mean and cruel.

We were barely scraping by in New York and living so cramped up in that tenement flat. I tried to watch Nolan carefully. I didn't think about it being one of the boys who would hurt you.

Then, when he put you in the convent, I was unable to keep you from that fate, but I had hopes that Luke could get you back, and he did.

You once told me that I was a weak woman, and you were right. I was. I did not have your strength and will.

I hope that now you will be aware of how much I truly loved you and Cassie. We are finally rid of Nolan, and I can protect the two of you with my very life.

That is all I have to give, my love. Please be happy and content. Marriage may not be your answer, but then again, it could be. Choose well, my love.

Mama

Armstrong rested his defense, and the two attorneys made closing statements.

Of course, Andrews argued that a handwriting expert should have been brought in, but the likelihood of that was so slight that most jurors were not influenced at all by this observation.

Jacob and Armstrong helped Kayleigh to the hall and to the small room they had been in previously. Once there, Armstrong advised Kayleigh and Jacob that it might take the jury several hours to a full day to return the verdict. So, when the three were called to re-enter the courtroom for a verdict after only one hour, they were shocked.

They returned to their seats, and the courtroom settled. The foreman rose, and the verdict of "Not Guilty" was read for Kayleigh. While the courtroom reacted and Jacob, Kayleigh, and Armstrong breathed in the relief of justice, Judge Winfrey brought the gavel down one last time.

"Let me make this clear," he looked directly at Andrews, Matthew, and Marcus. "I want these two men arrested on charges of Conspiracy, Perjury, Defamation of Character, and Extortion. What happens from there will be another jury's decision to make. I am not personally convinced that events transpired as the two Mr. O'Connors claimed." Then, while the sheriff and bailiff made their way toward Matthew and Marcus, Judge Winfrey declared the court dismissed.

The next morning, Jacob found a letter slipped under his door.

My dearest Jacob,

I will never be able to fully thank you for how you have helped me both in Faithful and now during the trial.

You have fulfilled every prayer that I ever dared to pray for a lifetime of love, and you are that to me, Jacob. There will never be anyone else. I have only, and will only, love you.

You have been the only man that I have dared to walk with and not away from. You gave your hand to me to hold and often to hold me up from despair. With you, I found myself planning the day around you, knowing that it would be better by simply seeing you. Believe me when I say that has never happened before.

I have only found small snatches of happiness here and there in this life, and perhaps that's all that anyone has. I thought, though, that there might be more with you. Whether you know it or not, you see the Lord well enough to show him to others. We all walk imperfectly, but you have looked past what I have been to show me what I could be.

My goal will be to live as that person, and I desperately want you to have every happiness. Sadly, I believe that you will achieve that better without me, for my past seems to follow me wherever I go, and now it is an open book to everyone.

When I return to Faithful, I will pack and be on my way to Canada. Mr. Leonardo's offer of being part of an artist colony still holds, and it will give me a purpose and a community.

Please find a pure and good woman who will be fully devoted to you and your life. I picture her as the Bible's description of a woman valued far above rubies. I will be taking the train back toward Faithful. I will then forge ahead to Canada. I still believe that God has a purpose for me, but perhaps it can no longer be in Faithful.

I love you.

Goodbye, Kayleigh

Jacob sat down for a moment and examined the letter. For a moment, he concentrated on the fact that she was taking the train. That would give him some time. He could beat the train with the long stop that it took prior to pressing on toward Faithful.

Then, he began to slowly focus on the handwriting. Part of the writing was in the circular curve of a school child's cursive, and part of it was in the sharp angular style of a more practiced writer. He drew in his breath and thought for quite a while. "It doesn't matter," he finally said aloud. "Even if she did somehow get there first and kill him and then came back to find her mother, it doesn't change anything. She'd had all she could take, and God is forgiving."

He then went down the hall to Kayleigh's room, but after knocking and calling, he could tell that she had already slipped out. It was time for him to write his own letter and find Caleb Spivy.

As Kayleigh began to board the train, Caleb came running up, carrying his valise and waving his derby hat in the air. "Miss O'Brien, wait up. I'm taking the train also."

She had thought that he would probably go back with Jacob, but perhaps he thought this faster than Jacob's wagon. They boarded together and looked for their seats. Caleb then talked an older gentleman into trading seats and tickets so that he could sit next to Kayleigh before the conductor made his way down the aisle.

She was somewhat amused, as was the gentleman who traded with him, but wondered why he had made the decision to ride the train and why he was so determined to travel next to her.

"Well, it's good to be getting back to Faithful," Caleb smiled as he spoke to Kayleigh.

"Yes, it is. Caleb, why are you not riding with Jacob?" she asked.

"Well, everyone knows the train is faster," he answered and laughed.

"Oh, and by the way," he continued, "I have something for you."

He fished about in his coat pocket and produced a letter. "Jacob wanted you to have this, Kayleigh." She took the letter slowly and put it into her small purse.

"Aren't you going to read it?" Caleb asked, somewhat disappointed.

"Of course," Kayleigh answered, "but I believe I'll wait until we're back in Faithful."

"Oh," Caleb said, at a loss for anything else to say. Then, being Caleb, he, of course, found his tongue.

"You know, Kayleigh, Jacob is a really good man. I wouldn't even be alive if not for him. Oh, he has his moments of impatience and vanity, just like most men, but he cares about people, and he reads a person's character quite well."

"You are preaching to the choir," Kayleigh said quietly. "I know as well, or better than anyone, just how good he is. Now, let's drop it, Caleb. It's a very personal matter."

"I know that, Kayleigh," he whispered, "but the two of you should be together. Any fool can see you love each other. I don't know what you put in that letter to him, and I don't know what he put in this one, but I wish you would go on and read it."

"Caleb, I've just been through a fight for my life. I have a lot on my mind and heart to deal with, and I need a little time, so please back off," Kayleigh finished.

"Alright," he agreed, "but please don't wait too long."

To Kayleigh's disappointment, the train stopped halfway toward Faithful for an hour, taking on more passengers and attending to the train engine before beginning again.

By the time they pulled into the station before Faithful, a team of horses and a wagon could have made it more quickly. She and Caleb hired a driver into Faithful, splitting the cost. The driver advised that he would go as quickly as possible but reminded them that it was sometimes hard to find a direct route to Faithful.

They said their goodbyes at the schoolhouse, and Caleb worked up the nerve to say one more time, "Kayleigh, please read the letter."

As he left, Cal Lindstrom stepped out of the shadows, startling Kayleigh a bit but not to the point of fear. It was more a question of curiosity as to why he was there.

"Miss O'Brien," Cal started with a nod of the head as he came closer to Kayleigh, "I heard about your being called to trial. I'm sorry about that. Do you feel more settled now? Will you stay in Faithful?"

"No, I don't think so," she answered. "If you don't mind, I'm really tired, and I need to pack."

"Oh, of course," Cal answered. "I just wanted you to know that I'd still like to go with you if you decide to live in Canada. I'm not suggesting anything lewd," he said, holding up one hand, "just what we talked about before."

"I'll keep that in mind, Cal," Kayleigh answered sincerely. "You know, though, it does look as though Jeanette might be highly interested in you. You might want to keep that in mind."

She then smiled and said, "Good night," while thinking of how to leave at the earliest possible time in the morning, although she was not ruling out Cal. She could love him in a way, and perhaps that would be enough.

She immediately began to pack her clothes. Most of her school supplies were still packed. When she had finished, she stopped, sat, and put her feet up on the little stool she kept in front of the fireplace. She closed her eyes for a moment and thought that she heard music coming from up the street. She wasn't sure what it was about, but she heard the melody of the piano and singing and clapping.

Kayleigh pulled the letter out of her skirt pocket, where she had transferred it from her purse, and began to read.

My Dear Kayleigh,

You are a very brave person in most of the arenas of life. I have always, and will always, be proud of you for that, and now I'm asking you to be brave in one more thing.

(This will be the point where he tells me goodbye, Kayleigh thought.)

I know that you are still reeling from the trial and the truths that emerged from it, but please consider this: my love for you. It's a love that wants to help you heal from the past.

I'm not looking for anyone else. I don't love anyone else. You are the one who gave my life new hope. I have loved you since the first day when you were wandering around lost.

If you leave, you'll never know what we could have been or could have had. Maybe you won't be lost again, but you may be unfinished, never having completed the life that we almost started.

I know that you have your own fortune, and please believe me, I consider it strictly yours. I want to give you everything that I have, Kayleigh. It may not be the most cultured or elegant or expensive, but it's real. It's a life of devotion, care, protection, companionship, passion, love, and faithfulness, but if I cannot give these things, I fear that they will turn into something hard, bitter, and unclaimed.

My deepest desire is to marry you and give you a home, a real home among people who have also spent much of their lives searching for a home. I will be your Tom Sawyer, and you, my Becky Thatcher, or the way they might have been if Mr. Twain had written them into adulthood.

If you would consider being my wife, there is a dance tonight at Lucy's. I will wait there for you. I will be the one looking hopeful and lovesick as I wait for a woman worth far more than rubies.

Jacob

She carefully folded the letter and put it back in her purse, which was over with the rest of her belongings. As she placed it there, she could see, through the little kitchen window, a few couples beginning to leave the dance for a quiet stroll.

Couples, she thought. *I never knew how that felt until Jacob.*

Suddenly, she realized that she had very little time left before the dance would end. Where was the dress? That was what was needed. Where was the second dress that Caroline had made for her? It was the same style as the blue one, but it was white with pink rosettes and interlaced pink ribbons.

With shaking hands, she pulled it out of her clothing trunk. Quickly, she took off the black skirt and white shirtwaist and put the new dress on, buttoning it clumsily. Then she was running down the street to Lucy's, her dress flowing out behind her and her feet barely touching the ground.

There was still a small crowd present at the dance, and Jacob stood at the bar. He had one hand on a beer, which still had not been drunk. He looked as though his world was falling in, but, being Jacob, he was trying not to show it.

Lucy was at the piano, still playing a few soft tunes for the couples still there and holding on to one another as they slowly danced. She occasionally glanced over at Jacob to make sure he was alright.

Kayleigh entered the inn, breathless and hoping that her hair was still in some kind of order since she had not taken it down. She spotted Jacob at the bar, his profile and serious look in plain sight. She smoothed her dress down and slowly approached him. Her entrance had not gone unnoticed by Lucy or many of the couples, and Lucy began playing a romantic tune.

Jacob glanced up to see her coming toward him. His saddened face changed in an instant, replaced by a smile and lit with happiness. He turned toward her and took her hands in his.

"May I have this dance?" he asked.

"Oh, I…you know I don't really dance," she had somehow disconnected from the fact that this was, in fact, a dance. "I know that's hard to believe, considering I worked in a carnival, but I really never learned."

"If you trust me enough to marry me, darling, then I think you can trust me enough to dance." He smiled and gently pushed a few stray curls back behind her ear.

She had to admit to herself that this made sense. She had to begin taking some chances. "Alright," she acquiesced, "but hang on to me and don't say I didn't warn you. I've been known to trip grown men."

He laughed and took her in his arms. "Hold onto me and don't let go," he instructed, and she felt inexplicably safe and heady at the same time. They were, in their minds, the only two in the room, the town, and the world.

They danced as Lucy played and smiled. They danced as other couples watched them with hope and approval, and they danced as Lydia and Maddie smiled at each other and thanked God.

They were married that night. The Reverend and Mrs. McKendree were seemingly ready for them, but then Jacob had arranged for everything to just seem ready to happen. The older couple was obviously so happy for them, as were the honored witnesses, Mr. and Mrs. Campbell. None of this was lost on Kayleigh, and she loved Jacob even more for it.

After the brief ceremony, Jacob turned to Kayleigh and said, "You understand that you're coming with me now and staying with me at my home, our home. There will be no more running."

"Of course, Jacob," she answered. "Only," she hesitated, "may I keep Sawyer?"

Jacob laughed heartily before replying, "Of course, but he'll have to understand it's my house, not his."

Kayleigh was baptized the next week. It made her feel more secure and complete in her own faith, and she and Jacob seldom spoke of her past or his.

One day, Neb Darius came by Kayleigh's new home, hat in hand, at Lucy's urging. He apologized for his previous behaviors. He explained that he had run from his own grief over losing his wife and child, and he asked if there was anything he could do to clear the situation. She thought a moment and made the "strange" request of buying one of his warehouses.

Her "wedding gift" to Jacob was the purchase of this warehouse. Jacob was hesitant to accept it at first, but then, putting his male pride aside, reveled in the fact that he would never be dependent on Darius again.

Cal Lindstrom and Mademoiselle Jeanette were married a week later. As Cal told Kayleigh once when they ran into each other in town, "She just needed a loyal man, and maybe a baby. Also, turns out she also wanted to know she had a man who wouldn't mind her having a business of her own. Don't bother me none. That's two paychecks for us to live on and be happy with along the way."

Noah Thomas and Mary Alice were married during the summer with a small church wedding. Those who attended were happy for both of them and still a bit surprised.

However, the biggest surprise was the union of Lucy and Neb Darius. As Beatrice Atwood related, she had heard them arguing one day as she passed the inn ("more like put her ear to the door," Maddie observed) and that Lucy had issued an ultimatum to Neb.

"Stop all this drinking and drunkenness. We've all had tragedies. It doesn't give you the right to act like a self-absorbed idiot. Be faithful to me and me alone. You are far too old to continue all this 'hound doggin'' about. It is already an embarrassment for you, and pay more attention to my adopted son, Ned," she instructed.

Rosemary Herd began a baking business, and Caroline kept her seamstress enterprise, sometimes working for Madame Jeanette. Both Mitch and Zach were now enjoying double incomes.

Jacob and Kayleigh were happy for them and for everyone who finally found each other in Faithful. They themselves were and are a rather wealthy couple, but they have never spoken of it or made an issue of it. However, many have puzzled over the "anonymous" donations made to the upkeep of the schools and the church.

They are very dedicated to one another and the life that they have built. Both, of course, were very proud of their son, Jack (actually named Joshua Luke McVale), and Kayleigh did give up teaching for a time.

This opened a position for her dear friend, Margaret Ruth, who came as fast as she could with "Professor Gallant" in tow. It should also be noted that Mrs. Margaret Ruth touched many of our lives as the principal of what came to be known as the "high school."

Interestingly, it is my cousin, Penny, who now helps my father and uncles run the business since Jack preferred to pursue medicine. It should also be noted that the business has tripled in its value.

Faithful is still not an easy place to find or even describe. Perhaps it will be renamed along the way or just fade away as some towns do. But, if you look for it and happen to find it, it's possible that it actually found you because you were in a place of need in a time of your own. Just remember what it did for its citizens long ago and could do again for those who prove faithful.

Now, my work is done. I hope I did a good job of telling the story for "my Miss O'Brien." I know that I'm happy that, somehow, the Lord did a good work in bringing my beloved Uncle Jacob and Miss O'Brien together.

(Oh, and just to prove that even the most distant dreams can come true, a copy of *Tom Sawyer* remains on their bedside table, and Jacob holds Kayleigh while she sleeps.)

EPILOGUE

Six months after our literary circle discussed *Jane Eyre*, I went by Aunt Kayleigh's house after finishing my teaching for the day. She was taking a nap, which she did more and more often, and sometimes, it was hard to take in the reality that my vibrant Miss O'Brien had aged. Oh, but there was still a twinkle in those green eyes and an empathetic intelligence.

"I understand that we have a writer in the family," Uncle Jacob smiled and hugged me as I came in. I was a bit surprised because I wasn't sure if Aunt Kayleigh had told him about our venture.

"Well," he said, motioning for me to sit as he folded his long legs into the kitchen chair and folded his hands on the old round oak table, "I'm a little glad it is just you and me. I want you to know the absolute end of the tale, Jennifer Anne."

I opened the small notebook that I had begun to carry, and Jacob began to speak.

"A few months after we married, I had to have my last say with Matthew. Kayleigh had finally admitted that she saw Matthew at an unmarked grave when she went to make sure her mother's and Cassie's headstones were placed. She also saw him placing something in a shallow hole next to the grave.

"We were very happy after we married, but she became somewhat depressed and quiet after about a month, so I confronted her about what was hanging over her and causing her sadness. That's when Kayleigh told me that she knew in her heart that her mother would not have killed Nolan O'Connor. It was not that he did not fully deserve it, but she did not feel that her mother had the act of murder in her.

"So, one day, without Kayleigh knowing, I took a week from work to go to Idaho Falls, pay a visit to Matthew in the jail, and try to extract a confession. I told her that I was going on business to the coast of California. She may have known that something was up, but she never asked. (Later, we had a talk about always telling the truth to each other.)

"I actually asked to speak to both Marcus and Matthew, but, somewhat to my surprise, they told me that Marcus had been killed. Truthfully, I thought someone might kill him based on his arrogance, and so they did, right within the jail. He made the wrong man angry, and my guess is that the guard just let it happen. Anyway, Matthew had been placed in solitary confinement in the basement, and that's where the guard led me. A police detective that my friend Caleb Spivy had contacted followed behind.

"It was cold and dark with that molded smell of an underground room. He squinted a bit as he looked at me. I guess the window in the room, which I sat in front of at a rickety table, was a shock to his eyes.

"The guard chained Matthew to the table and stepped just outside the door. He informed me that Matthew was ill with some type of fever and warned me not to sit anywhere close to him. With that, he closed the door almost the entire way, and I knew that his and the detective's ears were tuned to our conversation.

"'What do you want, McVale?' he said with an empty look in those dead dark eyes that he bored into anyone he hated.

"I got right to the point and told him that I wanted the truth about who killed Nolan O'Connor.

"He grinned that ugly sneer of his because he knew that he had something that I wanted. 'Well, I suppose Kayleigh did,' he said and laughed.

'Let me put it another way,' I said. 'how did you kill him? Was it with a Remmington?'

"He blanched a bit when I said that. His face was already ashen, but he became even paler.

'I didn't kill my own Pa!' he yelled.

"'Oh,' I answered, just as nonchalantly as possible, because I knew his game and his weakness. 'Then, I guess Marcus did, but he's not here to confess or tell that you did the deed. (I goaded and poked the bear, so to speak.)'

"'That's right, he ain't,' he yelled again. 'So just lie with the fact that your wife's a murderer.'

"'I would if I needed to,' I told him, 'but she's not.'

"'What did Nolan do that made you resort to shooting him?' I asked him calmly.

"'You might as well tell me, Matthew,' I said. 'I've already spoken to a detective and a very frightened and less arrogant sheriff. Everything points to you, and here's a little nugget that you might not have known. The Winchester that you turned in was known to be Kathleen's, and it had never been fired.

"'So what if I did,' he screamed. 'He wanted everything. I would have helped him get Kayleigh's money, but he wanted the farm and ranch that Marcus and I were building. He laughed when Cassie died—just out and out laughed.

"The last straw was when he set fire to the horse barn. I left Marcus to tend to that the best he could. Neighbors helped him some, and I chased Pa to Kathleen's. He had her backed to a wall with a knife to her throat when I came in.

"'You come at me and I'll slit her throat,' he said. 'By the way, how's your barn?'

"'What's she or the barn to me?' I answered. 'Go through her bedroom while I hold the gun on her,' I told him. 'Some of Kayleigh's money is bound to be in there.'

"He didn't go right off, but he finally let her go, and she cowered in a corner. I motioned for her to stay quiet.

"He came back out, the knife still in his hand, and his mean blue eyes narrowed.

"Are you trying to set me up?' he screamed and lunged at me with the knife.

"'I shot him before I even knew it,' Matthew said, and for a moment, he actually looked like a feeling human being.

"'Why did Kathleen hang herself?' I asked him.

"'I threatened her pretty strong, then Marcus barged in and told her that he would tell everyone that she killed Pa if she didn't keep her mouth shut, but I also told her I'd take care of all of it, and nobody need know. I guess she'd just had all she could take. She'd been pretty down since Kayleigh left, and Cassie went to the Langleys.

"He said all of this with a touch of regret. I did not think him capable of any emotion, but he may have had some humanity.

"'So where are your father's body and the Remington that you owned?' was my next question.

"I asked him straight out if they were buried together in the unmarked grave in the cemetery. I told him that Kayleigh had finally told me what she saw when she went to see the tombstones on her mother's and sister's graves.

"'Well, if you know,' he growled, 'why ask?'

Uncle Jacob stopped. His hand gripped the table tightly, and his eyes stared out the window as though painfully recounting the entire scene.

"'Is he still in jail?' I asked quietly.

"'He was placed in the state prison,' Uncle Jacob said calmly. 'The grave was located, and the rifle was extracted. Dr. Randall agreed to reexamine the body with the territorial coroner, and they confirmed that, to the best of their knowledge, the fatal wound corresponded to the Remmington that Matthew owned and the bullet that Dr. Randall had extracted from O'Connor.

'I had gone home by then, but they wired me that Matthew was standing trial for murder. Then, later, I had word that he had been put in prison for fifty years. Of course, he only lived a few more years after I had seen him. His health had already failed.

'When I thought that Kayleigh was ready to hear the outcome, I told her. She had tears of relief,'" Uncle Jacob finished with a peaceful finality.

I nodded. "You saved Aunt Kayleigh, Uncle Jacob," I said and smiled.

"God saved us both, and she found her faithful," he said, smiling, with his blue eyes back to their usual sweet calm.

BIBLIOGRAPHY

Birch, Harry & Gooch, William. *Reuben and Rachel*, (Boston: White, Smith, & Perry, 1871)

Bolton, Sarah. Paddle *Your Own Canoe*, (Indiana: Nathaniel Bolton, Harper's Weekly, 1850)

Bronte, Charlotte. *Jane Eyre*, (New York: Harper and Brothers, 1848)

Burns, Robert. *Auld Lang Syne*, (Scotland:1788), 1-11.

Dickens, Charles. *Oliver Twist*, (London: Richard Bentley, 1838)

Edwards, Jonathan. *Sinners in the Hands of an Angry God*, (Boston: S. Kneeland & T. Green, 1741)

Emmett, Daniel. *Old Dan Tucker*, (Boston: C.H. Keith, 1843)

Foster, Stephen. *Beautiful Dreamer*, (New York: William A. Pond & Co., 1864),

Foster, Stephen. *Oh! Susanah*, (Baltimore: F.D. Benteen, 1848)

Hawke & Rodney. *The Girl I Left Behind Me*, (Dublin: Exhaw's Magazine, 1794)

Johnson, George W. & Butterfield, James Austin. *When You and I Were Young, Maggie*, (Boston: Oliver Ditson & Co., 1864)

Montross, Percy. *Oh My Darling Clementine*, (Traditional: 1884)

Twain, Mark. *The Adventures of Tom Sawyer*, (New York: Harper & Brothers 1875).

ABOUT THE AUTHOR

Vicie Annette Allison lives in Nashville, TN, with her husband, Neal. She is a retired teacher with many interests, one of which, of course, is writing.

She is on a quest to use her doctorate degree in reading education as a writer. She finds inspiration from people that she has met during her career as a teacher and professor and in people that she holds dear.

Both her son and daughter have encouraged her to write books and begin another career as an author. This is her first full-length novel.

9 798893 335057